Praise for *Secrets of the Chocolate House*

"Brackston's vibrant story is on firm historical ground, with period details woven in nicely.... Time-swapping romance will please fans of Alice Hoffman." —*Publishers Weekly*

"*Secrets of the Chocolate House* has all the romance of the seventeenth century with a heroine that is every bit twenty-first: clever, fierce, and willing to put her own life on the line to rescue the man she loves."

—Ruth Emmie Lang, author of *Beasts of Extraordinary Circumstance*

Praise for *The Little Shop of Found Things*

"Brackston wonderfully blends history with the time-travel elements and a touch of romance. This series debut is a page-turner that will no doubt leave readers eager for future series installments." —*Publishers Weekly*

"Fans of Diana Gabaldon's Outlander collection will delight in Brackston's new series and eagerly await its second installment. A bewitching tale of love across centuries." —*Kirkus Reviews*

"A solid, enjoyable read with a hint of magical time travel." —*Booklist*

T0021401

SECRETS

OF THE

CHOCOLATE

HOUSE

Paula Brackston

ST. MARTIN'S GRIFFIN
NEW YORK

First published in the United States by St. Martin's Griffin, an imprint of St. Martin's Publishing Group

SECRETS OF THE CHOCOLATE HOUSE. Copyright © 2019 by Paula Brackston. All rights reserved. Printed in the United States of America. For information, address St. Martin's Publishing Group, 120 Broadway, New York, NY 10271.

www.stmartins.com

The Library of Congress has cataloged the hardcover edition as follows:

Names: Brackston, Paula, author.
Title: Secrets of the chocolate house / Paula Brackston.
Description: First Edition. | New York : St. Martin's Press, 2019. |
    Series: Found things; 2 |
Identifiers: LCCN 2019024261 | ISBN 9781250072443 (hardcover) |
    ISBN 9781466884113 (ebook)
Subjects: GSAFD: Love stories. | Occult fiction.
Classification: LCC PR6102.R325 S43 2019 | DDC 823/.92—dc23
LC record available at https://lccn.loc.gov/2019024261

ISBN 978-1-250-26986-7 (trade paperback)

Our books may be purchased in bulk for promotional, educational, or business use. Please contact your local bookseller or the Macmillan Corporate and Premium Sales Department at 1-800-221-7945, extension 5442, or by email at MacmillanSpecialMarkets@macmillan.com.

First St. Martin's Griffin Edition: 2020

10 9 8 7 6 5 4 3

FOR ALEX,

WHO HAS THE SHARPEST OF MINDS,

THE KINDEST OF HEARTS,

AND IS SO APPEALINGLY BONKERS

Do not tell secrets to those whose faith and silence
you have not already tested.

—QUEEN ELIZABETH I

Do nothing secretly; for Time sees and hears
all things, and discloses all.

—SOPHOCLES

SECRETS

OF THE

CHOCOLATE

HOUSE

{ 1 }

FROM HER VIEWING POINT AT THE TOP OF THE HILL, THE LANDSCAPE OF WILTSHIRE FELL away into the hazy distance of the cooling autumn afternoon. Xanthe shielded her eyes against the lowering sun, a breeze disturbing her golden, spiral curls. The hills and slopes of the countryside were flattened by her lofty perspective, the distant villages and farmhouses appearing impossibly tiny, as if they could never hold real people. As she listened to the whirring call of the curlew, the rising notes of its distinctive song seemed to sound an alarm, a warning against the apparent peacefulness of the setting. For secrets hid among the long shadows of the dwindling day, in the dark copses atop the stout hills, within the stone walls of the old farmhouses, beneath the flagstoned floors of the ancient churches. And secrets were anchored to their hiding places only with the steadfastness of trust and the weight of danger.

She breathed in the scents of the wiry grass and gorse of the hill, letting her eyes focus on the far distance of the vista before her. It was not hard to imagine the view as it would have been four centuries earlier. Little change had taken place. The settlement boundaries had crept outward. Here and there a minor industrial estate sat unobtrusively, quietly industrious. If she listened hard she could discern the swoosh and rumble of traffic on the main road that crossed the valley, but there were no motorways here. No cities. Small communities inhabited the ancient landscape, all concerned with families, with survival, with their own intimate futures and worries. What was harder to imagine were the invisible veins of energy that crisscrossed the verdant scenery, like so many electricity cables, buried deep. But ley lines were infinitely more powerful, their influence stretching not only across the miles, but over centuries. Xanthe knew now how to look for them. She found a church spire off to her left in the east, and then, narrowing her eyes, turned to another, set in a village on the river. Another half turn to the west and she found an ancient burial site marked by a treeless mound. The line would cut through these potent points on the map of human habitation, and in turn be bisected by another line, drawn between two further points of power, and two more beyond that, and so on and so on, crosshatching the whole of the countryside, a network of energy, a web of timeless connection. Xanthe knew only too well the transformative strength of that energy in certain places. Places such as the old blind house at the bottom of the garden behind The Little Shop of Found Things. Not for the first time, she wondered how different things might have been had she and her mother chosen a different town in which to start their antiques business.

The chalk horse drawing Xanthe was standing next to was so large that had she been careless enough to step onto it, her Dr. Martens would not have covered even one of its mighty hooves. The scale of the drawing, so artfully cut into the green turf, revealing the bright whiteness of the chalk below, always impressed her. The people who had taken the decision to carve the hill figure, hundreds of years before she came to live in Wiltshire, could not have known how long it would stand sentinel over the landscape. Xanthe found it heartening that the horse had survived weather, farming, battles, and the march of time itself to stand proud and steady all those long, restless years. It was a source of calm for her, so that she had come to enjoy visiting it, seeking out solitude and peace high above the county plains, whenever life's events felt as if they were getting the better of her.

She pulled her old tweed jacket tighter around her and sat on the wiry grass, dropping her hand to run her fingers over the compacted chalk of the great horse's noble head. She thought about how much had happened to her in the past few short months. Of how much she had come to understand things that only a short time ago she would have thought impossible. Even with everything so fresh in her mind it was still hard, at times, to believe it had all been real. To make sense of the fact that, with the help of the silver chatelaine, she had traveled back in time to 1605. That she had saved Alice. That she had met Samuel.

Getting to her feet again, she took a deep breath of the bracingly cool air. There was no point torturing herself with what might have been. With what she had glimpsed, felt, and lost. She had come to accept that she and Samuel could never be together. He inhabited his time, his world, and she hers. What she had felt for him, and he for her, she believed to be real, but she knew those feelings had been heightened by the danger surrounding the circumstances in which they had met. Magnified by that fact she had been so reluctant to acknowledge: that they would forever be separated by the centuries. This was where, and more important when, her own life belonged. She had people who needed her and cared for her here. And there was work to be done. If she and her mother were to make a success of their new business, Xanthe had to focus all her energies on it. Their financial difficulties were far from over, and Flora's health was unreliable at best. This was not the time to be distant. They were a team, she and her mother. That had to be her priority now. She would immerse herself in her work and turn her back on memories of the past. She said a silent goodbye to the great horse and followed the path back to the parking place where her cherished black London cab sat waiting for her. It was still her most treasured possession; a memento of her city life, and a boon when scouring the country for antiques.

By the time Xanthe arrived back at the shop the day had fallen into twilight and the little town of Marlborough was enveloped in a heavy fog. She shivered as she put the closed sign on the shop door and called out to Flora.

"Mum? I'm home. I'm going to lock up. Where are you?"

The sound of crutches on the tiled floor of the hallway to the workshop gave her mother away. Her arthritis might have made them a necessary part of her mobility, but that didn't mean she moved slowly.

"I was just putting the finishing touches to another mirror frame," she said as she hurried back into the shop. Her fine, fluffy hair was kept off her face by what Xanthe suspected was a polishing rag, rather than a scarf, but still Flora looked appealing, her English rose skin and deep-set eyes maturing kindly. Being in her fifties suited her.

"Leaving the stock at the mercy of shoplifters?" Xanthe smiled as she spoke, but there was a seriousness to her words. They had been warned about a spate of light-fingered browsers in the town recently.

Flora shook her head. "No one gets through the shop door without that old bell letting me know."

Xanthe thought guiltily about how many times she had done just that, sneaking in and out of the house so that her mother wouldn't know she had been there. Covering her tracks. Protecting lies. Keeping secrets. "I expect that's why Mr. Morris never got rid of it," she said.

"Well, if he used to restore things like I do he'd have needed it. I can't be in two places at once, love, and when you decide to go off on one of your walks . . ."

"Sorry, Mum. Just needed a bit of air. Clear my head."

"I'm teasing. Doesn't take two of us to man this place, not all the time. What does need your attention, on the other hand, is the stock. Or rather the lack of it."

"I know."

"Christmas may seem ages off, but we can't afford to miss the trade. People start shopping for gifts earlier and earlier these days. And if the things we find need some work doing . . ."

"OK, you're right. I should be out scouting for more stuff."

"If we don't have it we can't sell it." She paused, her face more serious for a moment. "We need these few weeks to be a success. Your father is still dragging his heels when it comes to agreeing to the divorce settlement."

"Still no news?"

Flora shook her head. "Why would he be in a hurry? He's got the family home and the income from an established business."

"Not to mention whatever his new woman brings to the party."

Flora tutted. "No use relying on any progress this side of the New Year. We just have to focus on finding treasures and making sales. And we have to prepare for our first Christmas in our new home! Nearly December and not so much as a pudding stirred."

The moment of tension passed as Flora gave way to her irrepressible love of the festive season. Xanthe made a mental note to make sure this would be a happy one, for both of them.

"Oh, and I want to get working on that lovely pine dresser we found in Devizes last week. We need to find a van from somewhere so we can collect it."

"No way that was going to fit in my taxi."

"Why don't you ask Liam if he knows where we can get one from?"

As always the idea of seeing Liam brought with it a tangle of feelings. He had already proved himself to be a good friend, had helped her when she had needed him. And it wasn't as if he was being pushy. But still it was clear his interest in her went beyond friendship. What he didn't know, what he couldn't know, was that Xanthe's heart was still bruised after having to leave Samuel.

She realized her mother was looking at her, waiting for an answer.

"Sure, Mum. I'll call him."

"Oh, look." Flora waved one of her crutches at the window. "No need. You can ask him now."

Liam was standing outside. He was wearing his favorite old, soft, leather jacket and had his hands deep in his pockets against the cold. His stubble, Xanthe noticed, had passed just beyond what was fashionable into something a little more rugged, yet still he was dangerously good-looking. He gave a rueful smile, his light blue eyes crinkling at the corners. Xanthe opened the door.

"I was passing. . . ." He grinned.

"Down a cul de sac?"

"I like to take in the sights. . . ."

"In this fog?"

"For heaven's sake, Xanthe, let the poor boy in and shut the door. It's chilly enough in here as it is. We were just talking about you, Liam."

"Oh?" He looked at Xanthe, who hurried to explain, the expression of hope on his face unnerving her.

"We need a van. To pick up a dresser."

"A lovely piece," said Flora. "We found it at an auction in Devizes."

"Mum wants to work her magic on it with paint."

"Do you have a van?" Flora asked Liam.

"No, but I know a man who does," he said.

"Excellent." Flora turned and stick-stepped her way toward the hall. "I was just about to muster up an early supper. Why don't you join us and we can make plans?"

"Oh, well . . ." Liam hesitated for form's sake, but Xanthe could see how keen he was to accept the invitation. "That'd be great," he said at last.

"Brave man," she muttered to him as they trooped upstairs to the little kitchen on the first floor. Her mother's singular approach to cooking was not for the fainthearted, and Liam had already chewed through one of her lunches, so he knew what he was letting himself in for.

In the few busy months since buying the property, Xanthe and Flora had transformed the dusty, cluttered shop into a wonderful, light-filled space, stocked with gorgeous things. The living quarters, however, had not received the same attention. There were still packing cases in every room and the sitting room was mostly given over to being an office, apart from the green velvet sofa on which they flopped when time allowed. Nothing had been repainted, and the floors remained covered in nasty carpet or cracked linoleum. In the kitchen, plates and general paraphernalia sat about in stacks and heaps waiting to be found homes.

"Find yourself a seat," said Flora, opening the fridge. She had given up apologizing for the mess. Xanthe suspected she no longer noticed it. It was only when visitors called that she herself saw their home with fresh eyes and felt a little embarrassed.

"We are going to redecorate up here," she said. "Eventually."

"Really? Can't think why," said Liam, moving a stack of *Antique Trader* magazines off a ladder-backed, pale pine chair. Xanthe recalled his own flat and realized that interior design, or the lack of it, was hardly a priority for him. He'd far more likely spend his time and money on his beloved classic cars. Just as she and her mother would rather be restoring a Georgian table, or reframing a set of Victorian prints, or repairing a crucial chip in a piece of powder blue Wedgwood china. She cleared some space on the old kitchen table and fetched bottled beers from the fridge.

"The dresser's a big one," she told Liam, handing him a bottle opener. "The base is over eight foot, three cupboards, and the top half has glass doors. Though we may have to abandon those."

"Nonsense," said Flora. "I've got the perfect set of hinges we can use."

"My mate's van will handle it, no problem." Liam paused to take a swig of his beer. "I'll text him. See when we can have it."

"You don't need to abandon the workshop; I can drive it," said Xanthe, taking a packet of spicy noodles from her mother and putting them back in the cupboard, selecting rice instead.

"Course you can," Liam agreed, "but you are going to need help lifting the dresser in and out of it, aren't you?" He had about him such an easy charm it was impossible not to feel a little better for simply being in his company.

Xanthe smiled at him and nodded. She admired his patience. Some men would have given up on her by now. Would have realized she wasn't looking for a relationship, taken the many hints she had dropped, and looked elsewhere. But not Liam. He was prepared to wait, and while he waited, to be a good friend. She couldn't help liking him for that. And their shared love of music and performing gave them a safe common ground too. He was a good lead guitarist. Better than good, in fact. She remembered the first time she had heard his band play at The Feathers, and the first time she herself had sung there. It was good to have a friend who understood what it felt like to stand up in front of a crowd, to make yourself so vulnerable, to give of yourself in that particular way.

Liam was an undemanding guest, and soon they were all seated at the table, a stub of a candle found for an orphan silver candlestick, more beers, and bowls of rice with chopped-up frankfurters, spring onions, tomatoes, and a handful of sultanas Flora had flung in while Xanthe's back was turned.

"Xanthe's singing in The Feathers again the week after next," she told Liam. "You will come along and support her, won't you?"

"Mum . . ."

"Try and stop me. Looking forward to it. Harley says takings go up every time you sing there, Xanthe. He's always telling people about how brilliantly you sing. What's the word he uses?"

"Stop, you're making me blush."

"*Stupendous*, that's it. He tells everyone you're stupendous!"

"He's a good publican. He's good at selling his events," Xanthe said with a shrug. In truth, she was, at last, enjoying her singing again, welcoming the chance to perform, and to earn some money of her own. She had intended to make herself choose new songs. Singing the ones that were of that distant time—Samuel's time—only made her melancholy. What was the point in wallowing? And yet, she still felt drawn to the melodies and sentiments of that era. Perhaps singing those ballads and love songs that Samuel would have known, just for a little longer, would help her ease away from him. Perhaps it was a way to prove to herself that she had accepted that she was never going back. The adventure was over. To return to him made no sense. It was too dangerous, and there was, ironically, no future in it for them. She had to focus on home, on work, on her singing. It was the right thing to do.

Liam interrupted her thoughts, checking a text on his phone. "Right, we can have the van on Thursday. That suit you?"

Flora answered for her, adding a liberal amount of brown sauce to her supper as she spoke. "Perfect. We've got a house clearance to do at Laybrook first thing tomorrow. I want to be back here by eleven at the latest so we don't have to leave the shop shut too long."

Xanthe nodded. "I took that booking. A lady who lived in the village all her life. The nephew is dealing with her estate. He said there's nothing large, as the family have taken the major pieces of furniture. Mostly paintings, china, rugs, some glassware."

Liam frowned. "Don't you find it creepy, sifting through a whole lot of stuff that belonged to someone who just died? Sort of ghoulish?"

"No," Xanthe said. "It's fascinating. We get a unique glimpse into someone's life through the things they chose to keep close to them. It's very revealing. And it's a privilege."

"Not to mention a treasure hunt," said Flora. "And Xanthe is always on the lookout for something that sings to her, aren't you, love?"

Liam leaned forward, gesticulating with his fork. "Your daughter has been very cagey about her special talent, Mrs. Westlake. Plays it down every time I try to ask her about it."

Xanthe helped herself to another beer. It wasn't a secret, the fact that some of the antiques they found spoke to her, giving her glimpses of their past, but it wasn't easy to talk about it without her feeling she must come across as a little bit bonkers. "Yes, well, I might find something special, I might not. Can't know until I get there. More rice, anyone?"

She let the subject drop, but privately she could not help being excited at the prospect of this kind of house clearance. By all accounts the old lady's house was something special in itself, and the village had a reputation for being one of the prettiest and best preserved in Wiltshire. They were almost certain to find some interesting and beautiful things for the shop, and that was what mattered. She told herself firmly that it might even be for the best if nothing in particular sang to her. No more mysteries. No more traveling back through time. She had to root herself in the here and now.

Arriving in Laybrook the next day, however, it was all too easy to believe she and her mother and even her black cab had journeyed to a bygone age. The little village was picture-postcard perfect, shown off to its best advantage beneath the flattering winter sunshine. The last of the russet leaves held fast to oak and ash, with evergreen climbers glossy over low stone walls. Road signs and markings had been kept to a minimum. Cottages, shops, pubs, and houses had all been painstakingly preserved, with not a modern window or clumsy extension anywhere to be seen. The National Trust had bought the village some years earlier and now managed it with meticulous care, but this was not a museum. Laybrook was a thriving community, and the beautiful houses were homes to real people living real lives. The house that had been home to Esther Harris for decades was a fine example of simple but elegant eighteenth-century English architecture. Lavender House was two stories of warm, tawny stone, its long windows balanced along classical lines with an imposing front door. The woodwork was freshly painted white, contrasting crisply with the rich stone, while the door itself gleamed in deep French navy. Dark gray stone tiles clad the steeply pitched roof, a chimney at either end. Unlike many of the smaller, terraced houses in the village, this one was detached, and set back from the street by a neat, paved front garden which was in turn enclosed behind a low wall topped with black iron railings. Two clipped bay trees stood guard on either side of the iron gate.

Xanthe parked the cab directly outside the house and opened the door for her mother. The fog of the previous day had gone so that the village was dressed in late autumn sunshine. Even so, she was glad of the old college scarf she had tucked into her vintage tweed jacket before they set out. She made a mental note to dig out her winter coat when they got home, and next time to team her tea dress with warmer leggings.

"Ooh," said Flora, planting her crutches firmly onto the pavement and taking in her surroundings. "How very lovely. No wonder they use this place for films."

"It is fairly gorgeous," Xanthe agreed. She felt a tingle of excitement, a prickling of her scalp, and wondered briefly if it signified something special inside the house. Something that was waiting for her. The thought, after recent events, caused anxiety to knot her stomach. Shaking off the idea, she told herself it was only the normal excitement of the treasure hunt.

"Let's get started," she said. "The nephew promised he'd be here by nine. His name's Lionel. Sounded like the whole business of inheriting anything is a bit of a chore for him."

They made their way to the front door and Flora used the key she had been sent to let them in. The hallway echoed as they stepped onto the broad boards of the floor. There were very obvious spaces where large pieces of furniture had already been removed, as well as light patches on the walls being the ghosts of the paintings that once hung there. A polished wooden staircase led up from the center of the hall, with a narrow passageway on one side toward the back of the house, and doors off right and left to the reception rooms.

Flora took her notebook from her backpack and consulted a list. "There won't be anything in here. Let's try the sitting room first. There should be a corner cabinet, a Persian rug, a chaise longue and, according to the nephew, 'a lovely fire screen.' We'll see. One man's lovely is another man's ghastly."

The screen turned out to be mediocre and the chaise too big to fit in the shop. The rug was somewhat marred by sparks from the open fire beyond it. Xanthe knelt down to inspect it more closely. It felt wonderfully soft as she ran her hand over the rich reds and blues of the pattern. As a child all such rugs had made her think of a magic carpet, and this one was no exception. She liked to think of all the children who had sat on it, perhaps playing with a favorite teddy bear, or driving a toy car along the geometric pattern at its edges. She wondered how many Christmas presents had been unwrapped on it, right there, in front of a crackling fire, and how many beloved dogs had stretched out upon it to luxuriate in the warmth from the hearth.

"It's not perfect," she told her mother, "but it's still nice. I think it would sell quite quickly."

Flora was scrutinizing the corner cabinet. "This is Victorian. Bit brown. Looks like this was used to display silver. The nephew must have already snaffled that. This is in good nick though."

"We could use it in the shop."

"Or I could rub it down and transform it with a new coat of paint. Dark wood's still pretty unfashionable. It would have a completely different feel if someone painted it . . . oh . . . mole's breath gray?"

"You're the woman to do it," said Xanthe.

Deciding they would make a low offer for the cabinet and think about the rug, they moved back through the hall and up the rather fine staircase. There were two floors of bedrooms and bathrooms. Xanthe let her mother check the ones on the first floor and took herself up the second flight to the attic rooms. She could hear the echo of her mother's crutches as she stick-stepped her way across bare floorboards.

"These rooms are pretty much empty already," she called up. "The beds might have been nice; pity not to have had a chance at those."

"We haven't room for beds, Mum," Xanthe reminded her. The smaller rooms on her floor would have originally housed the servants. The ceiling was boarded with modern insulation but still the unheated space was chilly. Xanthe could only imagine how cold the winters must have been for the maids living up in the rafters of the house. In times gone by the servants themselves served as insulation, helping to keep their employers warmer in the rooms below. Xanthe was reminded of how cold, even in autumn, her bedroom had been at Great Chalfield Manor. She thought wistfully of Jayne and wondered how her fellow kitchen maid was faring.

"Oh!" Her mother's delighted shout brought her back to the present. "A lovely escritoire! Come and have a look."

At last they went back downstairs to the dining room. As they let the door swing open, Xanthe and Flora gasped in unison. For Flora, it was the sight that greeted them that so impressed her. For Xanthe, it was the sound of a clear, high note, like the ringing of a celestial bell, that caused her to catch her breath and even throw her hands to her ears. Flora was too taken up with their find to notice her daughter's gesture. If she had seen how strongly Xanthe had reacted to the contents of the room she would have known instantly that something was singing to her. Some special object, filled with the vibrations of its own history, was calling to her. As it was, she was entirely focused on the treasures in front of her.

"Now that's what I call a collection!" she said.

The dining table and chairs had evidently been taken away, so that the main part of the room was empty. The far wall, however, had been given over entirely as a place to house the objects of Esther Harris's passion. On deep shelves, behind glass doors, sat dozens and dozens of chocolate pots. Some were copper, some fine china, some pewter, others silver. One or two were enameled. There were pots with wooden handles; pots with stirrers and pots without; pots with matching cups and saucers; pots with silver spoons and sugar bowls and tongs. There were graceful eighteenth-century porcelain examples with exquisitely painted decorations depicting flowers or finely dressed ladies. There were beaten silver pots engraved with swirling initials or coats of arms. There were sinuous pots in the art nouveau style and angular art deco ones with tiny wedgelike cups on ebony trays.

"Wow!" muttered Flora, hurrying forward to scan the shelves, taking in the range and beauty of what they had found.

Beyond the briefest of glances, Xanthe barely saw the true extent of the collection. She was irresistibly drawn to a single pot. She stepped forward, placing her hand on the glass, submitting to that unmistakable song, giving in to her gift. From anyone else this particular pot might not have earned a second glance. It had no elaborate rococo curls, nor was it fashioned from translucent French porcelain. This pot was made of copper, burnished to a deep shine over hundreds of years, dented in places, its simple shape and plain wooden handle suggesting that it had been made not for show but for function. Similar in size and shape to a modern coffeepot, the chocolatiere differed in one or two crucial details. The handle was set at right angles to the slender gooseneck spout. This was to allow the pot to be gently swirled as it was poured, the better to mix the grainy chocolate with the hot milk. The wooden half of the handle was shaped to fit the palm of the hand and to protect it from the heat of the pot. The lid had a hinged finial, which lifted to reveal a vital hole. Xanthe had seen such pots before and knew that a stirring stick, or "molinet" as it was known by aficionados, would be lowered into the liquid so that it could be stirred before pouring, to blend the mixture and keep it from separating, making sure that the chocolate was evenly distributed.

Xanthe closed her eyes. The glass beneath her hand seemed to vibrate. Above the keening note she could hear something else: a rumbling. What was that? Wheels, perhaps? Over a rough road, maybe? And something more. Water. Not the trickle of a brook or the rough sound of a rocky river, but a low thrum, suggesting a surge of deep, fast-flowing water. She waited for a vision, for a glimpse of what the pot was trying to show her, but nothing came.

Flora's voice reached her despite her dreamlike state. "Some of these are really special. Look, Meissen, Limoges . . . lovely bit of chinoiserie going on there. And those two have to be Viennese. Good grief! This lot must be worth a small fortune. Way out of our budget, I'm afraid. . . . Xanthe?" After a moment her daughter turned and Flora realized Xanthe's attention had been entirely taken by the single, unassuming pot. "Xanthe, love, have you found something?"

Xanthe opened her eyes and looked at her mother, her face confirming what Flora had already worked out.

At that moment they heard the front door open.

"Hello? Anyone about? Mrs. Westlake?" called a breezy male voice from the hallway.

Xanthe and Flora exchanged anxious glances. Both knew the price of the collection would be way beyond their means. And both knew that Xanthe absolutely had to have that copper pot.

"In here," Flora sang out as casually as she was able.

Esther Harris's nephew, middle-aged and middle management by the look of him, came striding into the room, hand outstretched in greeting, confidently accommodating Flora's need to adjust her hold on her crutches so that she could shake it.

"Lionel Harris. You got the key to work then? Well done. The front door can be a bit tricky. Poor old house needs some work. Apart from the outside, which the Trust insist is kept up, my aunt was inclined to let things slide. I see you've found her coffeepots. Can't think why she had such a fondness for the things. Don't recall her ever even drinking the stuff. But there it is, each to their own. I suppose one or two of the prettier ones have their charm."

Xanthe forced herself out of her reverie, shook the man's hand, and tried to avoid her mother's gaze. Lionel had revealed so much in such a short time it was difficult to process it. First, it was obvious to Xanthe, he had not known his aunt well. If he had he would surely have discovered what her collection really consisted of. Second, and here was the dilemma she knew Flora would be facing at precisely the same moment, he evidently had no idea how valuable the collection was. It was possible they could get a real bargain and turn a sizeable profit. But that would mean hiding the truth from him to strike a good deal. Xanthe could imagine many dealers she knew rubbing their hands together at the prospect of such a transaction. Less scrupulous members of the antique trade considered it no more than sound business, and if the seller was too lazy or too naive to find out the true value of what he had then that was his problem.

Flora, on the other hand, would never stoop to such low practices.

And yet, Xanthe could not walk away from that pot. Their only hope was that he might be prepared to split the collection.

Xanthe smiled. "Miss Harris must have been collecting for a long time."

The nephew shrugged. "My father and she weren't close. She hardly ever visited."

"And you don't want to keep any of these for yourself?" she asked.

Lionel Harris gave a dry bark of a laugh. "My wife said she won't give them house room. Mind you, that's not to say they don't have a value," he added, letting the thought sit there, waiting, presumably, for an offer.

Xanthe heard her mother tut under her breath. However much she prided herself on being a levelheaded businesswoman, to hear a lifetime of collecting reduced to nothing more than money, and to have so much craftsmanship and beauty reduced to a figure, would not sit well with her.

Xanthe nodded. "You're right," she said, knowing it was what the man wanted to hear, "some of them are quite sought after. And of course there is always a price to be had for silver." She let him enjoy his moment and then went on. "Problem is, a collection of this size, well, nobody's got room for it. We'd have difficulty shifting so many pots to the same person. And, to be honest, we don't have enough storage space for all of them. Ours is a small shop."

"I'm not surprised," said Lionel. "Business rates in Marlborough are a nightmare. How about you just choose the ones you think you could sell? I can let the charity shop take what you don't want."

Flora's mouth fell open at this. Xanthe knew they couldn't let him give away objects that could be worth tens of thousands of pounds without knowing their value. But if they talked the pieces up too much he might realize what he had and not let them have any. Xanthe thought quickly. It was true that the collection as a whole could be worth a great deal, but it was also a fact that few collectors existed who would be interested. Getting him to split it up might not be doing him out of what he could get, but they had to at least alert him to the real value.

"There are one or two that we're interested in. They'd fit with our stock, you see. Your best bet for the others would be to put them in an auction."

"Really? Would it be worth the bother?"

"Oh yes," Flora insisted. "We can let you have the number of a good auctioneer. He'll see they go into the right sale. You might be surprised how well they do."

"All right, sounds like a plan," he said. "Which ones do you want?"

Xanthe and Flora both waited, just for a moment, determined not to show any real eagerness, wary of seeming too enthusiastic.

Flora waved a stick at the shelves. "I'm quite taken with that flowery set with the cups and saucers. I think they might be Austrian. That silver one is Georgian and lovely, but a bit pricey for us, I should imagine. Art nouveau is always popular, so we could make you an offer for those two over there. And the one with the Chinese dragon, I like that. Xanthe, anything take your fancy?"

Xanthe's pulse began to race. The ringing in her ears grew louder. "Oh, you know me, Mum, I like the rustic stuff," she said, pointing at the copper pot. To her it felt so important, so filled with powerful history, she found it impossible to believe that Lionel Harris wouldn't be able to see how special it was.

"What, that funny old thing with the dents?" he asked. "I suppose you know what young people want. How much for those five then? Sorry to press you, but I've a lunch meeting in Salisbury, and there's the rest of the house to get round yet."

Xanthe didn't trust herself to handle the deal. Flora did her best to sound nonchalant.

"Well, if you throw in the little corner cabinet in the sitting room I think we could go to 3,000 pounds."

To his credit, Esther's nephew did a fair job of hiding his surprise. Even so, Xanthe saw a fleeting expression of delight cross his face. He cleared his throat and strode up to the shelves, studying the pots as if, suddenly, he knew what he was talking about.

"Three thousand, you say? Hmmm."

They waited. The sound of a church bell ringing drifted in through the thin glass of the window.

"Of course pretty china will always find a buyer," he said, looking hard at the set Flora wanted. "How about we make it three and a half?" he asked at last.

Xanthe tensed. Her mother's choices were sound enough, but it was still a niche market. And yet again she was asking her to spend money they scarcely had to buy something she wouldn't want to part with, at least not for some time.

Flora made a show of considering the offer, appearing to do some mental calculations. "Well, that is rather more than I'd like to pay, we do have our markup to consider. . . ." When Lionel didn't budge she smiled. "Tell you what, throw in the Persian rug and you've got yourself a deal."

An hour later, the rest of the house toured with no great finds, Xanthe tucked the bubble-wrapped copper chocolate pot safely into the back of the taxi, swaddling it in the rug, her hands trembling ever so slightly as she did so.

"Soon have you home," she whispered to the strange treasure. "And then you can tell me your story. Promise." At the same time she promised herself that whatever it revealed to her, there would be no more jaunts to the past. Not this time. It was just too dangerous.

She helped her mother into the passenger's seat, handing her some of her painkillers and a bottle of water. The village had woken up properly now, and even so late in the year there were tourists eagerly taking selfies in front of the stunning cottages. Not for the first time, Xanthe wondered at the power of such prettiness to draw people in. It wasn't simply the charming look of the place, of course she knew that; it was the presentation of an ideal. Chocolate box. A rural idyll. Harking back to a time long gone, when lives were simpler and the sun shone constantly. Except that, as Xanthe had found out for herself, lives were often far from simple, and the winters were just as bitter, the cold just as deadly. She climbed in behind the steering wheel and they set off for Marlborough.

2

THE REST OF THE DAY WAS TAKEN UP WITH GENERAL SHOP BUSINESS. NOW THAT THEY were open it had to be manned, and as Flora spent most of her time in her workshop repairing and restoring things, it fell to Xanthe to serve customers. Though the summer tourist season was over, most days there was still a steady flow of people. Some were true lovers of antiques. Others were on a day trip and drifted in and out enjoying looking at lovely things with little intention of spending any money. Flora called them "professional browsers." Xanthe pointed out that they often ended up making impulse buys. With such a new business and their finances still shaky, they couldn't afford to miss any potential sales. When they had arrived home from Laybrook, Xanthe had taken the copper pot, still wrapped, and squirrelled it away in her room. She wanted to look at it when she would not be disturbed, even if that meant waiting until after closing time. Flora set about the job of cleaning the other pots in her workshop. The cabinet went straight into the shop, where Xanthe found some nice pieces of glass and china to set it off. She tried to stay focused on what she was doing; tried to give her full attention to each customer. She almost succeeded. Almost. But the thought of what the little copper pot might reveal to her preyed on her mind. Until she had a chance to do some research she couldn't be sure of the date of the antique, but it looked old. Quite possibly seventeenth century. She knew that would be early for such a piece but found herself hoping that this was something rare. Something that could have come from the time she had visited. From Samuel's time. And as soon as she let that thought form in her head she felt unmoored. She shook her head against the idea.

That night, after a quick supper with Flora, Xanthe disappeared to her room, the singing object remaining an unspoken understanding between mother and daughter. Flora knew Xanthe had found something special and was accustomed to her need for privacy now. Xanthe's bedroom no longer held the stuffy heat of summer, built as it was into the slope of the roof, but had begun to reveal just how cold it might be in the months to come. She wrapped herself in an oversize fluffy jumper, found at a charity shop, tucking her feet underneath her as she sat on the bed. Slowly she peeled away the bubble wrap to reveal the pot, its bell-like song growing stronger and clearer as she did so. The metal felt cool beneath her fingers, the wooden handle smooth from the many palms that had held it. Lifting the lid, Xanthe inhaled. She had anticipated smelling the dust of ages along with a little cleaning fluid, but there was nothing so harsh. Just the faintest aroma of chocolate. She held the pot up to take in the simple but beautiful shape. Aside from a few scratches and one or two dents—with a rather noticeable one on the lid— it really was in very good condition. She imagined how many people must have used it. Listening hard she could again make out the sound of water, and that rumble that was hard to place.

"Where did you come from?" she asked. "What have you got to tell me?"

Again she waited for a glimpse of a face, or a building. Something. But nothing came. She felt both relief and disappointment. Setting the pot down on her bedside table, Xanthe fed words into a search engine on her phone. She scrolled down past some of the more obvious entries until she found a page she had used before when researching antiques. She read aloud what she found, as if hearing the words spoken would somehow nudge the pot into giving up its secrets.

"'Early chocolate pots followed a European design, often made from copper, brass, or silver, characteristically with a handle at the side, and a removable finial in the lid, sometimes hinged. The hinge suggests a later date. The earliest pots with sound provenance are dated around 1640, though rare examples may well predate this.'" She looked at it again. The opening in the lid was closed by a removable finial, but it was not hinged. She searched the base of the pot for marks and was able to make out something very faint. She retrieved her magnifying glass from her chest of drawers and looked more closely. As she did so, the ringing became much louder. Uncomfortably so. She squinted through the glass. There was something that could have been an S or possibly an F. She went back to her online search but could find no mention of any named manufacturers of chocolate pots before the early seventeen hundreds. She read that hot chocolate had become popular in the seventeenth century, and that chocolate houses existed before the more widely known coffeehouses, popular as meeting places often for people whose thinking was at odds with the mainstream. As such they had often been forcibly closed down by the authorities. The proprietors of those whose clientele were known to be rebels or dissenters often found themselves standing trial for crimes against the state, yet still the chocolate houses thrived. They were not, it seemed, places for genteel ladies, who would enjoy their chocolate at home, leading to a demand for more ornate and expensive pots in later years. Xanthe closed her eyes but still nothing came. She was at a loss to understand the way the pot was connecting with her. It was as if it was holding back, and she couldn't see why. This had never happened before. Any object that had sung to her had seemed eager to reveal its story. It occurred to her that if she took it into the garden, closer to the blind house, the pot would probably react. The thought frightened her. Before moving to Marlborough she had only ever heard or glimpsed the stories attached to the things she found. The discovery of the old jail in the corner of the garden behind their antique shop had changed everything. Sitting as it did on an intersection of powerful ley lines, it acted as a portal to times past. If she got too close she might fall back through time again. And go where? To what time? She didn't know when the pot had been made or who it had originally belonged to. She could end up anywhere. *Anywhen.*

She placed the pot on her windowsill so that she could still look at it without being close enough to trigger its louder sounds. Puzzled, she quickly changed into the man's cotton nightshirt she liked to sleep in and jumped into bed before the chill of the room could get to her. She half expected vivid dreams. Dreams that would give her clues as to the history of the chocolate pot and the people connected to it. But instead she slept heavily, deeply and blankly, failing to hear the alarm in the morning so that she awoke to the sound of Flora calling her down for breakfast.

The sun was still shining, so Xanthe tackled the job of winterizing the flower tubs and baskets at the front of the shop. Being outside, doing a bit of gardening, she reasoned, would be helpful for settling her unquiet mind. Wrestling her long curls into a loose ponytail, she pulled an old favorite, a khaki woolen army greatcoat, over her layered T-shirts and tea dress, with thick socks inside her Dr. Martens, and was glad of the extra warmth. As she emptied the old soil from the tubs into a recycling bag, she made a mental note to invest in some fingerless mittens. The geraniums had been frost nipped and were beyond saving, but some of the tougher plants in the baskets could be put away for next year. She decided she would see what the Saturday market had to offer by way of spring bulbs and something for a bit of color through the gloomy winter months.

After an hour of stooping and working with her trowel she straightened up, stretching her aching back. She noticed Gerri cleaning the windows of her tea shop on the other side of the cobbled street and waved. Gerri waved back and came to stand in the doorway. As always she was immaculately turned out in vintage 1940s clothing, her hair expertly rolled, scarlet lipstick flawlessly applied. Not for the first time Xanthe admired her friend's ability to bring up two children on her own, run a business, and look so wonderful. Her total commitment to vintage clothing was also impressive.

"Fancy some gardening work over here?" Gerri called, gesturing at her own displays. They did look in need of a bit of attention. Perhaps plants were actually something Gerri wasn't good at.

Xanthe called back. "I'm supposed to be in the shop, but I can come over after closing time and sort them out for you if you like."

"Wonderful! What's the hourly rate for expert gardeners?"

"Oh, two scones and a slice of Battenberg should cover it."

Gerri laughed but then her expression altered, becoming suddenly distracted and serious. Xanthe saw that she was looking past her now. She sensed rather than heard someone come to stand just behind her.

"You always did have a sweet tooth," said the horribly familiar voice.

Xanthe's stomach lurched. Before turning she made sure her face would not give away her shock. When she did turn, she looked her visitor squarely in the eye.

"Marcus. What an unpleasant surprise."

"Hey, Xan, don't be like that. After I've come all this way, specially to see you?"

"Uninvited."

Marcus hadn't changed. He was still a smart dresser. Still bothered about looking cool. Still had that edgy, restless appeal that women loved. That Xanthe had loved. Once. A long time ago. When she had left London she had fervently hoped that she had left Marcus in her past too, for good. She glanced through the shop window. If Flora spotted him there would be a serious scene.

"Aren't you going to invite me into your emporium? Show me what you're up to these days?"

"What part of your crazy brain thought I would want you here? Did you imagine me and Mum would welcome you with open arms? Lovely to see you, Marcus! Come in and have a cup of tea, Marcus! Let's talk about old times, like how you let me take the blame for your drugs stash, you remember? The one that got me sent to prison, Marcus? Just how did you see this going, really?" Xanthe couldn't hide her anger at his nerve in showing up. She was aware of Gerri still standing in the doorway of the tea shop, watching. Marcus took a step closer and Xanthe's whole body tensed.

"Come on, Xan, you know I never meant for things to end the way they did. We've stuff to talk about, you and me. Unfinished business."

She was on the point of telling him exactly how finished things were between them when an elderly couple went into the shop. She pushed past him.

"I'm busy," she said, pointedly shutting the door behind her as she followed the customers in. Marcus was not to be so easily put off, however. Xanthe heard the bell clang as he entered the shop. She continued to ignore him, engaging the couple in light conversation about a set of Victorian prints, while Marcus prowled among the displays picking up random objects.

"We saw them through the window the other day," the elderly gentleman was telling her. "We've thought about them ever since, haven't we, Mary?"

His wife agreed, adding that they had even picked out a place to hang them in their bungalow in Devizes. Xanthe's resentment of Marcus was increasing by the minute. These were genuine lovers of antiques who were considering a costly purchase. She should be giving them her undivided attention, not fretting about her loathsome ex-boyfriend, trying to figure out how she could get him to leave before Flora saw him.

She left the couple examining the pictures and hissed at Marcus.

"Will you just leave? We have nothing more to talk about. It's all been said. There is nothing left."

"You don't really believe that, do you?"

Xanthe heard the unmistakable sound of her mother stick-stepping down the hallway from the workshop.

"Just go!"

"Not until we've had a chance to talk. You and me."

Xanthe saw with a sinking heart that she wasn't going to get rid of him unless she agreed to hear what he had to say.

Seeing her hesitate he added, "Just an hour, Xan? For old times' sake?"

"If you promise that you'll leave me alone afterward." She bundled him through the door. "OK. But not here. I'll meet you at lunchtime."

"Name the place."

She thought of picking somewhere she didn't normally go. She didn't want this man in her new life. But then, it might be as well to be among friends. Marcus could turn nasty if he didn't get his own way. "The Feathers," she told him. "It's on the high street. Now go!" She shut the door behind him just as Flora came into the shop. Xanthe was thankful for the distraction of the customers, and drew her mother into the fun of closing the sale and wrapping up the set of prints.

The rest of the morning was mercifully busy, giving Xanthe little time to think about having to spend time with Marcus. As the hours passed she felt her anger grow. How dare he come to her home? How dare he expect anything of her after the way he had betrayed her, after what he had put her family through? And how had she allowed herself to be manipulated into doing what he wanted? One of the worst things about him turning up was that now she found herself having to tell her mother more lies. She knew how much Flora detested Marcus; seeing him again would bring back so many painful memories. Better that she never knew he had turned up. Better that

Xanthe deal with him herself. Even so, it was horrible to have to fib to Flora about what she was doing at lunchtime.

"Lovely that Harley's so keen to have you sing in the pub, wanting to sign you up for an extra stint," Flora called after Xanthe as she left the shop. "Make sure he agrees to free beer for your family at the next gig!"

"That'd be just you, Mum."

"Perks of being the parent of a superstar," Flora joked.

Xanthe closed the door and hurried away to The Feathers. She wished she was going there to sing instead of meeting Marcus. At least she would have the reassuring presence of Harley. Apart from the warmth of his person-ality and the fact that he was helping her restart her singing career, his interest in local myths and legends gave them another common ground. She had him to thank for discovering the intersecting ley lines in her garden where the blind house had been built. He was someone she could at least talk to about strange things, even if only theoretically, without feeling completely insane.

The pub was about half full, mostly of people eating light lunches, en-joying the good, simple food and the ambience of the ancient, low-beamed building. She found Marcus sitting at the bar, already halfway through what she guessed was not his first pint of beer. Opposite him, Harley stood, pol-ishing a glass furiously, not for one second taking his eyes off Marcus. De-spite his burliness, his tattoos, his wild beard, and his general hairy biker appearance, Harley was known as a mild-mannered Scottish landlord who kept a friendly inn. This was the first time Xanthe had seen him look men-acing. Clearly something about Marcus troubled him.

Marcus spotted Xanthe and raised his glass.

"Here she is! My girl. What'll you have, Xan?"

Xanthe took in Harley's reaction to this greeting. His bushy brows lifted in surprise.

"I'm not your girl, Marcus," she said quickly. "I'm not your anything."

"Chill! Come on, what can I get you?"

"Coffee, please, Harley," she said.

"Coming right up, hen," Harley replied in his rolling Scottish accent. "If y've a minute I need to speak with you about Saturday night?" he asked, tilt-ing his head in the direction of the far end of the bar.

"I'll be a moment," she told Marcus. "Look, there's a table over there." She pointed to a private seat in the corner.

Harley kept his voice low.

"Tell me it's none of my business, hen . . ."

"It is none of your business, Harley."

"But yon fella is trouble. I've a nose for it," he insisted, tapping the side of his nose.

"Thanks for caring, but I'm OK. Really."

"Really? Because there's trouble and then there's *trouble*, and he's not the sort you want messing with your head. I've seen his type before. They have a look. . . ."

She met his gaze. Harley wasn't a person to mince his words, but even he was reluctant to come right out and say what he was thinking.

"Is it that obvious?" Xanthe asked. Marcus had always prided himself in not conforming to the druggy stereotype.

"I've no wish to slander my own hometown and place of my birth, lassie, but I grew up in Glasgow, you know what I'm saying?"

Xanthe reached across the bar and briefly patted Harley's hand. "It's OK, I promise. I can handle him."

"Aye, well, you know where I am."

Reluctantly, Xanthe joined Marcus at the table. She took off her coat, not enjoying the way he watched her as she did so.

"Looking good, Xan. Even better than I remembered. I've missed you."

"What do you want, Marcus?"

"Hey, where's the Xanthe I used to know and love?"

"I'm not that girl anymore. Experiences change a person."

"Things went sour, I know it. But the past is the past."

"So why did you come? Why not leave well enough alone?"

"We were good together, you and me." He leaned forward and attempted to take her hands in his. She snatched them back. He opened his mouth to speak again but was interrupted by Harley arriving to slam the tray of coffee things down on the table and glare. Marcus waited until Xanthe's protector was out of earshot. "Like I said, I miss you. And I wanted to know that you were doing OK."

"I'm fine. Satisfied?"

"I'm glad, truly." He paused, taking a swig of his beer, and then went on. "To be honest, things haven't been easy for me. Not for a while. I made some bad choices, I know, but, well, I got let down too. . . . I lost the flat. Been sofa surfing since spring. . . ."

Xanthe sat back in her chair, staring at him.

"You've come here to ask me for money? Un-bloody-believable!"

"No, it's not that. But I do need to get my life back on track, and that means putting the band together again."

"You can't be serious."

"I've been writing songs again. They're good, Xan, I know they are. But they're for you to sing. No one else. Think about it. We can get out there, get performing again."

For a moment Xanthe was rendered speechless. It wasn't just the nerve of the man, thinking she would consider having anything to do with him after the way he had treated her; it was more complicated than that. Whatever else had happened, whatever else had gone wrong between the two of them, their shared passion for their music, for performing, for the band, that had been real. And if she was totally honest, she missed that. Missed being part of a band. Missed having songs written that were perfect for her voice. She shook her head, attempting to shake away the memories, reminding herself that there was no room for Marcus in her new life.

"I can't decide if you're crazy or if you think I am. After all that happened, after everything you did, you honestly think I'd want to work with you again?"

"Don't you miss it? Don't you want to sing again?"

"Who says I'm not singing?" She nodded at one of the posters near the door. It listed the lineup of Friday and Saturday night bands and singers for the coming month. Xanthe's name was clearly visible.

Marcus frowned and then quickly adjusted his expression. If he had been going to poke fun at her new venue he thought better of it. Instead he smiled at her. "You see? I knew it. I knew you wouldn't be able to give up on your singing. It's too big a part of you, Xan. We both know that. I'm so pleased that you are still singing. Really, I am." He hesitated and then went on. "What happened to you . . . OK, what I let happen to you. It was bad, seriously bad. If I'd ever thought that something like that could happen . . ." Seeing Xanthe's own face darken as she grimly stirred her coffee, he tried a different tack. "I want to make it up to you. Will you let me?"

"Oh? And how do you think you could do that?"

"Like I said, I've been writing songs. Songs for you." He became suddenly animated, his eyes bright with real excitement for what he was telling her. "They are good, I know it. But they need you to be seriously great. Your voice. It would be perfect. Let me play them for you. Just listen to them, then you can decide if you want to sing them or not. I know you won't be able to re- sist, not once you've heard them. You don't have to come up to London. We can find somewhere here. Even a one-horse town like this must have a decent keyboard in it somewhere." He laughed, letting his true opinion of provincial life show again just for a moment.

Despite what she knew of Marcus, despite everything he had put her through, just for a moment Xanthe let herself imagine what it would be like. Let herself think about how great it would be to be collaborating on new material, working with a proper band again. And then Marcus reached across the table again and took her hand, holding it tightly. Something about that gesture, about that connection, brought back all the hurt and betrayal. She pulled her hand back and got to her feet.

"I should never have agreed to talk to you."

"Wait . . ." Marcus got up, putting his hand on her arm.

"Go back to London. Don't come here again." She snatched her coat off the back of her chair but still Marcus held her arm. When she tried to shake him off he only gripped tighter.

"You can't just turn me away. . . ."

A shadow fell over Marcus as Harley came to stand close.

"Oh, I think you'll find she can, laddie," he growled.

"Call off your shaggy dog, Xan. This is between you and me."

Xanthe was spared the trouble of replying. Marcus might have been lean, but he wasn't small. Nevertheless, Harley picked him up by the scruff of the neck and the belt of his jeans and launched him toward the door. Marcus fell in a heap on the floor, his dignity further bruised by two young women all but falling over him on their way in. He scrambled to his feet, thought about taking Harley on, then thought better of it.

"This isn't finished!" he said to Xanthe. And then he was gone.

There was a moment's awkward silence.

"Sorry, Harley," Xanthe said at last.

"My pleasure, hen," Harley assured her, clearing the table as he spoke. "Any time."

"Oh, I think he got the message. We won't see him again," she said.

Harley gave her a look that said he thought otherwise.

Xanthe strode back to the shop, her mood darkening with every stride. She wanted to believe Marcus would stay away, but she knew him too well. Harley was probably right. Marcus was a certain kind of trouble, and he wouldn't give up so easily. As she walked she thought about how the men in her life seemed to cause nothing but trouble, each in their own way. Her father had wrecked his marriage and caused no end of financial difficulties for her and her mother. Her relationship with Marcus had been a disaster that ended up with her in jail for something *he* had done. Liam was being a good friend, it was true, but Xanthe's cynical mood questioned even that. And then there was Samuel. The one who still pulled at her heart, but the one who was forever out of her reach. By the time she got back to the shop her face gave away her mood.

"Goodness," said Flora when she saw her. "That bad?"

"What? Oh, no. It's all good with Harley. Just . . . you know, stuff."

"Right. Stuff," said her mother, seeing that Xanthe didn't want to talk about it. "Did you get any lunch? No? Come on then, I was just about to open a packet of soup."

It was after midnight before Xanthe managed to get to sleep, only to be woken again an hour later by a cat fight in the garden. Groggy and confused, she clambered out of bed and went to sit at the little window. There was a full moon that shone brighter than the streetlights of the town, so that the walled garden behind the shop was clearly lit. The arguing cats spat some more, their moon shadows jittering as they crouched and growled. Xanthe opened the window and whistled, watching as the distraction of the noise gave the smaller cat the chance to run away. The larger one thrashed its tail from side to side before stalking off, nimbly leaping to the top of the old brick wall and then dropping into the next garden. Xanthe shivered. If she had been dreaming she had no recollection of it, but she was too unsettled to attempt sleep again. And then the chocolate pot resumed its ringing. When she had first brought it to her room its sounds had been constant, so that she had even tried putting it, tightly wrapped, in the cupboard under the stairs. It hadn't made any difference, so she had retrieved it. It seemed if the found object was near, its singing would reach her, clear as if it was beside her. She knew she should not have been surprised at this: why should such a magical thing conform to the laws of physics, after all? Something that became clear to her was that it sang louder to get her attention if she tried to ignore it, or if she had been out of the house for a while. Like a needy child, it would call to her and would not be quiet until she attended to it. Xanthe ran her fingers through her hair. What was the point of the thing calling to her if it wasn't going to show her anything? Outside, at the far corner of the garden, the stone-work of the blind house gleamed beneath the nighttime illumination. As the garden plants began to die back for the winter, the little building was becoming more visible. Xanthe wondered how long it would be before her mother insisted they could make use of the space, filling it with stock for the shop. How could she explain to her the dangers of doing that? She could hardly tell her that the building was situated on a magical ley line, and that it had the power to transport her back in time. No, she would have to convince her it was irredeemably damp. She felt a burgeoning headache and the noise of the pot was making it worse. Suddenly, her patience ran out. She threw on her chunky jumper, jammed her feet into her boots, picked up the pot, and went downstairs. She had learned to avoid the floorboards that creaked and how to open the back door quietly so as not to wake up Flora. Once outside, she marched across the wiry grass of the lawn and stopped a few paces short of the old jail.

"Right," she spoke softly but firmly to the antique in her hands. "I'm not going any closer. No way I'm being whisked off anywhere. So, if you've something to share with me, now's the time."

She waited, feeling faintly foolish. Nothing happened. She risked taking a step forward. The sound of rushing water returned, louder than before. She closed her eyes. At first all she saw was darkness and blotches of moonlight on the insides of her eyelids. And then the vision hit her. Sharp and clear and shocking. Samuel! Despite the gloom she could make out his dark, shoulder-length hair, his strong, noble features, and his troubled expression. His eyes looked watchful, concerned, his mouth set, whether in anger or determination she could not tell. His hair was disheveled, and the velvet of his black jacket dull with dust. He was somewhere dark, his breath visible in the cold air. She could see that he too was lit by the moon, its rays slanting across his face. As her vision broadened, Xanthe could see that the moonlight was fractured through bars. He was in a jail of some sort! For a moment he vanished from her sight, and all she saw instead was deep, swirling water, dark and dangerous. And then she saw his eyes again, searching, trying to focus, almost as if he could see her.

"Samuel!" she called. "Samuel!"

And he turned toward her, as if he had heard her voice. Her heart lurched as their gaze connected. He seemed to search the darkness, his lips forming her name. Could he see her?

And then the vision stopped. The darkness descended once again. Xanthe opened her eyes, gasping. Although she could no longer see him, she could feel Samuel's presence, almost hear his breathing. And above all of what she had seen and what she could hear there was an unmistakable, powerful feeling of dread. She could not tell where he was incarcerated. She could not know how long he had been there or if he had heard her when she cried out his name. What she did know, beyond any doubt, was that he was being kept there against his will. That he was hiding very real fear. That he was trapped and threatened, and in great danger.

3

XANTHE HAD NEVER FELT SO TORN. SHE HAD PROMISED HERSELF SHE WOULD NOT TRY TO travel back in time again. She had experienced such dark confusion on her last journey home, there had been a moment she feared she would be unable to return. That she might be stuck hundreds of years before her own time, or worse even than that, lost in some timeless limbo. Apart from the risk of the transition, the seventeenth century was hardly a safe time for anyone to be living in, let alone a lone woman outsider who spoke strangely and had no family. And then there was Flora. She needed Xanthe. However independent she liked to try to be, she couldn't manage the shop on her own. Beyond that, there was the fact that in order to disappear for any length of time, Xanthe would have to concoct a string of lies to tell her mother. And Liam. And Harley and Gerri, who had all become important people in her new life in Marlborough. How could she take a step that would mean she had to deceive all of them? And what if she never came back? Her mother would never know what had happened to her. It would break her heart.

Xanthe knew all this. Her good sense and sound reasoning told her that to risk what she had, to risk hurting the people she cared about in such a way, was out of the question. But . . . but . . . When she had left Samuel, she had at least known he was safe. He was with his own family, leading his own life. Now, however, he was clearly in deep trouble. The sense of dread and peril that she had experienced during her vision simmered beneath the surface of her consciousness even now, in daylight, while she tried to go about her everyday life. Her gift might be as much a curse as a blessing, but it never lied. How could she not try to help him? What if there was no one else to go to his aid? His family had been Catholics at a time when that in itself was enough to get a person hanged. Their reputations, their work, their very lives were anything but safe. What if his father and brother were also locked up somewhere, awaiting a spurious trial, with no one to defend them? It seemed that the chocolate pot was directing her back not just to Samuel's time but to Samuel himself. What was the point of having a gift, of being capable of something as incredible as traveling back through time, if you weren't prepared to use it? She had come to realize, after helping Alice, that it was necessary that she do what she could to help those who called to her. To help those to whom she was led by the object that sang to her. She had a part to play in making sure history turned into the present, and ultimately the future, in the way that it should. It had been an epiphany for her, realizing that fact, acknowledging it. If she didn't answer the call, what might the consequences be? Not just for Samuel, but for the order of things. The way things were meant to be. She did not pretend to herself that she fully understood it all, but she knew what was right. She knew what she had to do.

As she dressed to go down to breakfast she was shocked to realize that she had already decided what she would do. What she *must* do. All that remained was to think of a workable story to tell her mother and summon up the courage to step back inside the blind house.

She was surprised to find the kitchen empty. She knew Flora was up, having passed her bedroom on her way downstairs. Then she heard the front door open and shut, the brass bell announcing Flora's return. It was strange that she had been out before breakfast. What was more worrying was the furious stamping of her crutches and footsteps as she made her way up the stairs. Something had put Flora in a rage. Something or someone.

"Mum?" Xanthe peered at her as she stood in the kitchen doorway clutching a pint of milk.

"When were you going to tell me?" she demanded. She snatched off the bit of scarf that was tying back her light brown hair and chucked it down onto the table. Her ordinarily placid features were hardened by anger.

"Sorry?" Xanthe tried not to panic, telling herself there was no way her mother could know what she was planning to do.

"I have just seen Marcus in the high street."

"Ah."

"How long were you planning to keep it a secret?"

Xanthe winced at the word. "Did you speak to him?"

"I didn't have a choice! He greeted me like a long-lost friend. Said how he'd loved seeing you again. How pleased he was that you had agreed to meet him."

"Mum . . ."

"That man is poison, Xanthe. I can't believe you sneaked off to the pub with him. Our pub . . ."

"I didn't sneak."

"You didn't tell me you were meeting him."

"I didn't want to worry you."

"Oh, and that always works, doesn't it? Hiding difficult stuff until it's become a disaster, and then you have to tell me."

Xanthe had to remind herself they were only talking about Marcus. "Mum," she said, taking the milk from her and setting about making tea, "sit down. I'll get us some breakfast and I'll explain everything. Though there really is nothing much to tell." She waited until her mother had, somewhat reluctantly, taken her place at the table before going on. "He turned up yesterday, out of the blue. He wasn't going to leave until I'd listened to what he wanted."

"Which was?"

"Me singing in his band again. Or money. Or both."

"Good grief."

"Exactly."

"I hope you told him to get lost."

"I told him, and Harley told him."

"Good for you. Good for him."

Xanthe put the mugs of tea, box of muesli, and bottle of milk on the table and sat down. A thought had occurred to her. An idea that was at once simple and yet somehow horribly manipulative. "Thing is," she said, choosing her words with care, "I don't think he really got the message."

"What, not even with Harley delivering it?"

"He's still here, isn't he? If he'd properly taken on board the fact that I want nothing to do with him he'd have gone back to London yesterday, surely?"

Flora considered this, taking a sip of her tea. Xanthe was relieved to see her anger was subsiding. She completely understood the way she felt about Marcus and wasn't surprised at how she had reacted to finding him showing up in their new life. What was harder to cope with was how hurt her mother was that Xanthe had kept a secret from her. A secret that was nothing compared to the one she was in the process of constructing.

Flora shook her head. "He's got some nerve, coming here."

"Marcus was never short of self-confidence."

"Loathsome man. I can't stand the thought of him hanging around, pestering you."

"I did tell him pretty plainly. And Harley, well, he has a way of making people see his point of view. Thing is," she hesitated, taking a breath, "Marcus is pretty boneheaded. He sees what he wants to see. He's not going to give up easily."

"Well next time I see him I won't be caught off guard. I'll tell him in no uncertain terms where he can go."

"He thinks he can persuade me. To sing with the band again."

"He can't. Can he?"

"Of course not! But . . ."

"But what? Xanthe, love, you're surely not thinking of having anything to do with him?"

"No. Absolutely not. But getting him to believe that . . ." She tipped cereal into a bowl and gave a shrug. "Maybe I shouldn't give him the chance to keep bothering me. Perhaps if I went away, just for a few days . . ."

"Away where? And why should you? This is your home."

"I know, and you're right, but, well, if I'm not here there's no point in him hanging around, is there?"

"You shouldn't have to run away."

"I'm not running anywhere. Look at this." She searched for a page on her phone and passed it to Flora.

"The Autumn Antiques Fair in Bristol. What about it?"

"Why don't I go? Find myself a B and B. Spend a couple of days at the fair finding us lots of lovely stock while also removing myself from Mr. Persistent-Pain-in-the-Arse's reach? Good idea or not, what d'you reckon?"

"I had thought we might go to that together."

"And close the shop? Again?"

And so it was decided. Guilt at how easy it had been to deceive her mother sat heavy as a stone in Xanthe's stomach, but she was relieved that she had found a way to do what she planned to do. What she *had* to do. Not that there weren't a dozen other things to be taken care of before she could go anywhere. She would have to convince Flora that she had booked a room at a bed-and-breakfast, without leaving her any details of it in case she tried to contact her and found she had never checked in. She had to assemble clothes that would not make her look like a madwoman in 1605. She had to pretend to leave, this time in her taxi, park it somewhere miles away, get back to the shop, and into the blind house in the garden without Flora seeing her. She had to make absolutely certain, of course, that she had the gold locket her mother had given her with her at all times. It was her ticket home and she would never forget how she had felt when she thought it lost forever. She also had to remember to "forget" to take her phone. Again. Leaving it in an obvious place in the house, so that her mother couldn't try to call her and then worry when she didn't answer. Or else think up a story about it not working. And she would have to find some antiques from somewhere; coming home empty-handed was not an option. And then there was the chocolate pot. Xanthe would have to make sure it was hidden somewhere in the garden so that she could quickly retrieve it and use it to step back through the centuries, having not had the chance to try it and see if it would work. Very quickly, Xanthe's initial relief at setting up the lie for her journey disappeared and was replaced by a level of stress that took a great deal of effort to manage without Flora noticing that something was wrong. Xanthe decided if her mother questioned her mood she would just blame it on having Marcus around.

She was sufficiently distracted to have forgotten that she was supposed to be collecting the pine dresser in Devizes with Liam. Flora had to remind her to be ready, saying that she would mind the shop.

"I can clean some of the silver while I'm in there."

"I suppose it will do you good to get out of the workshop, try your hand in the shop again," Xanthe told her.

"Might as well get used to it if you're going to be off gallivanting for three days."

"I don't even know how to gallivant. It's a stock-buying trip, remember?"

"Think I'll set up a little workbench in a corner of the shop. Make best use of the hours I'm in there. And don't forget we need to start planning Christmas."

"Mum, there's just the two of us."

"I know that, but we're still going to do it properly." Flora's tone was businesslike but Xanthe knew her too well. She knew how much her mother loved Christmas. This would be her first in twenty-five years without her husband. Her first with Xanthe in Marlborough. It mattered.

"Of course," Xanthe said, nodding emphatically. "First one in our new home. It'll be special."

"We'll need a turkey, even if it's a small one. There's an organic butcher's stall in the Saturday market. We can order one from there. It's got to be free range. And a tree, we need to find out where to get one of those."

"And where to put it," said Xanthe, thinking of the muddle that was their flat.

By the time Liam arrived with the van Flora was happily organizing her china repair tools and an angle-poise lamp in the shop, her head full of preparations for the festive season. The borrowed van was large and in good condition. Liam drove, and they took the main road out of Marlborough toward the auction house in Devizes.

"You OK?" he asked Xanthe after a few miles. "You are unusually quiet."

"Am I usually noisy?"

"You usually speak."

"Sorry. Thanks for taking the time to do this. Hope I'm not holding up a crucial bit of classic car restoration."

"You are, but you're forgiven. As long as we get lunch somewhere on the way home."

"I'm going away, did I say? Got a ton of things to do."

"Somewhere exciting?"

"Antiques Fair in Bristol. Mostly Victorian stuff."

"You antique women know how to have a good time."

Xanthe gave him a look. She leaned forward and tried the switch on the van radio. "Does this work?"

"Of course!"

"I didn't think they still made them like this. . . ."

"And you call yourself a lover of all things vintage? Here, you have to press that." Without taking his eyes from the road he prodded the right button and the elderly device burst into static and then song. "Wow! Gotta love a bit of Neil Sedaka," he declared, joining in with "Oh! Carol." His voice was melodic and rich, note-perfect and tuneful.

"Very impressive," Xanthe told him.

He paused to grin at her. "What, just because I play lead guitar you thought I wouldn't be able to carry a tune in a bucket?"

"I've seen Tin Lid perform, Liam, remember? I know you can sing. But driving at the same time? Well . . ."

"Some of us blokes can multitask, you know." He went back to singing, hamming it up for Xanthe's benefit. When she began to giggle he feigned hurt. "You could help me out here instead of taking the Micky. Come on, you'll know the words even if you think you don't. Here we go with the high bit. *'Darlin' there will never be another . . .'*"

Despite herself, Xanthe was unable to resist joining in. Their voices were good together and Liam quickly gave up playing the fool so that he could sing properly with her. Xanthe felt the tension in her shoulders easing.

Three songs and several miles later a news bulletin came on. Xanthe switched it off and they continued in companionable silence for a while. As they neared the town of Devizes, Liam spoke again.

"I saw Harley last night," he said. "He mentioned you'd had a visitor. From London."

"Did he?"

When Xanthe didn't offer anything else Liam let it drop for a while, but eventually curiosity got the better of him. "I'm guessing from what, Harley said, and what he said your visitor said, we're talking the toxic ex here. So . . . you gave him your new address? Only, I thought he was the baddest of bad from your dark past and you never wanted to see him again."

"Yeah, well, Marcus has never been very interested in what anybody else wants."

"So you didn't invite him?"

"I did not. Nor do I have any idea how he got my address. Might have pestered my father for it, I suppose. Oh, turn left here."

"What?"

"The auction house is to the left of the town center. We need to turn off the bypass."

Liam did as she instructed, taking the hint that Xanthe didn't want to discuss her ex any further. They soon arrived at their destination, parked, and got out of the van. Xanthe felt awkward not explaining things to Liam when he was giving up his time to help her, but he didn't need to know every detail of her life. Things were complicated enough without letting him get more involved. At that moment it was all she could do to concentrate on the practical details of her journey back to the seventeenth century. She felt bad for having allowed herself to forget that Samuel was in trouble. Here she was singing, enjoying Liam's company, when Samuel was in danger. Once again her head filled with panicky thoughts: what if she was too late? What if Samuel got moved before she could travel to his time? Time that seemed to move at a different rate to her own, so that she could not be certain how many days or weeks he was being held, or when he might face a trial. The clock was ticking, and yet in the present day she felt as if everything was moving with maddening slowness. As if she were in some awful dream, her legs leaden, her every action clumsy and unhelpful. She didn't have time to tell Liam everything he wanted to know. Didn't have the energy to worry about his growing feelings for her. Not then.

The dresser, when taken apart, fit snugly into the van. Xanthe spent some time tightening bungee cords and wedging blankets around its edges so it wouldn't get damaged on the journey. As she worked, it occurred to her that this could be a good place to park her taxi while she was away. Leaving Liam to make the final adjustments to the load, when she settled up in the office she checked that they wouldn't mind accommodating her vehicle in the car park for a couple of days. There was a cafe at the auction house so she was able to persuade Liam to get a quick bite there rather than seek out a pub.

A leisurely, chatty lunch was something Xanthe had neither nerves nor time for. On the journey home he was sufficiently sensitive to pick up on the fact that something was bothering her.

"You don't have to tell me," he said as he steered the van amid traffic swirling around a roundabout.

"Tell you?"

"About whatever it is that's bugging you. It's OK. We hardly know each other." There was a pause before he added, "That's where you're supposed to disagree and tell me that we're friends and of course friends share stuff...."

"Sounds like you can have both sides of that conversation."

"All I'm saying is, if your ex is giving you grief, well . . . I'm a good listener."

For all his joking she knew he was being sincere.

"Thanks," she said, and meant it. "If I need to talk, I'll . . ."

"Excellent! . . . Will you look at this plonker in front of us; does he even know he's towing a caravan? You can't throw an old banger of a car around like that. Give me strength. . . ."

Back in Marlborough, Liam maneuvered the van down the cobbled alleyway so that they could park outside the shop. Flora appeared in the doorway, eager to see their new acquisition.

"You're back quickly," she said.

"Liam is a demon driver," Xanthe explained.

"And your daughter has something against leisurely lunches," Liam added.

At that moment a man emerged from the shop behind Flora, who turned to smile at him. Xanthe thought he looked familiar but could not place him. She noticed how her mum seemed to like talking to him and felt a little lurch of love for her and a surge of hope. If her mother could enjoy working in the shop and meeting new people it would be so good for both of them.

"A happy customer?" Xanthe asked as the man left with a wave.

"Yes and no. He did buy that pinchbeck snuffbox we found last month in Melksham market, but he really wanted to talk to me."

"Oh?" Xanthe stopped hefting one of the doors of the dresser and watched her mother's face closely.

"I bumped into him in the Saturday market. He runs the artisan bread stall. I mentioned we have this place and . . ."

"He came looking for you."

Liam stepped out of the back of the van with another door. "Where do you want this, Mrs. W?"

"Oh, take it on through to my workshop, please."

"Mum." Xanthe wanted to hear more about the mysterious visitor. "The man from the bread stall? Did he come here to chat you up?"

"What, Graham? Don't be silly, love, he's a happily married man. No, he came because they are short a person for their bell-ringing team at St. Luke's. He wondered if I could help out. I think I rather like the idea. Thought I might give it a go."

"Bell-ringing? Well, that sounds . . . but what about your hands? Do you think you'd be able to manage?"

"Perfectly well, thank you very much. I'm not a complete cripple, you know."

"Mum!"

"Oh, don't look at me like that. I'm allowed to make jokes about myself, aren't I? It'll be fun. Do me good to get out of the shop and the flat every now and again. Now, come on, let's have a look at this lovely dresser and get it inside before it starts raining, shall we?"

Flora directed operations, with Liam and Xanthe slowly manhandling the dresser through the front door, along the hall, and into the workshop. Once installed they left Flora to enjoy inspecting the new treasure and went back outside.

"Here," Xanthe said, handing Liam the money to give to his friend for the use of the van. "Thanks. Really, I couldn't have done it without you. And it was . . . nice."

"Nice? OK, it's a start, I guess. Nice. Hmmm." Liam flashed her a smile and then climbed into the driver's seat.

"I should pay you for your time too."

"Not necessary," he insisted, starting up the engine. "But you could buy me a pint of Henge later. Deal?"

"Deal," she agreed, and found herself torn between wanting to show how much she appreciated his help and needing to prepare for the impossible journey she had to make.

As she was helping him reverse out of the narrow street Gerri came out of her tea shop.

"Was that a Welsh dresser I saw going into your shop?"

Xanthe nodded. "Mum can't wait to get at it with her paintbrush."

"I don't suppose it came with lots of lovely china, by any chance?" She left the doorway and came over to stand next to Xanthe, brushing icing sugar off her hands before wiping them on her pristine apron. "Been finishing off a couple of Victoria sponges. This stuff gets everywhere."

"We did get a box of assorted plates if you want to come in and have a look," Xanthe told her.

They found the box behind the desk that served as a counter in the shop. Xanthe let Gerri dig through the wrapping while she looked at the takings for the morning.

"Mum's done quite well for a weekday," she murmured.

"She'll be taking over your job as head of sales if you're not careful. . . . Ooh, that's a lovely strawberry pattern. I'll definitely take that one. Can't have too many plates," she said, putting it to one side.

"Actually, she's going to have to do everything for a few days. I'm going to an antiques fair in Bristol."

"Oh?" Gerri glanced at her just long enough for her surprise to register. Xanthe counted herself lucky to have made a new friend so soon after moving to Marlborough, but there were times when a person knowing the ins and outs of your working and family life had its drawbacks.

"Mum's been in quite good shape recently," Xanthe assured her. "The arthritis seems pretty manageable right now. And anyway I . . . I need to get away. Just for a while."

Gerri stopped rooting in the box, sitting back on her heels. "This wouldn't have anything to do with that good-looking stranger who called yesterday, would it?"

"Sort of. That was Marcus."

"Ah, the infamous Marcus. Well, easy to see why you fell for him. Is he trying to win you back?"

Xanthe pulled a pale cream tea plate from the box, running her finger around its fluted edge, which was decorated with tiny ivy leaves. "Let's just say if I'm not here he can't make a nuisance of himself. Here, you can have this one," she said, handing her the little plate.

Gerri smiled, picking up the larger one too. "Thank you! It will be put to good use. And this one is just the right size for a Victoria sponge. Fancy being paid in cake again?"

"This time, can I beg a favor instead?"

"Of course."

"While I'm away, could you just keep an eye out for Marcus? I don't want him bothering Mum. He really pushes her buttons."

"Do you want me to send him off with a flea in his ear?"

Xanthe smiled and shook her head. "Maybe just pop into the shop if you see him go in? Any trouble, Harley's your man."

"Sounds like I'm getting a good deal," Gerri said, admiring the plates as she left the shop.

"Happy hunting," she called over her shoulder.

As soon as she had left Xanthe began to assemble the things she would need for her trip. She could hear Flora singing along happily to Christmas songs in her workshop, deeply absorbed in her latest project. Xanthe's first task was to sort through their collection of old coins and pick out any that were the right date. There were worryingly few, and it was a slow business sifting through a deep box of worn coppers, holding each one up to the light to check the inscriptions. After half an hour she gave up, fairly certain that she was wasting her time. She chose a couple of simple silver rings instead. Precious metal was good currency in any era. She put her finds in a drawstring velvet bag and then helped herself to a small pocketknife. She had decided against taking such a thing the last time she went, but now that Samuel himself was in trouble, who knew what lay ahead. She had to be as well prepared as possible. Only now did it really begin to sink in that she was actually going to risk traveling back in time again. She felt a mixture of excitement and fear at the thought of it. She told herself, over and over, that if she was careful, if she used what she had learned on her previous trips, she would be fine. She would keep risk to a minimum. She would help Samuel, and then she would come home. To strengthen her resolve she allowed herself a moment to close her eyes and just think of him. To see if she could still summon up his face. To recall the sound of his voice. She had been trying so hard to forget him, and suddenly her head was full of him again.

"Samuel," she whispered, "where are you?"

Xanthe packed two bags. One to leave the house with, full of the normal, two-days-away sort of things. She felt more than a little crazy folding clothes as her mother watched and they chatted about what sort of things she would look for at the fair. The other bag, which she packed once Flora was busy downstairs again, was her canvas shoulder bag for her journey back to bygone Marlborough. Into this she put a woolen shawl, a hairbrush, the clothes she would change into before making the step through time, and some painkillers. She vividly recalled being in pain without any chance of relief on her last visit. The clothes consisted of a long peasant-style dress, leggings, a vest and long-sleeved T-shirt, a white cotton blouse, and a pinafore dress on top of it all. Her hair she would attempt to fix up with pins and tie a small scarf on it. She wished she had thought to just order a medieval-type costume but there hadn't been time. Luckily, her trusty Dr. Marten's would not look too out of place, and she decided on taking her First World War greatcoat. There were advantages to most of her clothes being vintage. She thought nervously about how cold it might be, given that she had no idea of the time of year she would arrive. That afternoon she sneaked out into the garden and hid the smaller bag and the wrapped chocolate pot in the bushes beside the blind house, doing her best to ignore the vibrations and sounds coming from it. Back in the house she fetched her overnight bag and looked in on Flora in the workshop.

"I'm off now," she said casually. As she hugged her mother goodbye she had to fight the urge to hold on to her just a little longer. This was supposed to be a simple trip an hour's drive away for a couple of nights. Flora couldn't know, must never know, how much danger her daughter was likely to be in.

"Spend wisely," Flora told her. "Remember our budget. And bring back lots of lovely things!" she added with a smile.

"Yes, yes, and yes. If Marcus turns up, don't tangle with him."

"All right."

"Just tell him I'm not here and send him away. And don't go overdoing things, Mum, OK?"

"Stop fussing. Off you go. Text me when you get there," she called after her.

As Xanthe went out she wedged a folded piece of card into the bell on the shop door so that it wouldn't give her away when she returned in a few hours. She had decided it was unlikely Flora would notice it wasn't working since it was so near to closing time.

The drive to Devizes took longer than usual because of what passed for rush-hour traffic. Xanthe thought of the gridlock she had been used to in London and told herself she had no right to be impatient. By the time she arrived at the auction house the building was closed and empty. She chose an out-of-the-way spot and parked her taxi before calling a mini-cab. She met the driver at the entrance so that it wouldn't look odd leaving her own car there. The closer they got to Marlborough the more nervous Xanthe felt. By the time they reached the outskirts of the town it was already dark. She asked the driver to stop near the church at the bottom of the high street, pulled on a bobble hat to hide her distinctive curls, and made her way back to the shop, keeping to the side roads and shadows. Her own cobbled street was deserted, Gerri's tea shop and all the other small businesses locked up and in darkness. She had always known this would be the most nerve-wracking part of the fabricated story she had told Flora, but knowing it didn't make it any easier to cope with. She waited outside the shop, straining her ears for any sounds, any clues as to where inside her mother might be. She was about to unlock the door when she remembered she was supposed to send a text. She checked her watch. A plausible amount of time had passed for her to have reached Bristol. Feeling ridiculous and dishonest, she took out her phone and wrote a quick message to Flora saying she was safely arrived and that the B and B was nice. Flora replied cheerily, wishing her luck at the fair and saying she was about to have a long soak in the bath. Xanthe waited a further ten minutes to be sure her mother would be happily wallowing, more than likely with some of her favorite music playing, and therefore unlikely to hear footsteps downstairs.

Once in the shop Xanthe removed the cardboard that was preventing the bell from clanging. She hesitated at the bottom of the stairs, having no idea what she would say to her mother if she appeared. The gurgling of the aged plumbing system and her mother's wavering soprano voice from upstairs reassured her enough to dash to the back door, go through it, and hurry to the dark corner of the garden to retrieve her bag. Her hands shook as she changed her clothes, a combination of the cold night air and her own nerves making her tremble. She hid her phone in the clothes she was leaving, switching it off. She had decided to say the battery died and that she got a new one later while she was in Bristol. She glanced up at the house. The curtains were drawn at all the windows. Finally, she buttoned up her coat and took the chocolate pot out of its wrapping.

"OK," she whispered to it, running her fingers over the smooth copper, struggling to master her anxiety at what she was about to do. "Show me," she said. "Show me Samuel. Make me believe."

She closed her eyes. The by-now familiar sounds started faintly then grew stronger. She saw stone walls, glistening wet, once again lit by moonlight. There was a figure moving in the darkness. Was it him? She couldn't be sure. She opened her eyes, took a breath, and pulled open the door of the old jail. In a panic she checked for her precious locket and was comforted to find it still securely on its chain around her neck. She took a deep breath. The smell of damp earth greeted her, and a musty warmth that should not have been there. As if the tiny building was inhabited by warm, unwashed bodies. She shook off the idea that another fearsome ghost might be waiting to meet her. "Not this time," she told herself, her low voice deadened in the ancient, windowless space. With her bag over her shoulder, clutching the chocolate pot tight, she stepped inside and pulled the door shut behind her, letting the darkness envelop her. She did not have long to wait. All at once the voices started up. Urgent. Pleading. Some wailing, others crying. Xanthe held her nerve and did her utmost to ignore them. She must think of Samuel. Only Samuel. It was for him she was risking everything.

She began to sway, dizziness almost overwhelming her, bile rising in her throat, the taste of it in her mouth acrid and bitter. She had the sensation of falling, and yet she could still feel the gritty earth firm beneath her booted feet. One voice rang out clear above the others. A man's voice. A man who wasn't Samuel.

4

XANTHE OPENED HER EYES. SHE WAS AWARE SHE WAS LYING ON A HARD, STONE FLOOR, somewhere cold and enclosed. It was so dark she could only just make out solid bare walls around her. With mounting dread she attempted to make sense of her surroundings, pushing herself up onto one elbow. For a moment she feared she had arrived in a jail or dungeon. How would she explain her sudden appearance to an incredulous jailer? Had she made the enormous leap through time successfully, only to find herself trapped with no one to help her, unable to save herself, let alone Samuel? Through the fabric of her blouse she checked that her gold locket was still in place. Feeling the smooth bump of it against her skin reassured her. Whatever else she could or couldn't do, as long as she had her mother's special gift to her she could return home. Taking a deep breath to steady herself, Xanthe smelled not the musty dampness of a cell, but the sweetness of apples. And pears. She could taste the acidic blend of fruit in the chilly air. Above this, there was the faint tang of onions, and the dry, warm earthiness of hessian sacks of flour or wheat. A storeroom then. A basement hoarde house. She recalled that when the chatelaine had drawn her back through time it had always taken her to a place where there was something she needed to see. Something connected to its story. Some clue or revelation.

She got to her feet, her eyes at last adjusting to the gloom. There was a slender, glassless window high up, which let in some daylight. She could see now that the space was orderly and well kept, free from cobwebs or dust. Turning, she saw a steep flight of wooden steps leading up to a heavy door, with light showing at its edges. As she climbed the steps she could hear the murmur of voices above. She leaned against the worn wood, listening. It was hard to make out words. The sound was more of a room full of people, some laughing, the occasional louder outburst, much general chatter. She lifted the heavy iron latch and pushed the door open a little. The room was low ceilinged, with heavy beams, and filled with rustic wooden furniture: tables, benches, and high-backed settles. A pungent fug of smoke hung in the room, supplied in part by the large open fire in the deep-set hearth, as well as by the many pipes that were being puffed upon, sucked, or chewed. For a moment Xanthe thought she had arrived in an inn, but then the truth struck her. It was so obvious she felt foolish for not working it out sooner: she was in a chocolate house! She stepped silently through the door, closing it behind her. She wanted to scan the room for any familiar faces. If she was close to where Samuel lived she might well see someone she had met on her earlier visit. But it was difficult trying to peer through the low light and smoky atmosphere of the space to study people without herself being seen. As she began to move cautiously around the room, keeping to the shadows and avoiding meeting the eye of any of the patrons, something struck her as odd. While the place had all the appearances of an inn, it smelled different. Here there was not the aroma of whiskey or sour ale. Nor the whiff of vinegary wine. There was none of the ribald coarseness she might have expected in a tavern, nor any drunken brawling or rowdy behavior at all. Instead there was an intensity to the discussions and conversations around her, almost a secrecy to the way the patrons huddled in small groups, deeply engaged in their talk.

A tall, skinny lad darted between tables delivering trays of cups and pots of chocolate. Xanthe sniffed. She could detect spices, cinnamon mostly, she thought. Perhaps also nutmeg and ginger. Looking more closely now she could see that there were copper pots and ceramic ones too, some on the tables, others at the counter which ran across the far end of the room, close to the door. Behind the counter was an elegant if aged woman who appeared to be in charge. She stood straight backed, keenly observing all that was going on in her establishment, occasionally issuing orders to the boy who ferried trays and pots back and forth, sometimes taking money from customers or engaging them in conversation. Even at first glance, Xanthe felt there was something about this woman, something singular beyond her faded beauty and regal demeanor. At that moment the woman turned and picked up a copper pot, swirling it by the wooden handle before expertly pouring a cup of velvety hot chocolate into a fine china cup. With a start, she recognized that this was *the* chocolate pot. *Her* chocolate pot. It looked younger, of course, less worn and a little shinier, but it was unmistakably the same one. Xanthe could even hear the high-pitched note of its song as it called to her. It had the same distinctive curve to the spout, the same dark brown wooden handle. She was uncertain of what to do next. Clearly this was where the pot had its origins. Its story was to be found here, and no doubt the owner of the chocolate house would have her part to play, but what of Samuel?

"Here, girl!" A gruff voice commanded Xanthe's attention only seconds before she felt an arm around her waist. She stumbled as the man seated at the nearest table pulled her closer to him. "I can find ye some't better to do than stand gawkin'!'" he laughed. Now that she was nearer the cups and pots on the table she could detect the faint smell of brandy. Clearly some patrons liked their chocolate laced with something stronger after all.

Xanthe smiled as she uncurled his arm from around her waist, not wanting to draw any further attention to herself. She reached over and picked up the large chocolate pot.

"Let me fetch more for you, sir. Can't have you sitting there thirsty, can we?" she said, slipping beyond his reach toward the counter. She heard his fellow drinkers laugh. As she was making her way toward the counter, planning to dump the pot and slip through the front door, she glanced out the window, and what she saw made her stop in her tracks.

"What's up, girl?" the man at the table wanted to know. "Changed your mind? Decided to come and sit on me knee instead, 'ave ye?"

While he laughed loudly at his own suggestion, Xanthe did her best to steady her nerves. Through the square panes of the little window she could see a broad bridge spanning a deep river. And on that bridge, set into its low wall and built of the same heavy, gray-brown stone, was a dome-roofed jailhouse. A blind house with fast-flowing water beneath it. Surely this was the one where Samuel was held! This was why the pot had brought her to the chocolate house. It made perfect sense. Spurred on by the thought that she was so close to Samuel, Xanthe strode up to the counter. If the woman behind it was surprised to see her she did not show it. Instead she studied Xanthe with a sharp gaze, almost as if she was trying to place her. Xanthe searched her memory but was certain she had not met the woman on an earlier trip, though it was possible she had been a guest at Clara's birthday party. In which case she would have seen Xanthe perform as a minstrel. She experienced a shiver as she came within reach of her own chocolate pot, and its song grew louder, more insistent, more urgent.

"The gentleman at the table over there would like more," she told the woman, setting the pot down on the counter.

She turned to go, but the proprietress called her back.

"Stay!" she said, her voice surprisingly melodic and youthful. "Why the haste? Will you not give me your name?"

Xanthe considered simply ignoring her. Just marching on out through the door and not looking back. It would certainly be simpler than trying to explain where she had come from, or why she was there. But if her other journeys back through time had taught her anything it was that she could not help anyone on her own. She needed allies. She certainly could not afford to make enemies. She paused, her hand on the door, turning to reply as lightly as she could.

"Forgive me, I am needed elsewhere. Urgently."

The woman came out from behind the counter and walked to stand close enough to Xanthe for her to be able to smell expensive perfume. Evidently the chocolate house business paid well. In fact, the woman did not have the appearance of someone who worked catering for others at all. There was something more refined, something more sophisticated about her.

"I do not doubt it," the woman said. "There will always be those who have need of your assistance."

Xanthe looked at her then. It seemed to her an odd thing to say. Did the old woman mean Xanthe's assistance in particular, or was she simply making a general statement? As Xanthe hesitated, the proprietress held out a graceful hand.

"Louisa Flyte," she said. "This humble chocolate house is both my living and my home. You are welcome. Will you not take a cup of chocolate to sustain you before you leave?"

Xanthe took Mistress Flyte's hand and felt her firm grip. For a moment the two looked each other directly in the eyes. The older woman's might have been dulled with age, but they had about them a noticeable strength of gaze and a quiet confidence. Xanthe felt her very soul being scrutinized. A little uneasy, she withdrew her hand.

"Neither yourself nor your establishment appear humble to me," she told her, remembering that formal good manners and flattery were the norm in the sixteen hundreds. "I thank you for your welcome and your kind offer, but I cannot linger."

"Where is it that you hurry to? I can have Edmund show you the way to the stage post, perhaps?"

Xanthe gave herself away by glancing in the direction of the little jail. She opened the door, speaking as she went. "No need. Thank you again," she said, closing the door before Mistress Flyte could ask any more questions. As she crossed the street she felt the woman's eyes upon her. The day was very cold and dry, with a clear sky, the sun beginning to lower. Xanthe registered the chill of the air against her skin. It made her walk faster, imagining Samuel locked in the damp, cheerless prison, surrounded by wet, heavy stones, the roar of the river beneath him. She had never seen a blind house built on a bridge before. Its location gave it a particularly lonely and isolated appearance. Nervousness gripped her as she drew level with it. Suddenly she was assailed by doubt. What would Samuel think of her appearing in his life again? Would she really be able to help him? What could she do? She had come without anything that could be called a plan, trusting only to her previous experience, hoping her knowledge of the time and the area would be all she needed to be of use. Now, though, she doubted herself, wished she had thought through what her next steps would be.

Before she had time to question the wisdom of her own actions further, she was there, standing at the door to the jail. A door which, to her surprise, was not wooden, but made entirely of thick iron bars. While this gave even less shelter from the low temperature of the day, it at least allowed a little more light into the building. It also allowed Xanthe to see inside. And to see that the jail was completely empty. No Samuel. No one at all. She gaped at the nothingness in front of her. She had been so certain of finding him. While part of her felt hope—he must have been freed—another part felt panic. Had he been moved to the county jail in Salisbury? Or elsewhere? And when had he been taken? He might already have stood trial for something. She might be too late to help him at all. Now what was she to do?

"Oh, Samuel," she murmured, "where are you?"

It was then that a shadow fell over her and she became aware of a tall figure standing close. A sense of unease took hold of her. Remembering that she had to appear of no interest, of no importance, had to pass unseen wherever possible she tried to ignore the strength of this unsettling feeling. Given her circumstances, it was natural to be on edge. She shouldn't read any more into her reaction than that. Even so, it was hard to shake off the intense and immediate anxiety this stranger triggered inside her. She attempted to slip away, not knowing where she was going, only knowing that she needed to find a quiet place to gather her thoughts, and to put some distance between herself and this man. But as she moved he stepped in front of her, blocking her path.

"Mistress, you appear perplexed. Do you, perhaps, search for someone?" he asked.

There was a flash of memory in the recesses of Xanthe's mind. Something triggered by the man's voice and, now that she looked at him, something familiar about his lanky, angular physique and long, straw-colored hair. She searched her memory in an effort to place him. He wore a wide-brimmed hat pulled low over his eyes. His clothes were not flamboyant, but they were expensive and fashionable. His jacket was quilted, cut tight to his body, worn beneath a short cape which was flung off his shoulders. The buckle of his belt gleamed the way only good quality silver could, and the leather of his long boots was supple and fine. These were the clothes of a successful man. A man of some standing and wealth. A man, therefore, of influence and power, and as such, someone Xanthe would do well to be wary of. She looked at him more closely but was certain they had not met before. Why, then, did he seem so familiar? Why did he spark such a reaction in her? She noticed that he was looking at her in a way that was similar to how Mistress Flyte had studied her. As if they knew her somehow. Almost as if they were not surprised to see her.

"I had thought the jail occupied," she said. "I was . . . mistaken."

"Had you come to gawk only?"

He watched her reaction to this. Xanthe considered allowing him to think this was the case; that she was just following a morbid inclination to look at some unfortunate people come to grief and incarcerated. It should not matter what opinion this man held of her, but it rankled her, the idea that she should be thought of as so shallow and unkind. Her hesitation gave him his answer.

"No, I thought not. You came seeking one who is of importance to you. What manner of person would that be, I wonder? To find himself brought so low and yet to command the attendance and concern of such an . . . unusual young maid?"

It struck Xanthe that this man's interest in her was of an entirely different nature to that of the ruffian she had been grabbed by earlier. His look was one of intense interest, but it was not lustful. Again she had the sense that he knew things about her; but how could that be? She wondered why he had been standing near the jail. It could have been coincidence, of course. The little town, wherever it was, seemed quite busy. He might just have been crossing the bridge as Xanthe appeared and seen her looking at the blind house. Somehow, though, his being there felt more meaningful than that. Might he know something about what had happened to Samuel? She had to tread cautiously. Not knowing what kind of trouble Samuel was in made it hard to tell who might be his friend and who might be his enemy.

"It is true, sir," she said carefully, "that I came looking for an acquaintance. I had heard he was in difficulty."

"An acquaintance?"

"I am a minstrel. I meet many people. This person did me a kindness once. I hoped to repay the debt."

"How curious. What help did you think to bring him? Were you planning to serenade him through the bars of his jail, perhaps?" A slow smile slipped across the man's face. It did nothing to add any warmth to it.

Xanthe was on the point of gingerly digging further for information about Samuel when their conversation was interrupted by Mistress Flyte calling from the door of the chocolate house.

"Girl! Once again you neglect your duties! I have had cause to speak to you of this before. Come, there is work to be done."

Xanthe realized at once that the woman was trying to get her away from the unsettling man. She was prepared to pretend that Xanthe worked for her in order to do so. She was risking publicly acknowledging someone she had scarcely met, someone who had just sneaked through her own home with no explanation. Xanthe could not know Mistress Flyte's reasons for what she was doing, but if she had to choose whom to trust out of the two people she now stood between, it would not be the man whose breath she could feel against her cold cheek.

"Forgive me, Mistress Flyte," she called back, grateful that she at least knew the woman's name. Without a backward glance she hurried back into the coffeehouse, where the owner firmly closed the door behind her. As soon as she was inside Xanthe turned, opening her mouth to speak, wanting to question the old woman, but she was not given the opportunity.

"Do not dawdle, girl. There are tables to be cleared and pots to be washed." Mistress Flyte clicked her fingers at the lad scurrying past with a tray of cups. "Edmund, fetch a clean apron for your new workmate. See that she knows what's what." So saying, she walked off to engage a table of regulars in conversation, busying herself with the job of hostess of the establishment.

"Make haste!" said Edmund breathlessly. "The mistress will not tolerate a laggard. Here." He took an apron from a shelf behind the counter and thrust it into her arms. "Put this on. You can leave your coat and bag over there. And, mind you, don't drop anything. If you break something it will come out of your pay."

For a moment Xanthe stood, clutching the starched apron, bewildered. She hadn't traveled back through the centuries to be a waitress. She was here for a reason, and at that moment she was still no further forward in finding Samuel. She glanced about her. The chocolate house seemed to be getting busier and slightly rowdier as the afternoon drew on. More patrons came through the old door, ducking to avoid its low beam, heading for a favorite corner or table. Edmund threw more logs onto the fire, sending up a shower of sparks. Mistress Flyte seemed to know everyone and made them welcome. Xanthe thought quickly. The woman had obviously been keen to get her away from the eerie stranger but was in no hurry to explain herself, or to question Xanthe. It seemed she was prepared to wait, and it looked as if Xanthe would have to be patient too. If Mistress Flyte had gone to the trouble of taking her in it stood to reason that she would be prepared to help her further. But in her own time. Perhaps, Xanthe decided, she would be more amenable, more willing to give the assistance she was going to need, if Xanthe put in a few hours' work for her first. It might even be some sort of test.

"Right," she said to herself, rolling up her sleeves. "How hard can this be?"

After three hours of running this way and that, carrying heavy trays laden with pots, pouring the hot chocolate into cups and tankards with increasingly unsteady hands, suffering variously minor burns and scalds, ribald comments from customers, and chastisements from Mistress Flyte, and even from Edmund, for being slow, Xanthe was worn out. Her feet ached, she was weak from having not eaten, and the pipe and woodsmoke in the room had left her with a sore throat and a fuzzy head. At last her new employer beckoned Xanthe, and she followed her through a narrow door and up a twisting flight of wooden stairs. They came to a small sitting room, neatly furnished with fine pieces; a rug, richly patterned in blues and golds, a chaise longue of darkest indigo damask, two small cushioned chairs by the little fireplace, a gilded mirror above the mantel, two delicate tapestries on the walls, and a writing desk in the corner. There was a bookcase, unusual for the time, with a precious row of leather-bound volumes behind a locked glass door. Xanthe could tell at a glance that this was not the room of a lowly cafe keeper. These were expensive, rare, and luxury items. Something about Mistress Flyte did not quite fit.

There were two small windows giving onto the street below and another view of the bridge and the river. As dusk had already deepened into evening they let in only the faintest glimmer of light from the town lamps. Mistress Flyte lit a spill from the fire in the hearth and applied it to candles set about the room. As she did so, she indicated a chair by the fire and invited Xanthe to sit.

"You appear fatigued, girl. Are you unaccustomed to labor?" she asked.

Xanthe tried hard not to resent the question, sinking onto the softly cushioned seat. "I am a minstrel by trade, ma'am," she explained.

"Indeed?" Mistress Flyte settled elegantly on the chaise opposite. "And what, pray tell, was a young minstrel, unaccompanied and unannounced, doing in a chocolate house in Bradford-on-Avon, apparently intent on visiting the blind house?"

If Xanthe had been expecting any sort of preamble to this question, any chance to feel her way with the woman, she clearly was not going to get it. While she had been waiting at tables downstairs she had at least had the time to come to a decision about what she would say to explain her sudden appearance. And about how much she would have to risk trusting this singular woman.

"I was, that is, I *am* looking for someone. I received word that he was in danger. I came to see if I could offer assistance."

"But you found the lockup empty."

Xanthe nodded.

Mistress Flyte turned to look into the fire, gazing at the dancing flames. "You are a little late, it would seem. The jail was indeed occupied until early this morning."

"It was? Do you . . . do you know who was being kept in there? Did you hear any name mentioned?"

"Oh, yes," she said, without raising her attention from the fire. "I know the name. In truth, I know the person."

"Would you tell me who it was? It might be that I was misinformed. . . ."

"I would prefer you give me the name of the man you so eagerly seek," she said. She turned to look directly at Xanthe then, her expression leaving no room for doubt. If Xanthe wanted to earn her trust then she would first have to confide in her.

"Samuel," she said as levelly as she could, annoyed at the tremor that crept into her voice as she spoke his name. "Samuel Appleby of Marlborough."

Mistress Flyte nodded slowly but did not speak. She seemed to be considering what to say, taking time to make up her mind about the strange girl in her home. Xanthe reminded herself that these were dangerous times. To trust the wrong person could prove fatal. A log cracked loudly in the silence. From downstairs came the sound of laughter. Mistress Flyte smoothed the cotton of her skirts with her palms.

"Two nights ago, Samuel Appleby was here, in the chocolate house. He and his friends choose to meet here, even though they must journey some miles. This is a place where it is safe to gather, to exchange ideas, to form alliances. That is to say, it has always been safe. Up until now."

"And now?"

"There are those who fear change. Those who seek to stamp upon burgeoning shoots of progress and grind them beneath their heel. Such men do not operate alone but are instruments of more lofty estates."

"The king's men, d'you mean?"

Mistress Flyte glanced at Xanthe, hesitated, and then continued. "His Majesty sees fit to send his agents abroad, to have them watch for any who might oppose him. Such opposition is no longer tolerated."

"But Samuel, the Appleby family, they are held in high esteem by many of the king's supporters. Their work as architects is in great demand. . . ."

"Which is the reason they have been left alone thus far. However, times change. The king feels more threatened, therefore he will strike before he is struck."

"What did Samuel do? To cause him to be locked up, he must surely have done more than talk to his friends."

Mistress Flyte got to her feet and began to pace slowly about the room.

"After the events of last autumn all who are not wholly committed to the king's views are seen as a threat. All are under suspicion."

Xanthe had to stop herself asking to what events she was referring. She had left Samuel in the first week of November. It was obviously winter now, but several months could have already passed since she had been here. A quick search of her own memory, of some of the names that Samuel and his brother, Joshua, had mentioned, reminded her of which event she had so closely missed. November 1605—the Gunpowder Plot. The ultimate act of treason, with the king and his family narrowly escaping being blown up by Guy Fawkes and his allies. Of course the situation for Catholics, for dissenters in general, could only have become far worse since that shocking day.

"Your friend," Mistress Flyte went on, "has of necessity surrounded himself with like-minded men. As I said, they meet here when they can. Not to plot the king's downfall, simply to ensure the survival of those about whom they care. Those, like themselves, who tread upon the precipitous edges of accepted society. It is, as you pointed out, his work that keeps him from persecution. Indeed, after he was summarily rounded up with his friends and thrown in the jail on charges of sedition, it was his talent as an architect and master builder that saw him freed. Those with him were not so fortunate. Fairfax had no use for them."

"Who?"

"Benedict Fairfax, whose ambition is exceeded only by his wealth, and that wealth gained through zealous service to the king. A man who ruthlessly pursues his own gains, playing the gentleman when there is not a gentle grain to his rotten soul." She stopped pacing and faced Xanthe again. "But you will have sensed his true nature, I believe. When you met him earlier today, did you not shrink from his gaze? Did not your very being recoil from his touch?"

"You are talking about the man on the bridge? He was responsible for freeing Samuel?"

"Because it suited him to do so. Just as it suited him to see your friend arrested to begin with."

"What? I beg your pardon, mistress. I don't understand."

"Nor do I expect you to. You will come to that understanding only in time. Know this: If you wish to help Master Appleby you will make an enemy of Fairfax in the doing of it. He will stand between the two of you."

Xanthe pulled her scarf from her head, wishing she could let her hair out of its tight bun. She rubbed her forehead, closing her eyes, trying to make sense of what Mistress Flyte was telling her. If Samuel was out of trouble it sounded as if his was a fragile safety, and that the threat of being charged with treason and facing a terrible death still hung over him.

"I have to go to him," she said. "I need to get to Marlborough."

"You will not find him there. Fairfax had him released only into his own protection, so that he could work on Laybrook Abbey. As long as the work lasts, so will Samuel's reprieve. I'd wager it will last not a day longer. If you wish to see him, you must travel to Laybrook."

Xanthe thought about how easily her stay could become prolonged. Samuel was no longer in the jail, perhaps she should be content to know that and simply return to her own time. But no, from what Mistress Flyte was telling her, he was far from out of danger. And besides, the chocolate pot must have brought her to Bradford, to Samuel, for a reason. She would see him, discover what it was she was being led to, do what she could, reassure herself that he really was safe and not still under threat from Benedict Fairfax; then she would go home. She got to her feet. "I have to. I have to see for myself that he is all right, and if there is anything I can do to help him get free of this man. . . ."

"You? A lone maid? A minstrel? With no family, no influence?"

"I have to try."

Mistress Flyte nodded and even allowed herself a small smile. "If it were any other I would tell them that to do so would be to seal their own violent fate. You, however, singer of songs, you might just be the one who could bring Fairfax down. *You*, I will help."

This puzzled Xanthe. Again she had the impression that her hostess knew more about her than she was prepared to reveal. Why would she think Xanthe was so well suited to rescuing Samuel, particularly when she doubted her own ability to do so? At least, she told herself, the old woman was willing to support her rather than ask awkward questions about how she had come to be in her chocolate house in the first place. Xanthe knew she needed an ally, and this person was, after all, a self-declared friend of Samuel's. "Thank you. I . . . I'm grateful. Truly I am."

"Save your gratitude. We do what we must. All of us. But plans for travel will wait upon the morrow. Tonight, you will work for your supper and lodgings. Edmund will show you where you can sleep after the chocolate house is closed. Come, quickly now, I hear thirsty patrons with money to spend."

Xanthe followed her new employer out of the little sitting room and back down to the buzz and warmth of the hostelry, spurred on by the thought that the next day she might at last see Samuel.

5

MISTRESS FLYTE'S ESTABLISHMENT DID BRISK BUSINESS IN THE EVENING. XANTHE, ALREADY tired from the leap back through time, the emotional upheaval of trying to find Samuel, and the hours she had spent on her feet serving at tables through the afternoon, blundered on, becoming increasingly weary and clumsy. More than once Edmund had cause to snap at her for spilling milk or dropping spoons. Inevitably she managed to break a porcelain cup too, earning a loud tutting from Edmund. Mistress Flyte had less time to talk to her clientele in the evening hours. Instead she was fully occupied with preparing the chocolate. Xanthe watched her heat the milk and then melt the crumbled cocoa into it. The temperature had to be hot enough to dissolve the chocolate, but not so hot as to boil the milk, which would spoil the flavor. The mixture had to be stirred constantly to stop it from sticking to the bottom of the pan. At the crucial moment, Mistress Flyte would add other ingredients, according to the customer's preferences. Sometimes she grated in a little nutmeg, with care and reverence, as she told Xanthe it was the most expensive spice they had. Other times a cinnamon stick was infused in the milk. Sometimes black pepper was added, or cardamom, so that by late in the evening the room was a heady mix of aromas. Some patrons, of course, liked the addition of a tot of brandy or whiskey. This earned the mild disapproval of the proprietor, not because of the effects of the alcohol, for she was no prude, but because, she claimed, it adversely affected the taste of the hot chocolate, masking the depths and subtleties of the cocoa itself.

✳   ✳   ✳

Much later, Edmund waited while Xanthe used the necessary house at the far end of the yard and then led her to a small space in the loft and directed her to a straw-stuffed mattress. The room was noticeably colder than the lower floors in the house and had the smell of a forgotten space, more than a little dusty and damp. Edmund handed her two rough blankets.

"You can sleep here. Don't mind the bats and they won't mind you," he teased as he went, leaving her with a stub of tallow candle. Xanthe set the precious light down next to her bed as close as she dared without risking a fire. There was a low window set into the roof which reminded her of her own bedroom back in Marlborough. She felt a stab of homesickness and wondered how her mother was, hoping that her arthritis had not chosen this week to flare up again.

She took off her boots, removed the pins from her hair and shook it loose and then, shivering, climbed under the blankets fully clothed. Exhaustion swamped her, so that within moments she had fallen into a profound, heavy sleep, where her dreams were haunted not by Samuel's darkly beautiful face, but by the pale, gaunt features of Benedict Fairfax.

Xanthe was woken before daybreak the next morning by Edmund shaking her.

"Up with you! The mistress will have something to say about sluggardliness. Quick sticks!" he urged her, before turning on his skinny heel and disappearing back down the narrow attic stairway.

Xanthe rubbed her eyes and crawled stiffly out of bed. In the half light that the lifting night allowed she tackled her hair, wrestling it into a bun and retying her scarf on top of it. The cold air of the loft space soon found its way through her layers of clothing so that she was eager to pull on her boots and descend to the warmth of the ground floor. She found Edmund setting a fire in the hearth.

"There's a washbowl in the pantry out back," he told her, not for a second taking his eyes off his important task. "Be quick now. Mistress Flyte likes the room swept fresh each morning before we have a bite to eat."

The pantry turned out to be a room several degrees colder than the attic due to the large slabs of stone and thick walls designed to keep milk cold. Hefty churns stood near the back door, some apparently empty, others with ladles hanging from their lids, filled with fresh, foamy milk. Xanthe found the washbowl and jug and prepared herself for the cold of the water. She had not, however, reckoned with a thin layer of ice which she had to break before she could fill the bowl and then splash her face. She gasped, thankful that she wouldn't be staying long enough to have to wash her body the same way. She all but ran to the little shed outside that housed the toilet. The slates on the roof showed a rosy sky through the gaps as dawn broke. Xanthe had to clench her teeth to stop them from chattering. This was no place to linger.

Back indoors, Edmund had succeeded in getting a cheerful, if smoky, fire going. He worked the bellows at it furiously, sending wild flames and sparks up the chimney.

"There's a broom behind you. The faster you sweep the sooner we eat," he told her.

Xanthe set to her task. The room still held the echo of men's laughter and chatter from the previous evening. With the smoke not yet having taken hold of the space, it smelled of polished wood and warm milk and brandy and, deliciously, tantalizingly, chocolate. Somewhere upstairs a clock struck the hour. Seven o'clock. Just getting light. Xanthe estimated that the time of year must then be mid-February at the latest. This puzzled her. On her previous trips to the past, she had calculated that time passed at a different rate than in her own day, and that difference meant that for every ten hours she was gone from the twenty-first century, ten days passed in Samuel's time. But this didn't fit with how much time had gone by since she last stepped back through the blind house. She had left Samuel just before August Bank Holiday in her own era, and approximately nine weeks had passed since then. Which meant months and months should have elapsed for Samuel. Years, in fact. But Mistress Flyte had talked of the "events of last autumn," referring to the Gunpowder Plot. Which meant only a few months had passed. In one way this was a relief. She had not stopped to think that several years might have passed in Samuel's life. How would he have changed? How would his life have moved on? It was comforting to think the gap had only been from November to February. What was worrying, though, was the dawning realization that this meant the time difference between the two centuries when she traveled was not fixed. Sometimes it went much faster in the past, sometimes it progressed almost at the same speed as her own time. Which meant she could never be certain, never plan her visits, never know for sure when she would arrive home. She felt a momentary panic. What if the system had reversed itself? What if weeks, months, *years* were passing back in her own century? What would poor Flora be going through? She shook away the thought, sweeping the floor with increasing vigor to stave off driving herself mad with such an idea. She couldn't know. Couldn't do anything about the movement of time, in Samuel's era or her own. She would just have to press on with what she needed to do as quickly as possible.

A hammering on the door made her start, she had been so deep in thought. Edmund scooted past her and drew back the bolts. The baker's boy carried in a large tray of loaves and cinnamon rolls, placing it on the counter. The aroma made Xanthe's mouth water.

"Mistress Flyte made you man of the premises, has she, Edmund?" he asked, wiping his brow with the back of a floury arm.

"She's not yet risen."

"All right for some." The baker's boy leaned on the counter and stared at Xanthe, taking in her less than normal clothing and inexpertly tied hair. "Got yourself some new help, I see."

Edmund frowned. "You'd better get yourself back before your father misses you. Doesn't take two minutes to cross the bridge. I wouldn't want to be on the blunt end of his bad temper."

"Oh, I'm not afeared of my father. Besides, can't leave afore I'm paid for the bread now, can I?"

Edmund's frown deepened. "I'll fetch you your money," he said, and hurried up the stairs to find his employer.

The baker's boy took the opportunity to stare openly at Xanthe. She stopped sweeping and put a hand on her hip, tilting her head, meeting his stare. "If you've nothing better to do I can find you a broom, you know."

"What, and leave off watching a person sweeping so finely? 'T'would be a shame. You are more refreshing to mind and soul than Edmund, I'll tell you that for nothing."

Xanthe was about to put him in his place when Edmund came racing back down the stairs.

"The mistress—she's not there!"

"What do you mean?" Xanthe could sense the boy's panic.

"Not in her bed, not in her rooms. Nowhere to be found. Gone!"

The baker's boy straightened up. "Mayhap she went out to fetch something."

Edmund shook his head, his eyes wide. "The door was bolted when I let you in. From the inside." He turned to Xanthe. "Had the milk been delivered?"

"Sorry?"

"Were the empty milk churns gone or are they there still?"

"I'm not sure, I think I did see some empty ones. . . ."

Edmund disappeared toward the back of the building and returned, breathless, only moments later. "The yard door is unbolted. . . ."

"Well, there you are then," said the baker's boy, shaking his head at such unnecessary drama. "Your mistress will have stepped out to fetch something. She'll return directly. I do not doubt it."

"But she never goes out before we have our bite to eat. Never. Not one morning in all the years I've been here! And never through the yard door. She only ever uses it to let the milkman in. Her bed has not been slept in. I tell you, she is gone!"

Xanthe could see the boy was truly distressed. She leaned her broom against the wall and put a hand on his shoulder.

"Don't worry, Edmund. I'm sure there's a simple reason for her absence. All will become clear. We'll look for her together. Will you help us?" she asked the baker's boy, who puffed himself out with importance at the thought of being needed.

"I shall go back into town and ask if anyone's had sight of her," he said, enjoying Xanthe's smile of thanks.

"Edmund, you know the town better than I. Come, we will go out the yard door and begin our search there."

"But we cannot leave the chocolate house."

It took her a full minute to persuade him they could lock up the premises and leave it for whatever time it took to find Mistress Flyte. After all, they could not throw open their doors to customers without her.

Xanthe ran upstairs and fetched her heavy greatcoat, Edmund pulled on a felted woolen jacket, and they re-bolted the front door, making their way out the back. The yard opened onto a cobbled street wide enough for the milkman's cart but comprised mostly of the backs of houses and shops, so that it was quiet and not overlooked a great deal. The cobbles felt uneven beneath Xanthe's boots, and it struck her how new and unworn they were compared to the almost flattened ones in her own little street in her own time.

They had gone no more than a few dozen yards when Edmund let out a cry.

"Oh my dear Lord in heaven! Look! Look there!"

She followed his horrified gaze and saw a figure, crumpled and twisted, lying in the gutter. It was clearly a woman, her skirts soaked in filth, frost upon them, her hair loosened from its pins. Edmund gasped, too horrified to look closer. Xanthe crouched down beside the stricken woman, gently placing a hand on her arm, knowing before she could clearly see her face that this broken, beaten creature was indeed Mistress Louisa Flyte.

Edmund could not bear to come closer. "Is she . . . ?" Nor could he form the word.

Xanthe put her fingers to the old woman's throat and felt a pulse. It was faint and stuttering, but a pulse nonetheless.

"She's alive! Mistress Flyte? Can you hear me?" Xanthe could see a nasty head wound and suspected some of her fingers were broken. It was impossible to tell what other injuries the woman had sustained, but it had clearly been a brutal attack, and one meant to kill her. Xanthe considered what she should do. She knew it would be dangerous to move her, but no ambulance was going to come to their aid. No paramedics running with a stretcher.

"Help me take her inside," she said to Edmund.

As gently as they could, they turned Mistress Flyte over. Edmund was a bony youth, but he was strong. He slipped his arms under his employer's, lifting her head against his chest, while Xanthe lifted her legs at the knees. Together they made their awkward progress back along the cobbles. At one point their patient gave a low moan.

"Oh!" gasped Edmund. "We are causing her to suffer more!"

"Don't stop!" Xanthe urged him. "We have no choice. Out here in this cold she will certainly die."

They struggled on. By the time they had reached the main room of the chocolate house the baker's boy had returned with no news and was able to help them take her upstairs to her bedchamber. It was pitiful to hear her moan as they moved her, but Xanthe told herself it was a good sign. She was regaining consciousness. There was hope.

"I will need to undress her to tend to her wounds," Xanthe told the men. "Edmund, why don't you go and make us all some hot chocolate? I'm sure you know how."

He drew himself up. "The mistress has me do it when she is occupied talking to the patrons," he assured her.

"Good. Bring me some in a shallow cup. Mistress Flyte must take some too if she is able."

After thanking the baker's boy for his assistance and promising him a hot drink for his trouble, Xanthe was left to do her best to nurse the old woman. It was slow work, taking off her filthy dress, some of which she had to cut away. Each piece she removed seemed to reveal another injury, and in places the fabric was pressed into the bloody flesh. Some wounds even bore the print of a boot.

"Who did this to you?" she asked, expecting no reply. Mistress Flyte's eyes flickered once or twice as if trying to make sense of where she was and what was happening, but she was not yet able to speak. "Who would do such a thing?" Xanthe knew that footpads and robbers lurked in all towns, preying on the unsuspecting and unwary. But Mistress Flyte was a woman of keen intelligence. She was evidently used to managing her own affairs. She would not, Xanthe realized, have opened that back door late at night without good reason. Without, perhaps, being asked to do so by someone she knew. Someone who had made the ultimate betrayal.

When Edmund appeared with hot chocolate and bread she sent him to fetch boiled water and clean cloths. While she waited she took a fine cotton nightdress from the linen press and tore it into strips for bandages. She thought about sending for the apothecary but decided to wait. Her own rudimentary first-aid knowledge would probably be as good as any quackery that might do more harm than good and, possibly, spread word of the fact that the old woman had not only been attacked, but that she still lived. If whoever had beaten her had meant to kill her, it was best, for the time being, that they thought they had succeeded. Xanthe didn't like to think of Edmund and herself having to fend off an attacker while also trying to nurse their mistress. She took stock of her patient's wounds. All the fingers of her left hand were broken, apparently stamped upon; she had extensive bruising over her chest, suggesting cracked ribs; her legs were also bruised and cut in places; and then there was the worrying head wound. It seemed her attacker had delivered a blow with some sort of blunt object, on the right side of the head, above the ear. As the old woman wasn't conscious it was impossible to tell if she was concussed, but it seemed likely. Remembering her schoolgirl first-aid lessons, Xanthe checked for straw-colored liquid in the ears—a sign of a fractured skull. She was relieved to find none. When Edmund brought the water he had also given her a pot of ointment, its ingredients indeterminate, which he assured her Mistress Flyte applied to all cuts and abrasions as it aided healing. Looking at the broken, bandage-wrapped person on the bed Xanthe feared it would take more than a sweet-smelling balm. She asked Edmund for small pieces of wood and strips of clean linen so that she could make a rudimentary splint for the damaged hand and then sat on the edge of the bed while she waited.

To her surprise, Mistress Flyte at last opened her eyes.

"Fear not," Xanthe told her gently, "you are in your own bed. You are safe now."

Mistress Flyte winced as she tried to move and quickly lay still again. She tried to speak but her voice was a whisper. Xanthe held the cup of chocolate to her lips and helped her sip. The old woman screwed up her face and found her voice.

"Ugh. Edmund has boiled the milk! He knows better than to do that," she said.

Xanthe smiled. "His mind was elsewhere. It is a good thing you will be here to remind him," she said. When Mistress Flyte raised her eyebrows Xanthe nodded. "You were close to death, mistress. Had Edmund not raised the alarm when he did, with your wounds, and the night so cold . . ."

The old woman closed her eyes. "He is a good boy," she said.

"Did you see your attacker? Who would want to do this to you?"

"We are none of us without our enemies. Do not leave the chocolate house to Edmund alone. He will not know . . . whom to trust. . . ." So saying, she drifted into a fitful sleep before Xanthe could question her further.

Xanthe had to acknowledge to herself, with a sinking heart, that there was no possibility of her going to Laybrook to find Samuel now. Who else would nurse Mistress Flyte? Her recovery was still not certain. And what if her attacker returned? She could not abandon her, not after she had helped her.

Once the old woman was sleeping a little more comfortably, Xanthe went downstairs. She found Edmund at the front door turning away customers. He was doing what seemed the most sensible thing, but was it? Surely business as usual would be better. People who knew her would be alerted to the fact that something was seriously wrong if she let her beloved chocolate house remain closed. Surely Edmund could make the chocolate and she could keep up with serving and playing host. Just for a few hours.

"Wait," she called after the would-be customers. "Gentlemen, stay."

A stout man with a drooping mustache stepped forward. "We understand Mistress Flyte is indisposed."

"That is correct, sir."

"So is the chocolate house open or no?"

"Our mistress would not hear of your good self, or any of her valued patrons, being turned away. Come, take a seat by the fire," she said, holding the door open and ushering them in.

Edmund's mouth dropped open. "What are you doing?" he hissed.

"It's what Mistress Flyte would want. We carry on. The chocolate house is open. And please don't keep telling everyone she is gravely ill. Don't tell them anything. Be vague, Edmund. Put your worry about your mistress aside and all your attention into making the chocolate. I know you will do a fine job. Now, show me what needs to be done."

The youth protested a little further but quickly gave in when Xanthe assured him his employer would be impressed and grateful if he managed to see to the customers. And that she would no doubt reward him. More than that, she told him, Mistress Flyte would be pleased that her careful training had enabled him to properly make the hot chocolate. At that, he turned the sign in the door to open, tightened his apron, and told Xanthe to follow him. Under his direction, they fetched flagons of milk from the churns in the pantry, stoked up the fire, set candles on the tables, put milk over a flame on the stove behind the counter to warm, unwrapped the precious cocoa, and laid out bread and cinnamon buns on pretty china plates. Within an hour, the room was nearly half full, and the murmur of soft voices gave the place a low-level buzz of good humor and lively conversation. Xanthe insisted Edmund show her how to make the hot chocolate, convincing him he couldn't do it all himself. It wasn't complicated, but there was clearly an art to getting the milk exactly the right temperature. And some customers were particularly picky, wanting this spice, or that strength, or this particular vessel. At first Xanthe found she and Edmund could keep up quite well, but by lunchtime they were overwhelmed and struggling. When a customer became irate because of the wait it was all Xanthe could do to resist giving him a piece of her mind.

At one point, without thinking about it, she snatched up the special copper pot, *her* copper pot. At once, it vibrated in her hand, setting up such a high-pitched whine that she fumbled with the lid and dropped it. It made a horrible clatter as it fell upon the unforgiving stones of the hearth in front of the stove. Cursing under her breath she picked it up and dusted it off.

As she checked the lid for damage she felt the hairs bristle at the base of her neck.

The lid had acquired the exact, straight-edged dent that she first noticed back in Esther Harris's house, in her own time, when she and Flora had found the collection of pots.

There was something deeply unsettling, something powerful about the thought that it was she herself who had caused this characteristic mark on the pot. That centuries from the moment when she stood in Mistress Flyte's chocolate house and dropped that lid, she would find the pot again, without knowing that it was she who had been responsible for its scar.

"Why do you stand and stare?" The panic in Edmund's voice was giving it a rasp. "For pity's sake, make haste! There is a merchant by the window who threatened to get me by the neck if I did not return at once with his fresh pot of chocolate, *with* the brandy added this time. And his companion emitted a fearsome growl. My mistress would not permit growling!"

"All in hand, Edmund," Xanthe assured him, sounding more confident than she felt. She quickly pulled herself together and put another pot of aromatic chocolate on a tray. "Here, have this one. Tell him it's on the house."

"What's that you say?"

"No charge! Now go on."

Although Xanthe made a point of running upstairs to check on Mistress Flyte throughout the day, she worried about leaving her, and was glad when the threat of snow prompted the customers to head for their homes. At last she was able to lock up, send Edmund to his bed, and take some bread soaked in hot milk up to her patient. She set the tray down on the small bedside table and lit more candles. It was hard enough changing dressings without trying to do it in the half dark. As she lifted Mistress Flyte's bandaged hand the old woman moaned softly and stirred from her slumber. Xanthe could tell she was in great pain and decided to try the painkillers she had brought with her. She quickly fetched them from her bag in her attic bedroom. The pills were chalky and easy to crush. She powdered them into the milk-soaked bread, hoping the taste would not be unbearably bitter.

"Here, let's sit you up." She plumped the pillows and gently moved her patient into a more upright position. She was as careful as she could be, but still Mistress Flyte moaned as she was moved.

"Forgive me," Xanthe murmured, trying to push away memories of nursing her own mother through acute bouts of her arthritis. "Please, try some of this. It will ease your pain." She lifted a spoon to the old woman's mouth and slowly succeeded in feeding her the drug-laced pudding. By the time she had finished, her employer was exhausted but suffering less.

"That is a truly miraculous concoction," she said. "I insist you give me the recipe."

"Oh, we minstrels have to look after ourselves on the road. We learn a trick or two," she said casually.

The old woman fought to focus on Xanthe's face, studying her in the way she had done when Xanthe first arrived at the chocolate house. Once again, she felt Mistress Flyte saw something in her; something she recognized.

"You must not fret about Samuel," she told Xanthe. "There is still work to be done at the abbey. He is safe as long as he is of use."

"And after that?"

"Then we will see what things you can bring about. Then we will see your true colors, singer of songs." She closed her eyes again and mumbled, her words too quiet and jumbled for Xanthe to make out.

"What is it, mistress?" She put a hand on her patient's forehead and was horrified to find it hot and damp. Fever. Xanthe doubted the old woman's beaten body could withstand an infection, but it seemed she was now in the grip of one. It seemed so sudden, but then the time of her attack could have been soon after everyone had retired for the evening. Hours spent bleeding and battered in the cold would have weakened her defenses and could well have hastened the collapse of her immune system.

"He will know you!" Mistress Flyte shouted suddenly, becoming agitated. "That rotten creature will know what you are, if he does not already. Beware, child!"

"Hush now, don't distress yourself. You must save your strength."

"You understand not the nature of what you face. Of the ruthlessness . . . the wickedness . . ."

"Mistress, please. Be at peace. I will not leave you while you need me. All else can wait."

Xanthe fetched fresh water and bathed the old woman's face and arms, remembering it was what Flora had done for her as a child when she had caught scarlet fever. The painkillers would help keep her patient's temperature down a little, but this was no virus, Xanthe was certain of that. It was more likely bone fever, brought on by the fractures, or possibly an infection in one of the wounds caused by laying in a dirty gutter for hours. If only she and Edmund had noticed their mistress was missing before going to bed. Xanthe sighed. It was no use torturing herself with what-ifs. She was doing everything she could think of, but she had to admit to herself that it was not enough. She went to the stairs and called up to Edmund, whose room was on the opposite side to her own. He quickly appeared at the top of the wooden steps, bleary eyed and anxious.

"What is it? Is our mistress worse?"

"You should fetch the doctor," Xanthe told him. "Do you know where to go?"

He nodded. "Doctor Philips lives on High Terrace."

"Will he come?"

"He will if he is paid."

"We will use the takings from today's business. Hurry now and tell him no more than that she is very unwell."

"He will discover what has happened. When he sees her . . ."

"Yes, well, leave that to me. The fewer people who know the truth the better, do you understand?"

He nodded again, dived back into his room to grab his jacket and boots and then hurried from the little house. Xanthe heard him slam the door hard as he left. In truth, she had no idea how she was going to explain Mistress Flyte's injuries. What she did know was that justice was not their main priority. The old woman had talked about enemies, and about how people like Samuel could be arrested merely for meeting at her establishment. If someone wanted her dead, it would be unwise to draw the authorities' attention to the fact. Xanthe did not know who she could trust. All she could hope to do was save Mistress Flyte's life. She must have powerful friends too. If she recovered surely she could call on them for protection, and then, with her help, Xanthe could go to Laybrook in search of Samuel. . . . If she recovered.

The doctor arrived twenty minutes later. He had the look of a man quickly risen from his bed and was not best pleased about it. He set his leather bag down on the table, put on a pair of thick spectacles, and peered at the restless old woman.

"How long has your mistress been so?" he asked Xanthe, Edmund having been sent to fetch more wood for the bedchamber fire.

"Less than an hour," she told him.

He gave her a look that said a little more information would have been helpful. When Xanthe did not elaborate he examined Mistress Flyte's unbandaged hand, scarcely glancing at her splinted one. He waved a dismissive hand at the dressings on her head.

"And beneath these . . . coverings, lies what, precisely?"

"A head wound, sir. Deep but not so much as to break the bone, I believe."

"Oh? And are you a physician?"

"A minstrel, sir."

"And your talents extend beyond singing to the skills of an apothecary perhaps?" he asked, looking again at the dressings and signs of nursing.

"When traveling, one must learn what one can," she said, wishing he would simply apply himself to helping his patient instead of questioning her.

He took an alarming-looking blade from his bag and set about cutting the bandage from Mistress Flyte's head. Xanthe had to stop herself from telling him to at least wash the knife first. He exposed the wound and squinted at it through his glasses.

"Hmm, there are signs of putrefaction."

"Really? I mean to say, I saw none when I cleaned the wound."

"That is because you do not know what it is you see. It would have been better had you called me when your mistress first . . . fell ill," he told her, his voice making it plain he knew what had happened but would rather not acknowledge it. To do so would be to involve himself in a dispute he would evidently prefer to steer clear of.

Mistress Flyte began muttering once more, her hands clawing at the bed-clothes.

"The fever must be brought forth if she is to survive it," the doctor said, shaking his head slowly. "A woman of this age . . . such an injury . . . a favorable outcome is by no means guaranteed, you understand? I will not be held responsible." He puffed out his chest, waiting for assurance that no blame would be laid at his feet were his patient to die.

"We would be grateful for any advice, any assistance you could give, sir," was the best Xanthe could muster. She felt no confidence in the man or his methods. "What course of treatment would you recommend?" she asked.

"She must be bled, and swaddled, in order to bring out the poison and draw the fever from her. It will place a burden upon her, being so old, but there is no other way," he said, taking a selection of blades from his bag. "Send the boy for a letting bowl. And the fire must be stoked further. Bring me blankets. She must be wrapped tight, the warmer the better, to induce the sweats."

What he proposed went against everything Xanthe knew about nursing someone with a high temperature. She recalled Flora telling her how when she was eight years old and delirious from scarlet fever she and her father had carried her out to stand in the cool air, sponging her down, spooning in anti-inflammatory drugs and analgesics in a desperate attempt to lower her temperature. To attempt to raise it seemed the height of madness. And the blood-letting, when Mistress Flyte had already lost blood from her injuries, and given the risk of further infection, was just stupid. But, Xanthe reminded herself, it was the medicine of the day. It was what people believed to be sound medical practice. The physician truly thought that he would be helping his patient. After all, he would be paid better, and his reputation enhanced, if she lived.

Xanthe faced a choice. Say nothing and watch him possibly make Mistress Flyte worse, or speak up and risk making an enemy of a local doctor, who could easily tell the wrong people of what he believed had happened, suggesting that the keeper of the chocolate house had brought violence upon herself by supporting rebels and recusants. What would happen then?

There was a great deal of bustling about as Edmund and Xanthe did as they were asked. As the doctor set about swaddling his patient Xanthe felt increasingly uneasy. She had called him because she feared Mistress Flyte needed more by way of medical attention than she herself could give, but her modern knowledge meant that she knew, in her heart, that this man could only make her condition worse. When he picked up a grubby-looking scalpel and was about to apply it to Mistress Flyte's arm to let blood, she could no longer stay silent.

"Don't," she said, stepping forward.

He looked up at her, knife poised. "If you are of a squeamish disposition I suggest you quit the room."

"It's not that. I . . . I do not believe this is what the mistress would want."

"She would presumably wish to be treated."

"She cares greatly about her skin. It is very fine, don't you see? She is a woman of some refinement. To put further scars upon her when she has suffered so much . . ." Even to Xanthe's own ears it sounded a weak argument.

"I was called here to act in my professional capacity," the doctor told her crossly. "It is my intention to carry out what procedures I deem suitable for my patient. Now, if you will kindly let me proceed, I will do my best for your mistress, and we may all return to our beds."

He leaned over and applied the tip of his knife to Mistress Flyte's pale flesh and Xanthe could bear it no longer. She jumped forward, grabbing the doctor's hand, preventing him from cutting any further.

"Stop!" she told him.

"What is this?"

"I'm sorry you were dragged from your home at such an hour, but I've decided we don't want her to have this treatment."

"You have decided . . . ? You understand you may be condemning your mistress to the grave?"

"I take full responsibility."

The doctor seemed to be about to protest further but then, with a sigh of exasperation, tossed the scalpel back into his bag, snapping shut the clasp. "Do not think to send the boy running for me again an hour from now when the consequences of your actions become clear, for I will not come, do you hear me? I leave the poor woman in your care, and may God help you both, for I cannot if I am not permitted to do my work." He stood stony faced. "I remain, I believe, in want of my fee?"

Xanthe could see there was little point in arguing with him. To do so would only delay his leaving, and now that she had decided he was making things worse she could not wait to get him from the room. She sent Edmund to the door with him, telling him to pay him from the takings and then go back to bed. The minute he had gone she set about removing all the extra blankets from the bed. She threw open the window, gasping as the cold night air blew in. She fetched more lukewarm water and bathed Mistress Flyte's face and neck. The old woman was mumbling, her head moving from side to side on the damp pillow, pulling at the bandages on her head.

"Hush now," Xanthe tried to soothe her, recalling how many times she had helped her mother through pain in the slow watches of the night.

"He will be waiting for you!" the old woman cried out. "He knows what you are. There is great danger. . . . It is not safe for you to go there. . . ."

"Fairfax? You mean Benedict Fairfax? I know, you've told me he is the king's spy. Don't worry. I will be careful."

"You do not understand . . . Oh!" She gasped as her agitated movements caused her broken hand more pain.

"Please, Mistress Flyte, do not concern yourself."

The old woman struggled to form her words, looking closely at Xanthe, using all her strength to make her point.

"Child, I know what you are," she insisted. "I know that you have traveled far more than a few dusty miles upon the highroad. The copper pot . . . it called you. You heard its song, did you not?"

Xanthe's heart skipped a beat. "I . . . Mistress, you are unwell. . . ."

Mistress Flyte grabbed Xanthe's sleeve.

"Know this," she gasped, her voice rasping, "Fairfax will have heard it too. For you are, *both* of you, spinners of time!"

6

XANTHE DID NOT KNOW WHICH WAS MORE SHOCKING: THAT MISTRESS FLYTE KNEW HOW Xanthe had come to be there and why she had come, or that this Fairfax, who by her account was a dangerous man, was also able to move through time. It was so much to take in, and yet she had so little information. She desperately wanted to ask questions, to know details, to understand how Fairfax knowing what she was might affect her. Might affect Samuel. But the old woman had slipped into a feverish state of semiconsciousness. Xanthe was unable to wake her even sufficiently to spoon down some more painkiller in the hope it might reduce her dangerously high fever. All she could do was watch and wait. And if the old woman died, what then? She would have to make her way to Laybrook and to Samuel without her help, but that was the least of it, somehow. There were surely many things Mistress Flyte could tell her about how the chocolate pot had called to her, and why. About why she, Xanthe, had been given this frightening gift. About what it was she was supposed to do to help Samuel.

As the evening wore into night Xanthe feared the old woman was fighting a losing battle. A rash had spread across her neck and face, and she seemed to have dropped into a deeper state of unconsciousness. Xanthe feared that what she was watching was the swift and deadly onset of sepsis. She had never felt so helpless. The old woman had been prepared to put herself at risk to help Xanthe. She had already protected her from Fairfax, and she understood about the way the chocolate pot had called to her through the centuries.

"Don't leave me now that I've found you," Xanthe whispered to her. She tried to decide what treatment would have been given to her patient in her own time. Fluids, certainly, and analgesics, both of which she had given as best she could. Above all what Mistress Flyte needed, though, were antibiotics. If there was an infection, being so old and frail and weakened from the beating, and if what had hold of her really was sepsis, nothing else would save her now. If she had been at home, Xanthe realized, even without assistance, she could probably have saved her simply by giving her strong antibiotics. The further irony was that Flora, because of her compromised health, always kept a stock of antibiotic capsules at home. She could go back and get them, but there were so many difficulties and risks attached to trying to do so. What if her mother saw her return to the house? How would she explain being there, or come up with a convincing reason for leaving again? And how long would it take her? Mistress Flyte could easily die in the time it took her, especially as Xanthe knew now that the ratio of one century's progression through time to another's was not fixed. Even if she spent only a few hours at home, weeks or months might elapse in the past. And where did that leave Samuel? He might be out of the lockup, but the chocolate pot would not have triggered Xanthe's gift, would not have insisted she travel back to his time, unless he was in very real danger. After all, Mistress Flyte had explained that once he had finished his work on Fairfax's house, once Samuel had served his purpose, he was expendable.

"How does my mistress fare?" Edmund peered around the door, his face showing a lack of sleep and a deep anxiety. He had reason to be worried, for Mistress Flyte was obviously not only his employer but the provider of his home and his place of safety. It was quite possible she was the nearest thing to family the boy possessed.

"She is sleeping," Xanthe told him.

"Ah, that is good. She must rest to become well again."

"Edmund, I have to warn you, Mistress Flyte is still gravely ill."

He took in her words, struggling to master his emotions.

"You are a fair nurse, and I thank you for your efforts," he said formally, trying to be the man of the house but giving himself away by his teary eyes.

"She is very weak, you see," Xanthe explained. "And, there is a sickness in her blood, because of her injuries."

He looked at Xanthe, his expression imploring. "Is there nothing more you can do? No further remedy we might try?"

Xanthe could not bear to see the heartache on his face, nor to think of this kind woman losing her life to the thugs who had attacked her. She made up her mind.

"Well, there might be something. I would have to . . . go and fetch it."

"A medicament?"

"That's right. I will be gone . . . a while. I can't say how long. I will be as quick as I can, but while I am not here you will have to look after your mistress. Keep her cool and quiet. Give her sips of milk if she will take them. Bathe her face and hands. Do you think you could do that?"

He nodded energetically. "It is no more than the mistress would have done for me, were I the one so cruelly used."

And so it was arranged. They put up a notice on the door of the chocolate house saying it would remain closed until further notice due to Mistress Flyte being temporarily indisposed. The note apologized for the inconvenience caused and assured patrons that once the doors opened again the first rum-laced chocolate would be at the expense of the proprietor. This seemed to satisfy Edmund that if his mistress survived she would have a business to return to. Xanthe made him promise he would not open the door to anyone he didn't know to be a friend. His only task was to look after his mistress, all else could wait.

Xanthe went up to her attic room. She closed the door firmly, fixing it shut with a chair. She had already said her goodbyes to Edmund, explaining she would slip out of the yard door at the back of the house when she left, and wouldn't disturb him on her way. He was so earnestly taken up with looking after Mistress Flyte that she was confident he wouldn't notice that he hadn't heard the back door slam shut. Xanthe took off her apron and let down her hair. There were so many unknowns, so many things to worry about regarding her journey back and forth that she refused to think about any of them. If she did she would lose her nerve. This was the old woman's only hope. She had to try. In an attempt to make sure she returned to her attic room, rather than some other part of Bradford, or Marlborough, she had taken the step of moving the chocolate pot upstairs, setting it down carefully beside her low bed. It thrummed as she handled it.

"You'd better bring me back," she told it, shaking her head at the thought that she needed the help of such a thing in the first place.

At last she could put the moment off no longer. She stood in the center of the room and fished the locket from beneath her T-shirt. In the dim light it still had the ability to gleam. She opened it, looking at the picture of her mother's smiling face.

"Hi, Mum," she said softly, and within seconds she felt herself falling, spinning forward through time once again. After a brief but dizzying moment where she feared she would land crashing onto the floor of the blind house, her transition slowed. She could hear the voices, but they were distant this time, whispering and less frantic. It was almost as if they—whomever they were—sensed that this was to be a fleeting journey. That she was not leaving, not properly. That this was all a necessary part of what she had come for. She had no time to understand these things any further, however, as with startling speed she found herself slumped upon the gritty ground inside the little stone building. She waited, giving her mind and body time to adjust, letting the nausea and giddiness recede. Slowly then, she got to her feet. She listened. The voices had fallen silent. The door of the blind house was ajar, as she had left it, so she was able to see that it was dark outside. Thanking her luck, she peered out. The garden was still and empty, save for a hedgehog making its snuffling progress across the lawn. It looked up at her, surprised, and then scuttled away to the cover of the shrubs against the tall wall. The fact that he was not in hibernation suggested it was still autumn. Another relief. Looking at the plants as much as she could tell in the gloom, everything was as it had been when she had traveled back. Gaining in confidence, Xanthe crept out, checking the lights at the windows of the flat above the shop. All were in darkness, except the one on the landing. A motorbike buzzed up the high street, its engine noise slightly muted by the fog that was descending. Everything suggested she had arrived in the small hours of the night. She hurried to the back door, using her own key to let herself in, and tiptoed up the stairs to the bathroom. As she passed her mother's bedroom she paused, holding her breath as she saw Flora sleeping heavily. The pill bottle on her bedside table suggested she had needed strong painkillers. Had her arthritis worsened? Was she going to be able to manage on her own? Xanthe shook such thoughts from her head. The quicker she did what she needed to do, the sooner she could return to help her mother. She moved on to the bathroom and slid open the door of the cabinet. There were two boxes of antibiotics, both within date. She took the strongest ones, which were capsules and would therefore be easier to empty into a liquid so that she stood a better chance of administering them to Mistress Flyte.

With her precious medicine tucked into the pocket of her dress, Xanthe hurried downstairs. She was on the point of leaving when she remembered a pair of tiny silver scissors that had recently been added to the stock. She thought how useful they would be for removing and preparing Mistress Flyte's bandages, so nipped into the shop to fetch them, risking switching on the lamp that sat on the desk. It was as she took them out of the glass-fronted case in the bow window that she became aware she was being watched. Slowly she turned. She had to stifle a shout when she saw a face looming at the window.

"Marcus!" she said aloud, a mixture of anger and relief making her forget for a moment that silence was essential. She unlocked the shop door, slipping outside quickly, being careful not to let the bell ring as she did so. "What are you doing skulking around here, frightening me half to death?" she questioned him in an urgent whisper. "It's the middle of the night."

"Couldn't sleep. Nor could you, looks like," he said, running his hands through his hair. He looked dreadful. Gaunt and pale with dark circles beneath his eyes. It was shocking how much of his youth and health were being sacrificed to his habit. Xanthe remembered how often when they were together he had been unable to sleep and had prowled the streets for hours. She stopped herself from commenting on his appearance, fearing that he might read her noticing as a sign that she cared.

"I've told you, Marcus, I'm not interested in having anything to do with you or the band, OK? All that is finished. Why can't you just go back to London? There's nothing for you here," she said, glancing up at the windows above the shop, worried that their words might carry. At least her mother's bedroom window was shut against the cold night air.

"Can't seem to tear myself away," Marcus said, stuffing his hands in the pockets of his inadequate jacket, shifting from one foot to the other. "Could do with a drink," he added.

"No way you're coming in." Xanthe shook her head. "Mum would go mad."

"So don't tell her. This is about you and me, Xan, no one else."

Xanthe realized that he wasn't just going to go away, just vanish back into the city and out of her life. If Harley hadn't put him off, if he hadn't already taken notice of what she'd said, he wasn't going to give up easily. She tried to think, tried to decide how best to deal with him, but all the time her head was full of what it was she was there for. Of Mistress Flyte dying if she didn't get back to her soon. Of Samuel, still in danger. Of the fact that she had to get back to the blind house as quickly as possible.

"Look, I don't have time for this right now."

"You've something else to do at . . ." he checked his watch, ". . . two o'clock in the morning?"

"Mum's not good. I don't want her disturbed again tonight," she said, inwardly flinching at the lie, hating herself for using her mother's illness. When Marcus showed no sign of going anywhere she knew she would have to promise him something if she was to get rid of him. It was setting up trouble for the future, but she had to get him to leave so she could slip back through the house. "We can talk again, if you need more convincing. Don't get your hopes up, I'm not going to change my mind."

"That's all I want, for us to talk. . . ."

"But not now, OK? I'll meet you in The King's Arms, it's the pub at the bottom of the high street."

"When?"

"Friday. Six o'clock."

"That's not until the end of the week. What am I supposed to do until then?"

"I don't know! For God's sake, Marcus, I have a life. My mother needs me. We are running a business here. . . ."

"And I'm paying for a bed and breakfast."

Xanthe sighed. "Some things never change, do they? Wait here." She dived back into the shop and took two twenty-pound notes from the cash box in the desk drawer, grateful they didn't have an electronic till system. "Here," she said, stuffing the money into his outstretched hand. "Just keep away from here and I'll meet you on Friday."

"Friday," he echoed, backing away up the cobbled street, watching her watching him until at last he turned onto the high street and was gone.

The second he was out of sight Xanthe went back into the shop, locked the front door, and hurried along the narrow passageway that led to the garden. She all but sprinted across the lawn, not giving herself time to worry about how difficult her journey back through time might be on this occasion, or where she might end up. There was no time to hesitate. She had to go back, and she had to go back quickly.

This transition was swifter than any she had experienced before. She barely had time to register the fact that she was blacking out, that she was traveling again, when she found herself back in her attic bedroom at the chocolate house. She was, as always, on the floor, breathless and giddy, but somehow less muddled, less unnerved, and the voices were quieter. Was she simply getting used to it? she wondered. Or could it be that she was, in some small way, beginning to take control of her movement through time? It certainly seemed to her that placing the chocolate pot where she wanted to return to must have had an effect, for there it stood, beside her bed, singing a high, clear note, as if it were a beacon signaling her way home. She shook off the idea that she could even briefly think of the seventeenth century as her home. Of course it was not. But after what Mistress Flyte had told her she knew there was more to her wondrous ability than she had first imagined. The old woman knew what Xanthe could do, and there were others who could do it too. What was it she had called them? Spinners of time? A memory, distant and faint, stirred in Xanthe's mind, but she couldn't pin it down. And this was not the time to be trying to find answers to riddles.

She got to her feet, moved the chair from the door, and hurried down to Mistress Flyte's room. She startled Edmund from his doze on the chair beside the bed.

"I did not hear you come home," he said.

Xanthe silently cursed herself for not having taken more care and was relieved when he told her how he had hated leaving the back door unlocked for her and was glad they would be able to put the bolt across again now that she had returned. She managed to tease from him the information that she had been gone only twenty-four hours. Mistress Flyte continued to be feverish, drifting in and out of a troubled sleep. She looked worryingly weak.

Xanthe took the antibiotics from her pocket and broke open two of the capsules, emptying the granules into a glass. She had no real idea of what dosage would be right. She reasoned that she should give the strongest dose possible, but Mistress Flyte would never have taken antibiotics in her life before. Would she be more sensitive to them? What if she had some sort of allergic reaction? It was a risk that would have to be taken. She poured in a little warmed milk and stirred.

"Here, Edmund, help me sit your mistress up," she said, perching on the edge of the bed. Together they lifted up the frail old woman, who moaned as she was moved. With great care and patience, Xanthe spooned the mixture into her mouth, allowing time for Mistress Flyte to swallow the medicine, waiting as she struggled to find each breath in between sips. At last it was done, and they laid the old woman back against the pillows. Xanthe checked the clock on the mantel. "We must give her more in two hours," she said. "We can let her sleep now."

"Will it work?" Edmund asked. "Will the cure save her?"

Xanthe put her hand on his arm. "She's a brave woman, Edmund. She won't give up without a fight. Come on, let's get that sign off the door and see if we can keep your mistress's business running. It's what she would have wanted." When he hesitated, reluctant to leave the old woman, Xanthe added, "I can't do it without you, Edmund. Will you help me?"

He hesitated, then nodded, and together they went downstairs.

The next day passed in a ceaseless round of nursing Mistress Flyte and working in the chocolate house. To begin with, as with the first time they had held the fort together, Xanthe and Edmund tripped over each other, made mistakes, and spent a fair amount of time making good their slipups and soothing the tempers of less-than-satisfied customers. Gradually, though, they settled into a rhythm, each playing to their strengths. Edmund, it transpired, was quite talented at preparing the hot chocolate, and Xanthe was happy to let him take over. Now that he was over the initial shock of what had happened to his mistress he made no more mistakes, focusing on the delicate task of producing the luxurious drinks to the clients' specifications with increasing confidence, his natural ability coming to the fore. Xanthe, on the other hand, was far more adept at handling the customers, keeping them cheerful even when things weren't done exactly as they had been used to. They seemed not to mind the unusual way she spoke, and no one was sufficiently interested in her to question where she had come from. Whenever anyone asked about her employer she told them the same thing, that she had taken ill with a heavy cold and would soon be up and about again.

She only wished she could believe her own words. The thought that time was passing and still she was no nearer helping Samuel was torture for her. She knew she could not leave while Mistress Flyte was so dangerously ill. Whenever possible, she or Edmund sprinted up the narrow wooden staircase to check on the patient. They bathed her, trying to reduce her fever that had her in a relentless grip. Xanthe changed the dressings on her wounds and could see no real change in the injuries. She comforted herself that there was no further sign of infection, but nor was there any noticeable healing taking place. Every two hours she had Edmund help her give Mistress Flyte more medication. Each time they both hoped for, searched for, signs of improvement, but there were none. In fact, by the end of the next day the old woman was so feeble it was even harder to get her to sip the medicated milk. That night, her feet aching from a long day serving downstairs, Xanthe sat in the chair beside the bed and watched the old woman as she slept. Would she ever wake again? Would Xanthe get the chance to question her further about what she knew of the time spinners? Were she and Fairfax the only two, or were there more? And how did Mistress Flyte know about them? Xanthe felt trapped. She could not desert the old woman, but she had to leave for Laybrook soon. Earlier she had overheard a conversation at the fireside between two carpenters who had mentioned Laybrook Abbey. Her ears had pricked up at the name, and she listened in for word of Samuel.

"That paneling was exceedingly fine, mind you," said one, leaning back in his chair to suck on a clay pipe. "I will not be ashamed to put my name to it."

"Aye, there is satisfaction in a job well done," the stouter man agreed, taking a swig from his pewter tankard of chocolate. "And glad I am that it is done, for I would not spend one swift minute longer in that place than my work compelled me to."

"Your work or your master." The pipe smoker shook his head. "I will not miss the company of Fairfax, no more will you."

"An exacting master."

"More than that, one who I believe will never find satisfaction in the work of another and will forever berate them, regardless of quality. Only yester-morn he did take me to task for the quantity of wood shavings left over from planing the lumber. Called it wasteful. I asked him what he would have me do, leave the wood the wrong size? He replied the shavings should be swept into sacks and put to some good purpose."

Both men had given a hollow laugh at this and just as Xanthe had started to think she would learn nothing of Samuel the pipe smoker had spoken again.

"Pity poor Master Appleby, for he must bide longer to see the work complete."

"Pity him more when 'tis done, for then Fairfax will have no further use for him beyond an offering for the king."

"You do believe he will do it? After all that Appleby has done to enhance the Abbey? After all the good standing of the family years past?"

"Ha, gone are the days such things counted. When a man has shown his colors, as Appleby has, he has put himself beyond the pale. These times are unforgiving, and no man more suited to them than Fairfax."

After that their conversation had turned to their own families. Once back in her garret room, Xanthe struggled to keep frustration from getting the better of her. She could not leave yet, but perhaps she could find more answers to the riddles Mistress Flyte had alluded to. She took up the chocolate pot, feeling it tremble slightly in her hands.

"Can't you show me anything? Surely there's something I could see, something to make more sense of it all. What do you want me to do?" She closed her eyes, waiting, hoping. There were whispers, glimpses of faces, shadowy and unfamiliar. She saw Samuel's face then, solemn and distant. And then Fairfax, with his unmistakable pallor and cold eyes. Eyes which, as she watched, seemed to turn toward her. To see her, their pupils widening, his expression altering from surprise to one of intense interest.

"Come quick!"

Edmund's shout from the floor below made her all but drop the chocolate pot. She raced to the top of the attic stairs. The boy below beckoned urgently.

"Come quick . . . 'tis the mistress!" And with that he dashed back toward the bedchamber.

Xanthe followed, fearing what she would find. As she entered the room she half expected to see a weeping Edmund standing over the lifeless body of Mistress Flyte. She could not have been more wrong.

"Why, Xanthe, how fatigued you look." The old woman's voice was thin but unwavering, and her eyes retained their focus as Xanthe came to stand at her bedside. "And poor Edmund is quite worn out. I fear the chocolate house has been a heavy burden, as have I . . . ."

"Oh, no, mistress!" Edmund insisted. "'T'was no trouble at all."

She reached out and patted his hand. "I am fortunate indeed to have such a young man as you in my employ. And Xanthe, has she proved useful?"

Xanthe fancied she saw the faintest smile on the old woman's lips.

Edmund treated the question with great seriousness.

"She has shown herself to be a fair apothecary, a good maid, and hardworking, but . . ."

"But?"

"She has no feel for the chocolate, mistress. Nor would I advise giving her the best porcelain to carry, not if you wish to see it returned in good order."

Xanthe could not help laughing at this accurate description of her talents. Edmund blushed deeply.

"Thank you, Edmund," Mistress Flyte said. "I will not keep you from your bed longer."

So dismissed he backed from the room, the relief of having his beloved mistress well again written all over his youthful if weary features. Once they were alone together the old woman reached for Xanthe's hand.

"I owe you my life," she said, already visibly tiring. "I am indebted to you."

"You took me in, gave a stranger a chance. . . ."

"I think you understand that I do not see you as a stranger, for I recall telling you that I know what it is you are."

"Ah, you remember that?"

"And more besides. You are a diligent nurse."

"To be honest, I wasn't sure what I was doing was even safe."

"You are a resourceful girl. As you will need to be."

"I have so many questions."

"I imagine so."

"The first of which is, do you remember who attacked you?"

"I did not see my assailant."

"But you unlocked the door, you went outside late at night. . . ."

"I heard my name called. I believed I knew who it was who called me. I fancied I recognized the voice." Mistress Flyte looked, for a moment, deeply saddened, and turned her face away. "Forgive me, I am fatigued. . . ."

"Here, let me help you." Xanthe made her more comfortable and then left her to sleep. She plodded back up to her own room, pausing only to remove her boots before falling into bed. The relief of knowing that the old woman would live, and that tomorrow she would at last be able to talk to her about so many things, removed the last of her determination to keep going, so that she quickly fell into a heavy, dreamless slumber.

{ 7 }

WHAT XANTHE HAD NOT CONSIDERED WAS THE FACT THAT MISTRESS FLYTE'S FIRST concern, now that she was well enough to fret, was the chocolate house. She had both Xanthe and Edmund running up and down the stairs all the next morning, bringing her a tally of chocolate and spice stocks, details of the takings, news of which customers had been in while she had been ill, and so it went on. Between meeting her demands for information and carrying out her instructions and serving in the chocolate house, there was no time for questions. No time to find the answers that Xanthe knew she must have before she left. She promised herself she would see Mistress Flyte on her feet, satisfy herself that the old woman's recovery was assured, and then she would talk to her. She dared not wait any longer.

Edmund rose to the challenge of continuing to keep customers happy, showing himself to be talented in at last learning the ways different patrons preferred to take their drinks. What he lacked, what Xanthe suspected he might never acquire, was the easy manner of a host. Nor did he have his mistress's interest in politics, so that he was quite oblivious to the whispering in corners and intense huddles around tables that went on in the business he was running. Xanthe began to notice there were cliques, or small groups of men who always sat together, always seemed engaged in earnest conversation, while others appeared to be more interested in smoking their pipes or enjoying their hot chocolate. She thought about how strange it felt not to see many women there. In the twenty-first century, chocolate was surely a predominantly female passion; she could imagine lots of her friends, Gerri and her mother included, who would love such a place. But there was evidently more to the chocolate house than its delicious and reviving beverage. It was about gathering. About a place to meet. A place slightly on the margins, so new and expensive was its delicacy. A place that was beginning to mark people out as having dangerous alliances, however. How much longer would people use it if they were going to be dragged across the road to the lockup on the say-so of men like Benedict Fairfax? Xanthe wondered.

It was nearly four in the afternoon before Xanthe finally had the opportunity to leave Edmund and go upstairs, taking two fine china cups of aromatic hot chocolate with her. She set them down on the bedside table in Mistress Flyte's chamber, drawing up a chair to sit near. She handed the old woman her drink, helping her to sit comfortably with it before settling down with her own.

"You have regained a little color, mistress," she told her. "Do you feel stronger?"

"Thanks to your ministrations and Edmund's chocolate I feel my strength wonderfully restored. On the morrow I shall at last rise from this sickbed and resume my duties. And you must make your way to Laybrook. I have detained you long enough."

Xanthe searched for the words to ask what she wanted, to start in on the difficult topic of traveling through time. Mistress Flyte saw her hesitation and read much into the silence.

"Ask what you will, child. You have earned the right. You undertook the dangerous task of journeying through time solely for my benefit. I, of all people, know what you risked."

"Please, don't tell me that. That's something I prefer not to dwell on."

"As you wish. Nonetheless, such action when you are so inexpert, that is to say, so newly come to the business of spinning through the centuries—well, it was courageous, and I will be forever grateful."

"Believe me, you took as great a risk as me. I wasn't certain how you would respond to the medication I brought for you."

"It was not as unfamiliar to me as you might imagine."

"Oh?" Xanthe was confused for a moment but then a realization came to her. "Of course, many of the old remedies, that is, the cures from this time, they must have contained antibiotics. I mean, the apothecaries and herbalists wouldn't have called them that, they might not have known how they worked, but I suppose trial and error would have led them to the right things sometimes. Like honey, doesn't that have high levels of antibiotics in it? Oh, sorry, silly question. You've never heard the word before now."

Mistress Flyte smiled slowly. "Let us say that a person does not reach my age without acquiring broad wisdom. Some sought, some given, all useful."

Xanthe leaned forward on her chair. "You told me, when you were feverish, that you knew who . . . what I was. You said something about spinners of time?" When the old woman nodded Xanthe continued. "Well, how did you know? How did you know about the chocolate pot, come to that? Can you hear it too? Do you connect with objects the way I do? And what about Fairfax; you said he could travel through time too. How do you know that? And how will he have heard about me?"

Mistress Flyte raised a hand, laughing lightly. "Upon my word, what a torrent of queries! You must allow yourself time to absorb all this newfound knowledge. It is a great deal to come to terms with. There will be some adjustment needed."

"I'm sorry, but I don't have the luxury of time. As you said yourself, I need to get to Laybrook and help Samuel, and anything you can tell me about this incredible ability that seems to have come to me out of nowhere . . ."

"No, not that. You have always had the gift of connecting with the past, have you not?"

"Well, yes, through some of the things I find."

"Or that find you."

Now Xanthe smiled. "That's what Mum always says. That a treasure hunt works both ways. And once something has found you, you shouldn't ignore it. It was meant, finding it, being found. . . ."

"Your mother is an astute woman."

"But I've always been able to detect the stories some of the treasures hold. When they want to show them to me, that is. This traveling backward and forward through time though," she shook her head, "this is something else! I worked out that the blind house in our garden, back in Marlborough, that it is some sort of point of energy which seems to change things. It sits on the intersection of two ley lines. It has the effect of changing the connection I have with objects from just showing and feeling to, well, going places." She laughed a little at the understatement of this. "But what if I'd never moved to Marlborough? What if we hadn't bought the shop?"

"You are prepared to believe that personal objects find you, why would you not accept the same of a building?"

"The shop, the blind house . . . they found us too? The way the chocolate pot did? And the chatelaine before that?"

Mistress Flyte shifted on her bed, her injuries still causing her pain and discomfort. "It is important you learn to relinquish control, child. Your path will be easier if you understand that it is one chosen for you, not the other way around."

Xanthe was too tired to decide if the old woman was being deliberately obtuse, or if it was simply a case of their use of language being so different. Either way she was struggling to fully make sense of what she was being told. She could see that Mistress Flyte was quickly tiring and had to hide her frustration. There were so many things she wanted to know, but the old woman's health was still fragile. She needed her rest, not least so that Xanthe would feel able to leave her to Edmund's care in the morning.

"I'm glad to see you recovered, mistress. Promise me you will not overexert yourself, not return to your duties fully too soon. I worry. . . ."

Mistress Flyte held up a hand. "You have nursed me to reasonable health. Do not concern yourself with me further. I will write you a letter to take to Samuel's cousin in Laybrook, by way of introduction. You can go there. It will be a safe place for you to stay while you do what you can for young Appleby. Now, to your bed. You will need your wits about you if you are to prevail over Benedict Fairfax."

Xanthe got to her feet. "Tell me one more thing. If Fairfax is a time spinner too, what would he want from me? He can travel to what time he wants without my help, presumably. And I'm no threat to him. I just want to protect Samuel."

Mistress Flyte turned and gazed at the pulsing flame of the candle beside her bed, and Xanthe saw again an expression of sadness cast a shadow over her fine features. She looked different, somehow, in these moments when she was caught thinking about Fairfax. "Who can fathom the workings of such a singular mind?" Mistress Fairfax said slowly. "What cannot be denied is that ambition can tarnish a man's heart. You will have to tread with caution. He is a Spinner of long standing, though he is not as gifted nor expert as he wishes to be. It happens that some are more natural in their abilities . . ." she smiled at Xanthe, ". . . while others must work harder to acquire the skills they need. And in that work, in that study, some equip themselves, over time, with further useful talents, such as the ability to detect the presence and activity of other time spinners. Fairfax knew you were coming. He was waiting here for you, was he not? It is entirely likely he was aware of your earlier journeys. You did not encounter him during your previous travels to this century?"

Xanthe started to shake her head but then experienced a vivid flash of memory. She saw, in her mind's eye, a tall, angular, pale man in a broad-brimmed hat standing across the green from her when she had visited Alice in the blind house. Now it came back to her. "Yes!" she said. "It must have been him. I knew he was somehow familiar. I saw him when I came to help Alice."

"And he saw you. Was it a seemingly chance meeting?"

"Well, yes. I mean, no one outside the household knew where I was going. And even they didn't know until practically the last minute, as I had trouble persuading Mary I should be allowed to go. Nobody could have told him. And it was cold, a stormy day. I remember that because I can remember thinking how bleak and awful it must have been for Alice to be locked up in that stone building with nothing to keep her warm. So it was odd that this strange man was apparently just hanging around on the green. It was as if he was waiting for someone. Expecting someone."

"Expecting you," said Mistress Flyte.

"He didn't approach me."

"Did he speak to you?"

"No. The jailer was around. And Willis, I think. But I have heard his voice. Now I know it was his, not just another of the many voices I hear when I am traveling. I've glimpsed his face too sometimes, when I've been falling through time. Yes, it was definitely him. Watching me. Stalking me, practically."

"Biding his time for the right moment. Which has come. Now that he has shown himself to you, made himself known, he will be ready to make his next move."

"Which is likely to be what? I still don't see why he needs me."

"That I cannot tell you precisely, child. Rest assured, he would not waste his energies on you if he did not consider you crucial to his own ambitious plans. There is something he wants from you." She closed her eyes for a moment, and it seemed to Xanthe that it was not her physical suffering that was causing her pain now as much as a memory, the echo of a past experience that made her look suddenly older and more frail.

"I am sorry to press you, mistress," Xanthe said, "but there is so much I need to understand. The more I know about how all this works, and the better I understand Fairfax, well, the stronger chance I have of helping Samuel."

The old woman opened her eyes again. "Chance has very little to do with it," she insisted. And then a thought appeared to come to her. She leaned forward, her voice urgent. "There is something that could help you greatly. I wonder . . . Yes, it would make perfect sense! The blind house led you to it. The chatelaine, the chocolate pot, why not this too? For is it not equally vital? Tell me, child, in all your collecting of found things, and indeed of those things finding you, have you perhaps been united with a very particular book?"

"A book? Which one? What's it called?"

"It may have no words written on the cover, or a single word, mayhap. It is so very old, it has been rebound many times, and different book binders have different notions about what would be suitable for a repository of such powerful knowledge. I saw it once, a long, long time ago. Held it in my hands. . . . Would that I had been able to keep it! Alas, such a prize provokes envy among those who know its worth. I know better than to believe I could keep such a gift, for it must go where it will. Where it is most needed. The time has come for it to have a new keeper, and I accept this." She sighed heavily. "The vastness of time swallows up small items. To find a single book in the midst of all that has been and all that will be is to locate a single grain of sand upon the shores of a great ocean."

As Xanthe listened to the old woman's words something in her own memory began to stir. Some faint image, a connection, a glimpse of something that had, at the time when she had seen it, seemed insignificant, but now appeared crucial to what she was trying to do. When she had sorted through the boxes of stock in the shop, the ones they had inherited from Mr. Morris, the previous owner, there had been books. Quite a number of books. Most of them had been water damaged or nibbled by mice or were marred by mildew, but some she had kept as part of the bookcase display. She remembered now the humble-looking leather-bound book that had worn gold lettering on it, flowing and deep set, making up the single word: *Spinners.* Excitement gripped her. She had dismissed the book as a dry tome about the history of a rural craft and not paid it any attention. It had to be the one Mistress Flyte was talking about. It had to be.

"I think," she said carefully, watching the old woman closely, "that I might just have found it."

Mistress Flyte sat forward. "Truly? You believe it is the very book?"

"Well, it's certainly old, and the only word on it was 'Spinners.' No author, no publisher, nothing else. I thought it was to do with wool. My God, I could so easily have thrown it out! I only kept it because the leather cover is still in good condition. People buy books like that to look nice on their shelves and bookcases, pretty much regardless of what's between the covers."

"You have it!"

"But it can't be what you say it is. I mean, if it's that important, and if it's about spinning time, and if I am a time spinner, then why didn't it sing to me?"

Mistress Flyte smiled, her whole face lit up with excitement on hearing of this discovery. "The book was waiting."

"Waiting?"

"For the right moment. The perfect moment to reveal itself, its true value, to the right person. To you."

"Well it might have ended up in the rubbish bin! I could have done with knowing about it sooner. If there are instructions about traveling through time . . . think of the mistakes and difficulties I might have avoided. Why didn't it sing to me when I found it, when I held it? Why wasn't that the right moment?"

Leaning back in her seat, wincing slightly at the movement, the old woman explained, "There is an order to these things. One that cannot be upset. From a child, you have been listening to the singing of objects and felt the vibrations of their stories. Now a grown woman, you found your way to the right place so that you could begin your work as a spinner of time. And so you have started your travels, each journey a test not only of your courage and integrity but of your suitability as a Spinner."

"But this is wonderful! It sounds like the book can really help me. I wish I had looked at it properly when I found it. You say it was waiting to sing to me, but what was it waiting for?"

"For you to come here, my dear. For you to find your way to me." So saying she closed her eyes, fatigue and pain taking their toll so that she was quickly asleep again, leaving Xanthe to clear away the cups and slip away to her own room to pack her few precious possessions. As she worked, her mind sped this way and that, cursing herself for not examining the Spinners book more closely and for not making the connection sooner. Her thoughts raced on to Mistress Flyte—what part had the old woman to play in Xanthe's time traveling? She had thought her simply connected to the chocolate pot, to this journey, this story, to helping with Samuel and learning about Fairfax. But if the book had waited for the two of them to meet before revealing itself, then surely she must be more significant than that. Must have a bigger part to play. Xanthe was almost too excited to sleep as she pondered the possibilities of what she would learn when she was reunited with that book. She was exhausted by her duties, fatigued by the cold of the room, weary from worry about Samuel, yet her mind would not be stilled. She marshaled her thoughts. She had come here for her own reasons, no matter what the chocolate pot, or the Spinners, or Mistress Flyte wanted from her. She would put all else from her mind and concentrate on what she had come to do: help Samuel. With this determined thought she chased a fitful sleep through the chilly night.

The next day was much colder, and a slow dawn revealed a rime of frost upon the little houses and trees of Bradford-on-Avon. As Xanthe crossed the broad stone bridge she glanced down at the water below. The river flowed full and silent, deep and deadly cold, making her shiver. She turned up the collar of her greatcoat and stuffed her hands in its pockets. She had Mistress Flyte's letter safely tucked into one, and the feel of the thick, coarse paper with its wax seal made her think of the note Samuel had written her. It seemed an age ago, though it had only been a matter of weeks for her and months for him. It was still painful to remember their parting, to recall how he had known she would leave him and had written down his thoughts and feelings for her to keep. What he could not have known was that his sweet words were doomed to crumble to dust before the year was out. Xanthe had seen how things she took back with her to her own time gradually disintegrated, not being able to make the journey through the centuries, or at least, not withstanding the effects for long. She had copied his letter, of course, as well as committed his thoughts to memory, but that hadn't stopped her heart breaking just a little more when the note had crumbled completely, his own dear handwriting lost to her forever. She wondered, not for the first time, if Samuel would even want to see her again. He might not want to have his feelings stirred up when there was no way they could be together. Or would time have altered how he felt? Or perhaps made him less understanding of how he had watched her quite literally disappear? It wouldn't have been unreasonable of him to have thought her some sort of witch. Why not? Wasn't she using magic that seemed to draw on something much more powerful than even she herself could explain? What was that if not witchcraft?

Xanthe felt awkward beneath the gaze of strangers as she made her way through the little town. They didn't know she was a minstrel, so her unorthodox appearance must have appeared curious, must have marked her out as different. As a stranger. She tugged at the scarf covering her hair, trying to make it sit more sensibly. The last thing she needed was unwanted attention or to have to explain herself to people. As she reached the coaching inn where she had been told she could catch the stagecoach that passed near Laybrook she also had to admit to herself that she had no clear plan of how she was going to help Samuel. How was she going to rid him of the threat of such a powerful man as Fairfax? Mistress Flyte had told her she had to get used to not being in control of her own life. She would just have to trust that she had been brought here for a reason. She had been summoned by the chocolate pot. Someone or something believed she had a purpose to serve, a mission to complete in order that history unfolded as it should, and keeping Samuel safe was clearly a part, at least, of what she had to do.

Xanthe sat between two elderly ladies, one of whom appeared to have bathed in copious amounts of lavender, and opposite a stout gentleman who insisted on eating sausages. Soon the air in the carriage interior was a nauseating combination of smells. Xanthe reached across and succeeded in opening the small window in the carriage door, allowing in at least a little breathable air. When one of her traveling companions complained of the draft she swapped seats, which meant she could at least watch the landscape through which they passed. Despite Xanthe's impatience to get to her destination, the picturesque Wiltshire countryside was a delight, and she felt her spirits raised by it. One of the first things that struck her was how few and far between the houses were. And how few people she saw, either in carriages, on horseback, working in the fields, or in the villages. She recalled that the population of England had only reached the ten million mark at the beginning of the twentieth century. What could it have been in the sixteen hundreds? Whatever the figure, the country appeared almost empty. It wasn't just the lack of actual people that made it feel so, it was the light touch that they had made upon the land. The stagecoach was traveling on one of the very few roads of any size, and even that was a rough and rustic affair. Most of the farmland was unfenced, giving it an open, slightly wild appearance, and there were far more trees. What Xanthe remembered in her own time as tiny copses or a handful of oaks and ash trees on the crest of a hill were proper tracts of woodland here. To the south, indeed, she was able to see only forest stretching away, dense and ancient. How many trees must have been felled since? Felled and not replaced. Winter had painted the landscape with a palette of soft browns and muted golds, with pale, pale greens where the grass and trees held the frost. Plowed fields had begun to show their winter crops as tough little beets and turnips poked their fat, flat leaves above the frigid soil.

The distance was less than ten miles, but the stage was on a slow part of its route—the ultimate destination London—and stopped twice, allowing what felt like an age for more passengers to board with their luggage. The further east they traveled, the more they found that the road had become boggy and rutted by the winter weather, so that the stage lurched and rattled, further slowing their progress. On rare stretches of good ground the driver whipped up the horses in an effort to make up time. The increased speed felt reckless, but none of the other passengers gave any sign of being alarmed.

At last they drew into the village of Laybrook. Now it was not the differences but the similarities between the modern-day version and this early one that astonished Xanthe. The village was eerily similar to how it was when Xanthe had visited it and found the chocolate pot, with only a few houses missing. One of them, Xanthe noticed, was Esther Harris's fine home. Being a Georgian addition to the street, it would not have been built for nearly another 170 years, and yet when she and her mother had visited it the house had seemed so antique. As Laybrook had been preserved and kept as authentic as possible in the name of historical heritage and tourism (not to mention its lucrative value as a film set) even in the twenty-first century it had not been spoiled with brash signs, road markings, or wires. She recalled stepping from her black cab and feeling as if she had stepped back in time again. It had made her smile then, wondering how many visitors to the area had the same feeling, and knowing that she was surely the only one for whom time travel was a reality! And now, looking at the little rows of houses, the shop with its sway-backed roof, the two inns with smoke pouring from their chimneys, seeing the old buildings as they had been when recently built, Xanthe experienced a strange disconnect. A sense of not being able to hold on to what was real and what was not. What was her reality, and what was someone, some*when* else's.

As no one else was getting off, Xanthe was able to swiftly secure her small leather shoulder bag, her only luggage, and step onto the muddy street. As she turned around to get her bearings, the stagecoach disappeared on its way with shouts and whipcracks from the driver. The largest of the two inns stood behind her, and a run of cottages and a similar set of little buildings on two other sides, forming something of a central square. Most of the houses were timber framed, showing their beams, some painted black, others natural wood. The spaces in between would have been made of wattle and daub, the plasterlike surface painted. Some were white, others pink, the charming color often obtained by adding oxblood to the wash before it was brushed on. One or two of the larger houses were built entirely of the local golden stone. These were not rough-hewn walls, but stones expertly dressed by skilled masons, making them almost as regular and smooth as bricks. An expensive option, marking the owners out as well-to-do. Xanthe recalled Mistress Flyte's directions and walked toward a narrow lane, using the spire of St. Cyriac's church as her landmark. All was exactly as had been described to her. A short row of half-timbered, black-and-white cottages, their upper floors and windows hanging out over the street, was set opposite the churchyard. There were no numbers on the dark wooden doors, so Xanthe simply counted along the terrace until she came to number three. She knocked and waited.

The young woman who opened the door was a tiny creature with watchful green eyes. Everything about her seemed tight and tense, from the neatly pinned cotton cap on her nut-brown hair, to her cinch-waisted apron and her tiny, restless feet. Xanthe put on her friendliest smile and handed her the letter from Mistress Flyte. It was fortunate that Samuel had once mentioned his cousin's ability to read within the older woman's earshot.

"My name is Xanthe Westlake," she said as the woman examined the seal. "You must be Rose. I'm hoping to talk to Samuel."

Rose shook her head slowly, unfolding the letter and reading as she spoke. "My cousin is not abiding here. His work keeps him up at the abbey."

"I thought he might be lodging with you and your husband."

"Master Fairfax prefers he be close at hand. The better to oversee the masons and such, see?"

"Of course." Xanthe's heart felt heavy. She had hoped to be able to talk to Samuel away from Fairfax. It seemed strange that he wasn't even permitted to stay with his family. After all, they were in the same village as the abbey. It seemed Fairfax wasn't prepared to let him out of his sight at all. She would have no option but to go up to the abbey, even if it meant confronting Fairfax. "Then that is where I must go," she added.

Rose looked up from the letter. "Mistress Flyte writes you are a good friend of Samuel's, yet I do not know you. Where was it that you made his acquaintance?"

"At Great Chalfield Manor, earlier this year. Samuel was working on the new screen for the great hall and I was able to assist him."

Rose was taken aback.

"Well, I never heard of a builder as was a woman!"

"Oh, no, I'm not. I'm a minstrel. I was employed at the house to sing at the birthday party of Clara Lovewell."

When Rose looked unconvinced, Xanthe tried again.

"As Mistress Flyte mentions in her letter, I have traveled a great distance to see Samuel."

"She says you wish only to help him. To defend him against any injustice as might be visited upon him. She does not name Master Fairfax, but it does not take a sharp wit to know it is he, the one who has Samuel's life in his hands. And held tight, at that."

"I will speak to Master Fairfax. I will plead Samuel's cause. First, though, I should like the opportunity to speak to your cousin alone."

"What reason would the master of the abbey have for caring what a minstrel from off should like?"

"None that I can think of. Which is why I would see Samuel first. Rose, I need to get to the abbey without being seen by the master of the house. Do you know a way?"

Rose drew her shawl tighter around her shoulders and took a step back, as if the very idea of going to the place frightened her.

"You wouldn't have to take me there yourself," Xanthe said.

"You won't find the way else," said Rose.

"Samuel needs my help."

Rose thought about this. "What can you do?" she asked.

Xanthe hesitated. She could see that, on the face of it, a young woman with no connections was not best placed to do anything of any significance. She couldn't tell Rose how much she cared for Samuel, or that his feelings for her meant that he would be likely to listen to and possibly consider acting upon any advice she gave. Nor could she tell her that she had unique knowledge that might help him. Knowledge that was for herself history but was for them the future. She knew that the present king would not remain long on the throne. She knew that great changes were coming. If she could make Samuel understand this, perhaps persuade him that in the short term it would be worth him giving up some of his allegiances, putting his political beliefs to one side, and waiting for the moment to come when he could again speak out without fear of prosecution. It wasn't much, but it might save him; if he was prepared to swear an oath of loyalty to the king, given how much he was in demand as an architect, it might just be enough. And then there was Mistress Flyte's insistence that Fairfax wanted something from Xanthe. Something that would help him spin time and develop his skills as a Spinner in a way that would fit in with his ambitions. There had to be a way she could use that, perhaps to strike a bargain with him. Aside from that, Xanthe believed that everyone had their weak point, their flaw that made them vulnerable. The more she could find out about Fairfax, the more likely it was she could find a way to use it against him if she had to. She put her hand on Rose's arm.

"I confess I am not yet certain, but I do have a plan. I know I am a stranger to you, but I think you believe Mistress Flyte to be a woman of good standing, and that is her letter of recommendation you hold. And Samuel chose me for his friend, did he not? If I don't try, once Fairfax has no further use for him, well, I fear he will not be permitted to return home."

She let the unspoken threat of a trial and execution hang in the air between them. Rose decided. She tucked the letter into her pocket, tied her shawl at her waist, and stepped forward, closing the door firmly behind her, leading the way without another word.

Laybrook Abbey was less than a quarter of a mile from the center of the village, and as they used a shortcut across the estate land instead of using the road and private approach, in no time at all they had reached the edge of the kitchen garden. The house was as unusual as it was imposing. Xanthe knew from what she had read after her twenty-first-century trip to the village that it had been a functioning abbey, housing a community of nuns, until the later part of the sixteenth century. After Henry VIII's dissolution of the monasteries it was a wonder the original building had survived at all, but it had, so that the larger portion of the house consisted of a Gothic structure, tall and angular, enclosing a set of cloisters around a courtyard. The more modern building that had been added gleamed golden beneath the chilly winter sun. Construction work was in evidence on all sides. This was an ambitious project indeed. Xanthe noticed that most of the work on the walls and windows had been completed, the scaffolding reaching roof level. A band of men crawled all over the steep slopes hammering stone tiles into place. Glaziers set about their work on the grander windows, some of which had stained glass. Masons could be heard hammering their chisels. However grand, the house was nearing completion. Samuel's presence would not be required for long. Weeks possibly, more likely days if he was not required to directly oversee all the works. His main expertise was for the construction of the interiors. How near to completion might that be?

Rose put a finger to her lips, signaling for Xanthe to stay silent as they made their way through the vegetable beds, past the fruit trees, and under an archway in the tall wall of the garden. This led into a courtyard around which the functional buildings that served the great house were arranged. There was a bakery emitting glorious smells of bread fresh from its oven; a washhouse, where maids labored, carrying baskets of laundry and pails of water; a hoarde house, where fruit and flour and vegetables were stored; a blacksmith's forge, fashioning shoes for the horses and plows for the fields; and a brewery in the far corner. Rose hurried to it and ushered Xanthe in. She spoke quickly to the elderly man who was tending the barrels of ale. After an exchange of tense whispers he left to go toward the main house.

"You are to wait here," Rose said, nervously glancing about her as if Fairfax might materialize from the shadows. "Taylor has gone to fetch Samuel. He will come when he can slip away unnoticed."

Xanthe squeezed Rose's hand. "Thank you," she said.

The young woman shook her head. "You are Samuel's friend. It is for him to send you away, which he will, for if he cares about you he will want you as far from Benedict Fairfax as you can be." She went to leave and then paused. "Come to us, after you have seen him. You can stop this night."

And then she was gone and Xanthe was left with her thoughts. She felt a nervousness that was less about being somewhere dangerous and more about being, at last, at the point of seeing Samuel again. She had considered how he might react to her returning, but she had done her best not to think about how seeing him, hearing him, standing close to him, would affect her. She had spent weeks telling herself that she had to forget him. That there was no possible way they could be together. That she had to weather the heartache

{ 8 }

FOR WHAT FELT LIKE AN AGE BUT COULD HAVE BEEN NO MORE THAN A MATTER OF seconds, they stood staring at each other. Xanthe's heart hurt before she had a chance to guard against her own emotions. So much had happened since she had last seen Samuel. And in that time she had convinced herself of the impossibility of ever being with him. She had accepted it. She collected herself, remembered her resolve, and tried to look at him as an old friend she had come to help, nothing more. There were, she noticed, subtle changes in his appearance; his incarceration, the threat of further imprisonment and possibly execution, and no doubt the stress of working for Fairfax under such conditions, all had taken their toll. There was a wariness about his expression, and there were shadows beneath his soulful eyes, though he was still darkly handsome. His hair was longer and less kempt, falling messily to his shoulders. His clothes showed signs of wear and lack of care. Xanthe thought too that he looked leaner, his black shirt hanging slightly loose on him. She opened her mouth to speak, uncertain what she could say that would be sensible, be appropriate. She got no further than muttering his name before Samuel strode across the room and wrapped her in his arms, pulling her close, murmuring her name into her hair. She breathed him in, allowing herself to give in to that fleeting moment of closeness, recognizing as futile her attempts to pretend, even to herself, that she had succeeded in distancing herself from him completely. What her head had accepted to be true her heart would resist a little longer. At last he stepped back, as if recollecting their situation and what was proper, forcing himself to rein in his own emotions.

"Let me look at you," he said. "Are you truly here, with me, or do my eyes play tricks upon me?"

Xanthe nodded, not blaming him for doubting her. Understanding his wariness.

"I am here, Samuel. Real as I know how," she said. Not for the first time she cursed her luck at finally finding a man who could truly move her only to have him inhabit a different century than her own. But that was the reality of it. She had promised herself she would not forget that. She let go his hands and moved away a little, putting on a bright smile.

"But how do you come to be here?" he asked.

"By stage from Bradford-on-Avon, and then Rose walked me from the village."

"Bradford?"

"Yes, I went there to look for you. I . . . I heard you were in the blind house."

"But how . . . ? Wait, give me no answer, for I shall not understand it." He hesitated, glancing back at the open door, and drew Xanthe to the corner of the room, keeping his voice low. "It is not safe for you here, Xanthe," he said.

The sound of him speaking her name made her start. She silently chided herself for being so foolish.

"I know. Mistress Flyte warned me. . . ."

"You are acquainted with Mistress Flyte?"

And then she tried to explain, gabbling on about the chocolate pot, and traveling a great distance to be with him, and seeing Fairfax, and how Mistress Flyte had helped her. Samuel looked increasingly confused.

"I would have come here sooner," Xanthe explained, "but something happened. Someone attacked Mistress Flyte."

"Dear God, does she live?"

"Yes, but she was badly beaten. Edmund and I looked after her. I couldn't leave her until I was sure she would recover. She is still in a lot of pain, but she understood that I needed to get to you."

"I am astonished she did not stop you. She knows the nature of the beast who confronts us. 'T'would have been better had she kept you in Bradford."

"And what use am I to you there? I went there because I thought you were still in the lockup. Once I knew you'd been freed . . ."

"Freed! I am as much a prisoner here as ever I was there. And I am the fortunate one. Others were taken either to the court at Salisbury or to London. Two are even now in the Tower."

"Oh, Samuel . . ."

"I am blessed with having a usefulness, but no worth beyond it. There is nothing you can do. My best hope is that Fairfax will be too taken up with matters of court to pursue me further. Once I have finished here I should put distance between myself and him."

"But where will you go?"

"We have distant family in Scotland . . . and yet . . ." He sighed, closing his eyes briefly. "If I leave he may take his ire out on my father and Joshua. In truth, I know I will not be able to bring myself to do it, though it is what they urge me to do."

"They are right, Samuel." Xanthe was reminded of how different Samuel was to his younger brother, and yet what a close family they were. "It won't be safe for you here."

"What would you have of me? That I become a fugitive? That I skulk in some unknown, dimly lit corner of the land, quaking at a stranger's footfalls, waiting for desperate news of those I hold dear? I cannot do it. I am deceiving myself to think otherwise."

"Then let me help you. Together we will think of something. Fairfax must have a weakness, everyone does. We find out what it is and we use it against him."

"I tell you, the man is made of stone, ironclad, protected by a shield of ambition and a guard of high-born allies. Weakness is not any part of him."

"I don't believe that. And there is more, something Mistress Flyte told me about him. It has to do with how I came to be here myself. I wish I could explain it better. . . ."

"You have risked much, coming here."

"You helped me when no one else would, Samuel. Besides, I . . . care about you. About what happens to you. And this is something I have to do. I can't make it any clearer, I'm sorry."

Samuel reached forward as if to stroke her cheek but then hesitated, drawing back.

"Xanthe," he said wistfully, his face suddenly sad. "I have dreamed of you these past months. Those words I penned, in my letter, they were the sincere outpourings of an aching heart." He dropped his gaze then, choosing not to look at her, turning away. "But I had thought never to see you again; that you were lost to me for all time. My life continued without hope of you. My obligations, my family . . ." He raised his eyes again. "There is something I must tell you."

The sound of brisk footsteps on the cobbled yard outside the brewery interrupted him.

"I am missed!" he said. "You must go before you are discovered."

"Appleby," said the unmistakable voice of Fairfax as he came to stand in the doorway, "who is it who takes you from your work?"

Samuel and Xanthe exchanged worried glances before he stepped forward.

"I was on the point of returning," he told his client.

"Do not be shy, maid, step forward," said Fairfax. "Let me see you. Ah, we have met, I believe. A stalwart friend you have, indeed, Appleby. I found this young maid searching for you at the blind house in Bradford."

Xanthe stood before him, reminding herself of her lowly position in this man's society but resenting having to humble herself before him. She had to repeat to herself what Mistress Flyte had told her: that Fairfax had the most powerful friends in the land, and that he held Samuel's fate in his hands. She knew he was playing the part of being surprised. If what Mistress Flyte had told her about him being a time spinner was true, he had sensed her presence. He had known she was close, and he knew what and who she was. It suited him to pretend otherwise. Xanthe decided it was safer not to show that she knew of his capabilities. Better to play along with this particular charade.

"I came to see for myself that all is well with my friend. I am reassured to find him engaged in work on such a fine house as the abbey, sir."

"Master Appleby is a man of talent. I am fortunate he is available," Fairfax said with a thin smile. "But were you not in the employ of Mistress Flyte? I understood she had been ailing recently. I am surprised you can be spared to go visiting at such a time. Does your mistress not have need of you at the chocolate house?"

"You are well informed, sir," said Xanthe as calmly as she could. How did he know about Mistress Flyte being unwell? And, more important, did he know what had happened to her? It seemed increasingly likely to Xanthe that he was behind the attack. Mistress Flyte said he was dangerous, but why would he want her dead? "I am happy to say my mistress is completely recovered, so that she was able to permit me to come to Laybrook. For a short visit."

"I had not seen you in Bradford-on-Avon before the other day. You do not, I must confess, appear to be a person who would content themselves with a life serving at tables."

"I am by trade a minstrel, sir. I take other work as necessity dictates."

"A minstrel? Ah yes, I recall you saying as much. That seems a better fit," he nodded, looking her slowly up and down, taking in her less than convincing historical clothing and inexpertly pinned hair.

Xanthe bobbed a curtsey. "Forgive me for interrupting Samuel's work," she said, making as if to leave, "I shall detain him no longer."

"Where will you go? There are scant lodgings to be found in Laybrook."

"She stays with my cousin in the village," Samuel explained, guiding her to the door.

Fairfax made no attempt to step aside but remained where he was, blocking the exit. "Surely, having come all this way you would wish to spend more time with Master Appleby. To satisfy yourself of his well-being."

"I hope to see him at his cousin's house this evening," Xanthe said.

"Alas, that will not be possible," Fairfax told her, a quite convincing note of regret in his voice. "I find your friend far too valuable to let from my sight. At least until his work here is complete. No, better that you come here. Yes, that would suit all, I believe. I shall have my cook prepare something in your honor, you may dine with us here at the abbey this night, and if I have impressed you sufficiently with my hospitality, mayhap you will in turn gift us with a song or two?"

Xanthe felt Samuel tense. She knew he wanted her gone from the abbey, out of harm's way, or at least, out of the reach of Fairfax. She also knew that the only real chance she had of stopping Fairfax from ultimately, at whatever time it suited him, sending Samuel for trial was to get close to the man.

To identify his weakness. To find a way to threaten or blackmail or barter with him. Perhaps to play on the fact that they were both Spinners. He had to have some manner of vulnerability, but she wouldn't find it by keeping her distance.

"That is a most gracious offer, Master Fairfax. I would be delighted to accept."

Fairfax smiled again though his features gained scant warmth from it. At last he stepped aside.

"Until this evening, then," he said, bowing as Xanthe walked past him. Addressing Samuel he said, "And no doubt you will work all the better, knowing your friend is close at hand. Come, I wish to discuss the window in the east wall with you. The stained glass is not yet to my liking."

Xanthe hurried across the yard, pausing at the gateway to glance back in time to see Samuel standing upon the threshold of the great house. He too turned briefly and there passed between them a look, a brief moment, before Fairfax ushered him inside, and the imposing door closed behind him.

By the time Xanthe had walked back to the cottage opposite St. Cyriac's church, Rose's husband, Adam, had returned home. A farm laborer, his day was shortened by the swiftly falling winter nights. As he invited Xanthe inside, the first flakes of snow chased their way into the little house with them.

In the parlor, Rose was stirring a stewpot which hung above the fire on a heavy chain. The room was smoky but snug. A small man with a thatch of sandy hair, Adam was every bit as tightly wound and nervous as his wife, and Xanthe thought how people of the day were at the mercy of men of power such as Fairfax. They were taking a risk simply by being distant relations of Samuel's. They were putting themselves further in danger by giving house room to one of his friends. Xanthe told them of her meeting with Samuel and that she must return to the abbey that evening.

Rose stopped tending the cooking pot. "I've never heard it said Master Fairfax had a liking for music."

"You must be on your guard," Adam agreed with his wife. "That man will want you there only to learn what he can of Samuel's allegiances. Would be better if you left the village, in truth. You can do Samuel more harm than good."

"I'm not going to run away. Who else is going to step up and do something? He's on his own up there. I won't just let Fairfax make use of Samuel and then send him to the tower." She regretted her outburst at once, realizing that it could be taken as a direct criticism of her hosts. Who was she to judge them? These people lived under the constant shadow of persecution, which could only have worsened since Guy Fawkes's attempt to blow up the Houses of Parliament and the king himself. "I'm sorry," she said more quietly. "I didn't mean . . ."

"'Tis no matter," Rose assured her. "You are afeared for Samuel. As are we all."

Adam was unconvinced.

"I tell you, if you wish to help him you would do better to leave now. Go and petition the king himself if you must, but do not tangle with Fairfax. He will twist your words, he will wheedle from you names and secrets, and before you know it more innocent men will be thrown in the lockups the length and breadth of Wilshire."

"I don't know any names," Xanthe insisted. "And I won't know how I can help until I try. Fairfax has invited me into his home. This is the best, maybe the only chance I might get to do something. I must go."

There was silence for a moment, disturbed only by the moaning of a thin wind that had risen, and the faint patting of icy snow as it struck the small window in the parlor wall. Xanthe shivered, fighting off the sensation that she was being watched, all the time, her actions and somehow even her thoughts being observed, being noted. She rubbed her arms, but the chill she felt was not induced by the cold of the winter's night.

Rose dusted down her pinafore. "Well then, if you are determined, we shall at least see you dressed for the occasion. Come," she said, leaving the room with a stern glance at her husband.

Xanthe followed her up the steep stone spiral stairs to the little low-ceilinged bedchamber where she had been given a bed.

"You will be comfortable here upon your return later this eve," Rose assured her. "'Tis not luxurious, but there is a good straw mattress and coverlets aplenty against the frosty air. Now, sit upon the bed. I shall fetch some more suitable apparel. And pins for your hair. Many, many pins."

It took a full hour of brushing and plaiting and taming before Rose was satisfied Xanthe's hair looked presentable. She held up a small looking glass.

"'Tis far from perfection," Rose announced, "but 't'will serve."

Xanthe turned her head this way and that, peering into the cloudy mirror. Somehow Rose had managed to smooth and twist her unruly blond corkscrew curls into a combination of braids and curls that sat neatly and securely, sweeping up and back, with tendrils left flatteringly loose about her ears and neck.

"Rose, you have worked wonders," Xanthe told her.

Rose insisted Xanthe borrow a crisp white cotton long blouse, a set of starched cuffs, and a high square collar. It sat well beneath her own felted wool pinafore. Rose apologized for not having a spare corset to offer her and inquired cautiously if Xanthe suffered some strange complaint that rendered her unable to wear stays of her own? It seemed easier to just say yes to this, which earned her a pitying sigh and the offer of a lace cap for her hair.

"Oh no, Rose, this is too precious."

"'T'will be easier to muster your courage if you know yourself to be presentable."

Xanthe smiled at this, thinking how down the centuries women had made the best of their looks in order to go into battle of one sort or another.

"I'm a minstrel. We have our own, unusual appearance. And you've made such a good job of my hair, I don't want to hide it," she said, handing back the lace, which she was sure would have been one of Rose's treasured and most valuable possessions.

Adam came to join them on the doorstep. Xanthe buttoned her greatcoat over her dress.

Rose tucked a sprig of dried lavender into her buttonhole. "Sing well," she said. "I will sit up for you and keep the fire burning in the hearth."

Adam handed her a tallow lantern. "Take the road. The fields will be too uneven in the dark and the snow is starting to lie."

"You have both been so kind. Please, don't worry about me." As she spoke thick snowflakes landed on her hair and the shoulders of her coat. Adam frowned and reached back into the hall. He took one of his own broad-brimmed hats from its peg and handed it to her.

"'Tis outlandish for a maid but will keep the weather off better than a bonnet."

Xanthe took it gratefully, lifted the lamp high, and hurried off down the narrow street. Her footfalls were silenced by the thin layer of snow, and her warm puffs of breath whipped away by the sharp wind that blew from the east. Snow clouds blocked out the moon and allowed no starlight so that her vision was restricted to the small pool of light from her lamp or the occasional streetlight. As she took the lane out of the village the darkness deepened, and the silence grew heavy. An owl hooted nearby. Her footsteps were muffled by the coating of snow upon the path. She soon came to the gates of the abbey and followed the sweeping drive that cut through its land. Lamps had been lit along the run of road that led to the house, casting their pale golden light upon the snowy ground. There were no winter crops growing here, more importance being given to the visual impact of approaching the great house. Tall trees lined the route, and as she rounded the top bend it was difficult not to be impressed by the sight that greeted her. An extravagance of lamplight illuminated the exterior of the house and candlelight flickered at windows that had not yet had their shutters closed or curtains drawn. The front elevation of the house was almost entirely new, from what Xanthe could see, with the older abbey buildings to the side and rear. The roof was freshly white with snow now, making the tawny stones stand out all the more, the deep, mullioned windows and their expensive glass, some plain, some stained vibrant colors, glowing against their muted backdrop. As she drew closer, Xanthe could see the ends of wooden scaffolding off to one side of the house, indicating the wing on which Samuel and his team of craftsmen were carrying out their improvements and extensions. By the time she reached the sweeping steps that led up to the grand entrance she was especially glad of her lantern, as the snow was falling faster and thicker so that it was becoming increasingly hard to see where she was putting her feet. She rang the bell and did not have long to wait before a liveried footman opened the door, bowing as she passed him. The entrance hall was awash with light, with elaborate candelabra hanging from the high ceilings. The space was paneled with what looked like new woodwork, waxed and burnished to the color of warm honey. There was a floor of pristine flagstones, and tasteful pieces of furniture were set about for show rather than function. Rich reds and deep indigos in the upholstery gave the whole place a sense of expensive taste, wealth, and lavish expense. Ancestral portraits adorned the high walls that rose with the elaborate staircase.

A maid took Xanthe's hat and coat. If she was surprised at the strangeness of one garment and the unladylike fashion of the other she was too well trained, or possibly too wary of a scolding, to let her astonishment show. She bobbed a curtsey and disappeared as her master descended the stairs.

"Ah-ha, our little minstrel! I am pleased to see you were not deterred by the inclement weather," Fairfax said, smiling politely as he bowed over her hand. Xanthe wished she had worn gloves as the feel of his flesh against hers made her want to whip her hand away. She resisted the impulse, knowing that she had to play the part of guest. For now. Fairfax was dressed in expensive, good-quality clothes and wore them as if it were his birthright to do so. The portraits on the walls around him showed ancestors with an unmistakable family likeness, particularly the blond hair and pale eyes.

"Before we dine," he said, letting go her hand at last, "permit me to show you how the house is being improved. After all, I am certain you would wish to see the fruits of Appleby's labors. Please . . ."

He offered her his arm and she took it. They left the hall through a door of light oak which opened onto an antechamber and then out into a courtyard enclosed by beautiful cloisters. Xanthe couldn't help a gasp of wonder.

"Yes," Fairfax smiled again, "they are impressive. The abbey was home to a community of nuns up until the middle of the last century. When King Henry decided to break with Rome and dissolve the monasteries, this building was rare in as much as all trace of its original purpose was not destroyed. The nobleman who first transformed it into a home chose to keep the cloisters. I, for one, am glad that he did so. There is something pleasing about their appearance, and they imbue the space with a contemplative air. Do you not agree?"

Xanthe suspected Fairfax was used to having his opinion agreed with. On this occasion, it was easy to say what he wanted to hear.

"They are very lovely, sir," she said meekly, choosing her words with great care, horribly aware that she sounded stilted and insincere. "I think it is good to keep a reminder of the history of the place."

"There are many other remnants of the old buildings. Might those interest you also?"

"Perhaps later?"

"Indeed. Here," he opened another door, "allow me to show you the latest additions to the house."

Xanthe stepped in from the cold of the cloisters into the slightly less cold great hall. There was no fire, so that the craftsmen who worked on even at night had to rely on warm clothes and the heat of exertion to stop them from freezing. There was an abundance of candles and lamps, but their combined warmth was no match for the harshness of the winter weather. There were six or seven men, all engrossed in what they were doing, evidently accustomed to having their employer inspect their work. One nodded in deference, another touched his cap, but none paused in their work. Two were lifting a wooden windowsill into place. A carpenter planed wood upon a bench in one corner. The far wall was covered in scaffolding, and a mason chiseled at a small alcove high up. Xanthe could see that the recess would house a statue, and that there were a dozen or so similar spaces all around the room. This was to be a statement; a hall in which to entertain and impress. And Fairfax was clearly nailing his colors to the mast, with a statue of King James at the top of the room, above the position the high table would take. A figure clad in dark clothes moved out of the shadows and into the lamplight. Samuel saw her at the same moment she saw him, and for a charged instant they held each other's gaze.

"Appleby," Fairfax beckoned him. "Come, tell your friend what it is you toil away at here."

Samuel made a polite bow and Xanthe bobbed a curtsey. It was frustrating to have her contact with him so acutely observed, but, she reasoned, it was better than not seeing him at all. His jacket was coated with stone dust and he looked tired, though there was a brightness in his eyes she recognized. It was the same flare of passion for his work she had seen before. How conflicted he must be to produce a thing of beauty for a man who would later sign his death warrant.

"As you see, Mistress Westlake, the new wing is nearing completion. We are working day and night to finish the interior. I am fortunate indeed in having diligent and expert craftsmen with whom to bring the great hall into being."

"Do you think you will complete the task soon?" she asked.

"God willing and with no more snow to impede deliveries of supplies, perhaps a week. Two at most."

There hung between them the unspoken conclusion to this statement. Two weeks, at most, before Samuel would be removed and his fate decided.

Fairfax was in a genial mood. "I am well pleased with your labors, Appleby. The hall will stand the test of time and fashion, I believe. You should be proud of it. Are you not impressed, mistress?"

"I could not fail to be, sir. The house will indeed impress all who see it, I'm certain."

"Let us hope so, else why am I sparing no expense and feeding all these workers? Ha!" He allowed himself a dry laugh at his own wit.

There was a shout from one of the men lifting a stone lintel, followed by a crash and a cry. Samuel rushed to see what had happened. Xanthe watched as he first checked that the mason was unhurt before turning his attention to the damaged piece of stone. From where she stood there did not seem to be any serious harm done.

Fairfax was instantly furious, the veneer of good-natured host quickly stripped away. "Remove that imbecile from my sight!" He pointed at the slightly dazed stone mason.

Samuel stepped forward. "Master Fairfax, the damage to the stone is slight. . . ."

"I will not have carelessness! I will not tolerate ham-fisted workmen. Call yourself master craftsman!" He glared at the mason. "You are not fit to work on my property. Get your things and get you gone!"

The man opened his mouth to protest and then thought better of it.

"If it please you, sir." Samuel's voice was measured and calm but Xanthe could hear the tension of restraint in it. "Harris is a good worker, skilled, trustworthy. Mishaps befall even the most cautious when working with such heavy items and without the benefit of daylight."

"It is curious how such accidents are never at the expense of those who and use it for eating wherever they found themselves. Fairfax, it seemed, was keen to embrace new ideas. There were even rudimentary forks, which were very rare indeed. As Xanthe took her place at one end of the table she couldn't help but think, with a stab of homesickness, what her mother would have made of such interesting antiques had they come across them at a fair or house clearance. She smiled ruefully to herself at the thought that it was a shame she could not take just one of those rare forks home for Flora. However tempting it was, she knew anything transported forward in time would not last more than a few weeks before it began to first dull, then disintegrate. She thought longingly of the love letter Samuel had given her when she had left him after helping Alice. She had treasured it and looked after it with such care but still she had been forced to watch helplessly as it became more fragile over time, falling to nothing at all in a few short weeks. She recalled how a dress she had been given during her time as a kitchen maid had also shown signs of falling to pieces when she wore it back to her own time. Nothing, it seemed, could make the journey forward in time if it had not originated there. She could not allow herself to think of home. There was too much at stake. She must give Fairfax her full attention and find out what it was he wanted from her, somehow, without giving away what Mistress Flyte had told her. The old woman had been adamant that Fairfax would know that Xanthe had traveled through time, and that he would know this because he too was able to do so. He would, the old woman had said, be able to sense her journey, and sense that she was close. And he had been observing her blundering attempts to travel through time ever since she started. Looking at him again there was no shadow of doubt in Xanthe's mind that this was indeed the tall, lone figure who had stood across the green from the blind house in Marlborough, the one that had held Alice, when she had visited the poor girl to offer her help only last summer, and yet it seemed a lifetime ago. She had felt someone watching her then and turned to see a man, this man, observing her from a distance. And then again, when she fell through the centuries to find Samuel, the face she had seen, those pallid, sharp features, had belonged to Benedict Fairfax. And the voice that had questioned her, during another of her journeys through time. What was it that she had heard? She remembered: *Where do you go?* He had sensed her traveling even then and had been able to make his presence felt, to make himself heard. What else had he seen? What else did he know? Had he watched her and Samuel together? Had he listened to her conversations with Mistress Flyte? Suddenly she felt unequal to the task of confronting him. What had made her think stepping into the lion's den was the best way to help Samuel? Rose was right; Fairfax was indeed a powerful man, more powerful than Samuel's cousin could ever know. And now Xanthe was alone with him, in his house, at his invitation, with Samuel shut away. How was she going to help him? How was she even going to keep herself safe? All she could think of was to play innocent as long as possible. To hope that his interest in her was something she could use to persuade him to let Samuel go.

"Now, Mistress Westlake, I sincerely hope you will enjoy this wine. I have it shipped directly from Portugal. It is very fine. Likewise, the food that has been prepared is of the highest quality. Dishes I'll wager you have never had set before you anywhere else. And if it pleases you to do so, after we have supped, I would hear you sing. I am told you have the voice of an angel, and I should very much delight in being serenaded by a member of the celestial choir."

The maid finished filling the Venetian glass goblets with dark red wine and Fairfax signaled for her to leave. After the door was closed and swift footsteps receded down the hallway he leaned forward on the table, his expression growing serious.

"But first," he said slowly, watching her closely as he spoke, "first I should very much like you to tell me how it is you come to be able to spin time."

XANTHE DID HER BEST NOT TO REACT. SHE PICKED UP HER WINE AND TOOK A SIP BEFORE responding. "Spin time? What a curious idea. I am a simple minstrel. . . ."

"Oh, come, come. Enough of this charade, I tire of it. We both know how you come to be here."

"I came to help my friend."

"You will persist in this?" He sighed. "I grant you that part at least is true, the *why* rather than the *how*. Very well, let us address your friendship so that it no longer stands in the way of more important matters. You and Master Appleby evidently had some manner of . . . friendship in the past. I do not dispute that. While it is laudable that you should put yourself at risk to assist him, I think that you do not realize to what breed of man you ally yourself. You sought him in the Bradford lockup for good reason. He has been freely associating with rebels and recusants; people who have openly set themselves against both the king and the faith of this land. Such blatant opposition to the monarch can no longer be tolerated. It is nothing short of treason. When he has served his purpose here he will face trial for his beliefs, both religious and political, as his fellows have done." Fairfax held up a hand to silence any protest Xanthe might have thought of making. He had not yet finished his attempt at crushing her loyalty to Samuel. "Of course, none of this may prevent a woman's heart from its illogical preferences, I am aware of that. There is something that seems to draw a tender soul toward a martyr, though for my part I cannot see the attraction. Nor do I presume to understand the workings of a woman's mind. No, what I think you may be more interested to learn is that the object of your misplaced affection would not be at liberty to return your love, even if he were not on his way to imprisonment, for he is now, and has for some weeks been, engaged to be married."

Fairfax leaned back in his chair, waiting to see what effect this news would have upon his dining companion.

Xanthe felt her stomach lurch. Engaged. She couldn't recall Samuel's family mentioning that there was anyone special in his life. He had certainly never said any such thing. It had only been a few months in his time since she and he had parted. Had he really moved on so quickly? Had there been someone else all along? Aware that she was being scrutinized she kept her face impassive, determined not to give Fairfax the satisfaction of seeing her upset. Whatever the truth of what he had just told her, Samuel's life was still in danger, and this man was the one who would send him to the Tower.

"As I have said, Samuel helped me once when no one else would. I am in his debt. I cannot stand by and see a friend in trouble and do nothing," she said.

"How noble. And how fortunate young Appleby is to have such a champion. He cannot know that you are quite possibly the only person able to alter his destiny."

She looked up at Fairfax then, trying to read his expression, waiting to hear what would come next, keen to discover at last what it was he wanted from her.

At that moment the maid and a footman returned with food. Fairfax did not seem to mind the interruption. On the contrary, he appeared to be greatly enjoying the game of confusing Xanthe, of giving her snippets of information and suggestions of what might or might not be true, and then observing her reactions. The servants set platters of roast meats and baked salmon on the table, along with freshly baked bread and pastries. There was a ridiculous amount of food for two people. Fairfax no doubt sought to impress but had not considered Xanthe's more modern perspective and how she would be appalled at such a wasteful use of food.

"So," he helped himself to some slices of lamb and pork as he spoke, "let us put aside Master Appleby's fate for the moment. I promise you, we shall return to it later. Of much more interest to me is the journey that you made in order to reach him. I wish to know not only where you came from, but how, specifically, and of course"—he stopped piling food onto his plate and smiled up at her—"*when?*"

Xanthe realized there was little point in continuing to pretend she didn't know what he was talking about. If Mistress Flyte was right about him, Fairfax knew the truth of it already. And from what he had just said, it was the fact that she had traveled through time that made her of importance to him. It would be some aspect, some detail of her talent that was of importance to him, and was, therefore, what she had to bargain with in order to get Samuel released.

"My home is in the town of Marlborough," she said, taking some bread and a piece of fish and putting them onto her plate. She would not let him see how confused she was by what he had told her about Samuel's engagement. Nor did she want him to think she was afraid of him. She tried some of the salmon. It was delicious, perfectly cooked, wonderfully fresh and flavored with fennel. She had not realized until that moment how hungry she was. She tucked in, deciding to make the best of the meal. Her previous travels had taught her that things could change quickly. Who knew when she would next get the chance to eat? It was only when she allowed herself to think of Samuel getting married that she found it hard to swallow anything.

"Excellent!" Fairfax clapped his hands and then swigged some of his wine, his narrow eyes suddenly animated. "And what, pray, is the date in which you inhabit your Marlborough home?"

"We moved there last year. In the year two thousand and eighteen."

He gasped, marveling at the thought of the centuries she had crossed so that she came to be seated across the table from him.

"How many wondrous things there must be!" he remarked. "Tell me, is there a king on the throne of England still?"

"A queen. Elizabeth the second."

"Indeed? And to which house does she belong?"

For a moment Xanthe had to think about what he was asking. The royal family had several official residences, but that was not what he meant. "Oh, the House of Windsor."

"Truly? Not Stuart? I have not heard of Windsor. And tell me further, is there a parliament?"

"Yes. In fact, the country is a democracy. The monarch doesn't have any real power anymore." Xanthe enjoyed telling him this, watching his face as he processed this information. "It's not always easy, choosing the winning side, is it?" she pointed out, trying a little piece of a meat-stuffed pastry in an effort to look calmer and more confident than she felt. She was surprised to find it laced with what tasted like port and mixed with sultanas. If the circumstances had been different she would have marveled at the food.

Fairfax frowned. "I, more than most, am aware of the truth of what you say. It is for this very reason that I believe you can help me."

"I don't know what you expect of me. From what I hear you are a Spinner yourself. I'm new to all this. Why would you need help from someone like me?"

"I wish to know . . ." he hesitated, showing an uncharacteristic nervousness, his hand going to the high white collar at his throat. "When you embark upon your journeys, what talisman is it that you use?"

"Talisman? You mean, something that helps me travel?"

"Yes. What facilitates your traveling? A timepiece, perhaps? A ring?"

"It's not just one thing. Different things sing to me. Don't they do that to you?"

"Sing?"

"Yes. I find some object, or it finds me, I'm never sure which way round it works. And that thing communicates to me. It has a story to tell. Of course it won't get me anywhere without the blind house. But don't you have that ability too? To pick up stories from different objects?"

Fairfax had stopped eating now. "Fascinating!" he breathed before getting to his feet and beginning to pace around the room. "Astonishing how our experiences differ in these regards. You say you use different objects and yet one place. No place ever enabled my travel, and only one object. An object that was so very dear to me." He closed his eyes briefly, remembering. "I would give all I have to hold it once again. Without it I am powerless to move through time. Without it I would not be alive to talk to you now." When he looked at her there was a light of excitement in his eyes. "You spoke of choosing the winning side and I have indeed found myself allied with those who were persecuted, those who had no chance of success." He took a breath and then continued, eager now to share his story. "I was not always the king's man. My birthright was noble, yes, but my family, in truth, had more in common with the Applebys than with royalty. We were Catholics, and our fortune had been made under a Catholic monarch. Through no fault of my own, I found myself cast out and ultimately standing trial for treason." He nodded at Xanthe. "Oh yes, I know what it is to be incarcerated. To wait upon the whims of others and the fickleness of fate for my destiny to be decided. My family were powerless to save me, and most preceded me to the scaffold." He stopped talking, the memory causing him obvious pain. "My family, and my betrothed." He closed his eyes again.

In that moment Xanthe glimpsed another side to the man. His grief was real and raw.

"I am sorry to hear that," she said.

Fairfax opened his eyes, waving his hand dismissively, collecting himself, evidently irritated to have let his guard down. He continued his story.

"At last the day came when I too was to be executed. Only my father's previous good standing with men of power saved me from a traitor's agony. Instead I was afforded the mercy of the hangman. I made the short walk from the Tower to the gallows alone, friendless, subjected to the scorn and jeers of the crowd. They came to see me dance." He allowed himself a slow smile. "But I denied them their sport!" He stopped pacing and came to stand beside Xanthe's chair, leaning on the arm of it, his face close to hers as he told his story. She was aware of the sourness of a nervous sweat emanating from him, the only sign that he was not in fact the supremely confident man he pretended to be.

"I had, for some time, been aware of a strangeness in my perception of the way in which time moved. For a number of years it was as if I caught glimpses of moments beyond the reach of my own life span. At first I put these imaginings from my mind, thinking them a possible intimation of a malady of the brain. Truth to tell, I feared them. And yet, as I grew from boy to man, I came to understand they were in fact the workings of a superior mind. A mind that was able to see what others could not. It was many

years before I found a way to harness this peculiar talent. It came about seemingly by chance, though I now believe that there is more order in the fates of
men than mere happenstance can account for. I met a man, an astrologer,
who spent his life striving to understand the course of the planets and the
significance of the stars. He had many fine instruments to aid him in his work,
and one of these was a small, brass astrolabe. This was not some fanciful
design, nor was it made to impress or for show; it was an instrument for plot-
ting the movements of celestial bodies. A system of dials and marks, all
constructed with great care so as to make it no larger than a timepiece. It
would fit into a pocket." He paused and closed his hand as if holding tight
this precious device. "It could be held in my palm, as if I were holding the
secrets of the heavens in my own hand!" He stood up then, turning to gaze
into the flames of the fire. Outside the wind blew icy snow against the win-
dowpanes. "The astronomer did not see the importance of the astrolabe and
readily sold it to me when I offered him more than any other would pay. I
hurried home with it, knowing only that there was something it could do for
me, something connected to my curious experiences and visions. When at
last I stood alone and held it aloft, willing it to show me what it would . . ."
He sighed at the memory, as if recalling the first attentions of a lost love. "At
first I thought I had experienced some manner of seizure, an aberration of
the brain, such was the strength of what I felt. There was a deal of chaos
around me, of movement, of noise. And voices. Many desperate voices. I fell
into blackness and then all at once into bright light again. I blinked against
the dazzle of it and it took me a moment to see that I was yet in my own
house, in the same room, the fire burning in the hearth, the sun falling through
the window. But at once I knew I was not in my own time! My furnishings,
my paintings and wall hangings, all had gone. There were no candles, but
strange lamps hung from the ceiling and were mounted upon the walls. Lamps
that gave off a clear and steady light but not any heat! And on the floor was
a woolen rug, brightly patterned, that covered the flags entirely. The chairs
were cushioned and large. The shelves were filled with books as if I stood in
a library. And the music! I found a small box with a silver front and from it
came the sound of an entire orchestra, a melody so pure and sweet, and then
a voice! Captured! My head was spinning from these wonders when the door

opened and a man entered the room. His clothes were simple, yet uncommon. His hair was cut short as a convict, though he had the step of the man of the house. And he saw me! He uttered an oath upon doing so, and I feared he might have me thrown into a cell, having found me standing like some robber in his home. Whether it was my own fear or the work of the astrolabe I cannot be certain, but I held it high again, letting the sunlight glint upon the inscriptions on its brass face, and suddenly I was falling once more. A moment and several centuries later I found myself returned to my own time, my own home."

He paused to see how his guest was receiving his tale. Xanthe sipped her wine and said nothing. He could not have known how greatly the story impacted on Xanthe. It wasn't that he had traveled through time: she had already known about him being a Spinner. What was sending her mind into turmoil was the fact that he was telling her he had traveled *forward in time.* Until that moment Xanthe had not so much as considered the possibility of this. Could she herself leap forward into the future? The idea terrified her. She snatched at the thought that as it was things from the past that caused her to travel there was no danger of this happening. But Fairfax had managed it with the astrolabe. There was no time for her to dwell upon the possibility or otherwise of her jumping ahead of her own time, however, as she had to concentrate on what Fairfax was saying.

"You know, mistress, what had happened to me. You too are familiar with the wonders of the experience. The thrill. The fear. Naturally, it took me time to fathom what I had seen. Took me time to use the astrolabe at will to venture into past or future. I only ever journeyed somewhere for the briefest of moments, but each time I saw something new and wondrous, and could barely comprehend what it was that I saw. I attempted to gain more control over my journeys, but alas, I developed little by way of mastery. I was compelled to content myself with such random travels as the device allowed me.

"Years went by. The tide of politics in England turned. My family, as I have already told you, found themselves on the losing side. And I found myself mounting the narrow wooden steps of the scaffold. Even as the hangman placed the noose around my neck I did not know, not with any certainty, if my precious device would work at my bidding. I clutched it, hidden, in my left hand, thanking God and the craftsman who made it that it was so small. I waited as long as I dared, for when I had tried to escape my cell it had not responded to my call. I believed I had one chance only, and that the greater my own state of agitation, the more likely was there to be some reaction from the astrolabe, some triggering of its power." His hand went to his throat and he pulled open his collar, leaning over Xanthe so that she could not fail to see the faint but clear discoloration of a line of raised skin.

"There was no long drop to break my neck. A trick to prolong the anguish of the accused and further stir up the blood of the mob, but for me it was a vital part of my deliverance. The stool was pushed from beneath my feet. The rope took my weight. I felt the fibers burn as they dug into my flesh and fought for the air denied me as the noose tightened. I closed my eyes, the better to bring my thoughts to bear upon the astrolabe and my desire to be gone from that deadly moment. The sweat of my palm made the device slippery so that I feared I might drop it, but no! The blackness that descended upon me did not signify my death, but my escape!" He smiled then, replacing his collar with practiced care. "My one regret is that I was not able to see the expressions and hear the terrified cries of those who were left to gasp at an empty noose."

Fairfax walked calmly back to his chair and sat down. Xanthe met his gaze.

"It sounds as if you can travel when you want to," she said. "What do you think I can do that you can't?"

Fairfax frowned, the look of self-satisfaction at his tale fading. "My ability to spin time was dependent upon the astrolabe. On that last occasion . . . it did not accompany me on my journey. When I found myself back to a point in my life before my fall from grace, my hand was empty."

"And you have not traveled since?"

He shook his head solemnly. "But you," he leaned forward, his expression altered again, his eyes lit up with the thought of the possibilities he believed Xanthe and her gift presented. "You tell me there are different objects that enable your movements through time. And that you are able to shift both back and fore, at will."

"It's not as simple as you make it sound."

"Yet here you are, moved of your own volition. Come to save your friend."

"The chocolate pot got me here. That and the blind house."

"Ah yes, the lockup. You have one at your home."

"I need both things. To go anywhere, I need something that wants me to travel, and I need to use the blind house to move back through time." Xanthe worried that she was telling him too much, but she had to think on her feet. Her plan now was to find something she could bargain with, so she needed him to believe she could give him whatever it was he wanted. Even if she didn't, in fact, know what that could be. She watched him as he absorbed the details she had shared with him. She could see he was working things out, so she should not have been surprised at his next question.

"So, as I understand it, you have spun time on several occasions before now. I can only marvel at your swift mastery of your gift. But what puzzles me is how you manage to return at will to your own time. You own no blind house here. And I cannot think that whatever calls you wishes you gone. How come you to return safely home, mistress? Tell me that."

Xanthe trod cautiously and had to stop herself instinctively touching the gold locket that sat hidden beneath her blouse. It occurred to her that there was something else different about the way Fairfax traveled; he went to the *future.* Xanthe had never done that; the objects that sung to her being all of times past. How, she wondered, was he able to move ahead of his own time without crumbling to dust like Samuel's letter or the dress she had worn in the wrong century? Could it be a power specific to him, or was it connected to his beloved astrolabe? Either way, she could see how being able to know the future could give someone an incredible advantage in choosing the winning side.

"You are overestimating my talents, sir," she told him. "I am not as expert as you suppose."

"Your gift far outstretches my own, however modest you wish to be. I had no say over the length of time I would spin through. Indeed, I could not influence the direction. When I made that vital transition from the place of my intended execution I did not know if I were to travel further forward in time or fall back to a date that preceded my own birth. Such an idea is sufficient to addle the strongest of minds," he said.

Xanthe was grateful that he was so taken up with sharing his experiences and having a person with whom he could discuss the wonders of time travel that he did not instantly press her for proper answers to his questions. It bought her a little time at least to think of convincing responses, and to not show her hand too early.

"There is so much I don't understand," she said. "So much that is risk. Chance. Out of my own control."

"Your humility does you credit, mistress, but it is misplaced. That you have succeeded in choosing the exact time you will move to, and more than once, is proof enough for me that you are practiced in this art. Which means, you can assist me in developing my own gift. More specifically, you can assist me in finding the astrolabe."

So there it was. Now Xanthe knew what he wanted. Would she be able to give it to him? Should she? Mistress Flyte had hinted at the dangers of an unscrupulous, self-serving person having the ability to spin time. What if Xanthe got him what he wanted and in doing so somehow helped him to alter things that he wasn't supposed to have power over? She couldn't imagine that Fairfax would care who he had to trample into the dirt in order to achieve his own ambitions.

As if reading her thoughts he told her, quite casually, how he intended to change events to suit himself. "I do not intend mounting those gallows steps a second time. The date of my execution was . . . *is* March twelfth, in the year 1610. Less than five years from now. When I traveled from that gibbet, I came back to my own life but six years earlier. Every thought I have had, every decision made, every action taken since that moment has been in the cause of altering my destiny."

"Which is why you have betrayed your friends? Turned against those people whose beliefs you used to share?"

"I see Mistress Flyte has been painting me in a poor light."

"Was she lying?"

Fairfax shrugged. "It is not an uncommon practice to shift allegiance to protect oneself, to build one's fortune, to secure a bright future."

"And sacrifice anyone along the way if necessary, no matter who."

"I have made many moves to change my fate. And yes, it is true I have had to shed old alliances and shore up new ones to this end. At first, it was all I believed I could do. But then I heard you. One night, last autumn, without any warning or preamble. I heard you calling the name of a servant girl, heard you cry out, sensed your presence as you manipulated time itself. I made it my business to listen, to watch, and to wait. I saw you for the first time outside the Marlborough blind house. You were most taken up with rescuing that girl, but still you noticed me, did you not?"

Xanthe recalled the way she had shivered at the sight of the stranger across the green. How unnerved she had been by finding him watching her. It made sense to her now, that she should have had such a reaction to him.

Fairfax rose from his seat and held out his hand to her.

"There is something I wish to show you," he said. When she hesitated he went on. "Appleby's continued existence in this world depends upon your cooperating with me, my little minstrel. One way or another you must sing for your supper. Now, come," he said. It was not an invitation but an instruction.

Xanthe got up and made herself give him her hand. He tucked it into the bend of his arm, patting it gently.

"Have no fear," he said. "We are to be partners of the most singular kind, you and I. Permit me to show you."

10

FAIRFAX LED XANTHE BACK ALONG THE CLOISTERS, WHERE THE SNOW WAS BEING WHIPPED up from the courtyard in dizzying whirlwinds and flung through the open stone arches. By the time they took a second staircase up through one of the towers at the north end of the great house her boots had white toes and she was shivering. Fairfax was eager to show her what lay behind the broad oak door on the top floor. With a flourish he bid her enter what was as far as Xanthe could tell some sort of observatory. There was a vast, floor-to-ceiling window at the far end of the room, in front of which stood a gleaming brass telescope, pointing at the night sky. There were charts and maps and models of planets. Two glass-fronted bookcases housed an impressive collection of leather-bound volumes. Knowing how expensive books were at the time, Xanthe calculated this collection to be the most valuable part of the room. Fairfax showed her a large astrolabe sitting on a walnut desk.

"I have searched far and wide for a replacement for the device that granted me the gift of time travel, but I have never found another. It seems that for me, *that* astrolabe was unique. I have tried to understand why it did not return with me and can find no explanation. Who will have the presence of mind to pick it up from where I stood? All had witnessed the impossible. A man vanishes before their eyes. What would they say about that?"

Xanthe gestured at the contents of the room. "You might want to be careful who you show this to," she said. "As I understand it, people of your time are quick to shout 'witch' at anyone they think might be dabbling in strange practices."

"I do not dabble!"

"But time travel is a pretty strange practice, don't you think? What if the king were to find out about your . . . obsession?" She walked around the room, examining the precious objects Fairfax had gathered in his search for another key to spinning time.

"Do not think to threaten me, little minstrel," he warned her. "You are in no position to so much as speak to anyone at court. And if you did, why would they listen to you?"

"Perhaps they wouldn't, but would you want to take that risk?" She knew she was on dangerous ground, but she was determined not to let him see how powerless she actually felt.

"I advise you to consider what paths you have to choose from. It is true, you could, should I allow you to do so, go from this place and travel to London in search of one who will hear the fantastic tale you have to tell them. You might even find some sympathy at the mention of my name, for one does not rise to prominence but one acquires enemies during the ascent." He came to stand in front of her and she could see how adamant he was that there was another way. "Instead, you might choose to work *with* me, rather than against."

"Work with the man who plans to send my friend to his death?"

"I am not unreasonable. Were we to form an alliance I would not be averse to considering your request for leniency toward Appleby."

"Leniency?"

"He is a recognized enemy of the crown. He cannot simply be allowed to continue with his treasonous thoughts and plans. . . ."

"Thoughts! Are you able to read minds now too? And what plans? You have no proof Samuel was planning anything."

"After the activities of Master Fawkes and his companions, everyone who chooses to set themselves against the faith and rule of the land in whatever small way must be considered a threat."

"If you were to speak up for him he would be left alone. If you declared yourself satisfied that he is a peaceable man . . . You could do that."

"I could. Had I sufficient incentive."

"What exactly is it you think I can do? I don't have your astrolabe. And I can't take you with me when I travel through time, not unless the idea of slowly disintegrating appeals to you. You might have been able to overcome that problem when you had the astrolabe, but I can't guarantee any such success."

"If we combined our knowledge. Put our experiences in the crucible of endeavor, here, in my observatory. With what you know, of the future and of the spinning of time, and with my resources, there is no limit to what we could achieve!"

"You are overestimating my ability. I've told you, I can't control every aspect of my journeys. I need specific objects. And they take me where they want. They decide where and when I go." Her mind briefly flitted to the book. Did Fairfax know of its existence? He hadn't mentioned it, but Mistress Flyte had been so excited by it, had insisted it was really important. Xanthe decided even if he had heard of it, he didn't know that she had it. It seemed sensible to keep it that way.

"But you have made many successful journeys, have you not? You have succeeded in moving backward and forward through the ages and suffered no ill effects."

"You don't understand the risks. There have been times I thought I wouldn't reach my destination. Times when I thought I would be lost in some sort of limbo. And what about how people will think of you if they find out what you are doing? You'd be accused of witchcraft, and if I was helping you, so would I. Your astrolabe saved your life. Can't you be content with that?"

"And sent me back in time, not safely ahead. Do you not see? How can I be certain I will avoid my fate when that time is yet to come?"

"I would have thought becoming the king's man and being willing to sacrifice anyone to gain more wealth and standing has worked pretty well so far. Laybrook Abbey looks to me to be the home of an influential and respectable person."

"You tell me your own time is ruled by a parliament and that the monarch is powerless. See how the tide can turn? Why would I satisfy myself with what is within the reach of so many well-born, clever men, when within my own grasp lies an ability to shape the very future itself? Imagine how you and I could use our wondrous gift."

Now the scope of his ambition was clear to Xanthe. This was what Mistress Flyte had feared, had suggested he would want. "Seems to me," she said levelly, "that you are not just interested in saving your own neck. You want to use the skill of spinning time to . . . what? Become more powerful than the king himself, perhaps? How many people would be sacrificed on your way up that dangerous climb, I wonder?"

"Better then that I have you by my side to moderate at least my ruthlessness, if not my ambition. Do you not see it as your duty as a Spinner to ensure that our gifts are well used? Perhaps this is the very reason you have been brought here, to this time, to my time. To me. We would be a match like no other."

"A match?"

"Alliances have ever been formed for the greater good of both parties. I care not for your affection. I would rather secure the availability of your gift. As my wife you would naturally be at my side."

Xanthe gave a shocked bark of laughter. "You want me to marry you?" Even as she phrased the question she could see that, for Fairfax, this was the obvious solution to his need. As his wife she could be with him all the time, her presence accepted, her background glossed over and forgotten when she became the chosen bride of an influential, wealthy man and the mistress of a great house. A stab of regret and jealousy assailed her heart as she thought of Samuel betrothed to someone else. Was that too a marriage of convenience? she wondered. Could it be that the match had been arranged by their respective families? It was ridiculous to be hurt by it, she told herself. If she didn't find a way to get past Fairfax, Samuel wouldn't live long enough to marry anyone. She made herself focus, keeping her tone businesslike and firm. "You need to understand something," she said. "If I agree to help you in some way . . . *if* . . . then it will be to secure Samuel's freedom and safety. I have a life of my own, in my own time, with my family."

"Why do you refuse to see the magnitude of what it is I offer you?"

"It seems to me your 'offer' amounts to nothing more or less than blackmail. If I don't do exactly what you want, you'll send Samuel to the Tower. That's the bare bones of the thing, isn't it?"

"You can achieve what you came here to do. You can see Appleby reprieved.

Why would you not wish to develop your stupendous talent to its fullest extent?"

"Why would I want to leave my family? And anyway, what makes you think you can keep me here if I don't want to stay?"

"I have considered this, naturally. Which is why," he lowered his voice, watching her face closely, "I earlier asked of you: How is it that you return to your own time? Do you, perhaps, need a specific place? Must the planets be in a peculiar alignment? Or have you some object that serves as sextant through the eons and delivers you home?"

Xanthe did not trust herself to respond or move. The slightest gesture toward her locket might give herself away. She played for time.

"I keep telling you that I have very little control over when or how I travel."

Fairfax looked disappointed at her answer. He drew back from her a little and she wondered for a moment if he might hit her. Did he think he could beat the information out of her? She felt herself tense, ready to move if he tried to strike her. But what then? He was, for all his bony frame, bigger and stronger than she, and the house was filled with his servants, his men. Xanthe felt suddenly trapped. Now that she knew Fairfax's intention was not simply to make use of her but to keep her, to make her his wife, she had to get away. Had to find some way to help Samuel at a safe distance from this obsessed man. She could see now that he had glimpsed a terrible power in the ability to travel to the future. He would settle for nothing less than total control over it. Another thought made her heart heavy in her chest. He would always use her feelings for Samuel to control her. Even if he called off the trial and let him go free now, there would always be the threat of what he might do to Samuel and his family if she didn't fully cooperate with him. Forever. What about her own life? What about her mother? She had to get away. In the moment it had taken for her to see this, Fairfax had come to the same conclusion. As Xanthe sprinted for the door he lunged after her.

"Let me go!" she yelled at him as he grabbed her. She kicked and struggled so that he was forced to grasp her clothing to keep hold of her. The cotton of her blouse gave way, ripping part of the collar. When she leaned over and bit his hand he cursed, shouted, and then slapped her hard with his other hand. Unbalanced and shocked, Xanthe fell back, landing heavily against the bookcase, shattering the glass in its doors. Fairfax took hold of her by the arms, hauling her to her feet.

"Such obstinacy! You foolish creature. It is a wonder you were ever chosen for a Spinner, when you are in possession of such witless reason."

"You're the fool if you think you can make me stay with you!" she cried, fighting to free her arms from his grip, feeling his bony fingers bruising her skin, his grasp tightening. She wriggled, turning, so that he stood behind her, one arm now around her neck, the other hand still clenched around her arm. Xanthe felt herself beginning to choke as his hold tightened on her throat.

Fairfax was enraged by her resistance and her refusal to accept what he saw as the only sensible course of action.

"I will never again suffer the humiliation and helplessness of being incarcerated. Never be the victim of another's ambition! Never await my lonely fate in a dark cell! I will become the most accomplished Spinner of time there has ever been and you will assist me. I will find ways to gain your cooperation. If you choose to fight against me do not be surprised if those ways are not in your best interests. I offer you a true alliance and you turn it down without a minute's contemplation!"

"I don't need another second to see what sort of monster you are." Xanthe let herself go limp and stopped struggling. Confused but wary, Fairfax loosened his hold on her. It was only a minute adjustment of pressure, the slightest lessening of force, but it was enough. Just. Instead of struggling forward against his hold, Xanthe dropped to the floor, and in one fluid movement, using the hem of her petticoat as a mitt, she grabbed a long shard of glass from the broken bookcase. As Fairfax reached down to take hold of her again she wheeled around as best she was able in her crouching position, swiping upward at him with the glass. She didn't have the chance to aim properly or think where her improvised blade might find its mark. There was a shriek as the sharp edge cut through Fairfax's flesh. He leaped back, staggering, clutching his face. Xanthe saw blood pour out between his fingers as he roared in pain and rage. She scrambled to her feet and ran for the door, not daring to look back. She raced down the twisting stone stairs of the tower, Fairfax's shouts following her as she went. She knew she had to get out of the abbey before his servants came to his aid. She threw open the nearest door and found herself back in the cloisters again.

"Stop!" One of the footmen, hearing his master's cries, had hurried toward the tower and saw Xanthe. "You there, stop!"

Xanthe jumped over the low wall of the cloisters and tore across the snowy courtyard. She could see the door to the main hall. Within moments she was there, fortunate that Fairfax's bellowing had drawn everyone who heard it toward him, leaving the front door unguarded. Xanthe hauled it open and ran out into the snowy night.

Heavy clouds blocked out the moon so that she was running almost blind, the dull gleam of the snow allowing only the tiniest amount of visibility. She ran down the grand drive, hesitating when she came to the gates at the bottom. Her instinct had been to run to the village, to return to Rose and Adam and ask for their help again. But Fairfax would look for her there. And then what hope for Samuel's cousins? With a stab of panic she thought of Samuel, still in the abbey. She couldn't risk going back to find him. Would Fairfax take his anger out on him? It pulled at her heart to think she might have actually made things worse for him. Sounds from the house told her horses were being fetched. She had to move on, had to run. If she stayed on the road they would catch her in a matter of minutes. Turning east, she climbed the low wall and raced off across the open meadow, heading for the dark cover of the woods at the far side. She reached the trees just as those sent in search of her thundered out of the drive, some heading for the village, others toward the high road.

Xanthe crouched at the base of an ancient oak, leaning against its great trunk. She had no coat, and the cold was already seeping through her clothes. She pulled the remnants of her torn blouse together and as she did so a wave of fear swept over her.

Her locket was gone.

She searched her panicked mind for when she had last known for certain that it was still around her neck. Had she lost it when Fairfax had ripped her collar? Was that when the chain had been broken? Might it have been caught up in her clothes? It could have fallen to the ground at any time while she was making her escape. It could still be in the abbey. It might be lying in the snow, soon to be covered by the fresh fall that seemed to thicken by the moment. Xanthe felt tears of despair stinging her eyes and angrily wiped them away.

"You idiot!" she said aloud, needing to summon up her fury to stop her-self giving way to desperation. Without the locket she was trapped, unable to return home. She would have to find it, but not now. If it was outside, the dark and the snow would make searching for it without a lamp impossible. She could not risk going back into the house. She knew the most likely place to find it would be Fairfax's observatory. Would he still be in there? How badly had she wounded him? It seemed unlikely he would have been able to ride out after her, not bleeding as heavily as he had been. She couldn't go back into the abbey, not with him still there.

Her teeth began to chatter. Staying hidden in such weather was not an option. She would not survive the night sleeping in the woods. She had to keep moving. She decided to head back along the road toward Bradford. She would have to hide from any riders, but at least she knew it was no more than about eight miles to the town. She would go to Mistress Flyte and ask for her help. It was possible, of course, that Fairfax would look for her there, but the old woman was clever and resourceful and would more than likely know of a place to hide Xanthe. And then together they could work out a way for her to retrieve her locket.

Xanthe left the woods, checked the snow-covered road, and then set off at a jog, heading west. She didn't slow her pace until she had left the village of Laybrook behind. The rough road was made a little smoother by the snow, but treacherous potholes and ruts still caused her to stumble and she had to move carefully to avoid a twisted ankle. As she walked she listened for hoof-beats and thought about how badly she had handled the situation with Fair-fax. She had gone there planning to bargain with him for Samuel's release and now she had enraged him and lost her precious locket. She was no use to Samuel and might never get home. She clenched her fists, digging her nails into her palms against her own weariness and the deepening cold. She had to find extra reserves of strength and think what to do next. She would go to Bradford and she would ask Mistress Flyte for her help. Together they could approach one of Samuel's friends, perhaps. Surely he was well enough liked and known, his family well regarded, that someone would help?

As the night wore on Xanthe's pace slowed further, so that after an hour she was trudging, stumbling more often, her fingers and toes numb. It was then she heard sounds of wheels and hooves. An approaching carriage, moving fast through the wintry darkness. She looked about her for cover, but she was on a stretch of road with no trees nearby, not even a ditch to jump into. She told herself it could not be anything to do with Fairfax, as it was heading toward and not away from Laybrook. Within seconds she could see lights as the carriage rounded the bend ahead and came hurtling toward her. She could do no more than step aside, head down, hoping that the driver would take no notice and simply pass her by. Just as it seemed they would do exactly that and drew level with her she heard voices, shouts from inside, instructions to the driver to pull up. Xanthe held her breath as the carriage slowed to a halt and the door opened. A figure took a lamp from the carriage and held it high, walking toward her. She could see that he was a young man, tall, his face partly obscured by the hat he wore. She searched her mind for a story to give this stranger as to why she was wandering the high road in the middle of the night.

"Mistress Westlake?"

At the sound of her own name, Xanthe started. She peered at the man who now stood only a few feet from her.

"Joshua Appleby!" She felt quite weak with relief at seeing Samuel's brother. "Oh, Joshua!"

"In the name of all that is holy, what are you doing out here, and in this weather? What has befallen you? No, do not trouble yourself to answer me. Come, I am on my way back to Marlborough. Let us get you into the carriage and out of this lethal cold."

He put an arm around her and helped her up into the carriage. His traveling companions were two young men, one of whom was asleep, while the other was cheerfully drunk and offered her his hip flask. Xanthe took a gulp of the fiery brandy as Joshua wrapped a blanket around her.

"This is my good friend William Barnet, and the snorer is Thomas Howard. A reprobate and madman and the soundest fellow you will ever meet."

"What?" William looked hurt. "No fine words for me? I am wounded, Joshua."

"We have been to the house of a friend some miles north of Bath, a man of some renown. It is another in our attempts to gain Samuel's release from Fairfax's dread grip."

Xanthe shook her head. "I came to try to help him. I think I have only made things worse!"

"You have seen him? You have been at the abbey?"

"Yes, but I was only permitted to see him briefly."

"How does he fare?"

"He looked tired, but strong as ever."

"My brother will not give his captor the satisfaction of seeing him brought low. Damn that creature!" Joshua thumbed the side of the carriage in anger and frustration. His sleeping companion stopped snoring but did not wake. William patted Joshua's shoulder.

"Courage, my friend. All is not lost."

Xanthe pulled the blanket tighter around her and took a long slow breath. She was not alone in trying to help Samuel. Of course his family were doing their utmost.

Joshua explained, "It is pure good fortune that we took it into our heads to return to Marlborough this night and not wait for the morrow. We feared the snow might render the route impassable by then."

"I am so glad to see you, Joshua."

"How came you to be on the high road in such a state and on such a night? You are near froze to death."

"Fairfax . . . he wanted to keep me there, but I got away. I had to. I'm worried about what he will do to Samuel to get back at me. Oh God, I've been a fool."

"But a pretty one," William insisted.

Joshua threw him a look that silenced him.

"Do not take on so. You are clearly distressed and weary. We shall have Philpott make you one of his famous hot toddies the second we arrive home. And then you shall sleep. In the morning you can tell me what has happened."

"Fairfax has sent his men to find me. We might meet them on the road."

"And if we do I shall send them on their way. Now, rest."

The events of the night, the effort of the walk, the warmth of the blanket, and the effects of the brandy combined to make Xanthe feel overwhelmingly sleepy. She rested her head on Joshua's shoulder and let the rocking movement of the carriage send her to sleep for the remainder of the journey. The next thing she was aware of was cold air through the open door, voices, some loud and some shushing, and then Joshua helping her out of the carriage and into his house. His two friends bid their farewells and headed off to their own homes, swaying slightly as they stomped across the whitened green.

Loyal servant Philpott appeared at the door to welcome them, despite it being the small hours of the night. He took one look at Xanthe and hurried off to find a warm shawl and reviving brandied milk. Joshua ushered her into the small sitting room and stoked up the fire. When Philpott returned he spoke quietly to his master.

"Earlier this night your father was roused from his bed by a great hammering at the door."

"Fairfax?"

"Not in person, sir, but his men, on horseback, sent in pursuit of Mistress Westlake."

"They searched the house?"

"Your father would not allow it. He is not, after all, a man easily intimidated."

"Saying no to Fairfax might be seen as foolhardy. Had I done such a thing my father would have berated me for my recklessness."

"If I might venture to suggest, sir, had it been Master Fairfax himself, your father might have been obliged to comply."

"True. Easier to send the henchmen off with a flea in their ear. They may well be back."

Xanthe looked anxious.

"I am putting you all in danger just by being here."

"This house will ever be a place of safe haven for you. Samuel would have it no other way, and nor would I. You are welcome here."

"But Fairfax . . . I have enraged him. I refused his proposition."

"Ha! He is certainly unaccustomed to being refused."

"Worse . . . there was a scuffle. I wounded him. With a piece of glass."

"The pity is you did not put an end to the unscrupulous villain." Seeing a look of reproach from his servant, Joshua added, "Fear not, mistress. Fairfax will not want it widely known that he was bested by a maid. Whatever he wants from you, he will have to take you from us to obtain it. And do not forget, he still has need of Samuel, who will not do his bidding if he harms you."

"It was Samuel I came here to help, now you are all having to help me."

"Enough. Here, drink your toddy, warm yourself by the fire, and then, and only then, I will have your story from you."

Once she had drunk half a glass of hot brandied milk and the feeling had returned, somewhat painfully, to her extremities, and Joshua was satisfied she was sufficiently recovered, she did her best to tell him what had happened. She had to tread carefully. It was hard to explain what had taken place in the observatory without mentioning time travel, either her own or the journeys Fairfax took. Her task was made easier by what Joshua already knew of the man. It was enough for her to suggest that he had asked something impossible of her, turned to violence, and that she had been forced to make her escape. Joshua was too gallant to ask for specifics. Too familiar with the ways a man might behave toward a woman, she recalled, remembering how he had come knocking on her door the first night she had stayed in the Appleby home. But Joshua was a decent man. He might have made inappropriate advances toward her, trying his luck, but he would never force himself upon her or anyone else.

"You say you saw Samuel when you were at the abbey. Were you able to speak to him alone?" Joshua asked, pulling her back to the present moment.

"Briefly."

"And you consider him in good health?"

"He looked tired, tense, but otherwise well."

"And the work? How near is it to completion?"

Xanthe turned and gazed into the fire. "Too near," she said quietly, the events of the night and her fears for Samuel threatening to overwhelm her again. She needed to regain her strength to be able to think clearly about what she must do next. This was no time to let her emotions get the better of her. She turned back to Joshua.

"Tell me," she said a little more brightly, "what news of my friends at Great Chalfield? Of Willis and Jayne and young Peter? I think of them often."

"The household thrives, under the stern eye of Mistress Lovewell. Her husband continues to entertain on a lavish scale in order to impress men he would do better to turn away from."

"But they keep their home safe, their servants secure in their work and their place to live?"

"They do. Willis creaks more with each passing winter but will never stop caring for his precious horses. He allows Peter to do a little more though I doubt he will ever entirely relinquish the reins. The boy is a child no longer but grows like a weed in a cornfield!"

Xanthe smiled at this, thinking of how small the boy had been for his age when she met him. Soon he would be a young man. "He will be filling Willis's shoes one day," she said.

"God willing."

"And Jayne?"

"The kitchen maid? The one who blushes so becomingly?"

"She would swoon simply to think you have noticed her existence. Mary was forever scolding her for lingering at windows when you were at the house."

"It is a brave girl who risks the sharp edge of Mary's tongue."

"She considered it a small price to pay for a glimpse of you," Xanthe teased him, enjoying a brief moment of respite from her own worries. "And Alice?" she asked carefully. "Have you had word of what happened to her after her release from jail?"

"She moved north. I believe Mistress Lovewell's conscience pricked her into recalling a distant relative who had need of a personal maid."

"I'm glad to hear it. A new position with a family who will accept her as she is, a girl with no family and a checkered past . . ."

"She owes you her life," Joshua said, his naturally lively face somber for once. "Without your help she would surely have perished. I have heard such tales of the horrors of transportation."

"I could not have saved her without Samuel, without all of you, Joshua. And now I must ask your help again."

She was on the point of telling him that they had to find a way to get his brother out of Fairfax's clutches, to spirit him far, far away, somewhere safe, and that she herself had to return to the abbey to search for her locket, but before she had time to speak again there came the sound of a carriage rattling across the cobblestones outside. Joshua ran to the window and opened the shutters a little to peer out.

"Fairfax's carriage!" He turned, grasping Xanthe's hand and pulling her to her feet. "Come!"

They ran from the room, along the flagstoned passageway, and out through the back door. The snowstorm beat against them as they hurried across the rear courtyard and into Samuel's studio. Xanthe recalled the basement hoarde room he had shown her and knew, with a sense of mounting horror, where it was Joshua was taking her.

Sure enough, he snatched a candle from a wall sconce and they descended the steps into the cellar. He handed her the candle while he dragged sacks of flour to one side, moving them until a wooden floor was revealed. Xanthe could hear her own heartbeat against her eardrums as she watched him lift the concealed trapdoor. He took the candle from her and held it aloft over the narrow gap that was now exposed.

"Samuel showed you this?"

She nodded. "The priest hole."

"There is no time to flee. You must get inside. Quickly now."

Xanthe took her courage in both hands, refusing to listen to the voice inside her head that was screaming at the thought of being locked in such a tiny space. She climbed down into the void, unable to ignore the fact that it was, of necessity, shaped like a coffin. She lay down, reaching up for the candle, but Joshua shook his head.

"It would be too dangerous and would give you away." He leaned over, squeezed her hand, and said quickly, "Fear not. Stay silent. I will return."

And then he pulled the heavy lid back into place. Xanthe forced herself to breathe slowly. By the time he had replaced the flour sacks there was not the tiniest crack of light inside the hiding place. For a moment she feared she would have no air, and then she remembered Samuel telling her that when he constructed the priest hole he had built in a special duct that drew in air from outside. She heard Joshua's dwindling footsteps, the cellar door shutting, and then silence. A silence so complete and heavy she feared it might crush her. She wished she could at least hear the moaning of the wind outside, or the rattling of tree branches against the studio windows. Anything at all, just to remind her that she was not entombed, that she was still alive. She thought about how Joshua would have to lie convincingly to Fairfax, who would be in no mood to believe him. What if he took Joshua away? No one else knew where she was. She told herself Master Appleby would look for her there, but then, if Philpott was taken away too, how was he to know she was even in the house? She could not afford to give way to panic. She had to use her imagination to take her to a different place. She tried to recall the words to the new song she had been learning. It was a ballad about a young girl who ran away to be with her soldier lover. It had been written a few years after the moment she now inhabited, after the terrible civil war that came later in the same century. She made herself remember, whispering the words, following the melody in her head.

"She up and left her father's house / she took to the high road with no backward glance / 'I'll be a soldier's bride 'ere the week is out . . .'" She stopped. She listened hard. She could hear doors opening and shutting. Footsteps. The house was being searched. Xanthe's heart pounded. There were men above, in the studio, she was certain of it. She couldn't make out what they were saying, but the voices sounded angry, urgent. The cellar door opened and someone descended the stairs. As they walked upon the floorboards of the basement she felt the vibrations jarring through the hard wood of the tiny space she lay in. The pacing stopped. There were dragging sounds. The flour sacks were being moved! She was trapped now. There was nothing to do to stop herself being discovered. Before she could begin to think of the consequences of being found, of what that would mean for herself and all of Samuel's family, the trap door was lifted and lamplight blinded her.

11

XANTHE INSTINCTIVELY PUT UP HER ARM TO SHADE HER EYES FROM THE SUDDEN BRIGHT-ness and to ward off any blows that might come. She was astonished to hear her own name spoken breathlessly and by a voice she knew so well.

"Samuel?" She sat up, blinking, feeling him take hold of her hand. He helped her to her feet and took her in his arms.

"Xanthe! That you should have to be in here!"

"But how did you get away? The carriage—we thought Fairfax had come for me."

Samuel released her, stepping back to look at her seriously. "You are in such peril because of me. Come, let us return to the warmth of the house. The cold causes you to tremble."

Xanthe allowed him to lead her from the basement and back to the sitting room. Soon they were seated in front of the fire, joined by Joshua. Philpott brought more drinks and lingered, evidently determined to hear the explanation for his master's sudden return.

Joshua helped himself to brandy without bothering to add it to milk.

"Brother, we are relieved to see you, but at a loss . . . how do you come to have the use of Fairfax's carriage?"

Samuel stood in front of the fire, clearly too agitated to sit.

"While we were working in the new wing we became aware of a commotion. There were shouts, servants could be heard running. The apothecary was summoned." He addressed Xanthe. "I questioned a footman and was told you had assaulted the master of the house and run out into the night. Fairfax had sent riders out after you but had been forced to tarry, being in need of attention. It seems you . . . wounded him, somehow?"

Xanthe nodded. "I was trying to leave. He was trying to stop me. I . . . I had to defend myself. There was broken glass. . . ."

Joshua gave a dry laugh. "Take notice, Samuel. Your fair friend has the courage to do what none of us has dared."

"I didn't think. I shouldn't have hurt him," Xanthe said. "I've only made things worse for you, Samuel. For all of you."

Samuel frowned. "To think of him laying hands on you . . . you had every right to do what you must to protect yourself. And it seems your blow struck home. There were howls of rage and pain from the east wing for some time."

"Pity the poor apothecary," put in Joshua. "His would be a thankless task."

"Whatever the risks," Samuel explained, "he succeeded in binding Fairfax's wounds. From what I was told, he was on the point of joining the search for you, Xanthe. He had his best horse readied, but then, as if by miraculous intervention, a messenger came from London."

"From the king?" A note of worry sounded in Joshua's question.

"Yes. Fairfax was summoned. He was compelled to abandon his pursuit and head to court. As soon as he was gone I requested the carriage."

Xanthe was confused. "But his servants, his men, they know you are being kept there. How did you persuade them to let you go?"

"They are expecting me to return with 'essential pieces' from my studio. I convinced them my work would be held up without these things and that I required the carriage to collect them. When they hesitated I insisted that if we waited the snow might become worse and they would have to answer to their master for the delay in the completion of his beloved house. Given his raving mood, they were not prepared to risk incurring his displeasure. I am pleased beyond words to find you here and unharmed, Xanthe. I must soon return to the abbey."

Joshua was appalled at the thought. "So that Fairfax can take out his rage upon you on his return?"

"The driver waits for me," Samuel reminded him. "I came only to see that you are safe and well. To flee now would be to condemn the man who let me go and the one who sits without this house to suffering Fairfax's vengeful temper. I will not be the cause of such a fate for them."

Xanthe searched for the words to properly convey to Samuel how she had failed to help him. "I know now what it is Fairfax wants," she said slowly, "and . . . it is not something I can ever give."

Samuel nodded, taking her hand in his. "And nor would I want you to," he said.

She could see from his expression that he thought Fairfax wanted her for himself, which was at least in part true. She let him think it, unable to discuss with him the details of his desire to keep her as his own, which went so far beyond taking her as his wife. Even if Samuel was prepared to believe all manner of impossible things about her, she couldn't speak of time travel and such madness in front of Joshua.

"There is something else," she said. "My locket. I lost it. When Fairfax attacked me. . . ."

"The one of gold that holds the miniature of your mother?" Samuel asked.

"Yes. You know, I think, you understand, Samuel . . . I have to have it. I cannot leave unless I have it."

"You too cannot mean to return to the abbey?" Joshua was incredulous.

"She must," Samuel replied.

"But Fairfax . . ."

". . . is in London. We have some time. Let us not waste it on further debate." He stood up, pausing to reassure Xanthe. "We will find your little piece of gold."

He smiled then, knowing and yet not knowing. Understanding little of what he had seen about the locket in the past, but just enough. Enough to accept that it was vital to her, though he could not be certain how. He was simply prepared to accept all her strangeness without question.

The weather outside had calmed a little, so that there was no wind and the snow had ceased to fall. It remained fiercely cold, however, and Xanthe's clothes, without her heavy coat, were insufficient. A search of the house produced a mop cap belonging to Abigail, the maid, and a velvet cloak with a wool lining that was Samuel's. Being tall, Xanthe was able to wear it without tripping up, and was grateful for its luxurious warmth and faint scent of the sandalwood soap Samuel used.

As they were getting into the carriage Samuel's father came out of the house, still in his nightclothes. Xanthe thought Master Appleby had aged noticeably since the last time she had seen him.

"Samuel." He put his hand on his son's arm. "Have a care. It is unlikely the king would summon Fairfax at such an hour and in poor weather for good news. He may return in a worse temper than he left. Do not let yourself, nor Mistress Westlake, bear the brunt of his ill humor." He nodded at Xanthe through the window of the carriage. Samuel assured him they would find her locket and then get her to safety. There was work still to be done on the house. There was still time for them to find a way to lift the threat of prosecution from him.

The driver steered the carriage around the snow-coated green, down the high street, and out of Marlborough. The thick snow clouds allowed no moonlight at all now, so that the horses navigated by their own superior vision, their familiarity with the road, and the meager cast of the coach lamps. At such an uncivilized hour there was no one else abroad. The horses' hoofbeats and the rumble of the carriage wheels were hushed by the snow. Inside the carriage Xanthe leaned close to Samuel, savoring the intimacy of the moment, storing up the memory of it for later when she would miss him. She reminded herself that he was engaged to be married now and shifted to sit a little more upright, a little more distant.

"Samuel, I understand you are to be congratulated."

"How so?"

"You are to be wed. I am happy for you."

He did not respond immediately. Xanthe sensed it was not an easy subject for him.

"I wished to have told you myself. I suppose that Fairfax relished delivering the news."

"He did seem to enjoy the moment. I admit, I was . . . surprised."

In the gloom of the carriage interior, with the fluctuating light from the swinging lamp, Samuel's face was revealed only in shadowy silhouette, his expression hard to read.

He spoke at last. "My father wished me wed. Alliances are all and everything for the survival of a family. And for my part, I had thought you gone forever. More, I knew that even should you return, it would not alter our circumstances. Better that we accept the way things are, so that we might both of us continue with our lives, without regret."

"Samuel, you don't have to explain yourself to me. Really, you don't."

"Henrietta's family and my own have long been close. They have been stalwart in their support, even now, with me so compromised. They are good people. Our families can help each other. She is a fine woman. Good-natured, wise, sincere. I believe we might have a good life together, God willing. Perchance a happy one. Xanthe, I would have you understand . . ."

"It's not my business. You were right, after all. I was gone. And I will be again soon. Your father knows what he's doing. And you are right; we cannot change the way things are."

They journeyed on in silence for a few miles until the lights of the village of Laybrook broke through the murky night.

"We should search the upper part of the drive," Xanthe said, leaning forward to peer out the window. "I can't be sure where I lost the locket."

"You do not think it to be inside the house?"

"It is probably there, but with more snow likely, I just think we should walk the last stretch, the part where I ran out of the house at least."

Samuel shouted to the driver to stop and he set them down, taking instructions to drive the carriage on to the east wing and have the men unload the pieces of cherrywood paneling Samuel had had the quick wit to fetch from the studio to shore up his story. Xanthe held the coach lamp high, searching for familiar landmarks, trying to recall her route.

"I made for the fence, and then the woods. I think if the chain was broken in the scuffle, the locket would have fallen free of my clothing as I ran. It is smooth, with a bit of weight to it. It couldn't have stayed in my clothes for many paces, so it's more likely still in the house, but I need to check. Here, look at the tracks. You can still make them out even though they are filled in a little. This is the point where I climbed the fence. Let's retrace my steps back to the front door."

Together they walked slowly, being careful not to disturb the snow, focusing only on the narrow route where Xanthe's Dr. Martens had left their distinctive treads. Soon they had reached the house and found nothing.

Samuel opened the door. The footman saw them enter and he waved him away, explaining he was to take Mistress Westlake to the observatory to await his master's return. As they climbed the stairs to the top of the Tower Xanthe felt her anxiety mounting. What if they couldn't find the locket? And what if Fairfax returned before she could leave? She was no nearer to helping Samuel than she had been when she'd first arrived, and now it seemed her own safety had become the priority.

As soon as they entered the observatory Xanthe hurried over to the broken bookcase, feeling increasingly certain that the locket must have fallen during her fight with Fairfax. That, or else it was somewhere in the snowy field or woods, which was too worrying a prospect to contemplate, as it would be impossibly hard to find there. Samuel had never been in the room before and was immediately distracted by its strange contents. He stared, amazed, at the glass ceiling, the telescope, the rows and rows of huge books, the charts of the stars and models of the planets.

"What uncommon curios Fairfax values. He concerns himself with the most arcane things. Is it magic he seeks in this unholy place?"

Xanthe crouched down among the shards of glass and splinters of the bookcase doors, taking care not to gather pieces in the hem of her dress. She picked up a piece of wood with which to search through the debris.

"You are closer to the truth than you know."

"Witchcraft, then?"

Xanthe paused and looked up at him, holding his gaze.

"Is that what you think of me? That I am some sort of witch? I wish I could help you understand."

"I cannot believe that, though the evidence of my eyes has told me you possess some method of . . . ensorcellment . . ." His expression suggested things were becoming clearer to him. "Is it this that Fairfax wishes to have from you? Is this what he asks of you? Some manner of ability he covets?"

"I can't do what he wants. It would mean staying here. Forever."

"Xanthe . . ."

"But I can't. We both know that. He does not."

Samuel walked over to her and joined in the search. Together they continued with the delicate work of moving the shattered glass. Xanthe was all too aware of the mutual unspoken longing that accompanied their task. And of the fact that Samuel was helping her do something that would send her away from him, again. Did he think it was for the best? Was it what he wanted, in fact, now that he was going to be married? Or was he doing what he knew Xanthe needed to do? Was she right in thinking that he truly understood that she had no real choice? She found herself staring at him, so that she saw his eyes light up suddenly.

"I have it!" he cried, plucking the locket from among the glass, gaining a small cut on his hand as he did so.

"Be careful!" she said, instinctively taking hold of his hand. For a moment they stayed, fingers entwined, the locket safe in his grasp, his blood warm upon her cool palm.

From outside the room came shouts.

Xanthe started. "Fairfax."

"He has returned so soon!"

They rose quickly to their feet but already they could hear pounding footsteps on the stairs. There was only one door to the observatory, and the room was placed too high in the building to escape through the windows. There was nowhere to run.

Fairfax flung wide the door and stood in the entrance. He was flushed from running, his normally pallid skin mottled pink. Xanthe was shocked to see that his left eye was covered with a patch and bandage. The thought that she had damaged his eye with the shard of glass, perhaps blinding him, made her feel sick.

"How fortunate for me I was intercepted by a messenger on the London road, informing me my presence was no longer required at court this night. Fortunate for me, if not for you," he said.

Samuel stepped in front of Xanthe. "Mistress Westlake was on the point of leaving," he said firmly.

"She does not have my permission to leave."

"Your mistake is in believing she requires it," Samuel said, turning to hand Xanthe the locket, closing her fingers around it, his look telling her he knew what would happen next. That he expected her to vanish, then and there, before Fairfax could stop her.

"Samuel, no, I can't . . ."

"You must."

"But what are you going to do? I can't leave you like this."

"I must have you safe. Away from here. I will not see Fairfax use you to who knows what end."

"Step aside, Appleby. Mistress Westlake is possessed of an unusually sharp and well-reasoned mind for a woman. The time she has had to consider her situation will, I am confident, have brought her to the conclusion that she can best help herself and you by accepting my offer."

"She will never be yours." Samuel took a step toward him.

"She will if she values your life as she claims to. Come, mistress, let us strike a bargain this moment. Your alliance, sworn and freely given, for the lives of the entire Appleby family. A fair exchange, do you not agree?"

"I will not allow it," Samuel told him.

"Oh? Do you have dominion over the maid? I understood you were be-trothed to the daughter of a minor nobleman from Sussex. Am I mistook? No, I see by your expression that I am not. Mistress Westlake is free, then, to make her own choice as to her future. Come, mistress, will you take that step toward a bright and wondrous future with me?" He gave a smile that, in his ruined and bandaged face, was strained and lopsided. He held out his hand and Xanthe saw that it was shaking. Whether from pain or suppressed rage she could not tell. She hesitated, unsure what to do. If she pretended to accept his terms, to go along with what he wanted, it would buy them some time. But could she trust him? Trust him to keep his word about Samuel and his family, and trust him not to take his revenge on her for injuring him? Whatever the risks, there seemed no helpful option. She could not simply leave Samuel now. She must find a way to use what Fairfax wanted from her to secure his safety.

She took a step forward.

Samuel gasped, putting himself in her way.

"No. You cannot!"

"I must, Samuel. It is the only way."

"We will find another. I will not have you in danger for my sake."

"Let her decide her path, Appleby. You are not, I think we have estab-lished, her master."

"And no more are you!" Samuel shouted, his anger at his own situation and his fear for Xanthe finally getting the better of him. He lunged at Fairfax, taking hold of him and forcing him back against the doorjamb. "Leave now, Xanthe!" he called over his shoulder.

"Appleby, you will regret this!" Fairfax promised him.

"I regret ever agreeing to come to this place. I regret letting fear for my family govern my actions. I regret that I ever allowed my talents to be used for your advantage. I will never regret doing whatever I can for the woman who once claimed my heart!"

What Samuel had not noticed, but Xanthe had seen, was that Fairfax was taking a knife from the belt at his hip. It was small, but lethal; a stiletto carried for self-defense or attack.

"Samuel, look out!" Xanthe cried, instinctively rushing forward to help him. Just as instinctively, she clutched the locket tighter in her hand. This action, the extra pressure of her palm upon the gold, coupled with her heightened state of anxiety and the agitated state of her thoughts, triggered the locket. Before she could stop it, she felt the charm working to send her back to her own time.

"No!" she shouted, doing her best to drop the locket, but the gold chain was wrapped around her fingers and already it was too late. The room seemed to spin, her balance disturbed, her vision blurred. As she watched, powerless to help, she saw Fairfax raise the dagger, saw Samuel grab his wrist, saw them struggle, and then the darkness descended, the pair were lost to view, and Xanthe plunged through the centuries once again.

{ 12 }

THIS TIME XANTHE FOUGHT AGAINST WHAT WAS HAPPENING TO HER. SHE TRIED TO RESIST the transition, tried to turn back. She even tried to let go of the locket she had risked so much to retrieve. She shut thoughts of home and of Flora from her mind and thought only of Samuel.

"No, no, no, I have to stay!" she shouted into the void. It was all pointless. It seemed however much she liked to think she had gained some control over when and where she spun time, once a journey was triggered she was unable to stop it. She arrived breathless and bewildered, slamming hard against the gritty floor of the blind house. She tried to marshal her thoughts, to see if she couldn't simply leap back again. In the darkness of the little stone building she felt around for the locket, found it, and put it on, tucking it beneath her blouse. Then she searched further, feeling around in a wider circle, seeking the chocolate pot. She needed it to make the jump back again. It had to be there somewhere. Like any other object, it could not return to the time when it originally existed, so as she stepped back, even though she would have been holding it, it would have fallen to the floor. Xanthe crept further across the uneven ground, the dirt damp beneath her hands as she frantically searched. It wasn't there! How could that be? It couldn't have journeyed with her, so that meant someone must have come into the jail and taken it. Without thinking, she clambered to her feet and pushed the door open, stumbling out into the dazzling light of a bright November morning.

And there, standing in the middle of the untidy lawn, leaning on her sticks, was Flora.

"Xanthe! Good grief, where on earth did you spring from?" Without waiting for an answer she hurried across the damp grass and gave her daughter a hug. "I didn't hear you come home."

Xanthe did her best to hide her own surprise and to come up with a convincing explanation for her sudden appearance. It was hard to know the right thing to say without being entirely sure of the time, or even of what day it was. Her mind was still in turmoil, everything telling her that she should go back to Samuel. How could she leave him to face Fairfax alone? Who could say what such a man would do if he believed he had been tricked out of having what he wanted? She had to go back, but at that moment her main concern was making sense to her mother. Which meant thinking up yet more lies. And, above everything because so much depended on it, finding out what had happened to the chocolate pot.

"Oh, I didn't want to disturb you when I came in," she said vaguely, playing for time, hoping for clues.

Flora laughed lightly. "I know I get engrossed in my restoration projects, but I've always got time to say hello to my only daughter, silly." From this reply Xanthe decided it sounded as if she had at least returned on the day her mother was expecting her, as she hadn't said otherwise. She was just processing this fact when the next question threw her. "What on earth were you doing in that filthy shed?" Flora asked, taking a step toward it.

"Don't go in there!" The words were out of her mouth before she could think.

Her mother looked at her quizzically. "Why ever not?"

Xanthe grasped at a flimsy idea. "You'll spoil the surprise."

"Surprise? Oh, does it have anything to do with the copper chocolate pot?"

"What?"

"I went in there yesterday looking for the garden fork and I found your special chocolate pot."

"You went in there?"

"Yes, I just said that."

"And you didn't notice anything . . . strange?"

"Only that you'd left your precious pot in there."

"Did you move it?"

"Well, yes, I don't think it's a good idea keeping it in such a damp place.

You spent ages cleaning it and it'll just tarnish. Copper's the worst for that you know, worse even than silver. Can't see why you'd want to put it in there in the first place."

"I wanted to try a quiet place, to let it sing to me. I thought it might be easier to hear its story away from, I dunno, lights and other sounds."

Flora nodded at this, easily prepared to accept that such a strange gift as her daughter's would prompt a person to do equally strange things.

"I still think it won't do the copper any good, love," she said. "Better to just keep it in your room and draw the curtains, don't you think? I've put it in the workshop for now. Gave it a bit of a clean for you."

"Thanks, Mum." Xanthe couldn't help thinking that the pot being moved out of the blind house might somehow have affected the link between the present and the past for her. Had that had something to do with her accidentally traveling back? Perhaps it was not only that she had handled the locket and that she had been upset. There was so much to think about, so much she still did not completely understand.

"Were you looking for it?" Flora was asking, still baffled by finding her daughter emerging from the shed.

"What? Oh, yes. I . . . missed it," she said.

Flora shook her head. "More than you missed me, clearly. Not one phone call to your old mum."

"I'm sorry, it was tricky, and I was . . ."

". . . busy. You don't have to tell me. I've been to more antiques fairs than you've had hot dinners, don't forget. I know how hectic they can be and how caught up in everything you can get. How did you get on with finding stock? I can't wait to see what treasures you've brought home."

Xanthe's head began to ache with the effort of such a complicated game of charades when all the time she was desperately worried about Samuel. She tried a smile. "Actually, you'll have to wait a bit longer."

"Oh?"

"Yes, it's all part of the surprise."

"Like what you've just put in the shed?" Flora's expression was becoming increasingly bewildered. "And why you're wearing those peculiar clothes?"

Xanthe instinctively put her hand up to her head. The mop cap she had been given had been dislodged somewhere in her transition and had not made the journey, but of course she was still wearing Samuel's cloak. She pulled it around her more tightly. "That's right," she said, already trying to construct in her mind a convincing explanation for such a buildup. "All will be revealed."

"You're being very mysterious. I hope you haven't gone mad with the budget."

"Of course not. I just, found some lovely things. And some of them I've got to go and collect, and . . ." She ground to a halt, completely lost for anything to add.

Flora narrowed her eyes. "I know what you've been up to."

"You do?"

"I know that look. You can't keep secrets from me, Xanthe, you never could. You've got Christmas written all over you."

"Christmas?"

"And here I was thinking you weren't going to be too busy to do much about it this year. But you know me too well. And this one will be special, like you said. Just you and me. Our first Christmas in Marlborough."

"Exactly what I've been thinking."

"You don't want to share your plans with me? OK, have it your own way." Flora smiled, holding up a hand. "I won't press you. Just promise me you haven't gone mad with my present. We can't afford big gifts this year."

Relief swamped Xanthe and she gave a little laugh. "I know, but you deserve something special, Mum."

"If you insist, I won't argue. Now come on, it's way past lunchtime. I want to tell you about my adventures in campanology."

"Sorry? Oh, you mean the bell-ringing."

"Yes, the bell-ringing. Honestly, Xanthe, love, sometimes I don't know where your head is. I've been for my first session. Well, not that I actually did much. But I watched and got the idea of what will be expected of me. Graham and Sheila showed me the ropes, so to speak." She giggled at her own joke.

"That's great, Mum. How did you get on with . . . ?"

"My hands? Completely fine, thank you. I actually think it might help, you know, strengthen them. They're better than some bits of me; might as well use 'em. Right, lunch. I know you think I never eat when you're not here but actually I've been cooking," she said, making her way toward the house.

Xanthe followed, realizing she had no choice but to eat with her mother. "Cooking? Really?"

"Yes. Must be the cold weather. I fancied a mutton stew."

"Good grief."

"Don't panic, I couldn't be bothered to go shopping and we were fresh out of mutton. So I used crumbled-up beef burgers instead. It's pretty good if I say so myself. . . . Ouch!" Flora stumbled, leaning heavily on one of her crutches.

"Mum? Are you OK?"

"It's nothing. My knee's been playing up a bit, that's all."

"Another flare-up? Do you want me to make an appointment for you to see the physio?"

"I'm fine, don't fuss. I just need a bit of grub and a sit-down," she insisted, striding off unevenly.

For all her protestations, Xanthe was not convinced. She suspected her mother was suffering more than she was letting on. The way she was moving, it was obvious she was in pain. She shouldn't be left to cope on her own. Xanthe couldn't help glancing back over her shoulder, taking one more look at the blind house, wondering what was happening to Samuel. Wondering what she would find when she went back. If she went back. Because now she had to find a reason for another absence and there were only so many stories she could come up with before she tripped over her own lies. And if Flora's health was deteriorating there was no way she could leave her, however much she wanted to.

Flora was determined to fix lunch, so Xanthe left her in the kitchen and hurried to her own room to change. As she folded the velvet cloak, running her hands over the dense, soft fabric, she could feel tiny particles crumbling. How long would it last? she wondered, setting it down on her bed next to Rose's white blouse. How long before both garments vanished completely? She had no time to think about it further. She pulled on jeans, a T-shirt, and a chunky jumper, for once favoring practicality over her preferred vintage clothing, and perhaps needing for once to root herself firmly in her own time. Downstairs she found her mother had succeeded in laying the table but was happy to leave Xanthe to sort out a meal. Flora was reluctant to talk about her flare-up, dismissing it, as was her habit. Xanthe did at least get her to agree that an appointment with the physiotherapist and the doctor should be made for the following day. As soon as they had eaten the strangely palatable meal, Flora headed for bed, reassuring Xanthe that using heat pads for her neck and shoulders would quickly ease her aches, determined to prove they would be wasting the doctor's time. It was a temporary setback, flare-ups came and went, and this one, too, would pass.

Xanthe went down to the shop and turned the sign to open, signaling the end of the lunchtime closing. A glance at the sales book on the desk showed her that Flora had not only found time to socialize with her new friends and her new hobby but had also been busy in the shop serving customers. While it was heartening to see that business was picking up, Xanthe felt even more guilty about not having actually been to the Bristol antiques fair. She was going to have to find some stock from somewhere, not only to back up her flimsy story, but to provide them with more treasures to sell. There were so many things she needed to do and so many places she needed to be. What might be happening to Samuel? She could not even be sure of how much time had passed since she left. It was so frustrating to be stuck, unable to return to him. She didn't dare go into the workshop to fetch the chocolate pot. She knew if she did she would be pulled even more strongly in the direction of the past. Right now her mother needed her. That was that.

Or was it?

There was something else Xanthe had not been allowing herself to think about until she had seen to her mother. Something that kept hope burning in her heart. Hope for Samuel. Now, at last, she could find out if this was false hope, an illusion based on wishful thinking and the obscure words of an old woman from centuries ago, or a real chance that she could truly learn to control the way she traveled through time. So that she could do it safely, certain about where she would end up and knowing that she could come home whenever she wanted to. Without mistakes. Without risk. Now she could find out if it really was possible for her to become a Spinner.

Nervously, she walked over to the glass-fronted bookcase that stood against the far wall of the shop, fighting off a memory of the one she had smashed into in Fairfax's observatory. She felt a wave of relief at seeing the book still there, nestled safely between a copy of *A Tale of Two Cities* and a collection of nineteenth-century poetry. She opened the case and took out the leather-bound book. It felt cool in her hands. It was nothing exciting to look at; just a simple, slim volume, its green leather cover worn in patches, the single word embossed in gold across its front slightly faded. She traced the scrolling lettering with a finger and whispered the title aloud.

"Spinners."

She opened it. To anyone else it might look like a fantasy novel, a work of fiction recounting the story of a group of people with a strange ability to spin time. To anyone else. Not to Xanthe. She knew what it was. It was a record of time travel, a book telling of the journeys made by people who were able to travel back and fore through the decades and centuries, beyond those of their own lifetimes. People like her. The contents were divided not, as she had half expected, into chapters regarding the technical aspects of time travel, but more like a collection of short stories. Each one looked like a fascinating tale, but it was far from being the instruction manual she had hoped for. She turned the pages quickly, searching for anything that might give a clearer indication of the how and the what of spinning time. There were illustrations—some simple line drawings, others more elaborate and quite beautifully worked—and there were maps, charts, and diagrams, but it was impossible at first glance to tell what might be relevant or useful.

"Stories are all very well," she said as if the Spinners responsible for writing them were there to hear her, "but I need guidance, clues, tips, warnings, damn it, something to tell me what I need to know. I don't have time to unravel stories!"

The jangling of the doorbell made her jump and snap the book shut. She knew the middle-aged couple now browsing in the shop could not possibly realize the rare significance of what she held in her hands, but still she wanted to keep it safe, keep it secret. At last she might find answers to some of her questions. She felt hope lift her. If there was one thing that might help her successfully balance the two lives, the two worlds she now inhabited, it was some level of mastery over her gift. It just might be that this dusty, tattered old book—something that the previous owner, Mr. Morris, could well have bought in a job lot and forgotten about—might at last give her control over her ability. Give her the skills she needed to travel when and where she was needed.

But it seemed that the running of the shop that day would not easily allow her to focus on what secrets might lie in wait for her in the book. A steady stream of customers required her attention, putting off further the moment she had been waiting for so eagerly.

Silly problems that she had brought upon herself now demanded her attention too. Like the fact that her taxi was still parked up in the car park of the auction house in Devizes. For a fleeting moment she entertained the idea of asking Liam to drive her out to collect it, but quickly decided she couldn't do that. She had asked too many favors of him already. It wasn't fair, and it was inclined to give him the wrong idea about how she saw him. He was a friend, and she valued his friendship, but she knew he wanted something more. At that moment she felt almost overwhelmed by the complexity of her situation. How much easier it would be to lean on Liam. To let him woo her. To allow herself to lower her guard and become closer to him. She glimpsed the comfort in that, the possible intimacy, the support, and the hope for the future such a closeness could give her.

She glanced at the two clocks on the shelf. One had stopped, Flora having forgotten to wind it, but the other was whirring and about to chime two o'clock. Xanthe calculated that her mother's pain medication, combined with her exhausted state, would most likely keep her asleep for a couple of hours. As soon as there was a break in the browsers and shoppers stepping over the threshold, she hurried upstairs, grabbed her wallet, went outside, and fetched her hidden car keys and phone from the shrubbery, ignoring the whispers from the blind house, hurried through the shop again, turning the sign to closed as she went and locking the door behind her. She took a mini-cab from the rank on the high street and was soon reunited with her own car. She made a detour into Devizes and all but ran in and out of two antique shops, buying a handful of random items. She was thankful that she and her mother were still relatively unknown in the area, even by other people in the trade. Eyebrows would most definitely have been raised regarding her business sense if anyone had recognized her and realized that she was purchasing china, jewelry, and glass at retail prices to sell in her own shop. By the time she returned to Marlborough her stress levels were high, her temper short, and her self-esteem at a very low point. She unloaded the two boxes of new stock, leaving them in the workshop so that Flora could look at them later, and parked the car. As soon as she returned to the shop she went upstairs. Flora had run herself a deep bubble bath and called through the door that she was already feeling much better. The genuine cheer in her voice lifted Xanthe's spirits. She made herself a cup of tea, sighing at the lack of milk or sugar in the house, seeing it as another sign of her own inability to keep everything together, and then felt almost ridiculously pleased at finding a packet of shortbread biscuits. Once back in the shop, she turned the sign to open again and sat in the captain's chair behind the desk, taking *Spinners* out of the drawer and setting the book down in front of her. As she took a quick sip of her Earl Grey she spotted the local newspaper on top of the stack of paper bags and tissue paper. It had been left folded open to show an advertisement for a pop-up antiques sale in a village hall in Ditton, a few miles west of Laybrook. The ad had been circled in green ink, and Xanthe suspected her mother had planned for them to go there together. It was unlikely she would be quite well enough, but Xanthe could still go on her own. There was the chance of some interesting finds for the shop, and at least she could pretend some of them had come from Bristol. Guilt curdled the tea in her stomach. More deceit. She leaned back in the worn walnut chair, the old leather seat creaking in protest, evidently in need of a bit of restoration work. If Flora had been well she would have noticed that and dealt with it straightaway. Xanthe rubbed her own aching neck, feeling the by now familiar jet lag that time travel left her with. She took a breath and picked up the book.

"Right," she said to herself, as much as to all the unknown Spinners who had gone before her who had set down their wisdom between those leather covers. "Let's see if this time I can find more answers than questions."

The remainder of the afternoon consisted of Xanthe trying to be patient with and attentive to customers, while all the time longing to read more of *Spinners*. The book was a treasure trove of stories about such wonderful time travelers that she could not believe they were all based on fact. Perhaps there were only one or two who had actually been able to move through time, and the others were just put there to camouflage the real ones. Some of the pages were beautifully illuminated with red and blue lettering picked out in gold. Others appeared almost to be written by hand, in flowing copperplate with thick ink and a worn nib. Could it have been the author's intention to record the exploits of the real Spinners for any who might come later but to hide them among fictional ones? Xanthe googled the name of the author, given only as M. Derive and not mentioned until several pages into the book, but got no results. There was nothing else written by him, or her, and no record of *Spinners* anywhere on the internet. There wasn't a publisher's name printed inside the book either. It was impossible to pick out what was, supposedly, fact from what was fiction. Most of the Spinners, like Fairfax, seemed to require one particular object to travel with. Only two she could find used lots of different things in the way that she did. One of those jumped so far into the future the story read like science fiction. Could that one really be accurate?

Something that struck her as she was reading was that this was no random collection of people. It felt more like a group or society, though it wasn't clear how anyone was chosen to be included in it. What were the rules? And if people *were* selected somehow, why would somebody as ruthless and unscrupulous as Fairfax be included? Come to think of it, why would she have been included? What had she ever done to show that she was a suitable person to take on the sort of responsibility she was beginning to understand was a part of the gift? If it could be called a gift.

Determined to make sense of it, she selected a page at random and read quietly aloud, as if hearing her own voice enunciate the words, clearly, sensibly, might give her an easier insight into their meaning.

Rowan hugged the swaddled babe closer to her, tugging the woolen blanket that all but hid him a little tighter. She glanced up and down the path once more before stepping out from the cover of the trees. Soon it would be dark, and the night would shield her. For now, she had only her wits, her sharp sense, and her youthful strength to protect them both. The ground was tinder dry from the summer drought so that twigs and empty acorn husks crunched beneath her feet as she ran. The noise sounded dangerously loud to Rowan. She had no way of knowing where her persecutors might be hiding; where they might lie in wait, ready to spring upon her and wrench her precious child from her arms. She could not let that happen. She would not. She bent lower over the sleeping bundle, breathing in the sweet, newborn scent of him as she ran, drawing strength from that visceral connection twixt mother and babe, knowing that there was nothing she would not do for him. Despite the courage this gave her, her soul still quaked at what she was about to do. If there were any other way she would gladly have taken it, but all options had been tried and found wanting. This, she had entirely convinced herself, was their only hope.

After an hour of running steadily along the fringes of the forest, the gathering dark beginning to cloak their progress, Rowan at last came to the stone well she had been told of. It was as the old woman had described; small, low set, unimportant. Its unique properties hidden. Its magic obscured. Out of breath, she leaned against the ancient stones, attempting to steady her galloping heart. The child reacted to the cessation of their movement by starting to whimper. Rowan hushed him, kissing the top of his head, scanning the darkening trees for sign of movement. At last a figure stepped forward, slender and straight-backed despite her age. The old woman pulled back her hood and came to stand close to mother and infant. "You are late," she said, reaching forward to touch the wool of the blanket. "How fares our newest Spinner?" As a reflex, Rowan drew the child still closer. "Tell me, is it safe, what you would have us do? My son will come to no harm?" The old woman's blue eyes, their brightness seemingly undimmed by age, regarded the girl soberly. "There is little in this life that does not carry with it a possibility of danger, child. You surely know that. I can give you no promise other than I believe this to be the best and safest course open to you, if the babe is to be saved. For one who has spent so little time on this earth, he has acquired powerful enemies. I will put you both beyond their reach. Come," she said, holding out an elegant hand. Rowan took it and permitted herself to be led toward the well.

"Wow," Xanthe muttered to herself, "she's going to travel through time with her baby!"

With a sinking heart Xanthe realized that the book was going to take time and close study if it was to give up its secrets. She shut the book, shut her eyes, and took a long slow breath. It all felt overwhelming. The person who could best explain it all to her was Mistress Flyte, who was well beyond Xanthe's reach at that moment. She needed help, needed someone she could talk to about it. Another mind to put to the impossible puzzles. But who? Her eyes sprang open. There was one person who knew more about all the mysteries, folklore, and legends of the area than anyone else she had met since moving to Wiltshire. One person who wouldn't laugh at what she needed to talk about. Someone outside the family who didn't have another agenda when it came to his friendship with her. Xanthe made a decision. She would talk to Harley.

At five-thirty she closed the shop and went upstairs to find Flora trying to get dressed.

"Mum, what are you doing?"

"What does it look like? I feel much better after a good soak. And anyway, I just stiffen up even more if I don't move around."

"Well, yes, but when you've had a bad day you have to go easy."

"How easy do you want me to go?" she asked, not really expecting an answer, wriggling her left arm into a cardigan sleeve. "Do stop fussing, love."

Xanthe had to put her hands in her pockets to stop herself helping her mother. It was hard at times to strike the right balance between helping when help was needed and letting Flora maintain her independence.

"OK," she said with forced cheerfulness, "let's get you into the kitchen. I'll make us some supper."

"I'm not hungry."

"You have to eat."

"I haven't done anything to work up an appetite."

"Mum, you can't take your medication on an empty stomach."

Flora stopped trying to do up buttons with her swollen fingers. The short silence that followed was filled with unspoken wishes and if onlys. Xanthe had learned to let these moments move at their own pace. To give her mother time.

Flora picked up her crutches and walked slowly out of the bedroom, maneuvering herself down the stairs with practiced caution. Xanthe followed.

In the kitchen Flora sat at the table without further protest while Xanthe took eggs and cheese from the fridge.

"How were sales today?" her mother asked. The moment had passed.

"Not bad. Two leather suitcases, a piece of harvest ware, a set of apostle spoons, um . . . what else, oh yes, a garnet ring, you know, the one set in yellow gold?"

"Did you get full price for that?"

Xanthe pulled a face as she cracked eggs into a bowl. "They beat me down by twenty quid."

"Oh, well."

"And the little table you painted white. A woman from the college bought that. She was very pleased with it."

"Sounds like quite a good day. Any beer left in that fridge?"

Xanthe opened her mouth to remind her mother that alcohol didn't help her arthritis but thought better of it. The tension eased, they ate omelettes and shared a bottle of local ale and talked of the shop and the new things Xanthe had found, some of which were downstairs, the rest to be delivered, and discussed the upcoming sale at Ditton. Flora quickly tired, and after supper she put up no resistance to being settled on the velvet sofa in the sitting room in front of the television. Xanthe explained she was popping out for a few groceries before the supermarket shut. She left her mother sitting in relative comfort, picked up her precious book, and hurried toward The Feathers.

Xanthe made a point of doing her bit of essential shopping on her way, knowing that she couldn't risk leaving it until later. She had to put her mother first. She raced around the supermarket snatching up fresh soups, bread, fish, and some tempting puddings. She remembered milk and sugar, beginning to wish she had brought her mother's wheeled bag, and then continued on her way to the pub. As she was going in, she met Liam coming out.

"Hey, Xanthe. Long time no whatsit."

She smiled. "I've been . . ."

". . . busy?"

"Away."

"Again?"

"Buying stuff for the shop."

"So, not another trip to Milton Keynes?"

Xanthe registered the mention of the specific place. It reminded her he had been complicit in some of the white lies she had had to tell Flora in the past. She had never fully explained all the strange requests for help she had made of him only a few months before. He had been good enough not to press her, even when he had had the chance to, but she sensed his patience was wearing thin.

"I'm sorry, really," she said.

He gestured at the pub. "Were you going for a drink? Will you let me buy you one?"

"Oh, thanks, no. I just needed a quick word with Harley."

"Are you singing this week?"

"Not sure yet." She knew she was being maddeningly evasive. She noticed Liam's naturally bright expression dim just a little. "Look, you have every right to be fed up with me."

"I'm not. Well, maybe a bit . . ."

"To be honest, I'm not good company right now. Mum's had a flare-up. Needs a bit of TLC." She raised her shopping bags by way of explanation.

Liam nodded. "Sorry to hear that." He paused, then added, "I did wonder if maybe you had someone else to think about right now."

"Sorry?" Xanthe's mind instantly pictured Samuel and then dismissed the possibility of Liam knowing anything about him.

"Your ex," he said. "Thought perhaps . . ."

"Marcus? You thought I was seeing him again?"

"Well, him turning up here, like that . . ."

"God, no. There is nothing left between us."

"Sure about that?"

"Completely."

"Not sure he is."

"He's been writing more songs. For me. He wanted me to sing with the band again."

"But you know that would be a bad idea, right?"

"Of course. Look, forget about Marcus. His life is in London, and that suits me fine."

Liam shook his head slowly. "I don't want to be the bearer of bad news but I saw him coming out of the off-license at lunchtime."

"What? Damn!"

"Looks like there's still unfinished business, at least as far as he's concerned."

"I can't be responsible for what Marcus does or does not think, but believe me, I have no interest in him whatsoever."

"Great. As long as you're not thinking about him, I'm not thinking about him."

"Our minds are both Marcus-free then."

"Not that I ever really had anything to worry about," Liam said with exaggerated swagger, turning up the collar of his jacket and standing tall. "Why would I?"

"Absolutely no reason," Xanthe agreed, and found herself wondering how different her life might have been if she had met Liam a few years back instead of Marcus.

Liam laughed and shoved his hands in the pockets of his old leather jacket. He looked at her differently then, his expression for once serious. "I've missed you," he said simply, and then, before she could respond, he went on, "Come and have a cuppa with me. I know you're busy, but just give me ten minutes?"

Xanthe fought frustration at not being able to get to speak to Harley. However much she liked Liam, she couldn't talk to him about the Spinners. She just couldn't be sure he'd understand. At least Harley had a declared interest in such things. It had to be him. At that moment, however, with Liam still looking at her the way he was, it was hard to say no to him. And anyway, she had to be a proper friend to him. It wasn't fair to keep leaning on him and then being so unavailable, so distracted, so busy all the time. Friendship was a two-way thing.

"Ten minutes," she agreed.

Liam grinned, taking her bags and leading her along the pavement and around the corner to his workshop. They went up the narrow stairs to his flat, which, while scruffy, was reasonably clean if not particularly tidy. Xanthe had to admit to herself that at least he managed to keep fresh milk in the fridge, which was more than she did most of the time. She sat down at the small kitchen table. Liam set about making tea, passing her the biscuit tin to dig into while he switched on the kettle.

"I recommend the shortbread," he told her, dropping tea bags into mugs. "You look like you could do with a bit of feeding up."

"Um. thank you?"

"Not that you're skinny."

"OK . . ."

"I mean, you're just right," he said, raising his arms and then dropping them in a gesture of exasperation. "This is not going how I'd hoped."

"Oh, and what had you in mind?"

"Me making witty remarks, you impressed, laughing, despite your natural inclination to cynicism."

"There you go again with the compliments."

He threw her a despairing glance.

"I'll just eat the shortbread," she said, taking a biscuit.

Tea made, Liam sat down opposite her, placing the mugs on the table. "Milk no sugar, right? See, I remember the important little things."

"So you do."

"So, I take it you are definitely not going to sing in Marcus's band again?" he asked suddenly.

"What? No." She dunked her biscuit in the steaming tea. "Although, I have to admit, him suggesting it did make me realize how much I miss being part of a band. Miss performing with other people."

"But you are singing again. You don't need him."

"I'm singing on my own. I never expected to end up being a soloist."

Liam smiled.

"Well, that is easily solved."

"It is?"

"Come and sing with Tin Lid." He leaned forward, his face lit up with the thought of what he was offering. "I have a band. You need a band. Join my band. And Marcus can sod right off."

"You haven't thought this through. I might not be a good fit for your band. What about the other band members? Don't you think you should discuss it with them before asking me? They might hate the idea. We might sound terrible together!"

"You and I sounded pretty good in my van, I seem to recall," he reminded her.

Xanthe hesitated, feeling herself tempted, unsure of the possible commitment. "It might be a disaster," she said.

"We'll never know unless we try, will we?"

Xanthe sat back in her chair and pushed her hair out of her eyes. "It's sweet of you, Liam."

"No, it isn't. I'm not sweet. Seriously, I've heard you sing outside the van and without Neil Sedaka helping you. You'd be great for us. For Tin Lid. What have you got to lose?"

"My self-respect?"

"I'm not asking you because I feel sorry for you!"

"My reputation as a singer around here? I was just beginning to get known for what I do and how I sing. . . . This would have to be something completely different, unless your band wants to start playing stuff that's four hundred years old."

"One song. Come on. Next time we have a gig you can be a guest artist for one song. You can't be too chicken to try that, now, can you?" He grinned, helping himself to another biscuit and enjoying watching her come to the realization that she was going to say yes to the idea.

At last she smiled. Smiled at the thought of the possibility of being part of a band again. At the thought, in fact, of spending more time with Liam.

By the time Xanthe left Liam's flat it was past eight. Conscious of the fact that her mother would be wondering what had happened to her, and that she would need help getting to bed with her arthritis as bad as it was, she opted for a quick phone call to Harley as she walked home. She asked if she could see him later to have a chat about something connected with local ley lines. He must have picked up on the note of tension in her voice as he didn't question her further but simply told her to come after closing when they would have plenty of time to talk without being disturbed. It would be late, but she had told herself Flora would be settled in bed by then, so it would be easier for her to slip out for an hour. Ordinarily her mind would have been filled with thoughts of what she had agreed to with Liam. It was no small thing, to undertake to sing with a completely new group of musicians. She had only heard them play once, and while she remembered them being good, she wasn't even sure their styles would work properly together. Would they truly want her? It might be what Liam wanted, but the other band members might resent her taking center stage. As it was, the matter of the book on Spinners was taking up so much of her thoughts that the whole business of any upcoming performances receded in her mind. There would be time enough to worry about that when she met the other musicians and they had their first practice together. At that moment she had something altogether more difficult to fathom, and she needed Harley's help to do it. He had studied all manner of legends and folklore and local history; he might just be the one person she knew who could help her unravel the mysterious book. Could it be that somewhere in all those wild stories lay a workable system, a method by which she could travel back in time when she wanted to? When she needed to? She already felt a little better just knowing that she would have Harley to talk to about everything. Even so, she struggled to imagine exactly how she was going to begin talking out loud to another person about the fact that she knew what it meant to travel through time.

13

FLORA'S CONDITION WAS MUCH IMPROVED SO THAT SHE ONLY NEEDED MILD PAINKILLERS IN order to get through the business of climbing the stairs to her room and getting into bed that night. Even so, Xanthe was concerned about leaving her again. She had to make sure she could journey with more control; that she could travel confidently, rather than feeling like a passenger. She needed to know she could come home when she wanted. For both their sakes.

By the time she returned to the pub it was nearly midnight and a sharp frost glistened on the pavement under the low glow of the streetlights. As arranged, Xanthe let herself in through the back door of the pub. Harley called up from the cellar.

"Be with you now, hen. Just finishing up with the barrels. Go on through to the bar."

She did as he suggested, perching on a barstool, enjoying the peace and quiet of the empty pub, which somehow still held an echo of the energy of the busy evening.

"What'll ye have to drink?" Harley asked, appearing through the hatch behind the bar, dropping the trapdoor behind him.

"Coffee would be great."

He made a face. "After the day I've had? I need something a wee bit stronger. And so do you, by the look of you, if you don't mind me saying so." He fetched two brandy balloons from their high hooks and drew doubles from the best brandy among the bottles suspended within handy reach. He came round to sit on the stool next to Xanthe and they silently toasted each other.

"That's wonderful, Harley. Good idea."

"Aye, one of my better ones," he agreed, swirling the dark brandy around in the ample glass. "I saw that fella of yours earlier today."

Xanthe waited, for a moment not sure if he meant Marcus or Liam, struck by the fact that neither of them was, in fact, her fella.

Harley went on, "Aye, he looked a bit worse for wear, if you know what I mean?"

So, Marcus.

"He's not my anything," she said.

"Thought he'd have taken himself back off to the big smoke by now."

"He can be . . . stubborn."

"Is that right? So, is it ridding yourself of the man you were wanting help with?" he asked.

Xanthe shook her head and reached into her bag. She took out *Spinners* and placed the book on the bar in front of Harley.

"I wanted to talk to you about this," she said, leaving the statement hanging, saying as little as possible, wanting to gauge his response.

Harley frowned at the book, his bushy eyebrows converging in scrutiny and concentration. He took another swig of his drink and then set the glass down. He didn't pick up the book, he just put his hand on it. It was a gesture almost of reverence.

"Have you seen this before?" Xanthe asked.

"I have not. But I have heard tell of it. Where'd you get it?"

"It was in with a bunch of other books. Along with Mr. Morris's stock that we bought when we bought the shop." There was another silence. It was as if they were both testing each other out, treading warily. Xanthe broke first. "Do you know what it's about? What the Spinners are? What they do?"

Harley was still gazing at the book as he replied to her question. "When I first moved here from Scotland I quickly became interested in the history of the place, as you know. It wasn't only the social history that I was into; it was the local myths, the legends, the stories. Some of those were well known. Others, they were spoken of in whispers," he said, lowering his own voice.

"So, who was it told you about the Spinners?"

"We had a regular customer, used to prop up the bar of The Feathers every night for an hour or so. Not a heavy drinker, but always a wee bit away with the fairies, if you catch my meaning. He came with the pub, more or less. Other regulars used to laugh at him a bit, telling me he was known to be soft in the head, but harmless enough." He shrugged. "Being a publican you get accustomed to forming opinions of people for yourself and, rightly or wrongly, those opinions are made based on how folks are when they are in here, often after they've had a dram or two. A barman listens to all manner of nonsense and bull dung. Goes with the job."

"But this man spoke a very specific kind of nonsense?"

Harley nodded. "Aye, he did. Rambled on about special people who could move through time, backward and forward. Said they looked like normal people, that you couldn't tell who was one," here he paused and then moved his gaze from the book to look at Xanthe, "even if they were right in front of you," he added pointedly.

Xanthe looked away, sipping her brandy. "But you never read anything about them? Not when you were reading up about ley lines and ghosts and stuff like that? I mean, I've read quite a lot of books about legends and ghosts and stuff like that, but I haven't come across anything mentioning the Spinners. Or this book. And it's not written as a textbook. There are no instructions or factual accounts. Just stories. All about different people and different times. Don't you think it's odd you've never found anything written down about them, not with all your research?"

"A secret society doesn't go about broadcasting its own existence, now, does it?"

"You've never mentioned them before."

"We've not known each other long, hen. You have to work up to that level of crazy."

"Is that what you think they were, though? Apart from crazy, I mean. An organized group, not just a bunch of random individuals?"

"No, I don't think that's what they *were*, hen. I think that's what they *are*."

"Yes, I think so too," she said, not quite picking up on what he said. Instead she opened the book, leafing through it to find a relevant passage. "Here, listen to this: *'She had not yet been fully accepted into the order. . . .'* Though it doesn't actually give it a name. And here, again: *'After returning from his third journey he was admitted into the fold, acknowledged as belonging wholly and properly. . . .'* It's a bit obscure but it does suggest some sort of organized group or society, don't you think?"

"Oh, aye, it does."

"So how does anyone get chosen for it? What are the requirements for members? I just wish it made things plainer. It's supposed to be really important, like the Spinner's bible, I was told!"

Harley narrowed his eyes at her. "Who told you, lassie?"

Xanthe hesitated. "I can't really explain. Just someone who knows a bit about these things."

"So why are you here talking to me instead of them?"

She took another gulp of her brandy, studying the book again, opting for a silent response. She wanted so much to fully confide in Harley, to share everything so that she didn't have to deal with it all herself anymore. But it was a big thing to talk about. Did she know him well enough? Would he understand? Would he even believe her?

Harley didn't seem surprised that she was reluctant to give an answer to his question. He tried another tack. "A bible, ye say? Well now, I'm no religious scholar and have ne been to church since Annie marched me up the aisle, but as I recall the Bible is all stories, and that's a rule book of sorts, is it not? The answers you need are in those tales somewhere, you just have to find them."

"But how? I mean, the stories, the drawings, they are all so . . . I don't know, random. How am I supposed to make sense of it? I mean, listen to this bit. . . . *'She had traveled so very many times before it had become second nature to her. Her first faltering steps as a Spinner were but distant memories. Her early fears and apprehensions faded. Now she could spin with confidence, with faith in her own abilities and skill forged in the furnace of costly experience.'* What cost?"

"I do not like the sound of that," Harley murmured.

"It would be helpful to hear what mistakes this girl made, but there's nothing more written about her story, not before this point. Some of the drawings make sense, like here, look, this seems to be a map of the south of England, don't you think?" She chose a page and angled the book so he could better see the image.

Harley leaned in, narrowing his eyes. "May I take a look?"

When Xanthe nodded he put down his glass and carefully took the book from her. He turned the pages slowly, his eyes widening as he scanned the text. "Astonishing! I could spend all night reading this." He glanced up at her. "But you won't want to let it out of your sight, eh? Don't fret, hen. I'd be reluctant to part with such a thing myself."

She shook her head. "When I think how close I came to throwing it out . . . Now I couldn't bear to part with it. I . . . I don't think I should."

"That's understandable. How would you feel about me photocopying some of the pages? Not the whole thing, but a chunk maybe? That way I could be getting some of it read and putting my mind to it."

"Great idea."

They left the bar and went upstairs to a tiny room in the accommodation above the pub. There was a desk sagging slightly beneath the weight of box files, in-boxes, paperwork, and so on. Harley muttered about neither he nor his wife having much time for admin as he cleared a path to the printer and put paper into it. "Right, which bit shall we start with, hen? Which story do you think is the most enlightening?"

"I wish I knew. There's one about a man who spins for the first time and ends up getting stuck for ages in the past. That might contain a few 'how-not-to' moments. And there's another about an elderly woman who traveled all the time, like she was taking a bus. That one makes it all look straightforward. I don't suppose there's much point doing the maps, though there is one that has marks on it that look suspiciously like ley lines. You'd be the best person to make sense of that."

As she flicked through the book and selected the right page she felt Harley tense slightly. It was only then she realized she was giving herself away. She had told him simply that she was trying to find out about the book. Or possibly the Spinners in theory. What she had just said suggested she wanted to apply what she could learn in real life. She closed the lid of the scanner gently onto the opened book. "Can you switch it on?" she asked, looking up at him.

To her relief Harley said nothing. He merely leaned across and pressed the buttons required to get the scanner going. There was a soft whirring as the machine sprang into action. They waited, watching the flash of light beneath the lid. Harley put his hand out to catch the copy as it was fed out of the printer. He turned it over in his hand. It was completely blank. Xanthe felt a chill wriggle down her spine. She and Harley exchanged glances.

"Nothing," he grumbled. "I'll bet the bloody thing is out of ink. Let me get to it."

She stepped aside to let him squeeze by, happy for him to check, but knowing somehow that ink was not the problem. Harley muttered oaths under his breath and put in fresh cartridges. She glanced at the doorway, hoping Annie would not become curious about all the late-night activity in her office and come to see what they were up to. It was hard enough explaining and yet not explaining things to Harley. She knew she wouldn't be able to talk about it to anyone else. At last he declared the ink replenished and set the thing to scan and copy again.

Still the pages came out blank.

Harley scratched his beard. "Well, I'll be . . ."

"Let's try this," Xanthe suggested, holding up her phone. They repositioned the book flat on the desk and she photographed a page. But the picture didn't take; the screen merely showed a blurred grayness.

Harley gave a low whistle.

"Come away back to the bar, lassie. I don't know about you, but I need another drink."

Back downstairs Xanthe perched on a barstool again, putting her hand over her glass when Harley tried to refill it.

"I'm confused enough as it is," she told him. She felt disturbed by the strange behavior of the seemingly normal book. She set it down between them on the bar again, sensing that Harley was waiting for her to speak. They had both just witnessed something impossible. She saw that this was a moment she hadn't planned for, but that she could not afford to pass up on. Harley would never be more prepared to believe what she needed to share with him than he was at that precise moment. She chose her words cautiously. "You know what you heard about the Spinners, well, now that you've seen how weird this book is . . . do you think some of what's written in it might be more than just stories?"

"Are you asking me do I believe there are some people who can time travel like Doctor bloody Who?"

Still she could not look at him but focused on the book in front of her, watching the low light of the room glint on the gilded lettering. "Yes," she said at last, "that's exactly what I'm asking."

"Oh? And what might these folk use for a Tardis, d'you reckon? Maybe an old, tumbled-down blind house?"

Xanthe's heartbeat echoed against her eardrums and she wished she hadn't let her nerves dictate the speed with which she had gulped her brandy earlier. She had underestimated her friend's interest in what she had already told him about the blind house. She had not credited him with a mind so quick he was already making connections between the merely bizarre and the plainly impossible. She tried to keep her voice level as she responded.

"Do you remember you showed me we have a point of convergence of two ley lines in our garden?" she asked.

"Aye. And I recall you wanting answers to questions regarding things that go bump in the night around here, not to mention taking a rare interest in that wee stone shed of yours."

"I guess that's what I'm after now: answers."

Harley drained his glass and wiped his mouth with the back of his hand. "Well then, hen, you'd best start asking the right questions. Or is it that you're wanting me to do that for ye? Would you be waiting for me to come right out and ask, bold as brass, is that what you think you might be, lassie? Are you telling me that you yourself are a real, live, bona fide, walking, breathing, back-to-the-future, eat-your-heart-out-H.-G.-Wells, time-traveling Spinner?"

There it was. The question, spoken out loud by someone as solid and real as anyone could be. The question Xanthe had to answer not just in the madness of the seventeenth century, but right there, in her own time. She hesitated, knowing that once said, once admitted to someone in her new life in Marlborough, there was no going back. She felt a little frightened, and more than a little bonkers. But more than that, she felt a mixture of excitement and relief. Relief that she wouldn't have to carry such an enormous secret alone anymore. And excitement, because Harley might just be the one person who could help her understand her gift. Maybe even master it.

She took a slow, deep breath, summoned up a bright smile and looked him square in the face.

"Yes," she said. "That is exactly what I'm telling you. I am a Spinner."

"And you've actually done it? Full-blown whizzing through the centuries? Actually traveling through time?"

"Yes," she said, beginning to laugh now, hearing how completely insane their conversation sounded, and yet knowing it all to be true. "Yes, I have."

"Christ on a bike!" Harley exclaimed before snatching up their glasses and heading for the optics again. "Don't you move an inch from that bar-stool, hen. This calls for another brandy, and I'll not take no for an answer. And then you are going to tell me everything!"

"I don't think you could handle hearing everything," she said, "and I'm pretty sure I couldn't handle telling it all either."

"But this is momentous, hen! Something truly wondrous." He took the stool beside her and handed her the glass. "I'm a wee bit jealous, I don't mind telling you."

"You shouldn't be. It's not been easy. At times it's been terrifying. Not to mention having to lie to my mother about it all."

"Flora knows nothing?"

"She wasn't keen on my going to Milton Keynes for the weekend; how would that conversation go, do you reckon. 'Bye, Mum, I'm just popping off through a portal to the seventeenth century where I may or may not end up burned as a witch because someone sees me appear out of nowhere. Don't wait up.' And anyway, she has enough to worry about right now."

"But still you went? You took the risk?"

"I had to. Mum was being threatened . . . does the name Margaret Merton mean anything to you?"

It was a long night, with so much to tell. Harley had endless questions and was reluctant to let her go at all. Eventually Xanthe had to insist. She was worried about Flora, anxious to be there if she woke up in pain again. And besides, it was curiously draining, unburdening herself, unloading all the details of her journeys back to the sixteen hundreds, trying to help Harley understand, and allowing him time to occasionally mutter oaths or gasps of amazement. She swore him to secrecy, mildly offending him for so much as suggesting he would not keep such a thing to himself. She knew he would hold her confidence tight and close. Later that night, as she lay in her own bed, fighting off her now customary sadness at having left Samuel, she recognized that she did feel somehow calmer. Somehow reassured. She had not, until recently, understood the loneliness a secret can inflict upon its keeper. At last she had someone she could talk to about all the incredible things that were happening to her. And it helped. At last she slept, and this time she was not disturbed by dark dreams or troubling visions.

The next morning Xanthe took her mother to the surgery for an assessment and a session with the physiotherapist. Flora insisted she didn't wait for her but return to the shop. Xanthe didn't fight against her wishes. She knew from long experience that her mother would not want her hanging around in waiting rooms. She also knew the best thing she could do for her was to take care of the business. She went back to the shop and had it open before Mr. Morris's ormolu clock chimed ten. While she was finding places to display some of the emergency stock she had bought in a hurry in Devizes, Gerri came in, carrying a basket, and accompanied by her daughter, Ellie.

"Hello." Xanthe smiled at the little golden-haired girl, who was blessed with her mother's large eyes. "No school today?"

"I've got a tiger," she said with all seriousness. "If you've got a tiger you're not allowed to go in."

Xanthe raised her eyebrows at Gerri.

"Impetigo," she explained, pointing discreetly at the small patch of slightly red skin on her daughter's cheek. "Completely harmless but very infectious, so she can't go to school. Needs another day, apparently."

Xanthe nodded, marveling at the way a five-year-old's mind worked. The word "impetigo" sounded to the child like "tiger" and the patch did look a bit like a stripe. That was logic enough for Ellie.

"I saw you helping Flora into your cab," Gerri said. "She did look a bit poor. Thought you might need a pick-me-up." She lifted the gingham cloth on her basket to reveal a glorious Victoria sponge, freshly baked and stuffed full of homemade strawberry jam and whipped cream.

Xanthe smiled, amused at how different Gerri's idea of a pick-me-up was from Harley's. "That looks fantastic!" she said, taking the basket. "Mum will be back before lunch. She'll love it, thank you."

"Oh, it's no trouble. I was whipping up a batch . . ." She hesitated, waiting until she could see her daughter was busy examining an old tin watering can, and then went on, keeping her voice low, "And how about you, Xanthe? Are you OK?"

"I'm fine, really. Mum and me, we are pretty practiced at dealing with flare-ups."

"Even so, it can't be easy."

"They pass. How's the tea shop going?" she asked, hoping to steer the topic of conversation away from herself.

"Good. Or it would be, if I didn't have a problem with the dishwasher. Wretched thing keeps breaking down, usually at the busiest moment. I've got someone coming in to have a look at it tomorrow."

"Hats off to you, running a business on your own. It's hard enough with two of us. And you have the little ones to look after."

"Thank God for grandparents and playdates. And the fact that both Tommy and Ellie like helping me out in the cafe. Chocolate brownies are good currency when bargaining with children. How is your lovely shop doing? Are you ready for your first Christmas?"

"I wish. We are still woefully short of stock."

"Even after your trip to Bristol?"

"Oh, I didn't find much there. Actually, I'm going to a pop-up antiques fair in Ditton tomorrow."

"Oh, that sounds like fun; digging around in all those interesting boxes, browsing the stalls. . . . I bet there will be some good china there."

"I can keep an eye out for suitable things for you, if you like."

"Yes, please," said Gerri. "I wish I could come myself."

"I'd be happy to have you, if you fancy it. We would be back by lunchtime, so you'd only have to shut up shop for a couple of hours. . . ."

"Oh, it would have been so nice to have some time off, but I've got the repairman coming tomorrow. I daren't leave him on his own. Got to get the wretched thing fixed."

"Next time there's a fair somewhere close by I'll give you the heads-up. A bit more warning."

"Lovely. And Ells should have gotten rid of her tiger by then and be back at school, shouldn't you, darling?" she asked her daughter.

Ellie had found a small, framed print of a bumblebee and pointed to it excitedly. "Look, mummy."

"Oh, that's one of your favorites, isn't it. Why don't you tell Xanthe what you call it?"

The little girl grinned. "It's a fuzzy buzzy pom-pom!"

Xanthe laughed. "That is a much better name for him."

Gerri took Ellie by the hand and led her toward the door. "Come along, we've got some scones to bake."

As Xanthe watched them walk back across the little cobbled street to the cafe she admitted to herself it would have been nice to have some company on the outing. Having unburdened herself to Harley there was nothing more she could do about going back to help Samuel. For now, she had to concentrate on the shop. Gerri's enthusiasm for the antiques fair would have helped with that.

As the day passed, Xanthe thought more and more about her conversation with Harley. Talking to him had helped clarify in her own mind some of the more confusing aspects of her recent experiences. Each time she thought about Samuel she told herself she could go back, she could see him again, she could make sure he was safe, but only when Flora was settled again and when she was sure she had more control over her journeys through time. She had to be certain she could come back when she wanted to, and that she wouldn't accidentally travel again. She had to be more able to control the where and when of her movements through time. In short, she had to become a better Spinner, and quickly. She took whatever moments there were during the afternoon to read more of *Spinners*. She felt conflicted by the fact that the shop was so busy. They needed customers, that was the plain truth of the matter, but somehow selling things, frivolous, largely unnecessary things, didn't seem anywhere near as important or urgent as learning all she had to know about what it meant to be a Spinner.

The next day was bright and cold, making Xanthe rub her hands together as she made her way to where her taxi was parked. Flora had returned from the doctor's the previous day tired and still uncomfortable but more able to manage her symptoms and definitely less panicked, insisting she would make the next bell-ringing session. Each time her condition got the better of her there was the underlying worry that this would be the time she did not regain as much mobility as she had had before. Each time she, and Xanthe, feared this was the start of an unstoppable downward lurch. Having been reassured and helped by the physiotherapist, however, and having accepted a slight increase in her medication from her doctor, things were looking considerably brighter. By the time Xanthe had cooked her supper she agreed she would not be up to going to the fair but insisted she would be more than capable of managing the shop for the morning. Not for the first time, Xanthe experienced the small high of relief at another episode survived, another setback in her mother's health weathered, with the prognosis not as bleak as they had both secretly feared. Now she could at least in part enjoy her trip out. She was doing something constructive for the business and for Flora, she was doing something straightforward and normal, giving her head a rest from the enormity of the Spinners, and distancing herself from the idea of Samuel. She repeated a silent mantra: it's impossible and he has someone else, move on. At first it sounded like the words of a wise friend, but gradually she was beginning to listen to what she knew was her own, sensible voice.

When she reached her cab she found the windscreen was heavily frosted and she knew it would take the aged heating system a while to clear it. She settled behind the wheel and turned the key in the ignition. The car made a feeble attempt to start, the engine spluttering. She stopped and tried again. There was the sound of the system turning over, but not sparking. At the third attempt the battery began to fade.

"Damn it!" For a moment Xanthe considered abandoning the trip, but they badly needed the stock. She couldn't be beaten by something as simple as the car not starting. It might just be the battery and could be fixed quickly and then she'd be on her way. There was only one person to go to for this. With a sigh, she locked the car and headed for Liam's workshop.

As she walked through the gates to his yard she could hear a radio playing and tuneful whistling. The doors to the workshop were open. There were several cars in various stages of repair, and Xanthe recognized the shape of Liam's beloved sports car under its cover in the far corner. The smell of oil and petrol and old smoky engines was powerful. She tracked the source of the whistling and spied Liam's booted feet sticking out from beneath an old Land Rover. As the song on the radio changed to something Christmassy Liam switched from whistling to singing. For a moment Xanthe stood and listened, enjoying the sound of his voice. He shifted on his trolley beneath the vehicle and Xanthe took a step back, her foot connecting with a can of grease that clanked loudly as it toppled onto a set of span-ners. She hurried to right it. Liam scooted out from under the car, smiling up at her.

"Well, well," he said, "look who's sneaking around my workshop."

"I was not sneaking," she insisted, staring at the gray-green grease that now coated her hands.

Liam stood up. He was wearing somewhat threadbare overalls, his face smudged with dirt and oil. He put down the wrench he had been using and took a rag from his back pocket, handing it to Xanthe.

"It's early in the day for a social call," he said. "Not that I'm complaining. Kettle at the ready, as ever."

"Business, not social."

"Yeah?" As she passed him back the rag he took hold of her hand and rubbed at a grease spot. "Missed a bit," he said.

"My car won't start."

"Oh, poor baby!" he said. Xanthe was pretty certain he was referring to the car rather than her.

"It turns over, just about, but can't spark up. I've tried it a few times but I'm just flattening the battery."

"Has she done this before?"

"Not recently. I did have some trouble with the starter motor a while back, but I had that fixed."

"Yeah, but fixed by who and in what way? Gotta watch out for cowboy mechanics, you know. They promise you perfection, charge you the earth, then just clean a few plugs or connections and work a temporary fix."

"He did say it would need replacing. One day."

"Ah. Could be that day has come. Might be tricky finding a replacement. They've been out of production a while. . . ."

"This is not what I need to hear. I was on my way to an antiques fair in Ditton." She glanced at her watch. "Do you think you could come and take a look at her for me? Now, if you're not too busy?"

"I could, but if it is the starter motor you won't be going anywhere in your gorgeous old girl today." Liam thought for a moment and then said, "Tell you what, how about I drive you to Ditton, bring you back with your purchases, and then I can take a look at the taxi? Once I know what the problem is I can start hunting down a new part, if that's what's needed."

"Oh no, I couldn't . . ."

"Oh yes, you could."

"But you're busy . . ."

"Nothing that can't wait. Besides, I've never been to an antiques fair in Ditton, and my horoscope this morning said I should keep myself open to new experiences."

Xanthe smiled. "You are a star," she said.

"Give me a minute to clean up so I can properly shine." He unzipped his overalls and disappeared into a small office that was built into the corner of the workshop.

Xanthe wandered around the drafty space, which was fairly crammed with cars and tools but still reasonably tidy. On the workbench, floor, and shelving units, the tools and tires and stacks of oil cans each seemed to have a proper place, and everything appeared to be well looked after. She picked up a badge that had come off a vintage Jaguar, running her thumb over the smooth, glossy chrome. She could hear Liam whistling again and turned to find that there was a window into the office. Through it she could see him. He had removed his overalls and was standing at a sink, running the taps. In a quick, fluid movement he pulled his T-shirt off over his head. His body was well muscled, making Xanthe wonder if he went to the gym. She didn't think anyone could get a body that fit just by working on cars. She realized how little she really knew about him. As he washed the oil off his hands and strong arms she noticed his tattoo. Standing at a distance she could not make out the detail but could see what looked like a classic sports car cleverly worked into a design of roses and thorns that centered just above his heart, reaching up across his shoulder and partway down one arm. As he was splashing water over his neck and chest, droplets coursing down his skin to the waistband of his jeans, he looked up and saw Xanthe watching him. He stopped whistling, his expression showing surprise but not a trace of self-consciousness.

Xanthe realized she was staring at him. Flustered, she turned away, feigning intense interest in a socket set on the workbench.

Moments later Liam emerged from the office shrugging on his old jacket over a clean T-shirt. "Right," he said, "let's get going."

"Um, we might not get many antiques in that sports car of yours," Xanthe pointed out.

"Don't worry, I have just the girl for us." He led the way outside to the far end of the yard. "Isn't she a little beauty?" he asked, indicating with a flourish the bright orange vintage Volkswagen camper van parked there. "Found her at an auction in Bristol a while back. Bodywork needs some time and effort, but mechanically she's sound. Popular things, these. Should turn a good profit on her. And roomy as you like. Come on."

Much to Xanthe's surprise the old camper started right up and they were soon zipping along the main road out of Marlborough. She was happy to feel the familiar slight tension in her stomach the anticipation of a treasure hunt brought on. She glanced sideways at Liam, the image of his half-stripped body still vivid.

"So, do you belong to a gym?" she asked.

He laughed. "God no. Terrible places." He paused and then added, "I have a set of weights in the workshop. When business is quiet I work out there. No posers or gym bunnies to deal with. How about you? I don't see you as the gym-loving type, somehow."

"I'm not sure how to take that! But you're right. If I get the time I'd rather walk up to the white chalk horse. Spend an hour marching about outdoors. Not that I've had much time for that lately, what with the shop, and Mum. . . ."

"How is she?"

"Up and down. Every time I think this is it, she's not going to get better. But every time she does. This time will be no different. I can already see her getting her strength back. She'll be fine, it just takes a little time."

"No siblings to come and help out?"

"Just me. How about you?"

"I'm a lonely only too," he smiled. "Not that I ever was. Lonely, I mean. My dad gave me my passion for cars. He has a BMW dealership in Salisbury. I practically grew up in the workshop. It was him got me my first apprenticeship as a mechanic. He was stoked when I set up my own workshop."

"I bet." She hesitated and then went on, "So, single guy with his own business, lead guitar in a band, not to mention a fine . . ."

He grinned. "A fine . . . ?"

"... selection of cars," she continued, pulling a face, "I'm surprised the local lovelies aren't falling at your feet."

"Who says they're not?" he laughed. "OK, they're not. Well, only sometimes. The band thing is a bit of a pull, not gonna lie. You must know that."

"Surely Marlborough is far too genteel and respectable to have groupies!"

"You'd be surprised."

"Right about that. And you never found a special one? One that mattered?"

"What? And give up all that breathless adulation from my screaming fans? Oh, here we are. Ditton in all its unvarnished splendor."

The village turned out to be an underwhelming collection of houses, set mostly along a short stretch of busy main road. Xanthe thought there was something familiar about it but could not recall ever having been there before. The shop and run of bungalows themselves did not strike any chords. The village hall made a good venue for the sale, being easy to find with ample parking. As Liam swung the VW into a space Xanthe was pleased to see most of the other vehicles were private cars, not vans or pickups belonging to dealers. She badly needed a few bargains and quality finds. When they entered through the double swing doors it was to find a happy buzz of browsers, mostly local people and a few tourists.

"What's the plan?" Liam asked as they went inside.

"A quick browse to see what's what, try and spot any gems. Single out the best stalls, then closer inspection."

"All the while not letting on your trade, I'm guessing."

"For as long as possible."

"Are you looking for anything in particular?"

"Nothing too huge or too expensive. Steady sellers. Things that would make good Christmas presents. Stuff Mum can get excited about."

Liam let out a low whistle at the sight of so many stalls all stuffed full of antiques and collectibles. "This," he said quietly, "is alien territory to me. Place is full of antique women!"

Xanthe gave him a little shove. "Come on, or all the best pieces will be snapped up. And I've promised Gerri a box of china, so you could look out for some of that if you feel like it."

"China, it is," he said, marching into the crowd with a determined step.

Xanthe scanned the room, her practiced eye dismissing tables of bric-a-brac and stands of heavily restored furniture. She was looking for quality so had to avoid cheap tat, and if Flora could add value by restoring an item, so much the better. No point paying for someone else to do what her mother could do so well. Xanthe strolled around the hall, making an initial sweep, keeping a mental note of interesting items and possible purchases. She noticed a couple of china stalls and made a note to hunt down some pieces for Gerri as she had promised. First, though, she needed to focus on treasures for the shop. One or two vendors greeted her enthusiastically, ready to draw her into a discussion about this little table or that glass lamp. She noticed Liam had stopped at a stand selling Victorian jewelry and was happily chatting with the rather attractive girl running it. Xanthe browsed on, investigating further, playing her cards close to her chest, even when she saw a beautiful Russian samovar that made her heart beat a tiny bit faster. It was best not to let her interest show too much. The price might be written on the tag, but the chance of beating the seller down dwindled in direct proportion to how much they believed the buyer truly wanted the item.

"It's a rare piece," a colorfully dressed woman said as she stepped out from a swathe of hanging kilims, a mug of coffee in hand. "And in fantastic condition," she added.

Xanthe smiled casually, turning the heavy samovar over while holding the lid firmly in place. There were marks of the maker and place of origin still clearly readable. It was silver plated, probably copper underneath, though it was hard to tell as the plate was still in a good state and not showing too much wear. Still, it was pricey, and the market for such a large piece was niche. She wondered, fleetingly, what would happen if an object from such a far-flung country sang to her. Would she be transported to St. Petersburg, perhaps? The thought was both exciting and terrifying. She was glad not to hear any of the telltale ringing. Nothing in the room seemed to carry that special connection. She had to admit to herself that she was thankful for that, this time. She had more than enough to cope with. It occurred to her that this might somehow register, somehow communicate itself. Could it be that a Spinner, when involved with an object and its story, when that mission was incomplete, could it be that she was unavailable to other found things in that way? As if she was taken, engaged in a task that she had not yet finished and so unable to take on another. She became aware that the seller was talking to her.

"Sorry?" she said, setting the samovar back down on the velvet-covered table.

"I was saying, it came from a family who moved here from Moscow two generations ago. The provenance is rock solid."

"It's lovely, but the price is a bit steep."

"It reflects the rarity of the piece. I haven't seen another one as beautifully worked as this in such good condition, have you?"

"Not recently."

The seller's expression altered minutely: she sensed another member of the trade.

"Where are you based?" she asked.

"Marlborough. It's a small premises, so I have to pick really carefully."

Now that the woman knew she was dealing with an industry professional her demeanor changed. She altered from friendly but ever-so-slightly patronizing to respectful but wary. She would now expect Xanthe to bargain hard, but there was also the possibility of selling her multiple items.

"What's your particular interest?" she asked. "I've some superb art nouveau bronzes and textiles."

And so the dance began. The vendor suggested things she thought might tempt her customer, while Xanthe parried her expensive selections, challenged the prices, and sidestepped the hard sell. She wasn't going to be pressured into paying too much, however lovely something was. On the other hand, the woman had a good eye and there were some intriguing pieces on offer. All that was required was that Xanthe get what she wanted for the right price.

"I don't want to blow the budget on one piece," Xanthe explained. "Oh, these are nice," she said, noticing a collection of small wooden items.

"Treen is always a good seller, don't you find?"

"Yes, if the piece is attractive." Xanthe could hear her mother's voice in her ear. *Inexpensive is not the same as cheap. Inexpensive is a bargain people are happy to get;*

cheap is low price for low quality. But the seller had a point. Treen was the name given to wooden household items, generally small ones, often kitchen based but not entirely. The word meant literally "of the tree" and tended to describe quite old antiques, as later versions of the same things would have been made from some sort of metal. Xanthe browsed through the selection. There was a snuffbox, a small chopping board, a mallet, three lace bobbins, and a salt box, which she picked up for a closer look. She ran her thumb across the surface of the lid. The close grain of the wood had been burnished over the years, worn smooth with use and polishing. The hinges were simple and small. There was a wooden bracket at the top, all cut from a single piece of wood that formed the back, so that the box could be hung on the wall above the fireplace to keep the precious salt dry. It smelled faintly of beeswax and salt. It was wonderful to think of how many kitchens it might have found a home in over the years. Of how many dishes it had salted; a pinch for pastry, perhaps, a spoonful for soup, a small scoop for a slow-cooked stew.

The seller smiled. "Lovely, isn't it? Old pieces like that sit really well in modern rustic kitchens. People will pay a premium for the history now. They enjoy something that shows it was loved and valued."

Xanthe nodded. "Pity the hinges aren't original, though. That would certainly make it more valuable."

The seller shrugged, sipping her coffee. If she was annoyed at being outwitted she was too much the businesswoman to let it show. "I could do you a good price on the whole lot," she suggested.

"I'm not sure I could sell the snuffbox. Redwoods are out of fashion at the moment. I like the bobbins." She didn't add that she knew Flora would be able to repurpose them as light pulls without too much effort.

"Anything else take your fancy?" the seller asked. "Always happy to do a discount for trade, if the purchase is worthwhile."

Xanthe moved along the three tables that formed the stand. As she brushed past a hanging rug she detected the smell of woodsmoke and incense. Patchouli and vetivers, she decided, conjuring at once a picture of the bohemian hippie home it might have inhabited. She rejected a stack of pretty quilts, reasoning that they would most likely require mending and cleaning. Sewing was not her mother's strong point now that her hands troubled her, and dry-cleaning would add to the final sale price of the items. The more Xanthe looked the more interesting finds revealed themselves, though still nothing that sang. For once it was a relief to simply enjoy the treasure hunt. She knew she would have to buy the silver-topped ebony cane the minute she spotted it, and could not hide her delight in a pair of small Staffordshire poodles in creamy-white china, their black eyes and noses and red collars still bright and their topiary tails perfectly intact. It became clear the samovar was too much of an outlay for one piece; she would do better to take a selection of good sellers.

It took a further half hour of offer and counteroffer, of negotiation and refusal, of air being sucked through teeth and heads being shaken until at last a deal was done. The two women shook hands, both ultimately pleased with the bargain that was struck. As the seller wrapped Xanthe's purchases, Liam came to stand beside her.

"How goes the treasure hunt?" he asked.

"Very well." Xanthe gestured at the pile of stock she had acquired. "Pretty much done."

"All from the same stall?"

"It works like that sometimes, if the seller has similar taste to ours. Now I just need to choose some china for Gerri and then we can go."

"I have not been idle. There are two stalls selling china. Follow me," he told her, clearly pleased with his own little bit of successful hunting.

Xanthe drew a blank with the first vendor but the second had some quality stock.

"That's nice," she whispered to Liam, pointing at a matching cup, saucer, and plate in chalky white with deep red roses on it.

"Don't you need a proper set? Where's the rest of it?"

"It's called a trio. Better buying them like this, so we get lots of different designs. It's a thing nowadays. People like to mix and match. These are Royal Albert. That one over there is probably Worcester."

"A trio," Liam muttered. "Who knew."

Xanthe selected two trios of Royal Albert china, the teacups a particularly pleasing shape, the Worcester, and two Laura Ashley. She struck a good deal on half a dozen breakfast plates too. They were not valuable, but in good condition and had an appealing bluebell design on them. She also found Gerri two large oval serving plates with sprigs of holly painted around the edges. It was easy to imagine them laden with freshly baked mince pies, making Xanthe suddenly realize how hungry she was.

With the china packed up and paid for, it was finally time to leave. As they crossed the room again, Xanthe's eye was caught by a stall partly hidden in the corner. It consisted entirely of rails of vintage clothing. She would dearly have loved to go and browse, to find things new to her for her own collection. She rarely shopped for clothes, and even from the other side of the room she could make out some gorgeous velvets and warm tweeds. She made herself resist, determined to keep her mind on business. Even so, a small idea began to take root in her mind, and she promised herself she would give it proper consideration later on. Together, she and Liam carted the found things out to the camper van. Xanthe felt a lightening of the weight upon her shoulders at the sight of all the new goodies she would be able to take back to her mother. Flora would be cheered by the new stock. The silver-topped walking stick needed some repair, as well as the Victorian footstool that would benefit from reupholstering. Her mother would approve of being able to add value, and both were things she could happily tackle, along with the bobbins. Most of the rest of the haul, including the poodles, the rest of the treen, two silver serving spoons, a string of jade beads, a box of assorted picture frames, and some colorful prints showing different varieties of roses, would all need nothing more than a bit of spit and polish.

As Xanthe settled Gerri's box of china onto the floor in the back of the VW, she glanced up through the window. She noticed a distinctive church spire in the distance. It took her a moment to recognize it. When she did she experienced a jolt of anxiety, a stab of fear for Samuel. It was St. Cyriac's church at Laybrook, which was only a couple of miles from Ditton. With the trees bare and the sky clear it was easily visible. Looking at it transported Xanthe right back to Rose and Adam's cottage in the village. To Esther Harris's house, where she had found the chocolate pot. To Laybrook Abbey. To Benedict Fairfax. To Samuel. She turned, determined to remain focused on what she was supposed to be doing. It was then she saw the pub at the bend in the road. It was nothing special in itself; there were any number of pubs in the area called The Swan, and this one, while clearly very old with timber frame and some black beams visible, was not particularly pretty. What chimed in Xanthe's memory, however, was its position, with the front door directly off the road. She remembered seeing it before, not in her own time. She had seen it with Samuel, on a journey from Marlborough to Great Chalfield. She was certain of it. Samuel had remarked not upon the pub—or inn as it then was—but the two unassuming cottages opposite it. One of them had been in the process of being built. It had no roof at that point, but was otherwise complete. She clearly recalled him telling her with unmasked pride that this was one of his commissions as an architect. He wanted to show her that he built more than jailhouses or extensions and improvements for rich nobles. This cottage had been commissioned by a kindly widow who had given up her Marlborough house to her son and his family and charged the Applebys with the task of designing and building a modest home for her to enjoy the countryside without being too far from town. Samuel had told her that as soon as he had finished the work he was then doing he would see that the cottage was finished. But Fairfax had called him away to work on the abbey and not allowed him out. The widow's little house would have had to have waited until after Xanthe had seen Samuel at the abbey. Until after Fairfax had released him from his tasks at the abbey and Samuel was again free to work elsewhere. She shut the door of the camper and crossed the road so that she could see the other side of it as it curved away from the pub. What she saw puzzled her. There was the neighboring cottage, a little older than Samuel's, still standing and still inhabited. Of the widow's cottage all that remained were a few stones of the original walls, overgrown with brambles and ivy. Xanthe tried to make sense of it. Perhaps it had fallen into disrepair and been pulled down. It was possible. Maybe there had been a fire. Or perhaps it had never been lived in at all; never been completed. A charge of icy fear shot through Xanthe's system as a terrible explanation for the disappearance of the cottage came to her. The shock of it must have shown on her face, as Liam peered at her with concern.

"You all right? You look rather shaky."

"Would you mind if we took a short detour, not go straight home, I mean?"

"Is anything wrong?"

"I just . . . I need to see something. To check something. In Laybrook. OK?" She was already climbing into the VW.

Liam hopped into the driver's seat. "Always happy to visit Laybrook," he said cheerfully, but his expression remained one of concern.

The journey to the village took less than five minutes. Xanthe had not the patience to use the car park and then walk in. She knew parking in the center was discouraged in order to leave room for residents, as well as to preserve the illusion of a timeless place. None of this mattered to her at that moment. There was something she had to do, and the more she thought about it the higher her anxiety levels rose. She directed Liam to a space at the side of the road, and without further explanation strode down the street and through the lych-gate at the entrance to the churchyard. The frost of earlier in the day had melted beneath the November sunshine so that the tombstones gleamed dully. Xanthe scrunched along the damp gravel path, moving quickly from the area of the churchyard where more recent burials had taken place, hurrying round the north end of the church, all the while searching for older headstones, squinting to read the faded inscriptions.

"Too new, too new, eighteenth century, nineteenth again . . ." she muttered to herself as she moved between the crooked rows of graves.

Liam caught up.

"Are you looking for something in particular? Can I help?"

"I don't know if this is the right place, or even if it would be here. . . . I'm not sure. It's just that . . . oh, these are earlier. Look, this one is 1699."

"Wow, some of these are pretty ancient. And very faded. Not surprising given that they are more than three hundred years old, I suppose. Bound to be heavily weathered."

There was a slightly damaged mausoleum which caught Xanthe's eye. It was the sort of thing a well-to-do family might pay for. She moved toward it, hardly daring to read the lichen-patched lettering.

"Watson," she read with relief. "Right date though," she said to Liam, pointing at the figures showing it to be the first half of the seventeenth century.

He leaned closer to read the inscription. "Must have cost a fair bit back then, I'd have thought. Were they rich, the people you are looking for?"

"Not rich, no, but successful. Comfortably off. Well regarded. At least, they were . . ." But had they remained so? If Fairfax had carried out his threat to have Samuel prosecuted, even if he had escaped the extreme fate of a traitor, he and his family would have fallen from grace entirely. In the end they would have more than likely had humble resting places.

And then she saw it. A modest headstone, leaning at a slight angle, set a short way apart from the rest of the monuments. She had to force herself to walk toward it, had to make herself step close enough to read the inscription. She knelt in front of the grave and rubbed at the moss that was obscuring some of the inscription. The letters were faded, patchy and worn, but still legible. She felt her heart tighten. She told herself it was nonsense to be so moved. Reminded herself sternly that of course Samuel was dead, and that accepting that was part of what it meant to have the gift—or the curse—of being able to spin time. Even so, it was beyond unsettling to stand in front of the grave of someone who meant so much to you.

Liam had come to stand beside her. In a soft voice he read the wording on the tombstone.

"'Here lies Samuel Appleby of Marlborough. Beloved son, cherished brother, a man of talent and a master builder. Delivered into the arms of our Lord . . .' Sounds as if he was well loved, don't you think? Xanthe?" Liam put his hand on her arm.

But Xanthe was no longer listening. As Liam had been reading she had found the courage to look at the headstone herself and to force herself to read Samuel's name. What she had not expected, what now caused her to have to quell a scream, was the date. In faint but clear numbers, the year of Samuel's death was carved into stone, waiting for her, unmistakable and horrifying: Spring 1606. He had not lived to a happy old age, had not enjoyed a long and successful life and career, had never married or raised a family. Had not, in fact, survived vengeful Fairfax. There was no avoiding the awful truth: according to this irrefutable evidence, Samuel had died only a matter of weeks after Xanthe had abandoned him to his fate.

14

SHE HAD TO GO BACK. XANTHE SAW NOW THAT SHE COULD NOT SIMPLY LEAVE WHATEVER it was the chocolate pot had taken her to. She had not completed her mission. The first time, when the chatelaine had sung to her, she had been challenged with rescuing Alice, and she had not stopped until she had achieved her goal. This time she had returned to her own era by mistake. She had left Samuel, and however much she was needed by her mother and her own life, he needed her more. She reminded herself that the things she did on her journeys back through time were crucial because they brought about the present as it should be. As it had to be. If she refused the call to action, if she failed in her task, things would never be right. She had not fully taken on board what this meant until now. Until she had stood in front of Samuel's grave. She had left things unfinished and this was the result. Not only had Samuel died young, but he had not lived the life he was supposed to have lived. The order of things had been upset, ripped apart. The cottage that he had shown her with such pride, had never been finished. It had never become the home it was meant to be, housed the gentle widow, survived as the neighboring cottage had, through the centuries. Because Samuel had not lived to complete it. What else had this rupture on the fabric of time resulted in? What other things, things she could not possibly know, had not happened or never existed because Fairfax had changed history? The effects would surely go beyond anything as simple as a cottage not being built. What about the people Samuel would have employed? Dear God, she thought, what of Samuel's descendants?

In that moment, reading the brutal truth of the date on his tombstone, realizing how far and wide the consequences of failing in her mission might be, Xanthe understood what it meant to be a Spinner. More than that, she understood that what she felt, her personal position in what she was called upon to do, mattered very little. There was far more at stake than her feelings. There was an obligation for her to use her gift, to do her duty. She had to go back.

Once again, Liam had shown himself to be a sensitive friend. It must have been obvious that Xanthe was upset, but he did not press her for an explanation. During the drive back to Marlborough he kept up a harmless chatter in an attempt to calm Xanthe and to show she didn't have to explain herself. Xanthe's mind was whirring. She felt furious with herself. She had believed Samuel would be all right because she was overcome with managing her own life. She had not allowed herself to think Fairfax might have killed him or had him killed because she could not see what she could do to prevent it. Refusing to look at the truth was no longer an option. She would have to go back to Samuel's time and she would have to do so straightaway. Which meant dreaming up more lies to tell her mother. It also meant leaving Flora when her health was not yet returned to its best strength, and the business needed her. The thought of such shoddy treatment of the person who meant the world to her caused Xanthe physical pain, but she had no alternative. If she did not go back, Samuel would die young and die violently, one way or another, at the hands of Benedict Fairfax. Xanthe let rage fuel her. She could not, *would not*, let that happen. One other thing she knew for certain: she could not go back without a plan. All she had done before was end up making things more difficult for Samuel and having him put himself in danger to help her. This time would be different. This time she would put herself in a strong position so that she could deal with Fairfax. Even as she thought about this she began to see something she could offer him. Something she could give him he would find impossible to resist. Something that would secure the safety of Samuel and his family forever. It was risky. More than that it was probably extremely dangerous, but it was the best chance she had. The time had come to use her gifts, to test her ability to spin time to its limits.

As Liam helped her carry the last of the new stock into the shop he put his hand on her arm.

"Are you OK? You seemed really shaken back there."

She nodded. "I'm fine, honestly. Take no notice, just a silly thing . . . something about history, you know, tombstones . . ." She knew she wasn't being convincing.

Liam waited, watching her face closely. For once his own expression was serious. "There was someone once," he told her, all his earlier flippancy on the subject gone. "Someone who mattered. But it didn't work out. And it was a while ago."

"Oh."

"Just so you know." And then he rubbed his hands together, his more usual lightness returned. "Right, give me the keys and I'll get to the important business of the day and see what your lovely little taxi needs to get her running again."

After her time spent studying the Spinners book, and ruminating on the way Fairfax worked, Xanthe had hit upon an idea for safeguarding both herself and Samuel. She knew Fairfax was not to be trusted. His word was too flimsy a thing to rely on for everyone's future survival. If she could use her skill as a Spinner to put some distance between him and the Appleby family, so much the better. And for her, a distance of time would be easier to achieve than a geographical one. She need only make sure that Fairfax was unwittingly guided by the way she spun time to where, and more significantly when, she wanted him to end up. Once she had the idea properly formed in her mind she felt galvanized, determined, completely certain that she should and could return to Samuel's time. What had to be seen to first, however, was how she could leave, what she could tell her mother, and how she could be sure Flora would manage without her while she was away. Again. More lies. More tying herself in knots trying to do the right thing for the people she cared about. At least this time there was one crucial difference from the other occasions when she had had to dream up an excuse for being away. This time she had someone she could confide in. Someone she could ask for help without having to tell a collection of half-truths and falsehoods. Harley.

When she returned to the shop, Xanthe was greeted by the sound of Flora belting out Christmas carols as she rubbed down a small table in her workshop. Xanthe paused for a moment, listening, enjoying every flat note and

improvised lyric, knowing that this was a sure sign her mother's spirits and
health were improving. A fact which went some way to assuaging the guilt
that had taken up residence in the pit of her stomach again. Flora was delighted with the treasures Xanthe had found and full of ideas for restoration
and repairs. The distraction of the new pieces could not have been better
timed. Xanthe had prepared her first necessary lie on the drive home and
quickly told her mother that Harley wanted to see her about a singing gig so
she was going to see him after the shop shut but before the bar got busy. The
rest of the day was spent manning the shop while secretly gathering the things
she would need for another trip back in time. Xanthe felt growing tension at
the thought of making another journey. Although she had moved the chocolate pot to her bedroom, she had hardly dared touch it since her accidental
return, doing her best to ignore its plaintive singing. Now she allowed herself to listen to its call again. She put together her collection of clothes that
would pass as seventeenth century, including the two pieces which actually
did date from that time. She held Samuel's cloak up to the light and examined it closely. There was some fraying at the seams and edges, and a slight
fading of the color, but otherwise it was still wearable, not yet degraded beyond use. Rose's blouse was similarly dulled, somehow, but wearable. Next,
she packed her leather shoulder bag with useful items, putting in painkillers,
a hip flask of brandy, a small LED torch, and another silver thimble for currency. She also spent a whole hour searching through their collection of coins
until she found one very specific one that was a vital part of her plan. She
tied a wide-brimmed felt hat to the straps of her bag. She had found the one
Adam lent her a Godsend, but she had left it at the abbey. She thought longingly of her army greatcoat, which she had been forced to abandon at the abbey. She would do her best to retrieve it. Until then, Samuel's cape would
serve.

When at last she was sitting opposite Harley in the small sitting room of
his flat above the public rooms of the pub, Xanthe realized she was at a loss
as to how to start to ask him for what she needed. The room was warm and
inviting, with a wood-burning stove glowing in the hearth and soft leather
sofas to flop onto. Harley's eclectic collection of biker memorabilia and local
history prints and maps gave the place a friendly level of clutter, but still she

found it hard to relax. They had left Annie downstairs manning the bar so knew that they would not be disturbed. Xanthe also knew she didn't have long, didn't have the luxury of taking her time to work up to the impossible subject she needed to talk to Harley about. Nor did she, on this occasion, have the assistance of vintage brandy to give her a little courage. Mercifully, Harley, who had evidently been thinking of little else since she showed him the book on Spinners, cut straight to the heart of the matter.

"You're planning a journey then, are ye, hen?" It was more of a statement than a question. Harley sat forward on the edge of the sofa opposite Xanthe, his expression intense. Xanthe was slightly thrown by the boldness of what he was saying. She was so used to covering up what she had been doing that to just come straight out and discuss it with someone felt both strange and risky. But she had to trust Harley. She needed his help.

"I have to. There is someone I have been helping. . . ."

"You mentioned a guy before."

"His name is . . . was . . . Samuel Appleby. When I left him last time, when I traveled home without meaning to . . . I left him in danger. I convinced myself he was better off without my meddling and because it's not a simple matter, to leave my life here and now and go back to him . . ."

"So what's changed?"

Xanthe looked at him and struggled to keep the panic out of her voice. "I saw his grave," she said. "If I don't go back he will die very soon."

Harley was silent for a moment, taking in what she had said, clearly trying to imagine what it must be like to see the resting place of a person who had been dead for three hundred years but who you had spoken to only days ago.

"I suppose there's no use me pointing out just how bloody dangerous flinging yourself back and fore through the centuries must be?"

"If he dies before he's supposed to it has consequences. Things that he's supposed to do, the life he's meant to live . . . they have to happen. I've got to go, Harley."

"Aye, I can see that you do. So," he slapped his thighs, sitting up straight, his manner suddenly businesslike, "how can I help? Tell me what it is you need me to do."

"You have no idea how much it helps just to be able to share all this with someone. Just to talk about it, out loud, without feeling I am losing my mind."

"*Tch*, you're one of the sanest people I know."

"You still think that? After all I told you last time?"

"Well, I confess, I did spend a wee while wondering if we'd a lunatic for a new neighbor, but then I got to thinking of how damn brilliant the whole thing is. And then there's that incredible book of yours—we both saw what we saw, and I like to think of myself as of sound mind, at least most of the time. Although next to you I feel like a shining example of normality myself, which is rare, I don't mind telling you."

"I hoped you'd understand."

"I don't know about understanding, but I am fascinated. And I want to understand. I want to know how it all works, how it's even possible."

"It's not an easy thing."

"But to travel though time! To actually be there, be *then* . . ."

". . . and get close to people who are then in danger, and you just make things worse for them." She couldn't keep the tremble out of her voice.

"*Och*, hen, you're too hard on yourself. I'm sure that's not the case."

"It is. Which is why I have to go back."

"You're a canny lass. And determined, that's obvious. I'm sure this friend, whoever he is, he'd be grateful for your help," Harley told her. "But . . ."

"But . . ."

"Well, if it was me heading off into the past I'd be bloody sure I had a plan. I'd arm myself if needs be."

"I don't think that'd work for me, do you?"

"Or, I don't know, take stuff that could be useful, helpful."

"It's impossible to know what that would look like. I try to take things like a torch, some money, though even that is problematic, so I just take valuable things I can barter if I have to."

"And your book hasn't helped?"

"I still haven't figured half of it out. There's definitely no list of what to pack!" She managed a smile, despite the stress she was having to manage. A thought occurred to her then, something that gave her a glimmer of hope. "There is someone who could unravel the secrets in *Spinners*, though. Of course!

Why didn't I think of it before? I'll take it to Mistress Flyte. She was so excited when she knew I'd found it. She'll be able to show me how to make sense of it."

"Well, that's a good place to start. With your natural pluck and the old woman to help you, it strikes me you've a fair chance of success. All you need now is a plan."

Xanthe nodded slowly, her stomach tightening at the thought of what she had decided she must do; of the only way she could think of that would guarantee Fairfax's cooperation. "Oh, I have a plan all right," she said. "I most definitely have a plan."

"Care to share?"

Xanthe sighed, pushing her heavy hair off her face. "It's a lot to explain, and honestly, I don't have time. I keep having to lie to my mum about what I'm doing and where I'm going as it is. I need to get home, spend some time with her, try to explain why I have to go away. Again. When she's only just over being unwell. Let's just say there's someone in the past who wants something really badly, and I think I might have found a way to give it to him." When she saw Harley's expression of alarm she added, "It's not what you think."

"Lassie, at this point, even *I* don't know what I think! But, if you tell me you've got it sorted in your own mind that's good enough for me. What worries me more is the actual . . . traveling. From what the fella who used to come into the pub and talk about Spinners told me, it is far from safe, and from what you've told me yourself, what you're attempting to do is not without very real risks."

"I have done it before. Quite a few times."

"Oh aye, and are ye telling me it never felt dangerous?"

Xanthe hesitated, and that brief silence told Harley all he needed to know.

He nodded slowly. "Is there nothing you can do to protect yourself more?" he asked.

"Not that I know of. I prepare as best I can. I think about my clothes, about what I can take with me. I've got a bit better at landing up where I want to, at least once I've got used to where each found thing is trying to send me. It always pulls me to a spot that's relevant in some way to what I'm supposed to be doing. Or to the person I'm supposed to be helping."

"That's something, I suppose. But how can you be certain you'll end up in the right time, never mind the right place?"

"I can't be. Not completely. All I know is that as long as the object, in this case the chocolate pot, as long as it's still calling me, it will take me to where I need to be as well as when I need to be there. Except that . . ."

"What?"

"Well, sometimes it's not where I'm expecting exactly, and that can cause problems. But the most worrying thing is I never know how much time will have passed. I mean, I thought I'd worked it out, when I made my first journeys."

"Meaning?"

"There seemed to be a fixed order to the way time moved in the distant past and in my own era. Ten minutes here equated to ten hours back then. Roughly. But this time, well, that doesn't seem to hold true. It's as if it's not actually fixed at all, that ratio. So, I never know if I'm going to get there and find months have passed instead of days or weeks. And the same goes for returning home. So far the time I've been away has stayed moving at the same speed as it did the first time I went, so I can spend days at a time in the seventeenth century and be missing from here only hours or a couple of days at most."

"What can I do to help, lassie? Just ask. Anything."

"It's something I'm going to have to figure out on my own, I'm afraid, and mostly just by the doing of it. There is something else you can help me with, though. It's not very nice, and I don't feel good about asking you to do it, but . . ."

"Ask away. I'm ready. I'm up for it. Consider me your stalwart companion in any and all matters of time travel!"

"I need you to lie to my mother."

Once Harley had recovered from his disappointment Xanthe explained. She would tell Flora that a friend of Harley's who lived in London and also ran a pub had heard of Xanthe singing at The Feathers and asked if she could go and do a couple of nights in his establishment. It would mean going to London for a couple of days. It was short notice, but Harley was to back her up, saying the friend had good connections, and it was an excellent opportunity for Xanthe to get her singing noticed again.

Harley agreed to do what she asked. "I'm a wee bit concerned at the deviousness of your mind, I'll tell you that," he said. "But I can see you need to reassure Flora. It's a story that could hold water." He got up and searched for pen and paper. "Best get our facts straight and not leave the details to my addled brain. Now," he sat down again, the sofa sighing under the weight of him. "What's the name of this lifelong friend of mine, and what shall we call his pub, eh?"

Together they thrashed out the necessary facts. It was also agreed that Harley would invite Flora to join him and Annie in the pub for a drink and supper at the moment when Xanthe would be leaving, meaning she would not have to go through the charade of pretending to head off to catch a train. It also meant she could get changed and get to the blind house with the chocolate pot without Flora seeing her. Already Xanthe felt a seismic shift in the way she was going to be making her journeys through time now that she had Harley to help. She noticed that the panic she was at constant war with regarding what might be happening to Samuel lessened a fraction now that she did not have to face doing everything alone.

When she got home Xanthe found her mother brighter, if tired from her activities in the workshop, and still with the slightly glassy, bright-eyed look of someone under the influence of painkillers. She was on the sofa in the sitting room watching a celebrities and antiques program.

"So," she asked, clicking the TV to mute, "what did Harley want? Has he got another singing date for you?"

"Yes and no," Xanthe said, sitting on the Queen Anne chair that had somehow not yet found its way into the workshop.

"Oh?"

"Yes, he has a date, but no, he doesn't want me to sing in The Feathers." She hurried on before she could lose her nerve. "He has a friend in London, Richard, runs a pub in Hackney called The Fox. Well, he wants me to go there and do a two-nighter."

"Hey, word is getting around at last; you're in demand. Two nights, you say? When does he want you to do it?"

"Tomorrow."

"What? Xanthe, love, what about Christmas? What about the stock for the shop?"

"I know, but he's been let down. He apologizes for the short notice. . . ."

"Short . . . !"

"But he'll pay really well. And Harley says it's a nice pub. The music there is known to be good." She picked at a loose thread in her skirt, unable to meet her mother's eye. She could hardly believe the lies were tripping off her tongue so easily. She plowed on. "Actually, according to Harley, they get talent spotters in. You know, record producers, people like that."

"Oh?" Flora shifted slightly on the soft cushions.

Xanthe hated herself but there was no turning back. "Yes. Singers get noticed there sometimes."

"Really? You never sang there when we lived in London, did you?"

"I think it's quite new, the live music part. But it's really taken off."

"What if Marcus is there?"

"What?"

"Well, you said he wanted you to sing with him again, and that he was getting the band back together. What if he goes there? You've only just got rid of him again. I don't think it's a good idea to be moving in the same circles as him again, do you?"

Xanthe had been doing her best to forget about Marcus. "Actually, Mum, he's still here in Marlborough."

"Still? I thought you and Harley sent him packing. How long have you known about this? Why do you keep things from me? It isn't helpful, really it isn't."

"OK, I'm sorry, I didn't want to think about him. I guess I was hoping if I ignored him long enough he'd give up and go away. Hasn't worked yet." Xanthe slid off her chair and knelt in front of her mother, taking her hands in her own, looking up at her now. "Not brilliant timing I know, but at least I'd still be out of Marcus's reach. And it's only for a couple of days, Mum. I'll be back before you know it. And besides, this is what you wanted, isn't it? I mean, you've been nagging me for ages to take up my singing properly again. To prioritize it. This could be a really great opportunity. . . ."

Flora nodded. "It does sound like a good gig. And you want to go, don't you?" She leaned forward and stroked her daughter's hair.

Xanthe did not trust herself to answer. She nodded, smiling, wishing there was another way.

Flora leaned back against the faded velvet of the sofa. "Of course you must go. In fact, I bloody insist on it." She laughed lightly then. "To be honest, I've had enough of you fussing round me. I'm OK, love. Sometimes you have to trust me to know how to get through these blips. Because that's all they are; temporary setbacks. And we are not going to let them stop you singing or me running this business, OK?"

"You'll be all right?" Xanthe could not stop herself asking the pointless question.

"I'll be perfectly fine. Without you around to distract me I'll probably get more repairs done. And you won't be able to flap about me going back to bell-ringing practice tomorrow." She held up her hands to ward off any resistance to the idea. "Sheila says I have a natural ear for the rounds. See, being subjected to your singing practice all these years is finally paying off. I have a natural ear," she said, theatrically indicating her head. "I wonder which one it is?" she added, making Xanthe laugh. "That's better. And I can get on with some Christmas cooking without you under my feet in the kitchen."

"OK ... What are you going to try this year? Just so I can prepare myself. ..."

"Never you mind. You're not the only one can pull off surprises. I have my ideas. ... Now, before you go you can help me position some of Mr. Morris's mirrors along the passageway so that I can see who's coming into the shop. That way it won't matter if I take a few seconds to emerge from my workshop."

"You're a star, Mum. Oh, and Harley has invited you over for supper with him and Annie at The Feathers tomorrow evening."

"Ooh, what have I done to deserve that?"

"He feels guilty about being responsible for me going away again."

"So he should. I shall enjoy letting him squirm through the main course, then forgive him over pudding."

"Sounds like a plan." Xanthe laughed, thankful the awful conversation was over. She got up. "I'll make us a cuppa. Then bed. I'm plum tuckered," she said, a little too brightly, keen to move the moment on.

"I'll have chamomile," said Flora. "By the way, I'm looking forward to my surprise," she added.

Xanthe paused on her way out of the room, trying to work out what her mother was referring to and then remembering, just in time, the conversation they had had when she'd emerged from the blind house. She had hinted at a Christmas present, and beyond that, a surprise connected to the period clothes she had been wearing. "Oh, you'll have to wait a while yet," she said.

"I'm intrigued. Is it something to do with the shop?"

"You'll have to wait and see," she insisted, briskly stepping from the room before Flora could press her more. In the kitchen she filled the kettle and struggled with a mounting sense of everything getting on top of her again. Just when she thought she had all the most difficult aspects of what she was trying to do planned out another element demanded her attention. Another of her lies nearly caught her out. Finding a gift for her mother wouldn't be difficult, but what about the rest of it? How was she supposed to make sense of her clothes and of building up to a reveal of something special when there was nothing? She would have to come up with something. She knew Flora well enough to know that she would not forget, that she would continue to ask questions. Her own behavior had been too strange for her mother to just let the thing drop. As Xanthe made the drinks she added sugar to her own tea, realizing she would have to stay awake long enough to come up with something.

$\{$ 15 $\}$

XANTHE NEED NOT HAVE BOTHERED WITH SUGARING HER TEA IN AN ATTEMPT TO STAY awake and think, as sleep proved largely impossible. The chocolate pot set up a near constant ringing, distracting her from the business of dreaming up a surprise for Flora. When she had at last come up with something workable and tried to get to sleep her mind was too busy, her thoughts too hectic, to allow sleep to come. She went over and over everything she needed to do before leaving; all the necessary steps to keep her complicated secrets. And then she thought about Samuel, and about Fairfax, and about the plan she had struck upon. It was risky, she knew that, but she could not think of another way. She feared Fairfax was not a man who would ever give up. She had to offer him something he desired beyond anything else. She had realized that he did not, in fact, want her, he wanted what he believed she could give him: dominion over time. It had occurred to her that the astrolabe could do this for him. True, he had not completely mastered using it, but he was quite obsessed with the idea of having it, or at least he had been until he had got hold of Xanthe. What if she could give it back to him? What if she could then somehow show him how to use it? Whether or not he would be able to do so safely she couldn't know. She was convinced, however, that he would jump at the chance to have it in his possession again. All Xanthe had to do was convince him that the way she had thought of getting it was feasible. Because it would be highly risky, particularly for him.

When she did succeed in getting brief snatches of sleep she was assailed by dreams. She hoped to have some sign of Samuel; that he was well. Instead all she saw was Fairfax's gaunt face looming at her out of the darkness, his eyes unblinking, so that by the time she woke up the next morning she had the eerie feeling that he was watching her every move. She passed the day in an agony of anticipation, wishing she could leave then and there, but knowing she must wait until the evening. A busy day in the shop helped a little, as did a short conversation with Gerri. Xanthe had popped over to the tea shop to buy some toasted sandwiches for lunch. The tables were all taken with customers enjoying Gerri's excellent home-cooked food. Despite how busy she must have been, Gerri looked as perfectly turned out and unflappable as always. She smiled at Xanthe as she saw her enter the tearoom.

"I was just coming to see you," she said, deftly slicing a lemon drizzle cake into generous pieces. "You seemed tired the other day, a little down, perhaps. I was worried."

"Oh, just a few things on my mind, you know, running a business, Mum, usual stuff. . . ."

"If you're sure . . . ?"

Xanthe nodded. "I just came to let you know I'm going up to London for a couple of days. Singing." The lie did not taste any more palatable on the second time of telling, especially when Gerri was so pleased for her friend.

"A bit of London glamour for a day or two will perk you up," she said, turning to warm more teapots with water from the huge copper urn behind the counter.

"Yes, I expect so. Um, I was wondering . . ."

"Would you like me to pop in and see Flora while you're away?"

"That would be great, but actually, I have a business proposition for you."

"Ooh, now I'm interested," she said, wiping her hands on her spotless apron and giving Xanthe her full attention.

"It's just a very unformed idea really, but I'd love you to put your mind to it. I want to run an early Christmas promotion, something to start off the present shopping, and I struck on the notion of a themed Saturday with maybe all the shops in our little lane taking part."

"Wow, that sounds ambitious. But you know me, always happy for a bit of dressing up. What sort of theme?"

"Seventeenth century."

"Oh, lovely!"

"You think?"

"I do! I could look up some recipes. The Stuarts loved their puddings and tarts."

"Did they?"

"Food history is one of my hobbies."

"I can't imagine you have time for a hobby!"

"Well, I can pass it off as work, can't I?" She stepped past Xanthe and delivered a tray of tea things to the corner table. Returning, her expression was quite lit up, already enthused by the idea. "I could get the children to dress up too, help with serving. We'd need to get flyers out, maybe an ad in the paper. I wonder if I could call in a favor from an old chum of mine at Radio Wiltshire. . . ."

Not for the first time that week Xanthe saw how lucky she was to have made such good friends in Marlborough. "I knew you'd be full of ideas," she said.

"When were you thinking of doing it?"

"How about the second weekend in December? That gives us a couple of weeks to get everything sorted. Oh, don't mention it to Mum yet. It's a surprise. Something I want to share with her when I come home."

After her conversation with Gerri the afternoon was easier, her concern about Flora and her worry about making good all her promises and excuses lessened slightly. It also helped to think that she would at least be doing something good for the business. And that would definitely please her mother.

At six-thirty Flora was ready to leave for her supper at The Feathers.

"You will take care of yourself in the big city, won't you?" Flora stood in the shop doorway, coat on, bag over her shoulder, clearly a little reluctant to say goodbye.

"Mum, I am a Londoner, remember? Six months away hasn't turned me into a country bumpkin," Xanthe told her.

"Yes, but you haven't been there in a while. And you'll be distracted, and a bit nervous, I should imagine."

"I will be fine. Now go, you'll be late. Don't want to keep Harley and Annie waiting." She gave her mother a hug and adjusted her woolen scarf a little. "You are the one who needs to take care. Make sure you take your extra medication."

"I'm allowed to fuss over you, I'm your mother. It doesn't work the other way around. Not yet, at least," Flora said. She seemed on the point of going but then hesitated, scrutinizing her daughter's face. "Are you all right, love? You look very pale."

"Couldn't sleep." Xanthe shrugged. "You know how I get before a performance."

"I wish I was going with you."

"And leave the shop to do what, exactly? Now, go. Have fun. Eat lots."

She stood at the door and watched her go, the clicking of her sticks upon the cold cobbles echoing down the narrow alleyway. At least this time Harley would keep an eye on her. He had tried one more time to warn Xanthe about going back before confessing to his own excitement at even talking about it. There was little he could do to help, much to his frustration. At least that meant he had happily agreed to getting a little closer to Flora if only to ease Xanthe's worry about leaving her.

Closing and locking the door, Xanthe forced herself to put her own problems to the back of her mind and focus on what lay ahead. She marched through the shop and upstairs to her bedroom. She quickly changed into her seventeenth-century costume—Rose's blouse, her own pinafore dress and leggings, and Samuel's cape. Already the garments she had brought forward with her through time appeared faded, their hems starting to fray, the lining of the cloak beginning to split and degrade. She double-checked the locket was in place, having earlier fixed the broken link in the chain. She picked up her bag, carefully tucked the Spinners book inside it, and last took hold of the chocolate pot. The note it emitted was so high and so piercing it caused her to wince.

"OK," she told it quietly. "I'm on my way."

Taking care to leave the doors closed and locked as they would have been had she left through the front door to take a mini-cab to the train station, Xanthe went out into the garden. It was already properly dark and very cold. Her breath preceded her as she hurried across the lawn, tightening Samuel's cloak around her and hitching her old leather bag over her shoulder. This

time she did not hesitate. She was a woman with a mission and a clear plan
of how to succeed. This time, she would be in control.

Xanthe had expected to feel disorientated and confused when she arrived back
in the seventeenth century. She sat still, kept her eyes closed for a while, willing her thundering heart to steady and slow, taking control of her ragged
breathing. She knew she needed to take a moment to recover from the singular journey. She clutched her bag at her side and felt the shape of the precious book safe inside it. As she slowly opened her eyes she found she was
once again in a dark, cold place. There were stones beneath her, but dry ones.
She had not, she realized with relief, arrived in another blind house. She could
make out the outline of a window, even though there was little light coming
through it, suggesting dusk or dawn, she couldn't tell which. The space was
very quiet and she was certain straightaway that she was alone, save for a scurrying mouse nearby. As she got to her feet she tried to identify what it was
she could smell. There was a mustiness, not unlike a mill or stable, but something else. Apples. She blinked, squinting into the gloom and at last could
make out shelves and barrels and sacks. She was in another hoarde house or
cellar. But whose? Where? It felt a little familiar, but it was too dark to be
certain. The sound of a door opening, the wood scraping against the flagstones and the hinge creaking in protest, caused her heart to thump again.
She stayed motionless, hoping that the darkness would conceal her presence.
Light fell through the doorway as someone came to stand at the top of the
flight of steps, candle held high. Xanthe could see, behind the flickering glare
of the flame, the figure of a woman. She found she was holding her breath.
Only when the woman spoke did she exhale.

"Well, girl, are you to skulk in the shadows all evening?" Mistress Flyte
asked.

Xanthe felt her relief quickly outweighed by frustration. She was in the
chocolate house again, in Bradford. Safe, but miles from Samuel. But then
she needed to talk to Mistress Flyte about the book. Was that why the chocolate pot had chosen to bring her there again?

She stepped forward.

"Good day to you, Mistress Flyte. I am pleased to find you looking so well. Are you fully recovered from your injuries?"

"I have survived worse," she said simply. And then she turned to leave, calling back, "Make haste. You of all people know that time does not tarry."

Xanthe followed her upstairs, through the busy chocolate house where she glimpsed Edmund fetching and carrying pots and cups, on up the next flight of stairs, and into Mistress Flyte's sitting room. The old woman set the candle down on the mantelpiece. A lamp burned on the table, and the fire gave off its own glow. Mistress Flyte seated herself on the neat cushioned chair within reach of the warmth from the hearth. Xanthe put down her bag, removed her cape, and sat opposite her host. She noticed with some astonishment that the color of the velvet cloak was beginning to refresh and return to its original richness. As always, she felt a little light-headed after her journey, and was glad of the warmth of the fire and the safety of sitting with a friend. More than that, she was with someone who understood where she had come from, and why she had come. She noticed that her host's face still showed some bruising, and her hand was still bandaged.

"Tell me, mistress, have you heard any news of Samuel?" she asked. As she formed the questions she realized she had no notion of how much time had passed since her last visit. Had it been hours, days, or weeks? Could it have been months? Nothing seemed fixed or reliable anymore. Might she be too late? The thought made her stomach lurch. "What day is this? How long . . . how long have I been gone?"

"From what I understand, you left the abbey a week ago."

"You heard this from Samuel? You've spoken with him?"

"Not directly. It was his brother who came here. Two days ago." She held up her hand to stop Xanthe's question. "His brother lives. He is yet kept at Fairfax's home. His work on the abbey is not complete."

"When I left, they were fighting. . . ."

"Joshua Appleby told me some of what had happened. Including the matter of you inflicting a grievous wound upon Fairfax."

Xanthe flinched at the memory of it. While she had good reason to hate the man, the thought of cutting anyone like that, of doing lasting damage, was awful.

"His eye . . ." she started.

"Will not be of use to him further."

"Oh my God." Xanthe shuddered with guilt at what she had done, and fear at how angry she might have made him. Would he demand revenge? And would he look for that vengeance upon her or Samuel?

Mistress Flyte leaned forward and took up the poker, prodding more heat from the fire.

"Save your sympathies for another more deserving of them," she said. "Fairfax brought about his own suffering. As he ever does. For now Samuel is safe, as the work continues. In addition, Fairfax knows young Appleby has a further value." She looked up then, meeting Xanthe's anxious gaze. "He surmises that Samuel will bring you back within his reach. Is he mistook?"

"I have to go back and put things right."

"You consider yourself able to do so? Have you not to this point only served to make the situation worse?"

"I was unprepared, I didn't really know what . . . *who* I was dealing with."

Mistress Flyte sighed. "Why cannot the young learn from their elders? Why must they insist upon burning their fingers on the glowing embers rather than considering the wounds of others as evidence of such folly?" She jabbed at a log, sending sparks spitting, before returning the poker to the hearth. "Tell me then, young Spinner, how it is you plan to get the better of Benedict Fairfax?"

"When I was at the abbey, Fairfax told me what had happened to him. He told me how he was on the point of being executed. He even showed me the scar on his neck from the noose. He said he had an astrolabe, and that it enabled him to spin time. Nothing else works for him."

"Which is why he is so interested in you."

"He was; he may not be now that I have half blinded him."

"You still hold the secret to manipulating time. He has tasted the intoxicating power of that gift. He will overcome his anger at you to get what he wants."

"He wanted me to stay with him here, in his time. He wanted me to become his wife."

Mistress Flyte gave a dry laugh. "Many young girls would be tempted by such a fine match, however corrupt the man."

"I am not in the market for a husband. And if I was, it wouldn't be someone . . ."

". . . who plans to kill the man you love?"

Xanthe caught her breath. "I was going to say, it wouldn't be someone who lives in a different century to my own. I have a life, a home, someone who needs me."

Mistress Flyte nodded. "What is it, then, that you can offer the man if not yourself?"

"I have to strike a deal, I know, and if I am not to be part of that deal, I have to give him the only other thing he truly wants."

"Which is?"

"The astrolabe."

"I believe he has amassed a collection of the things."

"I don't mean just any astrolabe, I mean the one that he used. The one that saved his life."

"But you cannot know where to search for it. It would be impossible to find. Fairfax has come back from a future point and changed the order of things, so he cannot know that it will ever come into his possession again. The last time anyone can be certain of where it was, was at the point and place of Fairfax's scheduled execution. A time that has not yet come to pass. The only way to get it would be to . . ."

". . . to travel forward to that date."

For once Mistress Flyte's mask of composure slipped and revealed the shock she was feeling. "You cannot mean," she said, lowering her voice as if she feared being overheard, "to take Fairfax with you to locate the astrolabe specific to his own tale, to take him to the point of his death . . . !"

"I admit, the idea is not without its risks, particularly for Fairfax. And now that he has altered things, well, we can't even be certain he will end up on the scaffold, can we?"

"If the world were rid of the man it would be a better place!" the old woman snapped, jumping up from her chair. "I am not concerned for Fairfax's welfare any more than you are yourself. What I cannot countenance is using your gift as a Spinner to enable the man to travel through time, first as your guest . . ."

"Not quite how I would put it . . ."

". . . and then to give him an object so powerful that he will, no doubt with your instruction, be able to move back and fore as he pleases." Mistress Flyte began to pace the room, her agitation obvious.

"Look, I don't see that I'm doing anything particularly reckless. Fairfax had the astrolabe once. He used it. He is a Spinner. None of that is new. And I don't intend teaching him to use it better, even assuming I'd be capable of doing that. The deal will be to take him to the astrolabe, to reunite him with something he had once before anyway. I don't see that I'm doing anything wrong, not if it frees Samuel and secures the safety of his whole family."

"Then you underestimate your adversary. Tell me, truly, what do you believe Fairfax will do if he obtains the astrolabe?"

"What he has always done; look after number one. Make himself richer. Improve his standing with the king. Make sure he's never on the losing side again."

"And you think he can achieve all this without it being at anyone else's expense?"

"At the moment he's trying to do just that at Samuel's expense. What's the difference?"

"None, save that you will not know who it is he cuts down on his way to the high position he is determined to claim as his own." Mistress Flyte sat down again, mastering her emotions, regaining her more customary composure. "But that is a small matter and for your own conscience. There is a greater issue at stake here. Something that goes beyond your own personal wishes, or even the safety of a handful of innocent people."

Xanthe felt weary. "Mistress Flyte, believe me, I've thought long and hard about this. I'm doing the best I can to make things right."

"Your motives are sincere, that I do not doubt. However, your reasoning is limited and your understanding of the situation lacking in insight."

Xanthe frowned. "I had hoped that you would support me."

"How can I support an endeavor that may enable an unscrupulous, amoral, dangerous man to harness the manner of power we are discussing? You cannot have considered the consequences. Given such a gift, Fairfax would not simply spin time, he would twist it! Once he realized what was within his grasp he would never be content with his current modest ambitions. Why should he? Nothing would be beyond his reach. No one would be able to resist him. He would be able to move through the decades, through the centuries, distorting and corrupting, giving no heed to the consequences of his deeds, caring only for his own advancement."

Xanthe was beginning to see, beginning to understand. "Just because you can, doesn't mean you should."

"The ability to spin time has to be governed. It must only be used responsibly, for the good of all, to assist those who have suffered an injustice, to allow good to triumph. Fairfax would burn those precious laws to cinders."

"OK, maybe he would, or maybe he'd just get rich quick and enjoy the high life. I don't know. I can't say. What I can say is that I came here to do something, and there is only one way for me to do it. Why do I suddenly have to be the keeper of this whole Spinner thing? I didn't ask for it. Nobody asked me if I wanted to be dragged through time, putting myself in danger, risking being marooned and separated from my family, with nothing to gain but heartache. It's not my choice."

"The chatelaine sang to you. As did the chocolate pot."

"Exactly, they called to me, not the other way around," said Xanthe, allowing her own anger to show now.

"And you answered that call."

"Because I heard someone in distress. Because I'm a human being."

"Because you are a Spinner."

"Well, let me tell you, it's not all it's cracked up to be!" she shouted, jumping to her feet. "It's made me lie to everyone I care about, it's making me risk everything. And there's no guarantee I will succeed. You don't know what it's like."

"I assure you I do."

"How can you? Nobody could, unless they were . . ."

". . . a Spinner." Mistress Flyte turned her face up to Xanthe, her eyes bright but her expression calm. "Precisely."

"You?" Xanthe felt as if she was losing her already flimsy grasp on what was real and what wasn't. "You are a Spinner too?"

"I was. Many years ago I chose a different path."

"But you have done it? You have traveled through time yourself?"

"Please, sit."

Xanthe forced herself back into her chair. "That's why the chocolate pot brought me here, isn't it? It brought me to you."

"I was once, as you are, a youthful, inexpert, and reluctant Spinner. The gift came upon me in much the same way."

"You connected with lots of different things? Not just one like Fairfax?"

"I did. And those things often led me to dangerous places, to frightening times, to situations that asked much of me. I was not always willing to give what was needed," she said, looking briefly sorrowful, making Xanthe wonder what sacrifices she had made. "Over time I came to see that I had a responsibility. That I had been chosen to join a group of individuals, most of whom would never meet, whose task it was . . . is . . . to use their gift to fight against injustice. To protect the innocent. To assist those who need us."

"But you gave it up? Eventually you stopped spinning. Why? What was it that was asked of you that finally made you say no?"

Mistress Flyte gave nothing away now, the inscrutable expression firmly back in place. "This is not the moment to discuss my history. All you need to know is that you cannot, you *must* not, enable such a man as Fairfax to grow in strength as a Spinner."

"If he's so bad, why was he given the gift in the first place?"

"Not all scoundrels are born that way. Some are formed by their experiences. Fairfax once had allegiances and sensibilities far closer to those of the Applebys than you might expect."

"Yes, I do remember Samuel saying something about that."

"Feeling the roughness of a noose around one's neck might well effect a shift in a man's character, don't you think?"

Xanthe shrugged. "So what do you suggest I do? Appeal to his better nature? Hope there is still something of the better person in there I can reach? I have to say it's not a plan I'd want to stake my life on. Or anyone else's."

"If you insist on taking Fairfax forward to the moment he last had the astrolabe in his grasp . . ."

"Assuming that's possible, given all the things he's changed."

"Indeed. If you succeed in this course of action, you cannot bring him back to this time with the instrument that will allow him dominion over time. He is not a person to be trusted with that gift. He will use it badly, as in truth he has already attempted to do."

"Actually, I have had a bit of time to think of this myself. At home. It's easier to think clearly there, somehow. My mind works better there. Then. I suppose I shouldn't be surprised at that. I'm not going to thrash about blindly like I did before and end up making things worse. Again. This time will be different. For two reasons. First because I have come up with a plan."

Mistress Flyte raised her eyebrows expectantly.

"I thought about it, and if I can succeed in taking Fairfax to the moment just before his execution, then I reckon I can influence his return journey too. He might be using the astrolabe, but what if there was a way I could send him out of harm's way?"

"Have him arrive somewhere other than the abbey?"

"Somewhere, or some *when.*" She reached into her bag and took out a small velvet pouch. Opening it, she dropped the contents into Mistress Flyte's outstretched hand. A single silver coin fell into her pale palm.

"How do you plan to use this?" the old woman asked.

"Look at the date."

She held the coin close to the candle beside her chair, turning it slowly in her fingers, examining every part of the inscriptions it bore. At last she gave a little gasp and then looked up at Xanthe, smiling.

"You are proving yourself worthy of the name of Spinner already, child."

"I'm a quick learner," Xanthe said, shrugging off the compliment. "Do you think it will work?"

"It is possible," she nodded. "Although there are words that might help you; things that Spinners use to help control and direct their travel. Such things need to be particular to the person and the task, however. It would be no good my simply telling them to you. They have to be right for you and for this journey."

Now it was Xanthe's turn to smile. "I might just have something that could help with that." She reached into her bag again and slowly took out the Spinners book. "This is the second thing that makes me believe I can really help Samuel this time. That makes me know that this time, things will be different."

Mistress Flyte's hands flew to her mouth in astonishment.

"You have it!"

"It was . . . waiting for me."

The old woman's face was aglow. "I knew it would find you," she said, nodding slowly. "Now you are equipped." She sank back in her chair with what Xanthe saw to be a mixture of fatigue and relief.

"Will you help me understand it? I don't have much time and I really need to understand it. You say there are words in here that could give me some control, make my plan work." She opened the book and leafed through it, scanning the pages once again for anything that might seem relevant. "It's just that it's really hard to know where to start. There are so many stories." She held the book out for her host to take.

Mistress Flyte shook her head. "I do not need to read it."

"You don't want to take a look?"

"I know well what is within its covers, for I had many years to read it. For a long time it was in my keeping, now it is in yours. It finds its way to the one who has most need of its wisdom."

"Can you tell me how best to use it to deal with Fairfax? I bet he'd love to get his hands on it!"

"It would be of no use to him. It would not reveal itself to someone un-worthy."

"Really?" Xanthe thought of how the book had resisted being copied in any way, but the words inside it, on its own pages, were clearly legible.

Mistress Flyte picked up her little china bell and rang it. Although the sound was thin and light, Edmund must have become attuned to it over time, above the low hubbub of the chocolate house, for he was soon pounding up the stairs and appeared, slightly out of breath, at the door. He looked sur-prised to see Xanthe sitting by the fire, but also, she thought, pleased. He grinned at her before nodding at his employer.

"Mistress?"

"Edmund, you were a keen scholar, I recall. You can read, can you not?"

"Indeed, mistress. My father saw to it I applied myself to my letters until I was accomplished."

"Quite so. Xanthe would like to hear you read. Would you be so good as to read us a short passage from her book?"

Puzzled, but ever eager to please Mistress Flyte, Edmund took the book from Xanthe and turned to the first page. He frowned, searching further into the book. "Alas, mistress, I can find no words here. Shall I fetch your Bible?" he asked, passing the book back to Xanthe.

As she took it from him she could clearly see the text on every page, and yet to Edmund they had all appeared blank.

Mistress Flyte dismissed him with a light wave of her hand. "No matter. Another time. Thank you, Edmund, you may return to your duties."

As soon as he had gone Xanthe spoke up. "He couldn't see any of it, could he?"

"Edmund is too simple in his thinking, too limited in his intellectual scope; he is not up to bearing the weight of such knowledge. As for Fairfax . . . you are aware of what manner of man he is. Not all who have the gift that enables them to spin time remain worthy of it. Fairfax is too self-serving and ruthless. Only those worthy in all ways can see what lies within. He has proved himself to be a poor custodian of the gift."

"Power corrupts. I get it."

"Ha! For the most part, Lord Acton was never able to convince me of the value of his political philosophies, but I will allow the truth of that statement."

"You spoke to the actual Lord Acton? If I remember my school history lessons he lived in the early nineteenth century!"

"Now is not the time for my history."

"But wait, Fairfax is a Spinner."

"As I said, not all who are wicked begin so. There was a time when he showed promise, when he cared more for the fortunes of others. Alas, he has chosen a dark path to tread."

"I . . . I showed it to someone in my own time," she admitted, thinking suddenly of Harley. "Someone trustworthy," she insisted. "He could read it. Does that make him a Spinner too?"

"Not necessarily. In fact, it is highly unlikely. There are so very few of us. No, it is more likely that he has sufficient wit and wisdom, sufficient sensitivity to the subject, and sufficient integrity to be permitted limited access to these words. You consider him a helpmate, perhaps?"

"You could say that."

The old woman shifted slightly in her chair, wincing at the movement and effort involved, and Xanthe was reminded of how badly she had been injured.

"I'm sorry, Mistress Flyte, I know I'm tiring you, but I have to know. . . ."

She held up a hand to silence further questions. "You seek to understand what is written by looking, that is to be expected. Of an ordinary person. But think, child, how is it that the special objects make themselves known to you?"

"They sing to me."

"Precisely. You hear them. If you would know which story is right for you now, which tale will tell you what you need to know, then you should not look, but *listen*."

Xanthe paused for a moment, stroking the cover of the book. The cool leather felt warmer under her hand now, not because of the proximity of the fire, but rather due to some mysterious activity within the book itself. As if it was stirring. Xanthe closed her eyes and did her utmost to still her mind. She opened the book carefully, letting the pages fall how they would, making no conscious effort to choose a particular chapter or story herself. At first she heard nothing, but then, gradually, a whispering began. She quelled alarm, recalling the mournful cries and entreaties of the people she heard calling to her as she traveled through the blind house. This voice, however, was different. This was not a clamoring crowd, but a single, bell-like voice, growing from a soft whisper to a bolder, richer sound. Each word was spoken clearly, confidently, with authority. It was a woman's voice, not one she recognized, and the accent and sentence structure suggested the west of England, probably in the late eighteenth or early nineteenth century. Xanthe gasped as the speaker addressed her by name, drawing her attention to her story in the book, telling her how she too had needed to travel with another, to direct that travel specifically.

"There is no room for error in such an endeavor," the woman warned. "All must be prepared and done so with the utmost care, for to misstep could result not in failure alone, but in calamity. Bind the accompanying traveler to yourself with these words. Likewise send him to the time and place of your choosing using these words once more, and do not omit any, lest the spinning fall short of what is required. For so it happened to me, and I paid a great price for my want of perfection."

She spoke on, recounting her tale of losing sight of her fellow traveler, of the two of them being separated by centuries, and of how long and lonely was the road back to each other. And then she gave Xanthe the words that she must speak at the point of departure. Xanthe listened closely, fearing that she could not possibly commit them exactly to memory. The moment the voice fell silent she opened her eyes and checked in the book. As she had hoped, it lay open at the exact page of the story, and there were the few, precious lines, precisely as the woman had said them.

She looked up at Mistress Flyte. "Did you hear her?" she asked.

"No, child. The book is for you now."

Xanthe felt deeply moved. She had not thought before about what it meant to be chosen. She had seen only the difficulties and challenges of being pushed and pulled back and fore through the ages. Now, having heard someone from the book speak her name and talk to her directly, not only to say she must do something but to help her, to guide her, to trust her with such a rare knowledge—now she felt that somehow, as astonishing as it might sound to anyone else, she belonged. On asking the old woman for ink and paper Xanthe was directed to Mistress Flyte's small desk in the corner of the room. Xanthe quickly wrote out the lines she needed from the story, tucking the paper into her bra. She smiled at her host, closing the book and handing it to her. "Will you look after it for me, please? Until I return."

"Until you return," she agreed slowly, taking the book and holding it to her heart.

Xanthe picked up her cloak and swung it around her shoulders, hitching up her bag once more and setting her broad-brimmed hat on her head. "I'll say goodbye to Edmund, and then I have a stagecoach to catch."

For once she felt determined, in control, and focused. A state of mind that was lessened slightly when she remembered she needed money and had to ask Mistress Flyte to buy the silver thimble off her. The old woman agreed, and as she closed Xanthe's fingers around the coins, she held on to her hand, just for a moment.

"Godspeed, young Spinner," she said to her. "Remember, you would not have been chosen were you unequal to the task."

"Maybe it's the being chosen that makes a person good enough for it, don't you think?" She slipped the money into her skirt pocket, taking care not to mix it up with the special coin she had brought for Fairfax. The fire crackled and spat and, outside, the wind had begun to moan. At the door Xanthe hesitated, turning, and asked, "Do you think he will go for it? Fairfax, I mean. Do you think he will agree to return to that moment? It's a terrifying thought, surely; to face your own death not once but twice."

"For his beloved astrolabe he would do anything. Just as he would sacrifice anyone. Do not forget that."

Nodding, Xanthe pulled her cloak around her, paused to bid a brief farewell to Edmund at the counter of the chocolate house, and then left for the stagecoach that would take her to Laybrook, to the abbey, and to Fairfax.

16

SNOW LAY FROZEN TO A CRISP RIME UPON THE GROUND AND THE NIGHT SKY SHONE WITH stars. The coach was only half full, so that Xanthe was able to sit in a corner, her hat pulled low over her eyes, her bag on her lap, and avoid conversation with her fellow travelers. The journey to Laybrook was not long, but long enough for her to resolve never to take Fairfax at his word. However much she had convinced herself that she was going to give him something so wonderful he would have no reason to want more from her, Mistress Flyte's words had struck home. He was a man of no principle. A man who had set himself apart from others already by changing allegiances and serving only himself. Who could say what he would or would not do once he was in possession of his astrolabe? She comforted herself with the knowledge that she not only had a plan involving the coin, but the words of the Spinners book to help her. For the first time she felt a part of something, as if she were being supported and helped instead of either thrashing around on her own or battling on without any real understanding of what she was doing or how things worked. She had learned to be cautious and to be ready. This time her encounter with Fairfax would be very different. She would remain in charge, in control, even if he was unaware of that fact, right up until the last moment. She had to make sure the Applebys were safe, and that she herself would be free to return home.

The weather was still sharply cold, with a wind that sought out gaps in garments and holes in teeth. Xanthe dismounted from the stagecoach and stood a moment, watching the swaying carriage as the six dark horses took up the strain and cantered on out of the village. She felt little nervousness now. She was clear in her own mind of what she had to do, and she had come too far and risked too much to turn back. She replaced the strap of her bag over her shoulder, turned the collar of her cape against the wind, and walked the short distance to the abbey. If the servant who answered her knocking on the grand front door was surprised to see her he disguised it well and took her to a reception room off the main hall without so much as pausing to take her cloak and hat. This did strike her as a little strange until she entered the room and found Fairfax standing with his back to the fire, waiting. It was clear he had been expecting her, a thought that made the hairs at the nape of her neck bristle. How much did he see of what she did? How much could he know of what she had planned?

"Mistress Westlake." He made a polite bow but offered her no chair. His bandage had been replaced by a padded eye patch and the side of his face showed signs of swelling and bruising. Xanthe wondered, briefly, how much pain he was suffering. To apologize for what she had done to him seemed both pointless and insincere. She hated the thought that she had damaged his sight, but she knew she would do it again if she had to. It gave her some inner strength to realize that he would know this too.

"Master Fairfax, you were expecting me, I think?"

"I may not have your skills, but I am still able to detect the whereabouts and activities of a fellow Spinner, should I choose to do so."

Xanthe had never thought of doing this, but she remembered how she had seen Fairfax's face before she had ever met him. Was that a part of it? If she tried, would she be able to discover where he was when she needed to? To watch him? Much as she wanted to, she could not press him for details of how he did this. She had to maintain her position of strength as best she could.

"Tell me, mistress, have you reconsidered my proposal? I am hopeful that your coming here indicates, perhaps, a change of mind, if not a change of heart?" When she hesitated he went on, "I am not expecting a love match. It matters not. In point of fact, I have no interest in love. I care only for an alliance, and one sealed by matrimony would be both binding and more, shall we say, socially acceptable."

"I think you should understand this: even if I did not have a life and a family in my own time to return to, nothing and no one would ever induce me to be your wife." She watched his face register this, watched it sour at the insult and the refusal, and then she continued. "However, I do have a proposal of my own to put to you. A bargain to strike."

"And what, pray, do you have in your gift other than yourself that I could possibly want?"

Xanthe waited a beat and then answered simply, "Your astrolabe."

Fairfax revealed a fleeting glimpse of excitement before covering it with skepticism. "You have it?" he asked, taking a step toward her.

Xanthe instinctively tightened her grip on her shoulder bag, but did not move and did not let it show how much being close to the man who had attacked her unsettled her.

"No," she said. "But I can take you to it."

"How do you propose to do that?"

Xanthe took off her hat and dropped it onto the table beside her.

"I'll tell you, but it will take some time." She undid her velvet cape, the heat from the fire beginning to make her uncomfortably hot. "How about some bread and cheese while I explain?" She sat at the head of the table, looking at him expectantly. She had learned to eat when she could while journeying, and though she would not enjoy sharing food with Fairfax, she wanted to keep up the pretense that she was calm, in control, and confident of her plan. She needed to convince herself every bit as much as she needed to convince him.

Although Fairfax was plainly impatient to hear what she had to say, he summoned a servant and sent for food.

It took nearly an hour for her to outline her plan and for them to argue the points. Fairfax had been first excited at the prospect of possessing once again his precious found thing, but was, not surprisingly, appalled at the idea of mounting the scaffold for a second time. As Xanthe explained the details of her proposal he unconsciously rubbed at his collar, loosening the button, exposing the livid scar on his neck. Food was brought, good bread and two different cheeses, with pickled walnuts, which were both sweet and sour and delicious. Xanthe ate partly to cover her nervousness. Fairfax ignored the supper altogether. He questioned her on every point of her idea, shaking his head as she parried his queries, responding with further what-ifs and hows. Xanthe let him ask, let him challenge. After all, it was, quite literally, his neck that was being risked. At last he began to see that there was no other way of getting the astrolabe back, and that, if he and Xanthe combined their talents and energies, there was a better than fair chance of success. A servant came in to add hefty logs to the fire. Fairfax was silent while the young man did his job. As the door closed behind him he leaned forward on the table, his damaged face ghoulish under the light of the candelabra.

"Do you not see how together we could achieve so much? Does the idea not tempt you? Can you truly tell me that a part of you, that part that is Spinner above all else, does not long to see what you could do? To test your abilities, your gifts, to their very limits?"

Xanthe dabbed at her lips with a napkin. "I am not staying here. We are not going to be a partnership of any kind beyond this task. It is important you understand and accept that," she told him.

He leaned back in his chair, disappointed, cross at being thwarted, but, she could see, prepared to settle for what she was offering. At least for now.

"And you would have me do what with your dear friend?" he asked, not even bothering to name Samuel.

"I want your word that the Applebys—all of them—will have the threat of prosecution lifted from them. That they will be free to get on with their lives and their work without any stain on their reputation. And I want it in writing."

"Just this? Nothing more?"

"We are not all like you, Master Fairfax."

"Indeed."

He sent for vellum, quill, and ink and wrote, under Xanthe's instruction, a document exonerating Samuel, vouching for the good standing of the family, declaring them all to be God-fearing men and stalwart supporters of the king. He signed it, blotted it, folded it, and applied his seal. Xanthe took it, getting to her feet.

"I will give this to Samuel myself," she said.

Fairfax surprised her by giving a small, thin smile at this. "As you wish," he said. "You will find him in the morning room." He rang a bell to summon a servant, who arrived breathless from scampering up the many stairs from the distant kitchen of the great house yet again. Fairfax addressed the young man without for one instant taking his gaze off Xanthe. "Escort Mistress Fairfax to the morning room. Wait for her there. She will return momentarily."

"Not here," Xanthe said. "I will join you in the observatory in fifteen minutes. Be ready." A thought occurred to her and she added, "And I have a coat. I left it here. I wish to use it. Have it taken to the observatory."

When the servant hesitated his master nodded at him, and he held the door open for Xanthe.

She was surprised to find that Samuel was not in the new wing, working, nor in his own quarters, which by all accounts served as his jail. Instead she was led back through the cloisters to an older part of the abbey and a small but well-positioned room toward the front of the house. She was more surprised to find that Samuel was not alone. In the elegantly furnished morning room with its blond oak furniture and fine blue-gold rugs and tapestries, Samuel stood silhouetted against the tall window and beside him was a slender, well-dressed woman, holding his hand. On seeing Xanthe, Samuel self-consciously and abruptly let go of his guest.

"I had not thought to ever see you again," he said, moving a step toward her before stopping awkwardly. With his back to the light it was impossible for Xanthe to see his expression, but the tension in his posture suggested this was not an easy situation for him.

"I . . . I needed to come back," she said simply.

Samuel nodded to the woman standing beside him.

"But I am remiss. . . . Mistress Westlake, permit me to introduce to you Mistress Henrietta Shelton. Henrietta, this is the friend I have spoken of."

Xanthe watched the couple together. The way Samuel used the woman's first name, the way he had been holding her hand, and the fact that they were alone together, meant that this had to be his fiancée. Here was the woman Samuel was to marry. However much she told herself it was an arranged match, that this was normal for the times in which he lived, that he was marrying for his family's future, there was no escaping the fact that this was the woman he had chosen for his bride. It was she who would be the one to share his life, his home, his bed.

Henrietta moved forward and bobbed a polite curtsey to Xanthe. Now that she was no longer silhouetted against the window, the young woman was revealed in the soft light of the room. She had a pleasant face, not beautiful, nor particularly memorable, but there was a warmth about her smile and a softness about her hazel eyes that was truly attractive. Xanthe found herself thinking that this was a face Samuel could grow to love. Her clothes were of good quality, modest but not boring, the colors quite bold and the lace and braid details eye-catching, suggesting a confidence and flair in the wearer.

"The minstrel?" Henrietta asked. "Samuel has spoken so highly of your singing. And he told me how you helped him with the screen at Great Chalfield. He is fortunate to have such an ally." Her voice was sweet and sincere. It was impossible not to like the woman.

"Oh, I did very little," Xanthe said.

"Helping Samuel with this beloved building?" Henrietta laughed lightly. "I cannot think that he would see anything connected with his work as insignificant. I am indebted to you. His work is his passion."

Xanthe glanced at Samuel before saying, "Forgive me, Mistress Shelton, I don't wish to appear rude, but I cannot stay long. I came only to tell Samuel, that is, to let him know . . ."

"You are leaving again?" he asked. "Must your visits be always so mercurial? You have returned, and yet you must depart almost at once, it seems to me. To place yourself in such peril, and to no purpose. Would it not have been better had you stayed away?"

Xanthe held out the letter Fairfax had written.

"I needed to give you this," she said. "I could not trust it to anyone else. I had to make sure it reached you."

Samuel took it. He raised his eyes when he saw the familiar seal.

"Fairfax guarantees your safety," Xanthe explained. "Yours and your family's. He clears you of any charges of treason. With this, you will be safe. All of you."

She heard a gasp of relief from Henrietta.

"Welcome news indeed!" she said. "Samuel has lived beneath such a dark cloud of injustice. You have lifted that from him. From us all."

Xanthe smiled at her. It was a measure of the woman, and of her family, that they had stood by Samuel when he was under threat of prosecution. She wondered if Henrietta had put herself and her own family in danger by doing so. Or could it be that, as they were engaged before he was forced into residence at the abbey to complete his work, before his arrest, that the connection was already known? In which case if she broke the engagement she would surely have been making Samuel look more guilty, more unacceptable, more likely to be abandoned by those he had called friends.

Samuel tensed. "What did you have to promise him in order to obtain such a thing?"

"There is something he wants and I'm going to help him get it. And then that's it. We will both be rid of him." Even as she said it Xanthe knew her task was not as simple nor as definite as she was making it sound.

"You returned to do this for me?" Samuel asked, his voice showing how moved he was. "And I can offer you nothing."

Henrietta took a step back, feigning interest in a silver inkwell on the table, tactfully allowing her fiancé to speak with the unconventional woman who clearly meant a great deal to him. Xanthe could see why he had chosen her to be his wife.

She looked at him again, trying to commit to memory once more the face that she had loved. She was relieved to find that she felt a distance from him that had not been there before. She had put what there had been between them in the past. She had moved on. Samuel looked drawn and tired and she wondered what it must be like to watch a person you cared deeply about disappear in front of you, not knowing if they were alive or dead, fearing that they would never come back.

"I'm sorry, Samuel," she said, "for leaving you like that. I didn't mean to. It was the locket, and the fight, I . . ."

"Do not concern yourself. I was content that you were out of harm's way."

"What did Fairfax do to you, after I went?"

"He was enraged at having you slip from his grasp."

"I was worried. I wanted to return but I couldn't. My mother . . ."

"I am, as you see, unharmed."

"I have to go now," she said, turning to address Henrietta again. "It was a pleasure to meet you, mistress," she said.

"I am glad to have had the opportunity to meet someone who has done so much for Samuel."

"Will you return?" Samuel asked. When she did not answer he nodded, and she saw both resolve and resignation in his expression. "Then things will be as they should be," he said, without knowing how much those very words had come to matter to Xanthe; to be her reason for doing what she did. He gave a low bow. "I am ever in your debt, mistress. Fare thee well." And she saw that he too had accepted the way things were. His future was with Henrietta. He must let Xanthe go. As if to underline this point he held out his hand to Henrietta. She stepped over to stand at his side and put her hand in his. There passed between them a look, while not of passion, that told of commitment, of loyalty, of true affection, and of strength. All the things they would need for a future together in the turbulent times in which they lived.

Xanthe moved toward the door and then paused, taking one more look at Samuel, offering him her brightest smile. "Look after each other," she said quickly, leaving without waiting for a response.

She found Fairfax in the observatory in a state of agitation. He was rifling through papers on his desk, picking up this book, discarding it, snatching up a map or other document, talking about the necessity of choosing a place to make a journey, of what he should equip himself with, of what measures to take for a safe and swift return. Xanthe let him do what he felt vital to his survival. She was attempting to maintain the quiet presence of someone confident in their own abilities and unfazed by what they were about to do. It was, for the most part, a bluff, and she was surprised Fairfax believed it. The fact that he did reminded her how readily people believed what they wanted to be true, however unlikely, when it truly mattered to them. Her army coat had been laid upon a chair. She picked it up, comforted by its warm wool and the familiarity of it, the smell of woodsmoke from the chocolate house still discernible, but the smell of home, her own home, a little stronger. She removed her cloak and slipped the coat over her shoulders instead. Giving up something of Samuel's felt significant. She trod her own path, with her own duties and responsibilities and attachments now. As did Samuel.

After a further hour of bluster and discussion Fairfax at last stood still.

He could find no more reasons to delay and think of no other preparations to make. The moment had come. For the first time, Xanthe believed she saw the shadow of fear cloud his face.

"No one is making you do this," she told him. "This is what you want, remember?"

He frowned. "I would remind you, mistress, that you alone hold an alternative course within your gift. It is your refusal to agree to a partnership of two Spinners, a rebuttal of my marriage proposal, that has brought us to this action. You must accept your part in our fate, whatever it may be."

Thrown for a moment by the truth of this statement, Xanthe busied herself with her own preparations. There were not many to be made. She opened her shoulder bag and removed from it the chocolate pot she had persuaded Mistress Flyte to lend her. The copper was cool beneath her fingers and in it she saw her own blurred reflection. She felt the dent in the lid with her thumb. The dent that she had made. The dent that she had felt when she first found the pot in Laybrook in Esther Harris's collection, more than four hundred years from the moment at which she now stood. The pot vibrated in her hands, starting up its piercing song. The connection was still strong, but would it be strong enough? The words from *Spinners* had given her safeguards to help her travel with, but she had not tried them before. They should not only protect her, but guide her journey, giving her a greater control, more accuracy, and a better chance of a successful spinning. Would they work? Her greatest fear was that by going somewhere, *somewhen*, other than that chosen by the chocolate pot, she would somehow unravel that connection so that it could not bring her back. Either to this time or to her own. If she wasn't where she was supposed to be, wasn't where the found thing had wanted her to go, might that affect her locket? Could she end up marooned in a third time and place? It was a possibility. She pushed the thought from her mind and set about her task. Mistress Flyte had recommended she make Fairfax the central point of the ritual. It was his extreme moment they wanted to travel to. She was also to avoid touching the locket or thinking about Flora or anything connected with home. Xanthe instructed Fairfax to empty his pockets, which he did without question. She then had him stand in the center of the room at a point removed from objects and clutter. Xanthe rebuttoned her coat, slipped her bag over her shoulder, and replaced her hat upon her head.

"Should I equip myself with outdoor clothing?" Fairfax wanted to know.

"You probably won't need it," Xanthe told him, not meeting his lopsided gaze as the true meaning of this observation struck home. If she did her job well and they arrived where and when they needed to be, Fairfax might well be a convicted criminal on his way to meet his executioner. As she came to stand close to him he took hold of her arm, his grip tighter than was comfortable even through the thick wool of her coat.

"Do not think to trick me, little Spinner," he warned. "I am not the helpless passenger in this journey you prefer to imagine."

Xanthe shrugged off his hand. "Let's get on with it, shall we?"

She made him take hold of the chocolate pot too. "Are you sure your pockets are empty?" she asked.

"Yes. What is the importance of this?"

"Personal items have strong vibrations and the associations can interfere with what we are asking of this object," she said, gazing at the copper pot. "This is your anchor to me and mine to this point in time. Now, close your eyes." As he did so she moved closer, not enjoying the proximity to him but knowing it to be necessary for more than one reason. She quickly slipped the single, special coin into the pocket of his shirt; the one she had so carefully selected from the collection in the shop and brought with her. Such a small, worn little coin seemed a flimsy thing on which to place so much of her hope. As she dropped it into his pocket she offered a silent prayer to whomever or whatever it was that watched over Spinners, asking for her small refinement to the journey home Fairfax would make to be successful. If he noticed her standing near enough to press against him he did not comment on it. "Now," she said more calmly than she felt, "you have to think of the cell you were held in on the night of your execution."

"But surely to imagine the astrolabe would be more appropriate?"

"And how many times have you done that and gone nowhere? No, it is the heightened state that the dangerous moment in your life brought about that will call strongest. That and me being here."

When he opened his remaining good eye to look at her again, questioning the wisdom of her instructions, Xanthe had to damp down her temper. The last thing she needed was him sowing seeds of doubt in her mind. Not now.

"If you want this, you have to do what I tell you to do, and do it without question."

He set his mouth but did as she bid him.

Xanthe steeled herself. She shut out thoughts of Samuel, thoughts of her mother, thoughts of anything other than the chocolate pot and what Fairfax had told her about his execution. She tried to bring to mind the voice that she had heard from the book. The voice that had made her know that she had been chosen because of her own special gift. The voice that made her feel that she belonged. That she was not, in fact, doing any of her traveling alone. She closed her eyes for a moment and listened and was comforted to hear her name being whispered softly but clearly. Opening her eyes again she took the piece of paper from where she had concealed it close to her heart and unfolded it. The few lines she had written looked insignificant for such a huge task. Trying to summon the confidence they had inspired only a few hours earlier, Xanthe muttered them now, under her breath, trying to obey the instruction from the Spinner that they were for her alone. She would not impart them to Fairfax.

Let the door through the fabric of time swing wide,
May I travel through time's secret rift.
Let the centuries spin at my bidding,
May my return be sure and be swift.

The metal of the copper pot in her hands quickly changed from cool to almost intolerably hot. She heard Fairfax gasp. She closed her eyes, shutting out that other darkness that she knew must descend. She was aware of the ground beneath her feet lurching, upsetting her balance. Fairfax stumbled, but he too held tight to the chocolate pot. Then came the voices; the cries of the desperate and the lost, some calling Xanthe by name, others crying out to a Spinner to listen to them, to hear their story. She noticed that none called for Fairfax specifically. The sensation of both falling and moving fast through the blackness caused her stomach to tighten, but this time she did not feel afraid. This time, more than any other, even though she was doing something new, she felt in control. This was her choice. Her idea. Her way of doing what she needed to do. She had the found thing that sang to her even as they traveled. She had the snippets of wisdom gleaned from Mistress Flyte. She had the words from the book of Spinners, laid directly onto her ear. She had her mission to help Samuel to spur her on, and her need to return home safely to Flora to lend care and guile to her actions. She would not fail.

As quickly as the movements and supernatural sensations had begun, they ceased. She and Fairfax fell heavily onto the ground. She heard him groan as he landed. For a few seconds she remained where she fell, winded by the brutal connection with what transpired to be a stone floor. She knew better than to hurry to her feet. She let her mind and her body readjust, settle, recover, just for a moment. Beside her Fairfax cursed and struggled, dragging himself up, doing so too soon and too quickly so that he fell again. He lay moaning as Xanthe got carefully to her feet. She blinked, regaining focus. They were in a cell. A single candle stub sat on a small table against one wall beside a cot of pallets and straw. The air smelled of damp and of urine and of fear. She could hear the cries of prisoners close by railing against their lot. She helped Fairfax to his feet.

"Look about you," she told him. "Do you recognize this place?"

He pushed his lank hair from his face, hastening to regain his composure, doing what she asked of him. "I . . . can't be sure. Wait. It could be . . . I recall the flea-ridden bed, and the stink. . . ."

"Those could be found in any seventeenth-century cell, I should imagine. Is this one *yours*?"

He staggered about the small space, running his hands over the rough wood of the table, glancing toward the heavy door with its high iron-grilled opening. At last he spied an alcove in the far wall. It was nothing more than a natural gap in the stones, but it formed a cleft. He hurried to it, put in his hand, and drew out a cloth-wrapped loaf. He held it up for her to see as if offering a sacred relic.

"This! My manservant, still loyal, brought me food the day before my date of execution. This is that bread." He nodded at her. "This is my condemned cell. How came we here? Surely I have changed my fate to some-thing better?"

"I'm sure you will have. You must have. You were the king's man. . . ."

"Yet here we stand!"

"I told you this was a possible point of arrival for our journey. This is how it has to be, clearly. Don't lose your nerve now. And anyway, the cir-cumstance cannot be exactly the same. If you are where you were before, as you were before, you will have the astrolabe, surely?"

Fairfax dropped the loaf and shook out the cloth, holding it up to the light of the candle before abandoning it to search the little alcove again, grop-ing in the darkness with increasing desperation. At last he turned to her, shaking. "It is not there!" he said hoarsely.

"You had it hidden the first time you were here?"

Even in the inadequate light Xanthe could see how shattered the man was, and when he spoke she understood the reason for his stricken expression. "I was permitted to bring nothing with me into this godforsaken prison. When my servant brought me bread he risked his own life to bring me what I needed hidden within. It should be here and it is not. I tell you, the astrolabe is gone!"

17

THE ENORMITY OF THIS DISCOVERY OVERWHELMED FAIRFAX.

"You told me you would take me to it! You told me it would be here! I risked all!"

"Calm down. We don't know the situation yet. You might not be awaiting execution. There might be a lesser charge, you might be going to return home...."

"I tell you I know what this place is! Oh, I was a fool to believe you capable of doing what you promised."

"I said there would be risks. We did know you might end up having to go through the execution again. We discussed this. We wanted to come to the time and place, but you went back and changed things. After you escaped your execution you went back and changed the course of your life, you said so yourself. It was more likely we would come to this moment and find you a spectator in the crowd. That's what we planned for. I could make no guarantees. You knew that. But don't give up hope. You changed your own future by your shifting allegiances after the first time you escaped the scaffold. When you went back to your own time you swore your loyalty to the king."

"And yet here I stand once more! How is my fate improved?"

"I don't know, not yet ... but the first time ... the astrolabe did not return to your own time with you. It's possible you dropped it and it lies in the mud somewhere under the scaffold...."

"I should not have agreed to such a course of action! To find myself incarcerated again, and this time without my astrolabe ... If it sits out there beneath the boards now it may as well be at the bottom of an ocean, for I will not reach it before I am dispatched!" He stormed across the floor of the cell and took hold of Xanthe's arms. "We must go back. Now. Use your damned talisman and take us back!"

At that moment they heard the sound of footsteps heralding an approaching jailer. Light guttered through the grille in the door. Neither Xanthe nor Fairfax had time to move or speak before keys jangled and the lock was turned. A heavy bolt was drawn back and the door shoved open. The jailer was silhouetted against the torch he had placed in the wall sconce before stepping forward. The fractured light faded back along the stretch of narrow passageway that led from the cell.

The guard squinted in at Xanthe.

"How came you here?" he demanded. As Xanthe searched her mind for a plausible response he added, "A fine start to my watch. I should have been told if any of the prisoners had been permitted company. How am I to perform my duties acceptably when I am not appraised of the facts?" he asked of no one in particular, evidently expecting no reply. He stepped aside. "Out with you, wench. Time you were gone."

"And I?" There was a wavering note in Fairfax's voice that betrayed his fear. "When am I to leave this place?"

"Huh!" The jailer allowed himself a little laugh at his prisoner's expense. "Were I in your shoes, my noble Lord, I should not be so eager to make that short journey! Come, slattern, leave the man to his conscience now." So saying, he shoved a jar of beer into Fairfax's hand. "You have a friend left who sent this. And I am instructed your keepsakes be returned to you, though what use you may have for them now . . ." He left the thought unfinished as he tossed a small leather bundle onto the table. As it unraveled, both Fairfax and Xanthe glimpsed the glinting bronze and silver of the small, beautifully crafted astrolabe that lay inside.

Xanthe was pushed into the corridor and the door was slammed shut, locked, and bolted. She craned her neck for a final look through the door and saw Fairfax snatch up the precious device and hold it eagerly up to the light.

After the jailer had shooed her from the premises Xanthe found herself on the grounds of the Tower of London, lost and unnoticed among the rowdy crowd that surged and seethed around the scaffold, waiting for the next condemned man to be led to his doom. In such a throng it was easy to remain hidden in plain sight, and her faux seventeenth-century clothes were a passable disguise. What was less easy to explain should anyone have cared to ask was why she was wearing a heavy coat, warm clothes, and a weatherproof hat when it was clearly a bright summer's day. She quickly removed the incongruous outer garments, rolling them up and tying them to the strap of her shoulder bag. Judging by how high in the sky the sun sat, it was mid morning. The trees were in full leaf and people in the crowd were tanned from a full summer. The warmth of the day and the close press of bodies made the air heavy with smells of salty skin and unwashed clothes, over which Xanthe could detect the unmistakable stink of raw sewage. She looked about her, taking in the variety of people, apparently from all levels of society, who were drawn to witness the execution of traitors and murderers and who knew who else besides. Children ran and played amid the throng. Here and there hawkers offered pies or beer for sale. There was an unsettling atmosphere of a fair day or carnival, with human suffering and violence at its center. Xanthe moved cautiously between the spectators until she found a spot beside a wall in the shade, a little way to the side of the main area. From there she could watch without being jostled and could keep reasonably well out of sight herself.

She tried to take stock of the situation. Fairfax was in the condemned cell, that much was plain. The fact that the astrolabe had not been in its hiding place told her that this was not the moment before his original execution. Something had changed, therefore it could not be. So, this was a version of the date after he had been through it once before. Two things about this fact confused her. First, if this was the case, why wasn't the astrolabe somewhere on the ground beneath the raised platform on which the executions were performed? If Fairfax had dropped it the first time, seeing it slip down between the boards, the most likely place for it to be was still there in the mud somewhere. It was possible it could have been found by someone, of course. But someone had sent the astrolabe to him in his cell. Someone had had it and known of its importance to him. How did Fairfax come to have such a powerful ally in this second version of his experience of this date? And how had he come to fall so low as to be condemned when in Samuel's time he had been a successful, wealthy man of the king? Xanthe could not find tence so that Xanthe was unable to hear, unable to discover his crime. She saw him searching the crowd for her but did not dare signal to him. There were two possible ways their perilous plan could now progress. Either Fairfax successfully spun time at the point of his imminent death and this time managed to take the astrolabe with him, or he would trigger the journey but, as before, drop the device. If this second version of events happened, Xanthe would seize the moment of confusion when everyone was shocked and astonished to see a man disappear in front of them. She would hurry forward, dashing between the upright supports beneath the wooden platform, retrieve the astrolabe, and use the chocolate pot to return to Samuel's time. If he took the thing with him she would simply find a quiet corner from which to travel.

There was, of course, another possible outcome, and one which must have been much on the mind of Fairfax as the executioner placed the noose around his neck. What if he failed to trigger the device? What if this time he was unable to spin time at all? Was she about to stand there and watch him hang? Could she do that, knowing that it was she who brought him to this point? And what could she do to stop it? How long dare she leave things before trying to help him? And how would she get close enough to be able to help him? And might that not, after all, be the surest way of keeping Samuel safe: to let him hang? No, that was not an option she could seriously entertain. In any event, Xanthe decided, she needed to be closer. She squeezed and elbowed her way through the crowd, who were, helpfully, far too focused on Fairfax to notice anything out of the ordinary about the girl threading her way toward the scaffolding. As Xanthe slipped around the back of the platform she could hear prayers being read out, a final act of stamping the king's rule over his subjects, imposing his choice of religion upon the hapless prisoner. The rear of the dais was not guarded, as there were no steps on that side and it would have been difficult for anyone to get up onto the platform and interfere with the proceedings. Xanthe scurried across the dry, grassless stretch of earth and dropped to her hands and knees, quickly crawling beneath the wooden planks. She waited to see if anyone had noticed and would raise the alarm, but all were far too intent on witnessing Fairfax's suffering. From where she crouched, Xanthe could see up through the gaps in the boards. She could see figures moving about; the shuffling feet of Fairfax as he was manhandled, his wrists bound, the slow pad of the priest as he stepped behind him, the heavy thud of the hooded executioner's boots as he tightened the knot of the noose at the nape of his prisoner's neck and then went to stand to one side, ready to kick the stool from beneath Fairfax's feet. There was a pause. The crowd fell silent. Xanthe felt sure the drumming of her own heart was loud enough to be heard. She thought she sensed Fairfax's thoughts, those of a Spinner summoning the ability to move through time, inexpert and garbled, tangled with voices of others sensitive to another journey being made. The air was filled with the pungent stench of hot urine.

And then there came a scream. Not from Fairfax. A woman at the front of the crowd was the first to react to the shocking sight of a man vanishing before her eyes. Pandemonium ensued. The priest called on God to protect them from the devil's magic. The executioner exclaimed and shouted at the guards. Men in the crowd shouted their anger; they had been tricked, duped, justice denied them. Women screamed and ushered their children away. The guards rushed this way and that in a fruitless search, during which Xanthe feared she herself might be found. She patted the earth around her in the half-light, checking for the astrolabe. She had not noticed it fall, but she had to be certain. She could hear footsteps coming nearer. The searchers would soon discover her, and then what? If they took the chocolate pot from her she might not be able to travel back to Samuel, and if they took away her locket she would be completely trapped. There was no sign of the astrolabe. Satisfied that Fairfax must have succeeded in taking it with him this time, she took the pot from her bag, held it close, closed her eyes, uttered the words she had been taught, and focused her mind with all her strength and concentration upon Samuel. She was aware of the shouts and curses of the guards as they discovered her at the very moment she spun time and went hurtling through the years once more.

Xanthe found it frustrating, but not surprising, to discover she had arrived yet again in the chocolate house. It was as if the pot would always insist on taking her there. As she moved groggily through the cellar of the old building she wondered if it would now consider she had completed her task. Into these muddled thoughts came the voice of Mistress Flyte.

"I am pleased to see you, but what of Fairfax? Tell me, what has become of him?" The old woman held a lamp high, meeting Xanthe on the stairs and taking her arm, searching her face for an answer.

Xanthe rubbed her eyes and when she spoke her own voice was hoarse and weak.

"He escaped the hangman a second time," she confirmed.

"And the astrolabe?"

"He has it. Or at least he didn't leave it behind when he traveled from the scaffold." Xanthe's legs suddenly gave way beneath her and she stumbled against the steps.

"You are fatigued by the spinning." Mistress Flyte helped her up. "Come, I will have Edmund fetch brandied chocolate and beef stew. As you eat you can tell me all that has occurred."

Once settled in the comfort and safety of Mistress Flyte's sitting room, and revived by the supper Edmund brought her, Xanthe did indeed recount the story of her journey with Fairfax, step by step. She did her best to give a detailed account, but even so the old woman probed for every moment, every aspect of their time spent traveling. She asked so many questions and Xanthe was still weary from such a risky and bewildering journey.

"I'm sorry I don't have all the answers you want," she said, closing her eyes for a moment. "All I can tell you is that I believe it worked. I think I did what I needed to do and fulfilled my part of the deal."

"Assuming Fairfax has safely returned. Of course you must have come to realize by now that such a man will not settle. Once he has the device in his possession he will want to use it, and it will not take him many days to discover he is untalented and clumsy. He is a Spinner of the most basic nature, and this conclusion will not sit well with him. It will also lead him to the conclusion that his wishes could be better served if he had both the astrolabe and you."

Xanthe nodded. "I had thought of that."

"Do you still believe he will honor his side of the agreement and let the Applebys alone? He is slippery as a buttered eel."

"I believe the document he signed will prevent him going back on his word. But no, I don't trust him. He will try his best to wriggle out of the bargain. Or at least he would have tried, if I hadn't made it just a tiny bit more difficult for him."

"Ah, the coin! You succeeded in making sure he had it with him when he traveled?"

"I slipped it into his pocket. I double-checked it hadn't got mixed up with the money you gave me. It was definitely the right coin."

"The one dated a year from now."

"That's right. I made him empty his pockets before we traveled, so that he didn't have anything personal to connect him with this date. I figured the observatory and the pull of his own character would draw him back to the right place, but that coin was in good condition, made of silver, with the date clearly readable. With nothing else to locate him in the exact date I felt sure it would take him to its own time."

"The abbey, then, but in a time not yet come? One year hence. Ingenious!"

"I reckon he'll figure out how to use the astrolabe more accurately when he has to, so he'll return to this time soon. But it will take him a while. For all his bluster and ambition, he was never good at spinning time when he had the thing before. I can't see him risking using it straightaway, not until he is certain he can do so accurately. I wanted to buy Samuel some time of his own. Time to restore the reputation of his family, shore up a few allegiances, before Fairfax can get back here and try to cause trouble for him. And of course," she hesitated, taking a moment to study Mistress Flyte's face as she went on, "I will be long gone by then. Out of his reach."

The old woman said nothing. Xanthe tried to fathom what it was she wasn't saying. What secret was she keeping in that silence? She had already begun to suspect that Mistress Flyte was holding things back, things to do with the Spinners. She was a hard woman to read, and Xanthe knew she had little chance of getting anything from her that she did not want to share. Why, for instance, had she been so interested in the journey she and Fairfax had made together? Her insistence on knowing every detail seemed to suggest an interest beyond just wanting to know that Fairfax would not present a threat, and even further than simply being the curiosity of a fellow Spinner, particularly a retired one. Xanthe was not surprised to see that her host did not like the thought of her returning to her own time. She wanted her to stay at the chocolate house. But what for? She needed to get her to explain.

"I'm sure you'll find yourself another serving girl, mistress. Bradford must have plenty to choose from. Nice warm work, with free chocolate, after all. I'm sure there are girls would jump at the chance."

The old woman sighed and leaned back in her chair, turning to gaze into the fire as she had done before, the shadow of sadness clouding her eyes. Xanthe recalled her looking just so during an earlier conversation. Another time when they had talked about Fairfax. Was she still frightened of him, perhaps? Was she afraid he would take his anger out on her if he returned and found Xanthe gone and Samuel safely beyond the reach of his influence?

"He will be too busy using his precious new toy to bother you," Xanthe told her. "By the time he makes his way back to *this* time he will have plenty to do explaining his absence to the king too, and making sure he doesn't end up on that scaffold for a third time. I don't think you have any reason to be fearful of him."

Mistress Flyte shook her head and when she spoke there was a slight tremor in her voice. For once, instead of an elegant mature woman with a powerful secret knowledge and a thriving business that kept her in touch with the mood of the country, she looked to Xanthe like an old woman struggling to manage on her own, beaten down by the experiences life had dealt her.

"You are a Spinner of rare ability, child. You have a singular gift, yet you are innocent in the dark ways in which this world works. You show promise in your thinking, for not many would so much as attempt to outwit Benedict Fairfax. And you have courage, that is plain to see. But you know not how great your talent could be, nor how much envy such a gift provokes in others!" She paused, composing herself, sitting straight backed once again, mustering her more customary control and poise. "You have been called, I believe you understand that now, at least. Has not the book finding its way to you convinced you of that? A Spinner of such caliber as yours cannot turn her back on that calling. You may have completed this task, but there will be others who need your help. Others for whom perhaps their only hope of justice is through the art of the Spinner and counting one as their ally."

"And this is Spinner central, I suppose? I know you want me to stay, but I've explained . . ."

"Not I! Foolish girl. Do you consider the wishes of an old woman of any importance? My duty is to keep the chocolate house so that free thinkers and those who would defend the innocent against such men as Fairfax, they have a place of safety in which to meet. In which to form true alliances. But such a haven has its limitations. What is more important is that I keep my home open to Spinners who are called that they might have a point of entry and exit for their travels. Do you not see that you have found your true place of belonging?"

"And what of my life? My mother?"

"Alas, such sacrifices are often asked of us. You will come to see where your duty lies."

Xanthe got to her feet, shaking her head.

"Look, I'm grateful for how you've helped me, really I am. But as I think I've said before, I didn't ask for any of this. I've done what I came to do. And now I'm going home. I'm sorry I can't do what you want. I can't be what you want. That's just the way it is." She got to her feet, buttoning up her coat once more. "I'll take my book now," she said.

The old woman got up and fetched it from her desk. As she handed it to Xanthe she said, "There is something you have forgotten, is there not?"

"Sorry?"

"The chocolate pot. You borrowed it."

Instinctively Xanthe put her hand in her leather bag, but it was empty. Confused, she thought aloud. "I used it to travel safely. That's why I took it with me to Fairfax's execution: so I could come back here. And it worked. It brought me back, right to the chocolate house." She frowned, trying to make sense of it all.

"You know an object cannot be brought back from the future to a time and place where it exists. If it did, that would result in two identical things inhabiting the same moment. That cannot happen. The pot traveled forward with you. . . ."

"Oh my God, have I left it there?"

"No, it will be at the point of your recent departure."

"Fairfax's observatory."

"Correct. It belongs here. With me. In the chocolate house. It must be returned here, you understand that, do you not?"

Xanthe experienced a momentary panic. She needed to return home as quickly as possible after seeing Samuel. Traveling back to Bradford once again would take up valuable time, and yet she knew that Mistress Flyte was right; the pot belonged in the chocolate house. It had to be returned. After some thought she said, "I will see that it is brought back," even though she was, at that moment, uncertain how she was going to make this happen. "When I go to see Samuel and tell him what has happened I will retrieve the pot." She tucked the Spinners book carefully back into her bag and fastened the straps.

"It is of the utmost importance that these things are left as they should be. A Spinner must recognize and take on such responsibilities. All found things are to be treated with respect and kept safe. Though, of course, you will not find Master Appleby at the abbey."

"I won't?"

"I am reliably informed that he has returned to the family home at Marlborough."

"I'm glad to hear it. He must be so happy to be free to come and go as he pleases. I know he will complete his work at the abbey—he won't want to give Fairfax any excuse to damage his reputation as an architect—but he has been a prisoner. At least now he will be working as a free man."

As Xanthe prepared to leave, Mistress Flyte put a hand on her arm. The old woman had recovered from her injuries remarkably well, so that Xanthe could see once again the spark of life and wisdom in those bright blue eyes.

"You have proved yourself a true Spinner, child."

"I could not have done it without your help."

"And without *your* assistance I should not be here at all."

"That's what we are here for after all, isn't it? To help each other."

"Spinners and less gifted travelers all," Mistress Flyte agreed.

"Tell me one more thing." Xanthe hitched her bag over her shoulder. "Who do you think it was who attacked you? Do you still remember nothing of that night?"

"There is a darkness in my mind from the moment before the attack until I awoke, broken and bruised, in my own bed days later. And yet . . ."

"Yes?"

"I would not have drawn back the bolt on that door, would not have ventured forth into the alleyway alone at night unless I believed I knew who it was who called my name." She sighed. "It is not uncommon to make enemies when one supports those some consider dangerous. Dangerous, that is, to the accepted order. I must accept it as part of my lot in life. As must you."

With that thought, Xanthe gave the old woman a light peck on the cheek and set out once more for the stage, this time not to Laybrook, but to Marlborough.

❧ 18 ❧

ON THE STAGE JOURNEY TO MARLBOROUGH XANTHE HAD THE CHANCE TO THINK ABOUT HER conversation with Mistress Flyte. She had been grateful for the old woman's support and help, and had begun to feel she knew the woman, but now she had the sense that there was a great deal hidden. That her life held many secrets, and that some of them concerned not only the Spinners in general, but Fairfax in particular. Now that she knew she had once been a Spinner and turned her back on what she clearly considered a calling, Xanthe had so many questions, and she believed Mistress Flyte could provide answers. If only there was time. And assuming she was ready to trust Xanthe with the secrets of her past. She evidently loathed Fairfax and was frightened of him, that much was clear. But Xanthe could not quite work out what Mistress Flyte had been hoping for when she had heard of her plan to retrieve the astrolabe for him. Had she secretly hoped the mission would fail and that Fairfax would be hanged? She certainly seemed dissatisfied with the outcome of him being at least temporarily stranded and out of the way. And there was something else that nagged away at Xanthe: if she was so taken up with the business of working as a time traveler, why had she given it up?

At last the stagecoach began to descend the hill into Marlborough. A nervousness assailed Xanthe. In part it was due to the way seeing the town in its earlier state, without her own home existing in it, unsettled her and made her feel homesick. More than that, though, it was the proximity to Samuel. Yet again she had come to say goodbye to him. However often she had to do it, it never seemed to become less painful. Would this be the final time she saw him? It was likely, and the thought hurt her more than it should have.

She recalled how the last time she had spoken to him he had been with Henrietta. Xanthe had to accept that the future she had won for him included his fiancée, not herself.

The day was fading into late afternoon, the light already failing, as the driver pulled the blowing horses to a halt outside the Quills Inn. As she stepped from the carriage, shivering in the east wind that raced along the broad high street, Xanthe attempted to cheer herself up by imagining what Harley would make of seeing his beloved pub in its youthful incarnation. It failed to lift her mood. She could not keep subjecting herself to this manner of emotional turmoil. This would have to be the last farewell she said to Samuel; there was no other way. She shouldered her bag and marched toward the Appleby house, determined to keep her feelings in check. She had done what she came to do. All that remained was to tell Samuel he would be free from Fairfax at least for a while, and then she could go home. Even as she formed this thought she had to stop herself glancing down the alleyway where her own house, and the shop, were not yet built. And would not be for another two centuries. The idea still caused her head to knot, her thoughts to fight against the impossibility of what she was doing.

Welcoming lamplight shone through the windows of Samuel's fine town house, guiding her up across the green. She knocked, expecting Philpott to let her in, so she was thrown when Samuel himself opened the door.

For a moment they stood looking at each other saying nothing. It was Samuel who found his voice first.

"I am happy to see you returned safe and well," he said.

Xanthe attempted nonchalance and gave a shrug. "I told you not to worry about me, remember?"

Samuel recovered himself enough to recall his manners. Stepping aside he beckoned her. "Forgive me, I should not keep you out on such a chill night. Come, Philpott is fetching supper for us all. Father and Joshua will be delighted to see you again."

Xanthe stepped into the hall but put a hand on his arm.

"I can't stay, Samuel," she said gently. "Can we talk? Just for a moment, and then . . ."

". . . then you will leave me again? 'Twas ever thus," he replied, his own attempt at levity no more successful than hers. He led her not to the sitting room, then, but through the house, across the courtyard, and into his studio. The space was barely any warmer than outside, but it was quiet and private. And, Xanthe told herself, it was Samuel's place. It was the right place in which to remember him. It was the right place from which she could leave him. The smell of the wood and plaster and resin and ink took her back to the first time he had shown her his studio and shared his passion for his work with her. How much had happened since then. How far they had both come in so many ways. She made herself concentrate on what she needed to explain to Samuel. There were so many details that were impossible to share with him, the barest facts would have to do. At least, by now, he was quite accustomed to her being mysterious and evasive. She walked slowly around the studio as she spoke.

"Fairfax has what he wants," she told him. "He will be away for some time."

"Away? Where has he gone?"

"Oh, far enough not to bother you or your family. For a while." She stopped and smiled at him. "It will be all right now, Samuel. I promise you. You can get on with your life. You have his letter, and by the time he returns, well, he will have other things to think about, and you will have restored the family name with the people who matter."

"Yet again, I am in your debt," he said, watching her closely. She sensed he was looking for any sign of how she felt about him, any chink in the armor she had put on to protect herself from more heartache. "And you, Xanthe?" he asked. "You are . . . content to return to your home once again?"

"I came here to let you know about Fairfax, Samuel. That's all there was left for me to do. Although, there is a small favor I need to ask of you."

"You have only to say it."

"It might seem a little odd. . . . When next you are at the abbey, I left something there. A copper chocolate pot. You will find it in Fairfax's observatory. It needs to be returned to the chocolate house in Bradford. Could you do that for me?"

"I return to Laybrook on the morrow; I will find the pot the moment I arrive at the abbey."

"It is really important. To me."

"I will do as you ask without delay. You may depend upon it."

She nodded, satisfied that he understood how much her strange request mattered.

Samuel took a step closer to her. She could detect the sandalwood soap he used now, sense the warmth of him. When he spoke his voice was low and tight with emotion. "I think you will not come here again."

She met his gaze then, thinking of how the four paces between them might as well have been four hundred miles, because the four centuries that separated them were a distance they could never cross for more than brief snatches of time.

"Be safe, Samuel," she said. "Be happy."

He lifted his hand as if to take hers but did not. "I would with all my heart that things were other than they are, but God, fate, and whatever it is that sent you to me, decrees otherwise. We have different lives to live, you and I. In our worlds that are worlds apart. Let us live them without regret. Without reserve," he told her slowly. When she nodded her understanding he went on, "Do you wish me to walk you to the blind house?"

"No, thank you. I think, this time, I will leave from here. If that's all right with you?"

"I would prefer it," he said, gesturing at his studio with a wave of his arm. "That way I shall think of you as being here, whenever I am at my work. I might fancy, at times when I am alone here, that you are at my shoulder."

"I will be," she said, "as long as you remember me."

He held her gaze, his dark eyes somber.

Xanthe expected him to leave her then, or at least turn away. But she saw that he was waiting for her to go. He had seen her vanish before, both times when she had not meant him to, when he had not understood. Now, this time, he would watch her and that was how they would part.

She could put off the moment no longer. Xanthe slipped her finger beneath her collar and hooked out her gold locket. It felt warm. Still looking at Samuel, she clicked it open. In her peripheral vision she saw her mother's face smiling from the tiny photograph. She took one last lingering look at Samuel.

SECRETS OF THE CHOCOLATE HOUSE   ❖ 263

"Goodbye," she whispered. And as she felt herself falling through time she heard his voice following her.

"Farewell and Godspeed!"

And then the other voices, the cries and whispers and entreaties of myriad people lost and wandering and in need, drowned him out, and he was gone, and Xanthe tumbled through the centuries again.

On this occasion the transition from Samuel's time to her own was swift and less disorienting than Xanthe had anticipated. She had learned that when her task was complete and the found thing that had sung to her fell silent, the final journey home was usually quite brutal, leaving her bewildered and unwell. She recalled coming home after the chatelaine was done with her and how she had had such a bad fall in the blind house that she had lain there for hours. This time was painless and calm. Xanthe was confused by this. What did it signify? What was different this time? Perhaps she was simply becoming more adept at moving through time, more practiced at making the necessary transitions. She dusted herself off and felt around on the floor of the little building for the chocolate pot. There was some light coming through the gap around the door, suggesting morning sunshine outside, but it was still hard to see much. Frustrated, she took her torch from her bag and searched again. Nothing. It was gone. Could Flora have come in and taken it again? She checked her bag for *Spinners* and was relieved to find that at least the book was where she expected it to be. She would have to find a safe place for it in the house, probably in her own bedroom. She felt the need to keep it close. Switching off the torch, she gave herself a moment to prepare her story in her mind. Next, she pushed the door open a fraction and peered out, relieved to find the garden empty. She crept toward the house, reassuring herself that at least her coat covered her unusual clothes, but still anxious about bumping into her mother while coming from the direction of the garden. She paused at the back door, which was firmly closed against the cold of the day. She put her ear to the old wood and listened hard. The radio was on, a talk program. Xanthe recognized it as one her mother regularly listened to while working, which meant she must be in her workshop rather than the shop itself. If she could sneak through and appear as if through the front door . . . She turned the handle and slowly pushed the door, wincing as it creaked a little. She heard a voice, her mother's, chatting in answer to the reporter on the radio. Flora's habit of holding one-sided conversations with radio and television reporters was an old one and at that moment Xanthe blessed her for it. She was too taken up with indignation at some recent political outrage to notice her daughter slip along the hallway into the shop. Xanthe saw that the sign had been turned to closed and the row of clocks declared it to be one-thirty. Lunchtime. Xanthe made a point of opening and closing the shop door noisily, the aged bell sounding its welcome.

"Mum?" she called out cheerily. "You there?"

"Hi, Xanthe, love. I'm in the workshop!" Flora's voice sounded stronger, back to her more upbeat, resilient self.

Xanthe went to her, shaking off the growing self-hatred that came with the moment of presenting her mother with lie upon lie about where she had been and what she had been doing.

"One last time," she said to herself under her breath. "One last time."

Flora greeted her warmly, hugging her in a way that reassured Xanthe the pain from her arthritis had receded.

"Well?" Flora pulled back to look at her daughter. "How was it? Tell me everything. What was the turnout like? And the pub?"

"Oh, it was a bit more low-key than Harley had led us to expect, but nice enough."

"Nice? That doesn't sound very rock and roll."

"It was fine, Mum, really. Just what I needed. Nothing flash and intimidating. Friendly people . . ."

"And Harley's friend, what was his name?"

For a moment Xanthe panicked, unable to recall what she and Harley had dreamed up. She told herself her mother had obviously forgotten too, so it didn't matter. "Richard, yeah, nice bloke."

"So, a nice bloke with a nice pub. That's . . . nice." Flora smiled.

Xanthe was relieved to see that it was a teasing smile, not a doubting one.

"Yes, so, maybe I'll go there again."

"I tried to phone you twice, just to see how you were getting on. Your phone is always switched off. Honestly, I don't know why you bother having the thing. I can never get hold of you while you're away."

"Sorry, Mum. I just needed to stay focused. And, well, sometimes hearing a sympathetic voice, you know how that can make it harder to be strong. Sometimes."

"Well a text message would have been nice, just to let me know how you are."

"Sorry," she said again, cursing the way that her own phone seemed to work against her.

Flora smiled then, her features animated. "Actually, I have something to tell you. I haven't been moping around here like Billy no-mates while you've been away."

"Oh?"

"No. Look at these." She held her hands palms up.

Xanthe was at a loss.

"Go on," Flora insisted, "look closely. What do you see?"

"Um. blue paint . . . beeswax . . . blisters?"

"Yes!"

"How did you get those?"

"Bell-ringing, of course!" She waved her calloused hands pointedly. "Graham let me loose and it was such fun!"

"And it was OK, pulling the ropes? I mean, your hands . . ."

"As you can see, they need to toughen up a bit. Only beginners get these, actually. Should stop once I've mastered the technique. And they play handbells too. Like Sheila said, I have a natural ear. I think you'd be impressed." She grinned broadly, enjoying her daughter's surprise. "What's more the shop has been hectic too. Sales are up. And I finished painting that little chest of drawers. You know what they say: if you want something done, ask a busy person."

The two fell to talking easily about how busy the shop had been and how many things Flora had been able to work on in the evenings without Xanthe there to distract her. If she thought her daughter's reluctance to talk about her singing was strange she didn't press the point. Xanthe decided her mother was probably being tactful, not wanting to make a big thing of it, just happy she was singing again. Perhaps she believed it would take time for Xanthe to build up her confidence and she needed to allow for that. To discover that Flora had made new friends and found a new hobby in her absence was immensely cheering.

After a half hour of catching up Xanthe said she would nip upstairs to change and then reopen the shop. As she got to the door she asked as casually as she could, "Mum, have you moved the chocolate pot again?"

"What? No, haven't touched it. I thought you took it up to your room."

"You're right. Must be up there somewhere."

"Can't you find it? Can't you hear it singing?"

It was only when Flora asked this question that Xanthe realized something was not right. If her task was incomplete the object that had called to her would continue to sing and hum and vibrate, that much she knew. If she had succeeded in her mission then it would fall silent, become simply another antique curio. But the chocolate pot had disappeared. What could that mean? She became aware that her mother was waiting for an answer.

"Oh, I've probably hidden it in a cupboard," she said with a dismissive wave of her hand. "You know, put it out of earshot one night when it was keeping me awake. I'll find it in a minute." Seeing Flora's uncertain expression Xanthe sought to change the subject. "By the way, you remember that surprise I was planning?"

"Ooh, yes!"

"Well, I can share it with you now. Gerri and I have been hatching a plan for a historical Saturday promotion for Parchment Street. All of us in seventeenth-century costume, showcasing our older antiques, Gerri cooking cakes and puddings of the time. . . . She thinks she can get her friend on Radio Wiltshire to cover it. Should make a nice change from the usual run-up to Christmas stuff. Help us find a few new customers. What do you think?"

"That's a wonderful idea! Now I get the clothes, which were outlandish even for you, I have to say. But why were you planning it in the garden shed?"

Without missing a beat Xanthe replied, "Mum, I know nothing gets past you; I have to go to some lengths to keep a surprise a surprise. Didn't think you'd come across the bits and pieces I've been putting together if I kept them out there."

"Ha! I'll know where to look next time you're acting suspiciously," Flora laughed, causing Xanthe a momentary flash of panic and making her wish she'd thought of something else to say. At least Flora was now focused on planning the event. "We will need to put a notice in the paper, and some flyers, I think. And you and I will have to dig through all the stock, see what's relevant, make a special display in the window. And maybe a discount for the weekend . . ."

"So you like the idea, then?" Xanthe felt her spirits lifted by her mother's instant enthusiasm.

"Love it. More than that," she stepped forward and put her hand on Xanthe's arm, "I love that you thought of it."

"It'll be fun. Seventeenth century and making money, what's not to like?" she said before slipping away to change her clothes. Once back in her room she sat on the bed for a moment, her head in her hands. She suddenly felt utterly exhausted. All that she had done in the seventeenth century; the ever-present fear of making a mistake and the possible consequences for Samuel, for herself, for Flora; the journeying through time itself; the lies upon lies upon lies that she had to tell her mother; the worry about her mother's health; and the heavy weight of heartache over finally parting from Samuel, all combined to drain her of every last ounce of strength and energy. Wearily, she untied her laces, kicked off her boots, took *Spinners* from her bag and hugged the book tightly, then pulled a woolen blanket over herself, curled up on her bed, and slept.

That evening Xanthe decided she needed to talk to Harley. The cold weather had begun to adversely affect the temperature in the attic bedrooms, so that she found herself digging out warmer garments. She selected a vintage corduroy pinafore, pulling it over a seventies flowery blouse and on top of that a deep red alpaca cardigan. Black leggings and woolen socks felt like the final acceptance that winter had arrived. She hurried downstairs and explained to Flora it was only polite to report back to Harley on how the gigs in London had gone.

Flora laughed at this idea. "Well, I hope he can get more out of you than your own mother can! Perhaps a decent glass of wine will make you feel more like talking about the performances. He'll want to know, I mean, it is his friend's pub after all."

Xanthe endured another onslaught of guilt as she agreed with Flora.

"Let's have a bite to eat before I go," she suggested.

"I do eat when you're away, you know," Flora assured her.

"I know, I just . . . I like looking after you, Mum."

"It's not your job."

"I don't see it like that, really I don't." Noticing the sadness in her mother's expression Xanthe tried to lift the mood. "If it was a job it would be better paid! Think I'll stick to singing and antiques to earn my living, thanks very much."

Flora relaxed, sitting down at the table. "Mind you, that doesn't mean you can't cook your own mum a plate of spaghetti bolognese from time to time. Have we got any Parmesan?"

Xanthe made herself feel significantly better about her treatment of her mother, about all the disappearances, the coming and going, and of course the secrets, by making them both a tasty meal. She fought off her own impatience at wanting to talk to Harley about all that had happened. Flora deserved something of her; it wasn't fair that her needs so often seemed to slip down Xanthe's list of priorities.

When she eventually got to The Feathers, Harley was delighted to see her and abandoned poor Annie to manage the bar without him.

"Seriously, Harley?" his wife protested, not unreasonably. "It's getting really busy. . . ."

"I'll be back directly, hen, I promise," he assured her, leading Xanthe upstairs to their comfortable if slightly chaotic sitting room. There were two overstuffed leather sofas and more motorbike memorabilia than there was sensibly room for. Xanthe sunk into one deep, squashy sofa and Harley took the one opposite her, perching on the edge of his seat. He was so eager to hear what she had to tell him he didn't even offer her a drink.

"So you've been? You've actually traveled back in time, done your thing there, and returned home, safe and sound and in one piece?" When she nodded he whistled, flopping back in the deep leather sofa, his bushy brows lifting high in astonishment at the thought of what she was telling him. "I mean to say, lassie, I knew that was what you *said* you were going to do, and that you said you've done it before, but after we talked, after the book . . . and now to have you sitting there telling me you've actually *done* it. Marvelous. Bloody marvelous," he said.

"I've told Mum as little as possible about my 'gigs' in London. If she asks you about it . . ."

"I will be vague to the point of unhelpful and change the subject," he promised. "But tell me, what was it like? How did it feel, to move through time like that? Were there noises? Sounds? It must have been scary as hell."

"I am sort of getting used to it."

"Imagine that!"

"But yes, you're right, it can be scary. Especially when you don't end up where you think you will. And there are people trying to communicate, calling my name; some of them sound desperate, frightened. . . ."

"That must be distressing for you. And then you get there and . . . what?"

"Mostly I just have to pitch straight in. To start with I feel groggy, a bit like I'm waking up with a hangover, you know?"

"I am somewhat familiar with that condition, aye."

"There isn't time to think about it, to be honest. I'm usually just dealing with what's going on wherever I've pitched up."

"And the book?" he asked. "Was it of any assistance? Were you able to discover how to use it at all?"

Xanthe thought about how much the book meant. About what Mistress Flyte had told her. It only revealed its contents to those who were worthy of hearing them. It had chosen her. Having the book come into her possession was a call to arms. The enormity of that returned to her now that she had Harley to discuss it with. "I did find someone who showed me how to use it," she said. "I couldn't have done what I did without it, that's for sure." Xanthe smiled. "Turns out only the special few can see anything in it at all."

"You don't say?" Harley went a little pink with the pleasure of finding himself to be included in that number. "Well, well!"

"It seems so. My friend . . ."

"The one who you thought would be able to help?"

"Yes, her name is Louisa Flyte. She explained that the book finds the person it needs to be with. That it found me."

The next half hour passed quickly, with Harley quizzing her, hungry for details, and Xanthe finding the process of sharing her experiences hugely helpful. She was unburdening herself, to someone who chose to believe, who genuinely accepted what she was telling him. It mattered. It went some way to stopping her from feeling she was going slightly insane. It even eased her sadness at having to leave Samuel a tiny bit, as if having someone to talk to about him made him still in some way close to her. Still real, if she could sensibly use that word.

At last Harley slapped his thighs. "Hen, you are a wonder! You set out to save your friend and it sounds to me like you did just that. And what an adventure you've had! It's incredible, and yet it's all true!"

"You don't know how much it helps to hear you say that."

There came the sound of brisk footsteps on the stairs. Annie appeared at the door.

"Any chance of a hand, Harley? Pub's filling up."

Xanthe got to her feet. "I was just going anyway. Sorry to keep him, Annie."

"No problem. Actually, I wanted to talk to you."

"Oh?"

"The Blues Mothers have canceled on us. I don't suppose you fancy filling in? This Friday night?"

Xanthe looked at Harley, wondering how much he'd told his wife about where she was supposed to have been. Did she think she'd just come from doing successful performances in London? Xanthe was uncomfortable with the idea that her lies to her mother on this occasion had involved Harley. It felt wrong, and less safe. The more people shared a secret, the more likely it was to be exposed. Whatever he might or might not have told Annie, it didn't alter the fact that she owed him, and Annie, a favor.

"Sure," she said. "I'd be happy to." She smiled at Harley and left, grateful for something approaching normal life to be picking up again, if only to help her forget about how final her farewell with Samuel had been this time. As she walked home she found that her mind kept returning to the matter of the missing chocolate pot. It bothered her that she had not kept her promise to Mistress Flyte. At the time it had felt reasonable to ask Samuel to return it. Surely she could rely on him to do as she asked. Now, though, she worried that she should have taken the pot to its proper home herself. Perhaps it mattered that she was not the one placing it where it should be, restoring the order of things. It was more than an insignificant loose end, it seemed. If one of the consequences of her decision was that she did not have the pot, what else had changed? What else had she altered, without meaning to, not only in her present, but in the years between Samuel's time and her own? She recalled what Mistress Flyte had told her about it being her duty to complete the tasks she was called to in order for things to be as they should. She had worked as much out for herself after the chatelaine had summoned her to action. The more she thought about it, the more she worried that she had been wrong to leave such an important piece of the puzzle to someone else, even Samuel. She should have taken the chocolate pot back to its rightful home herself. And if Samuel hadn't done it, did that mean he couldn't? What was stopping him? As she wearily climbed the stairs to her room she did her best to shake off the feeling that there would be consequences to her actions. What was done was done, she was home, she couldn't go back, it was too late to change things now.

19

THERE WAS SOMETHING IMPORTANT THAT XANTHE BADLY WANTED TO DO, SOMETHING difficult but necessary if she was truly to put the events of her trip to Samuel's time behind her. However, now that she was home, the shop and Flora, not unreasonably, demanded her attention. Added to which, she had committed herself to band practice with Tin Lid. She'd found several texts waiting for her from Liam when she'd returned, the last one just giving the date, venue, and time of the session, saying how much he was looking forward to seeing her there. Xanthe felt she had so much to cope with already, but she couldn't let him down. And beyond that, she wanted to do it. Wanted to sing. With a band. With Liam. She found the old school hall on the outskirts of the town the following day. The band members were already set up, and Liam introduced them.

"Spike's been playing the drums longer than he can remember, but then Spike's memory's not the best," he said, pointing at the slightly plump figure behind the drum kit. "Baz is on keyboards, Mike's on bass, and then there's me." Amid the general greetings and smiles Liam took hold of Xanthe's hand. It was a small gesture, but a meaningful one. He gave a gentle squeeze and looked at her. "I'm really glad you came," he said. "We all are. The lads heard you sing at The Feathers. Have you got something you want to do?"

"We're a bit rusty on the medieval stuff," Baz admitted.

Spike started beating out an ancient marching rhythm. "We can adapt, babe. No worries."

Xanthe laughed, feeling herself relax just a little. She had thought about what she would sing and decided against anything from Samuel's time. The music of his day would be too poignant for her. "Actually," she said, "I thought I'd do something more in keeping with what you guys normally play. Do you have anything that would suit my voice?"

This was met with relief and enthusiasm from the whole band. After various suggestions were challenged they agreed on a Fleetwood Mac number, *Dreams,* found the right key, and sorted out a microphone for Xanthe. She took up her place at the front of the band, next to Liam. Looking at him she realized how much she had missed being a part of a group. She also realized how much happier she was to be sharing the makeshift stage with Liam rather than Marcus. At last she was able to give herself up to the music, letting the melody lift her, winding her sinuous voice around the lyrics, feeling the combined talents of the band working with her. It was such a sweet release after all the anxiety and challenges of late, she reveled in it. When the number came to an end there was a moment of silence before Spike gave a heartfelt whoop of delight and then the others clapped and congratulated Xanthe, one another, and themselves, on making such a beautiful sound.

Liam beamed. "You were bloody fantastic!"

"No," Xanthe corrected him, "*we* were."

He nodded. "We need to get out there, show everyone what we can do together. I need to find us a gig really soon."

"Actually," Xanthe told him, "I'm supposed to be singing in The Feathers tomorrow night. . . ."

Liam's smile broadened. "Perfect," he said, holding her gaze, his eyes bright, his expression showing genuine delight. Xanthe knew he was happy with more than just the song, and for the first time she found herself enjoying the way he was looking at her. Found herself in no hurry to leave.

The rehearsal had gone on longer than planned, so that Xanthe fell into bed late that night, waking heavy from sleep the next morning, knowing that there were still many demands on her time. She would still have to put off revisiting Laybrook, just a little while longer. She shivered against the chill of the room, pulled on a warm chunky sweater over a cheesecloth shirt and boyfriend jeans, and pushed her feet into her beloved boots. As she did so, an image flashed through her mind, causing her to gasp. It was very brief, the merest of glimpses, but it was clear. There was no doubting she had just "seen" the chocolate pot. She all but ran down the stairs, out the back door, striding across the frost-crisp grass of the lawn. At the door of the blind house she hesitated just a moment before pulling at the handle. She dragged the door open just enough for the soft morning light to fall into the gloomy space, and as it did so it fell upon the burnished copper of the pot, making it gleam. Xanthe stepped forward and picked it up.

"There you are," she murmured to it. She wondered if she had simply not seen it when she had returned. Could it have been there all the time? No, she knew that was not the case. Something had happened, in the past, to bring about its return. Her heart leaped at the realization that Samuel must have taken the pot from the abbey and restored it to its rightful place with Mistress Flyte in the chocolate house. The fact that he had been able to do this reassured her that she had indeed successfully sent Fairfax to the time of the coin, and that Samuel was free to come and go as he wished. As she held the pot she listened closely. There was nothing. Not a sound, nor a vibration. The pot had fallen silent. It had nothing more to ask of her. Her mission was complete. Could her plan really have worked? Was Samuel safe at last? There was one last thing she needed to do, she *had to* do, to be certain. But that would have to wait. Turning, she left the blind house, happy not to be assailed by pleading voices and whispers as she went. She took the pot upstairs and put it on the shelf in her room. Ordinarily she was quite comfortable selling the found things that had once called to her. Once they stopped singing. But this one was different. This one, Samuel had touched, had held, had been connected to. This one she would keep.

Having told her mother about her idea for the historical Saturday there was much to be done to organize it, which came on top of the everyday running of the shop, which was getting increasingly busy as people started their Christmas shopping. Flora invited Gerri over after closing so that they could discuss the promotion. Xanthe had been in the shop all day and had barely had the chance to so much as think of what she was going to sing at The Feathers that evening. There was no time for her to drive out to Laybrook as she had hoped. Her very personal and poignant task would have to wait until the following day.

Over Darjeeling and warm honey flapjacks, Gerri, Flora, and Xanthe sat in the muddled kitchen above the shop and brainstormed plans for the upcoming event.

Flora stirred sugar into her tea. "I wonder if we could get some of the market stall holders involved? Just a few. They could set up down our little street for that day."

Gerri nibbled at one of her own flapjacks, impressing Xanthe with the way her scarlet lipstick stayed put as she did so. "Hmm, we might have a battle with the council about that," she said. "They have strict rules about pitches and pop-up shops."

"What, you mean they'd object to a couple of stalls for a couple of days?" Flora was indignant. "That's a bit small-minded, isn't it?"

"Mum, Gerri knows how things work around here. We're just the newbies."

"Even so . . ."

Xanthe sipped tea from a mug commemorating a long-ago royal wedding. "Let's try and do something that gets as many people on our side as possible. If this little event goes well we can think bigger next time."

Gerri nodded. "Took me ages to get the planners to allow me to put tables and chairs outside. Now everyone's doing it. Be patient but persistent, is my advice."

"I think costumes are a good idea," said Xanthe, safe in the knowledge she had a fair idea how to dress for the seventeenth century by now. She wondered how it would feel, turning the clock back on the whole street. A street that, in fact, had not all been built at that time. The three talked on, making plans, coming up with thoughts and possibilities that would make the event a success. Xanthe was happy to take a back seat, pleased for Flora, relieved to have, for once, done something positive for the business, even if the idea had come out of a lie protecting her own secrets. After an hour she was able to make her excuses and go up to her room to prepare for her evening's singing. She leafed through the sheet music and lyric notes she had amassed, choosing upbeat, simple songs this time. She would stick with the ancient folk tunes and ballads that she had had some success with already but decided to avoid anything too romantic or sad. She was having a hard time keeping her mood steady as it was. Better to use the music and the audience to lift her spirits rather than to tempt her into wallowing. And then, for the last song of the evening, she would be performing with Tin Lid. The thought gave her courage. As she showered and washed her hair she found herself wondering what Samuel was doing, whether he would be working, or eating a meal with his family, or spending time with his new fiancée. She still struggled to completely accept the fact that he had lived his entire life a very long time ago. To think of him continuing with his life without her was difficult enough: to think of him dead was even harder.

Night was falling ever earlier as the winter days began to shorten. Xanthe was restless in the time leading up to her performance. She and her mother shared a supper of sandwiches but she found she had no appetite. Flora was chatting on about how having done so much singing recently Xanthe must be well practiced and less nervous about her performance.

"Actually, Mum, I think I'll go for a bit of a walk first."

"But it's freezing out there."

"Just a stroll down by the river. If I keep moving I'll keep warm."

"You don't want to turn up all chilled and with a red nose."

"I'll wrap up, I'll be fine. Don't fuss."

"As if."

"I'll meet you at The Feathers, OK?"

Xanthe pulled her greatcoat on over a red daisy-print tea dress that had been a charity shop find years before. She had teamed it with opaque green tights as a nod to the time of year, and of course her trusty Dr. Martens. She left her hair loose, her tight curls a little tamed and protected against frizz by a quick application of Argan oil. Outside the air was cold enough to make her breath form puffs of cloud as she strode over the cobbles and out across the high street. She took the little road that led from the side of the inn down toward the river, planning to follow the narrow, fast-flowing stream to the edge of the town and back again. Half an hour's march without anyone to distract her was the best way she could think of to steady her nerves and clear her head.

She had got no further than the rear of the pub, however, when she suddenly felt she was being followed. She stopped, turning, scanning the narrow street, but there was no one to be seen. She waited a moment, letting her eyes become accustomed to the deeper shadows between the streetlamps, but still there was nobody in the road but her. She was about to move on when she heard a noise off to her left, in the open gateway to the yard behind The Feathers. She hesitated.

"Harley?" she called out quietly, wondering if he might be out fetching crates from the store shed. "Is that you?" Getting no reply, she told herself she was being silly and turned back toward the river. It was then that rough hands took hold of her arms and she was pulled backward before she had time to do anything about it. She cried out, swearing, trying to twist free, but she was held tight and being dragged into the dark yard. She kicked over a bin as she went, hoping the noise of the metal container crashing to the tarmac might alert someone.

"Let me go!" she yelled, stamping at her assailant's feet, but she was too off balance for her heavy heels to find their mark effectively. Suddenly she was spun around and pressed up against the wall of the yard. At last she could see who it was had hold of her.

"Marcus! For God's sake, what are you doing?"

"You were on your way to his place, weren't you? You were going to see him!"

Even in the patchy light from the streetlamps Xanthe could see how wild-eyed Marcus was. She knew that look. She's seen it before many times. It was the face of someone between hits. The face of someone strung out and desperate, a long way from his last line of coke, with the chance of more out of sight. This was bad Marcus, unreasonable Marcus, Marcus who was out of control.

Xanthe forced herself to stay calm.

"On my way to see who?" she asked, although she already knew the answer.

"Liam, your tame little mechanic. Why are you wasting your time with him?"

"It's none of your business who I spend my time with. Let go of me!" She shook off his hands but he was standing so close she was trapped against the wall. She could smell alcohol on his breath.

"You stood me up," he said. "We were going to meet. You promised."

"I was busy."

"I waited, you never showed up. Did you enjoy that, eh? Thinking of me sitting there like an idiot? Did the two of you laugh about it?"

"You're being ridiculous. You should go back to London. Why are you still hanging around here?"

"You know why. You and me, Xan, we're not done."

"How many times do I have to say it? I'm not interested, Marcus."

"You said. Same as you said you weren't interested in singing, but I hear you're going to do exactly that, right here in this twee little provincial pub tonight."

"I'm earning a living, but then you wouldn't know anything about doing that, would you?"

"You wouldn't sing with me, but you're singing with him, aren't you? I saw the name of the band on the flyers. I asked around. He's wormed his way into your life, hasn't he? I bet he fixes that idiotic taxi of yours, doesn't he? And now he's got you singing in his pathetic band."

"It is none of your business."

"He can't write for you, though, can he? He'll never have that connection with you, Xan, you know that. You'd do better singing in London, with me."

"Nothing would be better with you, Marcus. Just leave me alone!" An edge crept into her voice that gave away her anxiety at having to deal with him in such a condition. Marcus heard it. He reacted minutely, his expression hardening a fraction, knowing that he was getting to her.

Fortunately, someone else heard it too. A figure stepped out of the shadows.

"You heard her; leave her alone," said Liam.

Marcus wheeled round.

"Why don't you piss right off, grease monkey. She's way out of your league."

"I don't think Marlborough is the right place for you," Liam said lightly, refusing to be riled. "Isn't there a rock somewhere in the city you can crawl back under?"

"Xan and me have history. She'd do anything for me."

"From what I've heard she's already done more than enough."

Xanthe slipped away from Marcus, moving beyond his reach. He noticed her move and tried to grab hold of her again. She shouted, more in anger than fear, but it was enough to trigger an instinctive reaction from Liam, who lunged at Marcus. The two barreled into a stack of crates, sending them toppling, scattering and smashing empty bottles across the yard. Neither took any notice of the chaos they were causing as they grappled, slinging fists, cursing and kicking at each other.

"Stop it!" Xanthe yelled. "Will you both just grow up!"

The back door of the pub opened abruptly and the bulk of Harley blocked out the light from the passageway.

"Hell's teeth, hen! What goes on here? Oi!" he yelled at the fighting men. Marcus had Liam pinned to the ground now and was raining blows down on him. While Liam was in better physical shape he was clearly holding back from hitting Marcus. Xanthe thought he could more than likely flatten him if he took it into his head to do so. Marcus was in such an agitated state he had quickly gained the advantage, not able to restrain his temper and desperation. Harley grabbed hold of his collar and hauled him to his feet.

"Would ye mind finding somewhere else for your brawling?" He kept a tight hold on the flailing younger man, his weight and strength unmoved by Marcus's best efforts to free himself.

"Get off me! This is nothing to do with you!"

"Oh it's plenty to do with me when it's in my own backyard, let me tell you that."

Liam got up, wiping blood from a split lip. "You want locking up," he told Marcus.

Xanthe looked at his bruised face. "Liam, I'm so sorry. . . ."

"Don't do that," he said quickly. "Don't apologize for something that is his fault, not yours. Haven't you learned that lesson yet?"

His words stung. "I didn't ask you to step in," she said.

"Oh, and you were doing just fine when I found him attacking you?"

Marcus jabbed a finger in Liam's direction. "See, she doesn't want you interfering. This is none of your business."

Liam had had enough. "Why don't you piss off back to London," he snarled at Marcus.

Harley rolled his eyes. "I've a pub to run here, and yon lassie is due to sing, so you two can both take yourselves off and cool your heels." He flung

Marcus forward, away from Liam, toward the yard gate. "I seem to be making a habit of evicting you from my premises, laddie. And I don't like it. I don't like it at all. You show your face anywhere near my property again and it'll be the police for you, d'you hear me?"

Marcus ignored him and took a step toward Xanthe, who instinctively stepped back. Marcus looked as if he was about to lay hands on her again but looked from Harley to Liam and thought better of it. Instead he leaned close to Xanthe, his voice low.

"OK, you play at being a small-town girl, Xan. It won't last. You don't belong here with these nobodies. One day you are going to realize that. And I'll be waiting for you when you do. We are very far from over, I promise you." He spat in Liam's direction before turning on his heel and striding off into the night.

Harley let out a sigh. "Right, if that's that, I'll be about my pub. Xanthe, hen, if it's all the same to you, I'd prefer not to have that wastrel in my life, d'you ken?"

"Sorry, Harley."

"Xanthe . . ." Liam raised his hands in a gesture of exasperation, letting them drop by his sides.

Xanthe saw Harley watching her. She gave him what she hoped was a reassuring smile. "I'm OK, really I am. I'll be in in a minute."

He grunted, nodded, pointing at Liam's face. "You'd best tidy him up a bit. Don't want people put off their pints," he said, and went back inside.

Liam asked, "Are you sure you're OK?"

"I'm fine." She lifted a hand to turn his face to the light. She could see another cut over his left eye and his jaw was already beginning to swell. "We should put something on that."

"Do you think Harley would spare one of his sirloin steaks? Ouch!" He winced as she dabbed at the cut with a tissue.

Xanthe started to apologize and then stopped herself, not wanting to begin another argument.

"Thank you," she said instead. "For helping."

"I'm not sure being thrashed and having to have Harley wade in was really helping much, if I'm honest."

Xanthe smiled. "I like that you tried."

"My grandad used to say trying is OK when you're five years old. After that you have to succeed."

"Hard man, your grandfather. Keep still, this is bleeding a bit. Here," she said, taking his hand and placing it over the tissue on his wounded eyebrow. "Keep the pressure on it."

"Will I have a manly scar, d'you think?"

"'Fraid not." She looked at him differently then, considering how even battered and bruised his face had an appeal that was hard to ignore. He noticed her looking at him and smiled, causing her to blush and him to wince at the split in his lip.

"And thanks for not, you know, laying into Marcus."

"It was tempting."

"I'm glad you resisted." She stepped away, fidgeting from one foot to the other in an attempt to keep out the cold night air.

"You ready for your performance?" Liam asked. "The band is stoked about this. All of them."

"I was hoping for a peaceful walk to steady my nerves," she said with a shrug.

"After singing up in London two nights running I'd have thought you'd be over your nerves. Settling into your stride," he said.

Xanthe managed to hide her confusion, remembering that she was supposed to have been at Harley's friend's pub. The effort of more deception, especially when Liam had got hurt on her behalf, was wearisome.

"Oh, you know, home crowd . . ." she said.

"But this time you're not on your own. You've got Tin Lid. You've got me," he said suddenly, his face serious.

Xanthe looked away. "Liam, I . . ."

"I know, I know. You don't have to say any more. Let's hope that charming ex-boyfriend of yours has finally got the message that he's not welcome. That'll be one less thing for you to worry about."

"Let's hope," Xanthe agreed.

He took the padding from his brow to check the bleeding.

"I think it's stopped," Xanthe told him. "You'll live."

"You sure?"

"Well, long enough for me to buy you a drink, anyway. Come on, it's bloody freezing out here. Got to get you tidied up before our set."

"Yeah, Harley won't be pleased if takings are down because of my ugly face." Liam smiled, flinching as he did so, taking Xanthe's arm, his grasp firm and reassuring as he led her toward the door of the pub. "Oh," he stopped, "in all the excitement I nearly forgot." He reached inside his jacket pocket and took out a small packet, inexpertly wrapped in tissue paper. He offered it to her. "I wanted you to have this. A good luck charm, for your performances tonight. Solo and with us."

Xanthe took it from him and undid the wrapping. Inside was a finely worked gold pin in the shape of a horseshoe, studded with tiny pearls.

"Oh, Liam! It's lovely, but . . ." She remembered then how he had spent time at the Victorian jewelry stand at the sale in Ditton. Even then he had been thinking of her, wanting to buy her a gift.

"Well, I know how much you like our white horse up there on the hill, and horseshoes are meant to bring good luck, aren't they?"

"It's too much . . . I can't . . ."

"Yes, you damn well can. I want you to have it." He took it and gently pinned it to the lapel of her dress. The gold looked lovely against the red of the print and the luster of the pearls gleamed beneath the low light of the yard. "For luck," Liam insisted.

"It's gorgeous. Thank you," she said, leaning forward to kiss his cheek.

Inside, the main bar was packed. Xanthe didn't flatter herself thinking they were all there to hear her sing, as Annie had only booked her at the last minute, and the posters had been scrawled on in black marker to alert people to the collaboration with Tin Lid. It had been Xanthe's idea to try out singing with the band. Practice had been so encouraging, and she had felt her nerves slipping away. It would be so much better to work with them. It would take time to work out their unique sound, to meld her voice with their playing, but she was confident it would work.

As Xanthe hung up her coat in the passageway behind the bar she glimpsed her mother and Gerri finding seats in the far corner. She had long ago trained her mother not to sit too near the front. Having someone she knew in her line of vision inhibited her performance. She thought about the fact that she was here, in the twenty-first century, singing for her supper, just as she had done the first time she had traveled back to the seventeenth century. For a moment her thoughts took her back to Samuel's day and to the time when she had sung at Clara's birthday feast. He had held her hand that evening, and saved her from having to dance when she didn't know the steps and might have been revealed as a fraud. It all seemed so long ago and so far away. She was aware, however poignant the memory, of a shift in her feelings, a subtle alteration in her emotional response to the memory. It all felt more distant, somehow. More completed. A part of her life that was over.

"You up for this, then? Ready to do what you do best?" Liam's question brought her back to the present. Even with his swollen face he exuded a calm, upbeat confidence that was hugely welcome at that moment.

"Yes." She smiled back at him. "Yes, I think I am."

20

XANTHE WAS UP EARLY THE NEXT MORNING, THE SUN NOT PROPERLY RISEN, SO THAT THE town was revealed in an eerie half-light. There was a heavy frost, and she had to scrape ice off the windscreen of her car. As she did so she thought about how the black cab was a constant reminder of the London life she had left behind. Was she wrong to hang on to it? Could there even be some truth in what Marcus had said about her not belonging in a quiet place like Marlborough? Was her taxi a sign that she had not, in fact, entirely closed the door on that life? After all, when she was singing was when she felt most at ease with herself and most able to cope with what life threw at her. It was in itself a type of forgetting. She finished her task and got into the car, turning up the heating and rubbing her hands together against the cold. The vehicle felt comfortingly familiar. And it was useful; not many other cars would be able to accommodate so many antiques when she and her mother went on a buying trip. She ran her hand around the large, cool steering wheel. No, she decided, this was one link to her past she was not prepared to let go.

It was not quite seven o'clock as she drove out of town. The November day was slow to get under way, so that the countryside remained largely hidden, the sun not yet high enough to properly illuminate the rolling fields and hills that spread away into the distance. There was very little traffic. In less than half an hour Xanthe was turning into the main street of Laybrook. She parked up at the side of the road and walked through the sleepy village. At the lych-gate of the church she hesitated, gripped by a nervousness she had been doing her best to ignore. This was something she had to do, but that made it no easier. Once she had seen that gravestone, once she had read the words and, more important, the date inscribed upon it, there was no unknowing what she would discover. She stood for a moment, her eyes closed, picturing Samuel, for once not fighting the memory. Had she done enough? Would Fairfax have returned before Samuel had a chance to shore up his standing with the king? She did not trust the man to keep his side of the bargain, and he was likely to be furious at having been tricked by Xanthe. Would he have taken his anger out on Samuel? She told herself that the chocolate pot returning meant Samuel had at least succeeded in taking it back to Bradford. That gave her hope.

"Can I help you?"

A gentle voice broke into Xanthe's thoughts. Embarrassed, she opened her eyes and found a short, middle-aged woman in a duffle coat and woolen mittens. It took her a few seconds more to notice the clerical dog collar.

"Oh, thanks, I was just . . ." She waved her hand vaguely at the churchyard.

The vicar waited. When Xanthe said no more she smiled. "I was about to unlock the church, if you want to go inside . . . ?"

Xanthe shook her head. "I'm just looking. Just . . . visiting."

"Well, if you change your mind, feel free," said the vicar before going through the gate and heading for the church.

Xanthe waited until she had gone inside. She was sure the woman meant well, but at that moment the last thing she needed was to have to try to explain what she was doing, or to share how she felt. She was having a hard time explaining it to herself. The narrow path that wound around the church was slippery with frost, the grass at its edges fuzzy with ice. Under the shade of the yew trees frozen moss formed little cushions of silvery green velvet. From nearby oaks a parliament of rooks began their morning noise, while a wood pigeon cooed its mournful, repetitive song.

At last Xanthe came to the place she was looking for. A few paces ahead of her a modest headstone stood slightly apart from some of the others, age and time having given it a slant and a weathered appearance. She forced herself to walk up to it, to stand directly in front of it.

She took a breath.

"Right," she told herself, her voice loud in the stillness of the day. "Let's do this."

She peered down at the stone, narrowing her eyes to make out the faded and worn lettering that had been carved into it so many, many years before. Moss and lichen obscured the wording, so that she had to reach out and rub at the surface of the tombstone. Gradually the inscription revealed itself. She forced herself to read out what was there, determined to take it in and accept it, however painful that might be.

"Here lies the body of Samuel Appleby of Marlborough. . . ." She paused, assailed by a jolt of pain that she should have been expecting. To read of his death, however much she had prepared herself, was still a shocking thing to do. She went on. "Architect and Master Builder of Renown, Loyal Subject of His Majesty King Charles. . . . Charles! Not James?" Relief swamped her. As far as she could recall, James I ended his reign in 1625. She raced on to the next line. "Taken into the arms of the Lord, 1648." She let out the breath she had been holding. Forty-two years after the date she had left him. Which meant he had lived on until his early sixties. Suddenly she found herself shedding tears of relief. She had not failed him. He was safe. Whatever Fairfax had done next he had not taken his revenge on Samuel. By modern standards dying before reaching even seventy seemed harsh, but given the times Samuel had lived in it was a fair age. There were other lines of the inscription, written below, the lettering a little easier to read, being a few years younger. Xanthe read it aloud to the rook sitting on a low branch opposite her.

"Here lies also the body of his beloved wife, Henrietta Appleby, left this earth for a better place 1661."

Of course Samuel would have married Henrietta. She was a good woman, and she would have made him a wonderful wife. A beloved wife. It was to be expected. It was as it should be. Xanthe was truly glad for him; that he had been happy. That he had found love. She knew then that she had done what she had been called by the chocolate pot to do. She had rescued Samuel from Fairfax and he had lived the life he had been meant to have. All was as it should be, order restored. Her duty as a Spinner fulfilled.

After leaving Laybrook Xanthe took the road that passed through Ditton. There was one more thing she wanted to check. One more thing she needed to see if she was to truly believe that she had done her work as a Spinner. She slowed the car as she approached the village, glancing first to the left at The Swan Inn, and then to the right. And there it was. She stopped the car in the middle of the road, taking advantage of the lack of traffic. The widow's cottage. Samuel's work. Showing signs of rot in some of the window frames but otherwise wearing its years lightly. It had been completed by Samuel, just as he had intended. Just as it should have been. It had survived all those long years afterward, giving shelter and a cozy home to four centuries of people. It would continue to do so for years to come. Order had been restored. The damage to history and the possible future threatened by Fairfax's actions had been repaired. Because a Spinner had done her job.

On the way home Xanthe began to feel calmer. If Samuel was safe, there was no reason for her to return to the past. No reason for her to take the risks that she had done before, for him, for Alice, and for her mother. The chocolate pot was where it belonged. It no longer sang to her, no longer thrummed with an urgent message. Xanthe had done what was required of her. Whatever Mistress Flyte had told her about her calling as a Spinner, there was no necessity for her to risk traveling again. Surely she had played her part. It was over. She would not have been surprised to find *Spinners* blank next time she opened the book. Perhaps she should put it back in the shop and see if it found someone else? She decided if it was blank that was what she would do. She had her own life to think about now, in her own time. With Flora. With the shop. With the band.

Marlborough was properly awake when Xanthe swung the black cab off the high street and down the cobbled lane. Passing the shop she saw lights on upstairs. Flora was up. She would need an explanation for finding her daughter out and about before breakfast. Xanthe drove to the small parking area for residents at the far end of the street. She locked up the taxi and headed back toward the shop. She was glad there was so much to be done for the business. She needed to keep busy and to keep her mind off Samuel. The Christmas trade would soon be revving up, and there was the historical weekend to organize. She wished now that she had chosen a different era, Victorian perhaps, anything other than Samuel's time. It was too late to change things now. Gerri and Flora were already making detailed plans. Xanthe would just have to ride it out, see the event as a final farewell to her wonderful adventure. And now she was singing again, and thankful for that. With Tin Lid, and Liam, to push her to take on more gigs she would scarcely have a free moment. She would throw her energies into the life in Marlborough that she and her mother were building. Samuel, Mistress Flyte, and the Spinners would all have to stay in the past where they belonged.

Two days before what everyone was referring to as "the medieval fair" (despite Xanthe constantly reminding them that it technically wasn't) Gerri came over for supper so that the three of them could discuss final details for the event. Xanthe opened the shop door to let her in.

"Brace yourself," she told her, "Mum's in a Christmas cooking frenzy."

"I thought your mum didn't really cook."

"She doesn't, but she does Christmas. Last year it was a plum pudding," she said, leading her through the shop and up the stairs, which were festooned with quantities of tinsel.

"How did that turn out?"

"Mercifully Mum got carried away with pouring brandy over it and the thing was lost to the flames."

In the kitchen Flora appeared as if at the center of a storm cloud of icing sugar, a red and white Christmas hat keeping her hair off her face, and an apron shaped like a Christmas tree bearing the brunt of the fallout.

"Ah, Gerri, a professional! Just the person I need," she said, thrusting forward a batter-covered wooden spoon. "Try this. Tell me what you think."

"Mum, let Gerri get her coat off at least."

Gerri handed Xanthe a bottle of red wine and smiled at Flora. "OK, happy to help. Um, can you give me a clue . . . what is it going to be?"

"Stollen. Made from an authentic German recipe."

Xanthe raised her eyebrows. "You actually followed a recipe?"

"I looked at one. All seemed simple enough. Though I did have to improvise a bit. Well . . . ?"

There was a moment heavy with expectation as Gerri took the spoon and tried the mixture. "*Hmm*, good consistency . . ."

"Yes . . . ?"

"Plenty of dried fruit, I like that. Candied peel . . . A bit of cinnamon in there."

"I did use cinnamon. It's *the* Christmas spice, don't you think?"

Gerri nibbled a little more and frowned. "There's something else. I can't quite place it...."

Xanthe groaned, being all too familiar with her mother's fondness for using unexpected ingredients.

"Try and guess," Flora insisted. "Go on, you being an expert...."

Gerri's face registered surprise and a little puzzlement. "I want to say mint, but..."

"That's it! Well done." Flora went back to beating the mixture some more.

"Really, Mum? Mint? In stollen?"

Gerri shrugged. "It's... different. What made you choose it?"

"It rather chose me, in fact. I only glimpsed the label, saw the first two letters and thought I was adding mixed spice. But I can really see it catching on. Now, Xanthe, love, have you finished with the oven? I want to get this in."

After a fair amount of clearing and juggling of dirty dishes and packets of ingredients, Xanthe put the shepherd's pie she had prepared onto the table and they all sat down to eat. Liberal quantities of Shiraz oiled the wheels as they went through an exhaustive checklist, ticking off all the things that were already settled, circling the one or two tasks that remained to be done. Flora squeezed a little more brown sauce onto her plate.

"I must say, Gerri, I am impressed," she said. "You are the living embodiment of the idea that if you want something done you ask a busy person."

"I've really done very little," Gerri insisted. "Xanthe's the one with all the ideas, and you've seen to the lion's share of the advertising and promoting."

"Mum loves to organize," Xanthe said. "Though some might call it being bossy...."

Flora rolled her eyes. "We must each of us play to our strengths. You've been busy with running the shop and with your singing, which is as it should be," she added quickly. "I like to plan things. We've got a lot riding on the success of this day. People are watching the pennies; they need a little persuading to part with them. And with Christmas being make or break for many small businesses, we have to compete. We're newcomers. We need to do a bit of flag waving to get noticed. This is very tasty, Xanthe, by the way."

Gerri nodded. "It's nice to eat something that I haven't had to cook myself for once."

"How are the recipe tryouts going?" Xanthe asked.

"Some more successful than others. The children have been very keen on helping me with the puddings. Tommy declared my marchpane roses the best sweets ever, and Ells is very keen on anything custardy, so she's enjoyed some of the tartlets. They are less happy about the idea of roasted sparrows with the heads still on."

"Good grief!" Flora was horrified.

"Fortunately, Waitrose was fresh out of sparrows."

Xanthe took another swig of Shiraz. "Best to steer clear of anything that still has the head attached," she suggested.

Gerri laughed. "Don't worry, I'm sticking to mostly simple recipes. Some of the things people loved in the sixteen hundreds would cause an uproar now, and rightly so. Poor sparrows."

"I guess it's no worse than eating chickens," said Xanthe.

"Ellie is teetering on the edge of being a vegetarian herself. It's a good thing I make more cakes than anything else. Here," she pulled another sheet of paper from her bag. "I've made a list of the food I'm doing. Most of it is already prepared. I've got a few hours more baking to do tomorrow though. I've gone with things that lend themselves to a bit of a buffet; things people can nibble at. I'll cut the bigger pies and tarts into small slices."

Xanthe and Flora leaned over the list of recipes. There were lemon possets, ham-hock pies with cranberry middles, pear tartlets, apple puddings, ginger biscuits shaped like lions, and tiny homity pies made with root mash and savory pastry.

Xanthe could not help but think of Clara's birthday party at Great Chalfield. Working as a kitchen maid for such an important occasion in 1605 had given her firsthand experience of what wealthy people of the day chose to eat. She wished she could share what she knew with Gerri, explain to her precisely what it felt like to toil away in the big kitchen of such a house and to wait on the gentry while they feasted. She herself had eaten some of that food. She recalled the roasted meat and sweet pickles with lots of raw fruit. People used to believe that cooking was a quick way to make some foods decay, as the evidence of their own eyes showed them that a baked apple spoiled far more quickly than a raw one carefully stored in a cool hoarde house. And yet they loved their puddings, as Gerri's selection suggested.

"Wow, Gerri, this is terrific," she said, promising herself that she would one day share what she knew with her friend. One day. "These will really give the thing an authentic feel."

"You've put so much work into it," said Flora.

"I've loved every minute. Makes a change from lemon drizzle and chocolate brownies."

Xanthe put down her fork. "If you ever stop making lemon drizzle cake we'll have to leave town. Mum's hooked on yours; we'd have to find another baker."

"No need for panic; I've got one in a tin in my bag. Thought you might be running low."

Flora dabbed at her mouth with a paper napkin. "That's very thoughtful of you, Gerri. Addicted indeed! At least I get some exercise to burn off all those sinful calories. Which is where I'm off to right now, in fact."

"Mum, I'm not sure bell-ringing counts as a workout."

"Says she who's never tried it. We're having a run-through with the hand bells tonight. You wait until Saturday, then you'll hear what I've been practicing so hard. She got to her feet, hooked her bag over her shoulder, and shrugged on her warm, quilted coat. "I shall leave you girls to your nattering. Just make sure there's some of that cake left for when I get home." So saying, she stick-stepped her way down the stairs.

"She's a marvel, your mum," Gerri said as they heard the bell of the shop door clanking.

"Don't let her hear you say that. It will either make her cross because she doesn't want to be seen as a martyr, or go to her head. Depends which day you say it. But yes, she is a marvel. I'm so glad she's found new friends and a new hobby."

"Had she ever shown any interest in bell-ringing before?"

"None at all. I think she'd have done whatever her new friends suggested, to be honest. It's as much about doing something without me as it is about meeting new people or doing something fun."

Xanthe cleared away the plates and picked up the bottle of wine. "Come on, bring your glass, let's move to the sofa."

She went through to the sitting room, which was in its usual state of chaos, so that she had to clear a space on the coffee table to set things down.

"Make yourself comfortable," she told Gerri, removing a stack of unframed botanical prints from the sofa and giving the worn green cushions a quick pat.

"Nothing like a velvet sofa," said Gerri, flopping onto it, kicking off her shoes, and curling her feet up underneath her.

Xanthe went to the window to close the curtains. "Oh, look! It's starting to snow." Small but determined flakes were falling onto the cobbles of the street below. Xanthe felt the usual excitement stirring in her. What was it about snow that did that to a person? She couldn't help imagining how the Wiltshire landscape would look in her own time under a covering of icy whiteness. She had, of course, seen it thickly coated with a deep fall in the seventeenth century. The strangeness of this fact, that she was, in some ways, more familiar with where she lived as it had been four hundred years ago than it was in the present day, brought on a sense of disconnection. A momentary feeling that she was not sure where she truly belonged anymore. It was easy to feel rooted in her own time while she was talking to her family and friends, planning ordinary things in everyday life, things that made sense. But at other times, when something jolted a memory or triggered a recollection, she felt unmoored. She might have completed her recent task successfully, but she was still a Spinner. Would she always feel like this now? she wondered. Was this what her future held? She thought then of her favorite carved white horse, high upon the hill. She had been too busy to visit him recently and she missed the sense of peace she found up there, close to the ancient chalk figure that kept watch over the valley. Over the centuries. She decided she would make time to go there after the historical event, perhaps on the Sunday. She needed space to clear her head. Needed that different perspective to help her find her way forward.

She joined Gerri on the sofa, reaching over to top up both wineglasses. "It must feel odd being child-free for a couple of days," Xanthe said. "Do you ever get used to it?"

"Not really. Their father doesn't have them often enough or regularly enough. Never a man for commitment, obviously. One of his failings as a husband and father. And human being, come to that. But the kids still love him, and he's still their dad. . . ."

"We haven't got many good examples of men between us, have we? There's your ex, my ex, my own father. . . ."

"From what I could see your ex is very attractive in a dangerous sort of way."

"Yes, well, the clue is in the description. . . ."

"And your parents' marriage was good for years, I suppose."

"Until it wasn't."

"It's enough to make you give up on them, isn't it?"

"Gerri, you are young and clever and gorgeous and one day someone worthy of all that will come along."

"*Hmm*, I wish I could believe that."

"There are good men out there too."

"Name three."

"OK . . . Harley. He's been great, supporting me with my singing, and . . . everything."

"And Annie seems happy enough with him; always a good sign. OK, I'll give you that one. Next."

"Um."

"See, you're struggling already."

"Father Christmas?" They both laughed before Xanthe, a little shyly, suggested, "Liam?"

"Ah-ha! I knew it."

"Knew what?"

"That you'd fall for him."

"You asked for three good men! I didn't say I was interested in him."

"Xanthe, please. He's good-looking, single, solvent, fit . . ."

"Are you sure you're not keen on him yourself?"

". . . he plays in his own band, which he's invited you to join . . ."

"We both like music . . ."

". . . he's clearly keen on you."

Xanthe had no answer to this. She knew it to be true. She shook her head, though. "I'm not looking for a relationship," she insisted, thinking about everything that had happened in her life in a few short months. "I'm not ready for someone new yet."

"I can see Marcus would be a difficult person to get over, particularly if he's going to keep turning up here. But from what you've told me he was bad news, Xanthe. You deserve someone who will treat you well."

Xanthe sipped her Shiraz, content for that moment to let Gerri think it was Marcus she needed time to heal from. What she hadn't realized until then, faced with Gerri's challenges, was that there was something different about the way she thought of Liam. During the time they had spent together there had been a subtle shift in their friendship. She could see that now. There was something new in the way that she responded to him. Something altered in the way she felt about him. She thought about the dear little golden horseshoe upstairs on her bedside table. She raised her glass. "Here's to good men, then," she toasted, and Gerri joined in.

{ 21 }

XANTHE STOOD IN FRONT OF THE TALLEST OF THE MANY MIRRORS THAT STILL FILLED THE second downstairs room in the shop. She experienced a tremor of excitement as her seventeenth-century reflection gazed back at her. She had secured her hair up beneath a mop cap that Flora had obtained from the fancy-dress shop where she had found her own outfit. Xanthe could not help comparing it to the one she had borrowed from Samuel's kitchen maid. Flora had insisted she let spirals of her dark blond hair fall out from under it in a way that was flattering but far from authentic. She still had Rose's blouse and decided as she hadn't been able to return it she would wear it, one last time. It was so fragile that when she had slipped her arms into the sleeves the seams had torn a little. She regretted agreeing to borrow it from Rose, sorry that she had not been able to return it. Xanthe wore her own pinafore that had already served her well. It would be strange mingling with other people openly dressed in such a way. For everyone else it was a fun day to celebrate the advent season. For her it was a powerful reminder of her most recent adventure. Only Harley would know where she had traveled in this very outfit. Where and when. She was aware of the need to ground herself in her own time. Her own place. Her own future. With a small smile she touched the horseshoe pin she had decided to fix to her pinafore.

"Xanthe?" her mother called from the front of the shop. "Are you ready? We need to open up."

"Coming!" She took a steadying breath, speaking to the old-fashioned version of herself. "Right, this needs to be a success. To business." While trade had been good, the shop was still a new venture and they needed all the sales they could get. It was vital that their time and what funds they had been able to invest in the event paid dividends.

In her rented costume, Flora made a passable Stuart woman of some wealth. Her dress was made of a damask fabric more suited to curtains than clothes, but it was an attractive burgundy and the right cut and shape to give the desired effect. Flora had borrowed some of the costume jewelry from their stock to set it off, finding a chunky gilt pendant and rings with glass rubies. Her face glowed with excitement. "There you are. There's no time to fiddle about, come on. Gerri's already got the cafe open. Look, she's written up a special blackboard with the menu on it and directing people to the shops for free samples up until lunchtime."

Xanthe peered out through the window. There had been no more snow, but the day was still bracingly cold. Any idea of outside seating or stalls had been altered; signs had quickly been drawn up to coax people inside instead. Each of the shops in the little alleyway had agreed to join in, and Gerri would be trundling in and out of them with trolleys and trays of food to try. She was already loading up the first trolley, with the able help of a local girl taken on for the day, and the less skilled but hugely enthusiastic assistance of Tommy and Ellie. Further up the street the art supplies and framing shop had put paintings and prints in its window that, if not exactly seventeenth century, had the right sort of look. The sweetshop near the top of the alleyway needed no alterations to look as if it had come from another time. All the shopkeepers had agreed to dress up and sported an array of costumes, some homegrown, others hired, none stupidly expensive, and all showing a deal of creativity and fun. Xanthe and Flora had both been touched by how willingly their neighbors and fellow shop owners had entered into the spirit of the thing. It felt good to be doing something for their immediate community and helped to make them feel that they belonged. Xanthe and Gerri had been out earlier that morning putting up blue, red, and gold streamers, and all the windowsills were decorated with holly. Most of the town already had its Christmas decorations up, although the official switching on of the lights was not for another week or so. There was a generally festive air, which Xanthe hoped would encourage shoppers to make some purchases, rather than simply browse.

"Here, let's move this closer to the door so people see it more easily," said Flora. Xanthe turned to find her attempting to push a hefty wooden coffer across the floor.

"Mum! Don't try to shift that on your own," she said, hurrying to help. The heavy box was big enough to sit on, solidly made, and would have housed all manner of valuable things in its time. The wood was naturally such a dark brown it was almost black. The pattern on all four sides was quite rustic, but nicely carved, with deep scallops overlapping and ears of corn at each corner. The lid was finger-snappingly heavy.

"That is a lovely piece," said Flora, straightening up to admire it. "And perfect for today. I'd stake my reputation on it being pre-1700."

"Let's hope someone thinks it will make a perfect Christmas present. Though it will have to be someone with pretty deep pockets," she added, looking at the four-figure sum on the price tag.

"Worth every penny. A solid investment, in every sense."

Liam appeared at the door, staggering under the weight of two large boxes.

"Oh, are those from Harley?" Flora asked.

"He spotted me on my way and I offered to drop them in. Where d'you want them?"

They found a space on the desk that was also the counter. The contents clanked as he set the box down.

"Thanks for bringing it over," Xanthe said. "You always seem to get roped in to help somehow."

"I volunteered this time, remember? Who could pass up the chance for a bit of free food and booze? Though I'll leave the dressing up to you, if you don't mind," he said, pointedly gesturing to his own favorite soft leather jacket. He'd put a sheepskin-lined hoodie underneath it, and was wearing a plain black beanie over his cropped hair, which suited him well. He evidently expected to have to be sent out into the cold throughout the day.

"I owe you."

He grinned. "Don't worry, I'll think of a reward later."

Xanthe made a face. "Mead or apple puddings are what's on offer. Just so you know."

Liam took in the costumes and decorations. "All looks very medieval in here. You antique women know your stuff."

"The sixteen hundreds were not, strictly speaking, medieval," Xanthe reminded him.

"And if you go on calling us 'antique women' you might not get your mead," Flora added before bustling off to readjust a display of pewter tankards and copper cooking pots that were not quite to her satisfaction.

Xanthe unpacked the shot glasses they were going to use for the free drinks. Liam helped her set out the bottles.

"Hey, this stuff is quite strong," he said, studying the label. "Didn't monks used to drink it? They must have been permanently half cut."

"They made it to sell, mostly. And anyway, people drank more alcohol than anything else in the seventeenth century. Milk was for babies and invalids, and water was downright dangerous, though they didn't know that, exactly. They thought it was too 'cold' to be good for them."

"Maybe life wasn't so bad back then after all."

"Believe me, it's not as much fun as it sounds." When he gave her a look she hurried on. "Actually, they did have hot chocolate, those who could afford it. They drank it good and hot. It was really delicious, apparently."

At that moment Gerri appeared at the door carrying a tray of tiny jars. "Possets!" she explained, plonking the tray down on Flora's beloved blanket chest. "I'll bring the apple puddings over later; they're just warming through."

Gerri, as Xanthe could have predicted, was beautifully turned out. She had opted for the guise of a seventeenth-century cook and had gotten her costume spot-on. She had an immaculate, starched white pinafore over a wheat brown dress that fell to just above her ankles. The fall of the skirt suggested she had found the perfect petticoat so that it achieved the shape that was fashionable at the time, swelling out gently over the hips and falling straight. Even her shoes looked right, soft leather with hard soles and buttons that looked as if they needed hooks to work them. She had detachable white cuffs and collar too, and a cap that sat securely on her sleek hair that would not dare show so much as a single stray wisp.

"You look fantastic," Xanthe told her. "And so do the little ones! Remind me to talk to you about an idea I've had, when we get a moment. A business proposition."

"Oh, that sounds intriguing. Tommy, darling, those puddings are for customers. Come on, I've got hot chocolate on the go for you back in the tea shop. Do you want me to fetch you a cup, Xanthe?"

"Ah, no thanks, I'm fine right now." Just the idea of drinking freshly made, high-quality chocolate unnerved Xanthe a little. She knew the taste would forever take her back to Mistress Flyte's chocolate house. Every time she thought of the mysterious old woman she found herself with more unanswerable questions, many of which asked something of herself. About what her role as a Spinner might be in the future. About whether or not she could truly accept another challenge, with all that was at stake. With all the risks that were involved.

"Right!" Flora clapped her hands together in a determined fashion. "I do believe we are ready." Xanthe and Gerri nodded their agreement. As if on cue, two of Flora's new friends arrived carrying hand bells. With a great deal of giggling they went back outside and rang them in a well-practiced round, signaling the start of the fair. Soon shoppers were drawn down from the high street, attracted by all the noise and the bright colors of the decorations. Flora and the other shopkeepers welcomed them along the length of the little lane, explaining there were free refreshments for browsers up until lunchtime and ten percent off all marked prices throughout the day. Soon the shop was filled with keen treasure hunters, Christmas shoppers, and general browsers. An hour later the steady stream of people showed no signs of stopping. Among those nudging their way through the door Xanthe spotted Harley and Annie. Harley had embraced the theme in his own individual way and was wearing a multicolored jester's hat, complete with bells. It looked wonderfully incongruous with his biker's leather jacket and Viking beard.

"Wow, Annie, he's let you out of the pub!" Liam teased.

She laughed. "Only because we've got extra Christmas staff on at the moment."

Harley shrugged. "Let's test them out before the season gets properly under way. Find out what they're made of. Now, have ye any of that mead left, or have all these thirsty punters drained the last drop already?"

Liam stepped forward, brandishing a bottle. "It's good stuff. Here you go."

Harley necked a shot, shuddering, causing the bells on his hat to jingle. "What a vile concoction that is. Best taken swiftly so ye can ne' taste the stuff."

As Annie drifted off to look at some jewelry and Liam went to help Gerri with more trays of tartlets, Harley beckoned Xanthe into a quiet corner.

"How have ye been, hen? No more treasures singing to you?"

"No, and I'm not sorry about that."

"I don't blame you. Still, it can't be easy, settling back down to what passes for normal life around here after, well, all you've experienced. Not sure I could do it, not just like that, you know?"

"The business has kept me occupied," she said, gesturing at the bustle in the shop. "That's helped."

"Aye, well, if you need to talk. About . . . things . . ." He put a hand on her shoulder. "You know where I am, hen."

"Thanks, Harley. You don't know how much it helps to have your support."

"*Och*, what did I do? Mind, should ye ever need a traveling companion. . . ." He tapped the side of his nose in a conspiratorial manner, his jingling hat making his seriousness more than a little ridiculous, but nonetheless sincere for that.

The day passed in a blur of activity. At one point Xanthe had to force her protesting mother to sit down for ten minutes and eat something. Gerri's food was a great hit, and people took to the idea of spending time, asking about the antiques and collectibles while enjoying a glass of mead and an unusual snack. Liam stayed all day, fetching and carrying trays of food, clearing away glasses, and carting the larger items sold from the shop to people's cars. One customer, a glamorous young woman, particularly enjoyed having Liam help her pack her purchases into the back of her BMW. She flirted with him shamelessly, maintaining eye contact and resting her hand on his arm at every opportunity. Through the shop window, Xanthe found herself watching the two of them together and felt her stomach tighten. The woman took a pen out of her bag, lifted Liam's hand, and wrote something on it. Her number,

Xanthe guessed. Liam smiled and waved as the car drove slowly away over the cobbles. As soon as it had turned the corner into the high street he looked at his hand, licked his thumb, and casually rubbed away the number. Xanthe's stomach relaxed a little.

It wasn't until six o'clock when they finally shut the door of the shop and turned the sign to closed that she and her mother had a chance to talk.

"Well, Xanthe love, that was fantastic!" Flora threw her arms around her daughter in a celebratory hug.

"All the hard work paid off, Mum."

"Teamwork, that's what made it special. We must do something to thank Gerri."

"She told me she sold out of just about everything. The historic food was a real hit. She shut up an hour ago and took the children home. They were so good; it's been a long day for them."

"We'll have to make it a regular event. A pre-Christmas date all the locals can look forward to."

"Not to mention boosting our bank balance. Sales have been terrific."

"Told you I'd sell that coffer. The man who bought it lives in a gorgeous seventeenth-century house just outside Marlborough. Said it was going in his hall. I even got full price for it."

Xanthe smiled. "He probably didn't think it quite proper to haggle with you dressed like that. You do look quite the lady of the manor."

Flora gave a little lopsided twirl on one crutch and Xanthe said a silent grateful prayer that her mother's health had held up and not spoiled the day for her.

"I've had another idea for the shop," Xanthe told her.

"Oh, another money spinner?"

Xanthe felt herself react to the word and quickly brought her focus back to the business.

"I hope so."

"Let's hear it."

"Well, Mr. Morris's mirror collection is at last getting smaller."

"Thanks to the power of the internet and some extremely competitive pricing."

"I believe we can put that room to better use. What do you think of the idea of vintage clothing?"

"You mean, as in most of the clothes you own?"

"Sort of, but not just wearable things. Beautiful, collectible pieces too. We could give the whole room over to it, make it a collection people would travel to see, if we can source quality items, not just jumble sale stuff. I thought I'd pick Gerri's brains about it."

"You know, I think you may be onto something there. Let me give it some thought when I'm not so exhausted. And yes, talk to Gerri." She put her hand on her daughter's arm. "I love that you are enjoying our little shop," she said. "That means so much to me."

At that moment the door opened, the bell ringing almost wearily from so much activity. Liam stuck his head through. "Do you want these streamers taken down? It's starting to snow again. They'll be a soggy mess by morning."

Flora made as if to go outside.

"No, Mum. Liam and I can manage. You go and put your feet up."

"But . . ."

"We'll be in for a glass of something in a bit. Go on."

Outside, the winter darkness was offset by a single streetlamp and the tiny fairy lights that the shopkeepers had set about their windows. There was not the slightest breath of wind, so that the snow fell soft and silent, each flake glinting for the briefest moment as it landed. Most melted away, but some were starting to stick. Liam had fetched the stepladder and moved it from place to place letting down the streamers while Xanthe packed them into a box.

"You've been such a help, Liam. I honestly didn't think we'd be this busy."

"Not a problem. I've been fueled by mead and Gerri's cooking. Here, last one," he said, dropping the scarlet crepe paper.

Xanthe watched him as he folded the ladder and leaned it up against the side of the shop. She tried to imagine Marcus spending the day being supportive and useful but couldn't. She wondered, fleetingly, if Henrietta helped Samuel with his work, and was surprised to find the thought of him no longer caused her any inner turmoil. Surprised and relieved.

Liam came to stand next to her.

"Another successful event on your hands," he said. "First opening day, then your gigs at The Feathers, singing in London, and singing with Tin Lid, of course."

Xanthe smiled. "Still a highlight," she assured him.

"You make a very good medieval person."

"Seventeenth century."

"That."

He reached forward and touched a lock of her hair that had fallen from beneath her cap.

"You're getting snowed on," he said.

"So are you," she pointed out. "We should go in."

"Wait. I've something I wanted to . . ." He dug in his jacket pocket and pulled out a somewhat squashed twig with small green leaves and white berries.

Xanthe peered at it through the darkness.

"That is the saddest piece of mistletoe I've ever seen."

"I've been waiting for the right moment."

"It's hardly Christmas yet, Liam. And anyway, in the seventeenth century people didn't use it in the way we do now. Pagan traditions were frowned upon, and . . ."

"Xanthe," he interrupted.

"Yes?"

He slipped an arm around her waist and pulled her toward him, holding her close.

"Fortunately, we're not living in the seventeenth century," he said. He raised the mistletoe sprig high and leaned in for a soft, tender, lingering kiss.

For a moment Xanthe thought to pull back, but then, as she felt his mouth on hers, his strong body warm against her, felt safe and close and wanted as he held her, she found that she didn't want him to let go. Didn't want the kiss to stop. She felt herself responding to the sweet moment.

When at last he broke away he kept her close, making no effort to step back. Instead he looked into her eyes, searching, trying to read her reaction. Xanthe didn't quite trust herself to speak, unsure of how she felt. Liam grinned, waving the mistletoe gently. "I reckon this thing's good for at least one more kiss. What do you think?"

Xanthe hesitated and then slowly slipped her arms around him inside his warm jacket.

"I think it might be," she said. And this time she was the one who did the kissing.

As soon as it was light the next morning, Xanthe pulled on warm clothes, shrugging her army greatcoat on top, twisted her hair up beneath her broad-brimmed hat, and grabbed a pair of fingerless mittens. She left the house quietly, not wanting to wake her mother, who was sleeping deeply, recovering from the hectic day before. Xanthe fetched her cab and drove down the high street. The town itself appeared to be moving at Sunday speed too, with most shops still shuttered and silent, and only the occasional dog walker up and about. Snow had continued to fall throughout the night in a gentle fashion, so that the roads were still clear but the countryside had received a light dusting, like a sprinkle of sugar on one of Gerri's cakes. The car's elderly heating system struggled to raise the temperature of the interior and keep the windscreen clear. Xanthe drove with purpose, knowing exactly where she wanted to go, spurred on through the chilly morning by the thought of spending a little time with the great white horse she had become so fond of. Unsurprisingly, there were no other cars parked in the space at the top of the hill. She locked up the taxi and followed the narrow path that led out to the chalk figure. As always, as the vista was revealed to her she felt her spirits lift. Even with the air still heavy with snow clouds and the dawn only recently broken, she could see for many miles in all directions. See the cottages and farms like toy buildings in the distance. See the patterns that the hedges made as they poked through the fragile layer of snow. The landscape was reassuringly familiar, even dressed as it was in its winter clothes. She walked to the head of the great horse. The snowfall was not nearly enough to blur the edges of the artwork as they were cut deep into the soil.

"Did you miss me?" she asked it. "I know, I haven't been for a while. Things have been . . . busy." She smiled to herself at the understatement of this. So much had happened since the last time she had stood beside the ancient sentinel. Since the chocolate pot had sung to her. She thought of how different her journeys back to the past had become; how they had changed. Her traveling back no longer felt overwhelming, sometimes involuntary, often as if she were a mere passenger. She had come to see that now, as a Spinner, she did have a measure of control. With the book, and with the help of Harley and Mistress Flyte, she had started to learn how to move through the decades and centuries when she wanted. True, there was still a great deal to learn and much she didn't understand, but she was not the same person. She felt that she had changed on a deep, fundamental level. Not only because she had become more adept at spinning time, but because she had come to accept why she was called upon to do it. She had come to understand what was expected of her. And she had learned that her personal feelings, her wishes and desires, would always take second place to the duty that her gift placed upon her. While this might once have made her sad, when her feelings for Samuel were so heady and unguarded, now she felt strangely freed by the notion. Strengthened by it. Her place was in her own time. What she did when the found things sang to her she did as a traveler, as a visitor, as a Spinner. Her own present day was where she would always belong. And now there was Liam. Liam.

Xanthe turned her collar up against the cold air and walked with determined strides along the length of the ridgeway, letting the exertion steady her thoughts, allowing the December air to invigorate and restore her. At last, after a brisk half hour, she circled back round to the noble horse. She paused and blew him a kiss. "I'll come again soon," she promised before making her way back to the cab.

Marlborough was still quiet when she drove back up the high street. She waved at Harley, who was out to fetch the Sunday paper. As she turned down Parchment Street she could hear the church bells ringing. She parked up at the end of the lane, making a mental note to buy more antifreeze for her precious vehicle. She rubbed her hands together as she walked across the cobbles, wondering if her mother would feel like sharing a full English breakfast with her.

She was about to go unlock the shop door when something made her stop.

She paused, listening, waiting, searching for a reason for her sudden unease. She heard voices. Not real voices from real people standing close—the street was devoid of shoppers—but distant, ethereal, lost voices; the ones she heard when she was spinning time. But she was doing nothing remotely connected with journeying through the centuries. She was at home, in daylight, away from the blind house, without any treasure singing to her. Why, then, could she suddenly hear the cries and pleas of so many desperate people? She needed to turn around, to scan the area, to look for an explanation, but she found she was frightened of doing so. Her breathing and heartbeat accelerated, panic stirring within her. She must turn. She must look. She must see! It took all her willpower to step back from the door of the shop and turn. She had the sensation that icy fingers were stroking the nape of her neck. The cobbled space was clearly empty, even though she felt as if a hundred souls were crowding it, pressing forward, clamoring and pleading, demanding her attention. And then she saw it. Standing at the entrance to the narrow alleyway, a figure. He was silhouetted against the light from the broad high street behind him so that Xanthe could not clearly see his face. He wore a wide-brimmed hat, and his clothes were an unconventional shape. The man began to move toward her, and as he did so, he emerged from the shadows and into the growing light of the morning. Even before she could see him properly, something in Xanthe told her that danger was close, that a darkness was approaching. Even so, she had to steady herself against the shock of discovering that the man who now stood before her was none other than Benedict Fairfax.

ACKNOWLEDGMENTS

I'd like to thank the many owners of antiques shops who have tolerated my endless questions about their stock. Likewise, the curators of historic houses in Wiltshire who have had to put up with me and have been so very helpful.

Thanks, of course, to my editorial team, for their patience and for sharing my vision for this story. I am truly fortunate to have them.

I am grateful, as always, to the whole family of hardworking people at St. Martin's Press who each do their crucial bit to bring my books into being. The thrill of seeing a new title in print, and to hold it in my hands, never gets old.

And thanks this time to my readers for their enthusiastic response to the series, which gave me the confidence and courage to continue the story.

READ ON TO SEE HOW XANTHE'S STORY
CONTINUES IN THIS EXCERPT
FROM PAULA BRACKSTON'S

THE GARDEN OF PROMISES AND LIES

THE MOON SHADOWS IN THE GARDEN CREATED UNFAMILIAR SHAPES BENEATH THE TUMBLING climbers and chaotic shrubs. From the window seat of her attic bedroom, Xanthe had a clear view of the muddle of borders and the barely tamed lawn as they began to emerge from the chill of winter. The roof-scape of the sleeping town beyond the redbrick garden boundary glistened under a light frost. She thought of how quickly the weeks had passed. Christmas and New Year had come and gone in a blur of activity in the antiques shop and extra bookings for the band. Then there had been January sales to organize, and work on the room of mirrors in order to accommodate the new vintage clothing venture. And now it was the first day of March, and their first spring in Marlborough, with the slumbering garden at last beginning to properly reveal itself again after the bare winter months.

In the corner, the gray stone of the little blind house stood without the softening cover of its deciduous rambling dog roses and honeysuckle, so that it appeared all the more solid, aged and humble. There was nothing about its size, nor its proportions, nor its worn, heavy door to give a hint of the magic that it contained. There was nothing to suggest that within those damp, bleak stones lay the secrets of the past and the means for some people—a few, special people—to journey back to times gone by. Not for the first time, Xanthe felt a sense of wonder at what had happened to her since she and her mother had opened The Little Shop of Found Things. What had begun as a new home and a new business for both of them in a quiet Wiltshire market town had turned into the greatest adventure of her life. On the first few occasions she had travelled back down the centuries she had done so without control, falling through time as if pushed from the top of a cliff of immeasurable height. Her trips to the era where she had faced danger and found love had been the floundering actions of a beginner in the art of time travel. Now though, after many more journeys, she knew that she did have some control over what she did. And now she had the book of the Spinners. To discover that she was part of a group who shared her ability to move through time and to hold their collected wisdom in her hands had given her courage. There were others like her and she could learn from them, and she was hungry for that knowledge. Slowly, she was starting to uncover their secrets. To understand who and what she truly was. However dangerous her journeys to the past had been, she was no longer afraid. That early fear of what she had been doing, and of all the possible perils, had been replaced by an excitement, a thrill, a deep, precious joy at the thought of what she now knew herself to be. Nothing, though, had prepared her for the shock of seeing her nemesis, Benedict Fairfax, standing at the top of her street, in *her* time. She had used her skills as a Spinner to send him away from Samuel, and in doing so, somehow, she had enabled him to travel forward to the present day. No matter how he had achieved this feat, she had to accept some responsibility for it. She was the one who had helped him get the astrolabe. It was she who had tricked him into travelling to a time not his own to ensure Samuel's safety. She could not, no matter how hard she tried, shake the belief that it was her own actions that had led him to appear so close to her home, to her mother, to everything that now mattered to her. It was up to her, then, to hone her skills, to be better able to protect those she loved. In short, to become what Mistress Flyte had told her it was her destiny to become: a true Spinner of time.

What was it that Fairfax wanted? Why had he come? Still she did not know, for since that first brief, heart-stopping glimpse of him standing at the end of the alleyway, she had not seen him again. She had attempted to convince herself, at first, that she had imagined seeing him. That the vision was simply the product of a tired mind, an overactive imagination, and a confusion brought about by the tumultuous events of her life at that time. But she knew, truly *knew*, that she had seen him, and that he had really been there. Flesh and blood, not a ghost or shadow of a person long dead. Real and calm and cold and dangerous as he had ever been. And knowing Fairfax as she did, she could be certain that he had not chosen to appear in front of her without good reason. He had meant her to see him. He had wanted her to know that he was close. That he could choose when to confront her. And yet, so far, after so many weeks, he had not. She had been watchful, nervously checking she was not followed if she went out at night, vigilantly locking the doors of the shop, taking care not to leave her mother alone for longer than was absolutely necessary. But she had not seen him again. What was his plan? she wondered. Did he want revenge for what she had done, for how she had tricked him? She couldn't be sure. As time went by she wished he would show himself so that she could face him, once and for all. The waiting and wondering had become intolerable, and she knew that she had begun to let her guard down. It was impossible to stay alert to the danger forever. And the not knowing when or where he would show himself again was taking its toll. The only thing she felt with absolute certainty was that he would come again. One day. And that he was capable of anything.

She pulled her woolen shawl tighter around her shoulders and got up from the window seat. Morning would come soon enough, there was work to be done and nothing to be gained by hours spent worrying over things she could not change. When Fairfax made his move she would have to be ready for him; losing sleep in the meantime was pointless.

Having at last fallen into a deep slumber, it was after eight when Xanthe descended the stairs from her attic bedroom to the kitchen on the first floor of the tall narrow apartment that sat on top of the shop. She could hear her mother singing along to the radio, raising her voice to compete with the sound of the whistling kettle.

"Ah, there you are. I was going to give you a shout. Coffee's nearly made. Sit down and help yourself to breakfast. We don't want to keep Gerri waiting when she gets here. Can't have been easy finding someone to man the tea shop." Flora pivoted on one of her crutches as she reached for the jar of ground coffee, deftly snatching a spoon from the draining board as she did so. She had become so adept at managing the restrictions her arthritis placed upon her that most of the time Xanthe forgot how she had been before it had encroached upon her health. Before she had needed sticks for support and painkillers to sleep. "It's going to be such a help, having her input on this. I can't think of anyone better placed to advise us on buying vintage clothing," Flora went on, waving the spoon at her daughter. "Apart from you, love, of course."

"I think of myself more of an enthusiast than an expert." She gestured at her own seventies floral dress and sleeveless Shetland jersey. "I can't hold a candle to Gerri. How she always manages to look so perfectly turned out with two small children and a business to run single-handedly amazes me."

"Not to mention her scarlet lipstick," said Flora, pouring water into the coffeepot. "Never a smudge in sight. How come it always ends up on my teeth if I try it?"

She smiled, taking in her mother's fine, fluffy hair which was even now escaping from the random bit of scarf she had tied around it. She glanced down at the plate of food on the table in front of her. "Another experiment, Mum?"

"There's nothing particularly outlandish about crumpets."

"Crumpets, no. Crumpets covered in avocado and—is that broccoli?"

"We had some left over from last night. I've added some grated cheese. It'll be fine. Come on, eat up. Green food is healthy, isn't it?" She sat down opposite her daughter and squeezed brown sauce from a plastic bottle onto her own breakfast. Xanthe poured coffee for them both, grateful for its aroma and hopeful it would make the food more palatable. Despite the twice-weekly food markets in Marlborough High Street which her mother enjoyed browsing, Flora still preferred to cook whatever she found in the fridge, almost regardless of the end result.

"And don't forget," she said, sipping the hot coffee, "you've got the sale at Corsham tomorrow. We need to get as much done to the new room today as possible. If I'm manning the shop and finishing that escritoire in the workshop I'll have my hands full."

"Still can't believe you're letting me go and do the buying at a sale like that on my own. Stately home clearances are your favorite."

"I can't be in two places at once. And besides"—Flora beamed—"we had a good Christmas, and now is the perfect time to invest in stock. A sale like that could yield all sorts of treasures. You know what you're doing, most of the time."

"Thanks. I think."

"But if something sings to you . . ."

"I know, don't go mad."

"Of course you will have to get whatever it is. Just don't blow the whole budget, is all I ask. We have made so much progress with the shop."

"Proved the doubters wrong, eh?"

Flora nodded. "Your father among them. Not that I care, of course."

She chose not to pick up on the reference to the man she now thought of simply as her mother's ex-husband. Instead she stayed on safer ground. "Like I did with the chatelaine, you mean? We did get a good price for it in the end, you know."

Flora smiled. They both knew that when something sang to Xanthe, when it triggered her gift of psychometry, she wouldn't be able to resist it, whatever the cost. The ability to detect information about an object—its past, its origins, its story—was a rare thing and unheard of by many, but to the Westlake family it was simply a part of their daughter. Nothing would change that. "We need saleable items, love. Preferably small things. A little more jewelry wouldn't go amiss. Seems popular. And if you see a little dresser for me to paint, or a pair of decent bedroom chairs . . ."

"I will keep my eye out. Don't worry. Business head firmly screwed on, Mum."

"Why don't you see if Liam is free to go with you?"

"You think he's a sensible influence?"

"I just thought it would be nice."

"Mum . . . he has his own business to run."

"He likes helping you. Spending time with you."

"I'll see him tonight at band practice. We spend plenty of time together already." She shook her head at her mother's shameless attempts to encourage her relationship with Liam. It was nice that Flora liked him, of course, but she refused to be rushed. Since the medieval weekend—since that kiss—

they had agreed to take things slowly. In truth, Xanthe had insisted upon it and given him little choice. She valued their friendship too much to risk it. She knew she was still on the rebound from Samuel. And now that she was a full-time member of Tin Lid, her closeness to Liam had several aspects to it, all of which were woven into her new life. She didn't want to jeopardize a possible future they might have together. As friends. As band members. As lovers. She gulped down her coffee. "Come on, Mum, eat up. I need to unlock and let Gerri in. We've work to do."

The room that the previous owner, Mr. Morris, had used to house his collection of mirrors was behind the main shop, and had only a small window. Xanthe had thought it rather dark and cramped, but since they had removed what turned out to be more than fifty mirrors, the space had grown. They had ripped up the old carpet, sanded and polished the floorboards, applied pale gold paint to the walls and white gloss to the woodwork. The window had been left without curtains to make the most of the natural light, and three vintage standard lamps had been carefully placed to give the room a warm glow. Some of the mirrors had been a useful part of the transforma-tion. A full-length rectangular one had been given a makeover by Flora, its pine frame painted and decoupaged with roses in soft greens and pinks. Two smaller mirrors, one elaborate French gilt, the other a smooth white plaster, had been hung to reflect the daylight and allow customers to view themselves from several angles when trying on the vintage clothing. The tasks that re-mained included setting up new rails and a hatstand, positioning and filling the glass-fronted display case, and unpacking the stock they had amassed over the preceding few months.

"Right," said Xanthe, rubbing her hands together. "Let's start with these boxes.

Gerri, who had arrived on the dot of nine o'clock and was dressed as a Land Army girl in dungarees, hair expertly twisted under a gingham scarf, lipstick perfectly applied, started to pull garments from the nearest crate, handing them out for inspection. "What have we here? A houndstooth-check winter coat, good and roomy. A suede jacket with tassels . . ."

Flora gasped. "Oh dear . . . does anyone actually wear tassels anymore?"

"Mum." She took it from Gerri and gently smoothed the fringed sleeves.

"Don't be so quick to judge. It's all about putting a look together. You'd be surprised what some people would do with that."

"Xanthe's right." Gerri held up a Laura Ashley dress. "It's a matter of seeing the potential in things."

"Well, I'm very glad I've got you two to do that," Flora said. "To me it all looks like jumble. All thrown out for good reason."

Xanthe shook the folds out of a maxi skirt. "Some of it's a bit down-market, I grant you, but fans of vintage stuff know what works. We just need to make sure we have some high-end items too."

"Yes, designer pieces!" Gerri's eyes lit up at the thought. "I bought an original Biba blouse the other day. It wasn't cheap, but it'll hold its value."

Flora tried on a dusty bowler hat, peering at herself in the gilt-framed mirror. "Hmmm, I think it's a bad idea to wear vintage if you yourself are vintage," she decided, making the others laugh.

"The trick is," Gerri said, minutely adjusting Flora's hat to a more flattering angle, "to always choose clothes that suit your own shape and coloring. That's the secret to avoid giving the impression you're in fancy dress." She thought for a moment, removed the bowler hat, and replaced it with a beret, artfully positioned.

Flora grinned at the result. "As long as you agree to be my personal dresser, Gerri, I'll give it a go."

Xanthe started slipping blouses onto hangers. "The challenge is going to be locating the fine, expensive items. We want to get known for quality as well as range."

"Can't we find things on the internet?" asked Flora.

"If only," said Gerri, frowning at a lurid green skirt before dropping it into the rejections box for recycling. "People are much more clued up about the value of things nowadays. Good pieces are in demand. You can end up paying over the odds."

"I'm going to the dispersal sale tomorrow," Xanthe told her. "Corsham Hall, out toward Bath. Do you know it?"

"Oh, that was the house of the Wilcox family. They were fabulously rich, once upon a time."

"Let's hope the late owner secretly hoarded all her ancestors' clothes."

"There might be flapper dresses in the attic!"

"Well, if there are, I'll snaffle them. That's exactly what we need to elevate this little lot."

They worked on, steadily sorting the wheat from the chaff, ignoring some of the faces Flora pulled at the more outlandish items. Xanthe was happy to have Gerri's support for their new room. She knew her mother had agreed to it to please her, and it helped to have the input of a person whose taste they both trusted. Even though they were no longer in the financial difficulty they had been when they first bought the shop, every space in it still had to earn its keep. Mr. Morris's mirrors had been taking up too much space and moving too slowly. She had been forced to swallow her pride and call Theo Hamilton again. She did not enjoy having to contact her rival antiques dealer and offer him the pieces after turning him away the first time, but needs must. Fortunately he had still wanted the mirrors as a job lot, though he had not been above making her work at getting his forgiveness for his previous wasted journey when she had changed her mind about selling them. In the end his eye for a bargain had won out and they had agreed on a fair price. Her hope was that the vintage clothes would attract new browsers, extra shoppers who might not otherwise visit an antiques shop. Once over the threshold, who knew what they might be tempted to buy?

"Oh, look at this, love." Flora held up a black, sequined dress. "You could wear it for your next performance with Tin Lid."

Xanthe laughed. "Not unless we start booking gigs in a jazz club, Mum!"

"I think you'd look lovely in it," she insisted. "I bet Liam would agree with me."

"He usually does."

"Such a nice boy."

"He's smart enough to know how to get round you," she said, taking the dress from her mother and hanging it on the rail. "Anyway, he doesn't really notice what I wear."

Gerri raised her eyebrows. "From what I've seen, he notices every little thing about you."

"We're just good friends."

"With benefits?" Flora asked, giving a pantomime wink.

"Mum! You know full well what that means. Don't pretend you don't."

"I'm assuming friends who help and support each other?" she replied innocently, while Gerri tried not to laugh. "He's been so good, running you around when your car broke down, driving the van to pick up bigger pieces of furniture . . ."

"Right, first—*please* don't ever use that expression again. Second, Liam and I are perfectly happy with the way things are between us, thank you very much."

Flora and Gerri pointedly exchanged looks that clearly told her they thought otherwise.

Later, after she had shut the shop for the day, Xanthe said goodbye to her mother and headed for The Feathers. Her irregular but increasingly frequent chats with Harley had become an important feature of her week. While Benedict Fairfax might not have shown himself again, he was still ever on her mind, and her determination to be ready for him the next time she saw him occupied her thoughts whenever she was alone. However, between the shop, Flora, the band, and, of course, Liam, it was difficult to find clear time to focus on the madness of what she had experienced since moving to Marlborough. Sometimes the pull of normality and the wish to believe all was safe and sensible prevented her from facing what she knew, in her heart, had to be faced. The fact that Fairfax never did anything without a reason. The fact that he was not a man to give up on something he wanted. The fact that he had proved himself capable of doing anything in order to further his own interests. Which was why she felt blessed to have Harley—publican, local historian, hairy biker and true friend—as a confidant. He alone knew the truth of where, and more important, *when*, Xanthe went when she was away from Marlborough. He knew about the Spinners; she had shared their secrets and their precious book with him and no one else. And she had told him about Fairfax. Speaking with Harley about so many impossible things made her feel just a tiny bit less crazy, and a tiny bit more in control of what was happening. And now that she had decided to properly study the Spinners' writings she was eager to test her theories about its contents with him.

She found Harley fixing new window boxes to the sills of the pub. He was a burly man, big rather than fat, but not in the best of shape. She heard him puff a little and curse quietly in his endearing Scottish lilt as he wrestled the heavy, soil-filled boxes into position.

"I've never thought of you as a gardener, Harley. Will you be arranging flowers next?"

"You are so bloody funny. Don't just stand there, hen, hand me that hammer, would ye?" He gestured at the pile of tools on the pavement. Passersby were forced to step into the street to avoid the muddle.

"Must be spring," said Xanthe, passing him the hammer. "Window boxes going up, Harley sighted out from behind the bar."

"Not for long," he said, taking a large staple from the pocket of his biker's leather jacket, placing it through the flower box stay, and bashing it in to place. She watched him work for another five minutes. At last he was satisfied, brushed mud from his hands and picked up his tool kit. "Right, that's me done. I'll leave the tending of the plants to Annie. Come away inside. Winter might be over but it's still cold enough to freeze a man's ears off, if ye ask me."

The pub was in its late-afternoon lull: lunch service over, evening meals not yet started, and no live music scheduled. Harley grabbed two bottles of Henge beer from behind the bar, removing their tops with practiced ease, signaling to his wife and the young man working with her that he was going upstairs. Xanthe, after pausing to say hello to Annie, followed him up the slightly wonky staircase to the apartment on the floor above. The sitting room was warm, comfortable, and in its customary state of barely contained chaos. Harley moved a stack of motorbike magazines from one of the worn leather sofas and subsided onto it, handing her a beer as she joined him.

"Did you bring the time travel manual with you?" Harley asked with the now familiar note of awe that crept into his voice when he spoke about the *Spinners* tome.

She nodded, taking the old leather volume from her bag and passing it to him.

Harley took a swig of ale and wiped his beard with the back of his hand, wiped his hands on his trousers before carefully, almost reverently, taking the book from her. "This is an incredible thing you have in your possession, hen."

"I read a little every day and still there is so much to learn. It's not just the stories; there are maps, drawings, poems, recipes, spells even. It's crammed full of stuff. The tricky thing is working out what's real. I mean, what's instructions, and what's just, I don't know, cautionary tales?"

"Aye, it's not your straightforward user's manual, that's true enough."

"Sometimes I feel stupid not being able to properly understand what I'm reading. Some pages make more sense only because I've been back in time. I can relate parts of what is written to my experiences but, well"—she gave a shrug—"it's easy being wise after the event. What I need is clues for what I do next. How to use what I've learned to travel better. Safer. With more control."

Harley smiled. "I'm just pleased I can see anything written there at all," he said, referring to the fact that *Spinners* did not reveal its contents to everyone. Xanthe had wondered about this fact since they had first discovered it. The book could not be copied, nor could it be read by just anyone. Why had it chosen to let Harley see its secrets? He did not have her gift of psychometry, nor did he ever glimpse the past. No objects sang to him, and when she had taken him to see the blind house in the garden he had detected nothing strange or magical about it at all. In the end, she had concluded that *Spinners* wanted him to be able to help her. It shared its wisdom and stories with him just enough for him to be able to give her his support and input. The subtlety of the way the book guarded its knowledge astonished her. It also made her feel all the more privileged. It was as Mistress Flyte had told her. She was a Spinner. Her journeys through the centuries had not been random experiences, caused by stumbling upon powerful objects and coming to live near the blind house. It was all meant to be. She was learning who she was, or at least, what she could become. She briefly entertained the thought that one day she might be able to travel back and visit her friend and mentor, and the thought of having such control and such freedom thrilled her.

"Do you think it's what your man is after?" Harley's question broke into her thoughts.

"*Spinners?*"

"Aye. Is that why he's found his way here, to this time?"

"He wants something, there's no doubt about that. And I'm actually rather hoping it is the book he's come for. Because if it's not, then the only other reason he would go to the trouble and the risk of spinning time to get here is—"

"For you," Harley finished her sentence.

"It's not a pleasant thought."

Harley gave a snort. "You're right about that, hen. From what you've told me the man's a right bastard." He took another long gulp of his beer, his expression thoughtful. "Way I look at it is, whether it's the book he's after or taking his revenge on you for tricking him the way you did, well . . . one way or another he's trouble. But you've not seen him again?"

"No, still just the one time, standing at the top of our street. But I know he's close."

"You sure you're not imagining that? I mean, it's understandable you're spooked, but if he hasn't turned up again maybe it was just a one-off and he's gone back to wherever—whenever—he came from."

"I wish I believed that, but I don't. I *know* he's still around. I can sense his presence, sometimes really strongly. I think he's waiting for something. And then . . ."

"And then?"

Xanthe drank deep from her beer bottle. She paused, taking a breath. "Mistress Flyte was right. He's not a fit person to have something so powerful. A Spinner should respect the order of things, the way things are meant to be. They shouldn't change them to suit their own purposes."

"No pressure then." Harley shifted his not inconsiderable weight, making the leather sofa creak. "In the meantime, you've plenty on your plate with the band. Annie says we're lucky to book you now!"

She smiled. "I'll always find time for The Feathers, you know that. Actually, it's Liam who's elusive at the moment. He's been very busy with work. He's up in Oxford today delivering a recent restoration. A beautiful blue Jaguar."

"Hell's teeth! Has he won you over to classic cars too? He must be even more bloody charming than he looks."

Xanthe recalled the first time she had seen Liam and how his good looks had made her wary of him, her experience of beautiful men up to that point not having been entirely positive. He had worn his hair cropped short then, giving an edge to his appearance. Lately he had grown it out a little, causing her to tease him about being a secret surfer. The truth was, he'd look highly appealing either way. "I'm just quoting him," she said. "He's been so passionate about the thing it would be hard not to remember what it was. Anyway, he's doing a second one for the same enthusiast. He said it'll take another few weeks. He should be more available for gigs after that."

"Let's hope so. We miss your singing, lassie."

"Trust me, the other members of Tin Lid won't let him get away with much more shirking."

As always after her chats with Harley, Xanthe felt reassured. She was not dealing with everything on her own anymore. Whatever her future as a Spinner held, she had a confidant. A part of her was sorry it wasn't Liam. Their friendship mattered to her and they had become closer since Christmas, so she was increasingly uncomfortable about keeping secrets from him. And time travel was a pretty big secret. She wondered, briefly, what would happen if she allowed herself to truly care for him. If she let herself fall for him she knew he would be waiting with open arms to catch her, but would she ever be able to tell him about the Spinners? Could he understand? Would he even be able to believe her? It was a lot to ask. And then there was Flora to consider. The more people who knew about her other life, the greater the chance that her mother would find out. Would she be terrified at the thought of what her daughter had been doing and, Xanthe knew, would continue to do? Would she beg her never to step through the blind house again? If coming to terms with her own abilities and true identity was challenging, sharing it with people who cared about her seemed one of the biggest challenges. And yet increasingly she was drawn to the idea that she should tell her mother everything. In fact, there were days when she came close to doing so, when her excitement about being a Spinner came close to making her blurt it all out. Flora had long accepted that Xanthe had the gift of psychometry; surely she of all people would be the most accepting, even of something so incredible.